HARMONY

HELEN GARRAWAY

Published by Jerven Publishing

Cover designed by 100 Covers

eBook ISBN: 978-1-915854-21-6

A CIP catalogue record for this book is available from the British Library.

Sign up to my mailing list to join my magical worlds and to recieve further information about forthcoming books and news at: www.helengarraway.com

First Edition

HARMONY

For Jennie

ALSO BY HELEN GARRAWAY

Sentinal Series

Sentinals Stirring (Free when you sign up to my newsletter)

Sentinals Awaken

Sentinals Rising

Sentinals Justice

Sentinals Recovery (Novella)

Sentinals Across Time

Sentinals Banished

Sentinals Destiny

SoulMist series

SoulBreather

DragonBound

OblivionGate (July 1, 2024)

Standalone Novel

Harmony

CONTENTS

1

"What is the point of life on Harmony?" Annie muttered, ignoring the curling plume of misty breath trailing on the evening air. A frost was already descending, icing the wooden buildings with a glittery wrapper as if it could disguise the destitution within.

All she ever did was wash, starve and sleep. Her shift at the laundry always finished late, and she never got paid extra. The thought of washing one more piece of clothing, ever, made her grit her teeth in frustration. There had to be more to life than this constant drudgery, not that she dared to ever speak that thought aloud.

Annie was running late again. Mind racing, she hurried home as she tried to figure out how she could fit in going down to the creek before curfew sounded to, yes, wash more clothes, but their own for once.

Once she reached the unit she lived in with her parents and twin brother, she changed into her brother's old trousers and shirt, the material catching on her chapped skin. Her brother's clothes always lasted longer, as he got a clothing allowance from Comptech.

Even late as she was, no one was home. The hearth was dead, no fire warming the chill air, no dinner cooking, not that there was anything to cook. She wondered where her mother could be and then shrugged the thought away. She didn't have time to linger if she wanted to get her washing done.

All day she had scrubbed other people's clothes, and the little time she had away from the tubs, she would do more. Bundling up her washing, she shoved a tiny piece of soap rind into her pocket. She had managed to salvage it on the first day of that week's shift.

After slipping out of the housing unit and scurrying down the alley that ran between two lines of terraced houses backing onto each other, she hopped over the rubbish and the putrid remains littering the ground, skirted the edge of the quadrant, and then veered off into the denuded tree line. Only the stunted grey trunks of the once vibrant trees remained, standing in straggling lines like grave markers.

Annie slid down the bank, catching the bole of a tree at the bottom to stop herself from falling into the water. She scowled at the meagre stream, now ice-rimmed along the edges. The water level was down again; soon, there would barely be a trickle, and what was left would freeze solid. Wasn't it time winter released its grip on the sectors?

Wishing for warmer breezes, or heat of any sort come to that, Annie checked to make sure that she was alone. She stripped and washed herself as best she could with the tiny piece of soap. Once clean, she shrugged her brother's clothes back on over damp skin.

As she soaked her hands in the clear water for a moment, she wished…She didn't know what she wished, only that life was better. That there was more to life than this daily drudge. Her brother's frustration suddenly made sense.

Time was passing. Scrubbing the clothes on the rocks,

she wrung them out as much as possible before stretching them back out. Once she'd smoothed out most of the creases, she folded them over and climbed back up the bank.

The jingle of harnesses made her shrink back. Many horses were approaching, and nothing good ever happened when horses arrived in the quadrant.

Annie slid back down the gully and hid among the tangled, moss covered tree roots. At least her clothes blended in with the mud. If she had been in her work shift, she would have stood out like a beacon. She tucked her clean washing inside her shirt and listened.

A sharp voice barked a command, and Annie's heart sank. They wanted access to the water. A whole troop of Devenders were stopping on the path above her. What were they doing there? What could possibly bring Devenders to the forty-fifth sector?

A stocky man dressed in a khaki uniform, with many canteens strapped crossways over his shoulders slithered past Annie, so close she could have reached out and touched him. She hid her face and tried to disappear.

Please don't see me, please don't see me, she chanted over and over, gripping the tree roots tight with trembling fingers.

The horses shifted restlessly on the road above her. The clinking of their bridles was soft and surprisingly soothing in the evening air. Relaxing a little, she listened to the desultory conversation above her. The speakers didn't sound particularly pleased to be here, either.

"We should have taken the coastal route," a harsh voice said. "At least the view would have been pleasing."

The responding voice was deep and calm. "But we would have been another three days on the road. Let's get this over with. I want to return to Maincore."

"Got a girl waiting, have you? Might've known a

Gallante would have them on tap. Lucky bastard. I wouldn't touch any of this lot. Infested, all of 'em."

"They don't have much choice, now, do they? And from what we can see here, I would think one of the nodes has failed. No doubt, Comptech is overcompensating and draining the life from this place."

"C'mon now, Kiefer. You would've thought Harmony would be more accommodating, wouldn't you? Isn't that what the original brochure said? Welcome to a world of harmony, where nature meets technology and flourishes, accommodating all requirements."

"Ha," the deep voice snorted as the horses shifted impatiently. "I expect the definition of harmony over a thousand years ago was a little different to what we have today."

"True, very true. Where is that man? Is he boring for water? Hey, Jeffers, get a move on!" the harsh voice shouted down the bank.

"Coming, sir," Jeffers responded from almost on top of Annie. The man hesitated and then continued to clamber up the bank.

Annie froze as a low-voiced conversation murmured above her. She only made out the 'Really?' before the deep voice, Kiefer, Annie labelled it, said. "Enough. We don't have time for this. We're already behind schedule, and one drab is not cause enough to delay us further. Come on."

"A bit of sport, Kiefer. A rabbit chase," the harsh voice said, rising with a touch of excitement.

"You can volunteer for the next clearance run if that's what you want. You'll break your horse's shins in this tangle of roots. Onwards. Let's get this check done and leave. We're going to have to stop for the night in this godforsaken place as it is."

Annie breathed a sigh of relief as the column finally moved on. Climbing up the bank, she peered around a tree trunk. One of the Devenders, leading the pack mules, was looking back down the road as he rounded the curve at the end. Annie ought to let them get far ahead, but she was running out of time; curfew would be sounding soon. She hurried down the trail towards the housing quadrant.

As she reached the curve, she saw a pile of horse droppings on the road. She searched for something to carry them in; dried, they would burn well. Not seeing anything of use, she scooped them up in her hands. The droppings were still warm and smelt, funnily enough, sort-of clean. The fresh smell of shit, strong enough to clear your lungs and rarely experienced in the quadrant. Devenders could be useful for something after all.

Why were they in the sector, and what was the check for? Devenders usually protected cities, like Maincore, and the sub-core installations, patrolling for rule-breakers, hackers, and the like. Restoring order and maintaining the peace.

Not that there were any hackers anymore. Only the controllers had access to the net, and that was protected by more Devenders. The world was in its current state because hackers had destroyed the foundation on which Harmony was supposed to run. They'd corrupted the programs that supported the colonisation of the planet, undermining the very principles the original settlers had signed up for, leaving a system that had degraded over time and was just about spent.

Annie wondered what the original vision of this planet had been. Her weekly orientation class never covered it, only the new rules that were being put in place to protect them from the threat of the dead zones, the contamination that spread through the depths of the Wytchwards. She frowned. Why weren't the Devenders out there, clearing the infection out of the fringes? That would be a better way to protect the cities.

There was no sign of the Devenders as she approached the quadrant. No doubt, they would be ensconced in the hospitality of Comptech. She scuttled up the alley towards their unit as the curfew rang out.

Her mother exclaimed at her tardiness as she entered, but once Annie had told her about her close encounter with the Devenders, her mother was even more horrified. The droppings were carefully laid out on the cold stone hearth to dry. Her mother took the damp clothes, now somewhat less damp from enforced contact with Annie's body heat, and hung them up to dry.

Annie realised both her brother and her father were not at home. "Where's Chiva and Da?"

"Chiva had a late pass, something to do with the academy. Your father has a double shift today."

A double shift was usually the punishment for something. Annie swallowed as she looked at her mother. "What did he do?"

"Nothing. He did nothing wrong. One of the processors they were working on failed, and they haven't been able to repair it, is all. They have to stay until it's repaired. Jonni came by. His da was held back as well."

"What if they can't repair it?" Annie whispered, and her mother's lips tightened at the thought.

"They will; they have to. Come. As it was just us two, I thought we would finish the last of the flour and have a treat, a fresh flatbread between us. Look." Her mother's face brightened as she displayed the flatbread.

Annie looked at it and then at her mother. Her mother's mouth trembled, and Annie rushed to hug her. "Ma, you are a wonder. Thank you. You take the first bite. After all, you baked it."

"No, we both take the first bite." Her mother tore the bread in half and smiled at her daughter. "One day," she said. "One day, we will be able to make fresh bread every day."

"Of course. Harmony will protect us; she will provide for all," Annie replied. "Harmony bless us and the food we eat, by your leave," she murmured as she stuffed a piece in her mouth, savouring the fact that she was actually eating solid food. She chewed so long that it got stodgy, and she struggled to swallow it. Closing her eyes, she nibbled another piece. "What about Da and Chiva?"

"Chiva will eat at the academy. I got your da an egg."

Annie sat back in her chair. "Where in the world did you get an egg?"

"Now, that would be telling," her mother said, pursing her lips.

They looked at each other across the table. Her mother's faded blue eyes were set in a prematurely wrinkled face. Annie couldn't remember a time when her mother's hair hadn't been grey, yet she still sat straight and proud, kept her tiny home clean, and managed to scrounge up food out of nowhere.

Annie didn't press too hard. She was sure there was some black-market trading going on, but what her mother had to trade, she couldn't imagine. Was this what she would become? A homemaker for some man who rarely came home? Her life spent in the laundry, if she was fortunate? What was the point of it all? Why would Harmony allow them to be reduced to such straits? She could see why Chiva was itching to get out: to have a better life. But why couldn't she have one, too?

Chiva sat in the Computer Lab, his fingers flying over the keyboard. He had a real project for once, in the live lab, not the test lab they were usually restricted to. His stomach tightened with the thrill of it. The controller had called on the students to reprogram the processor that had failed. The technicians couldn't get it online, and they couldn't find the fault. Every student had been roped into searching the code for the error.

There was a rumour circulating that a troop of Devenders had arrived just as the facility was failing. They couldn't have timed it any worse. The double-supe was in a frenzy, afraid of being held accountable.

Chiva frowned at the screen as he easily translated the sequences in his head. He typed a couple of corrections and moved on, forgetting in his eagerness that he was supposed to get them approved. Scrolling down the lines of code, he saw the same error was repeating. He raised his hand. "Supe?"

"Yes, Chiva?" The double-supe skittered over to Chiva's workstation.

"There's a repeating blocker here, sir. I need a replacement command. If I remove them all, it will become a circular loop."

The double-supe leaned over Chiva's shoulder. "Stay. I'll check the manual." He was back in a moment, reciting a command.

Quickly updating the code, Chiva did a find-and-replace, and scrolled back to the top for a final manual check.

"Let me know as soon as you've finished," the supe murmured, and then he went to each station to give the students the new command.

Chiva frowned at the logic. Should he speak up again? Twice in as many minutes was pushing his luck. He hesitated a moment and then raised his voice. "Supe?" he called.

"Yes?"

"This subroutine, isn't it contradicting the prime command? I can't see its purpose."

The supe shoved him out of his chair, sat in his place, and carefully scrolled down the page. The lab door cycled, interrupting his concentration, and the supe looked up with a frown. A tall, lean man with broad shoulders and black hair cut short and swept back off his face stood at the entrance. His dark eyes swept the room.

"Who's in charge here?" the man demanded as he strode forward. The artificial light revealed the deep-brown uniform of a Devender, and a commander at that, according to the reflective stripes on his collar and sleeves. He still wore his muddy riding boots, though he had shed his outer garments.

The double-supe lurched to his feet. "I am. Double Superintendent Floris, sir."

The piercing brown eyes searched the supe's face and moved on to Chiva. Stiffening under the acute inspection, Chiva took a step back.

"I understand the sentinel core processor failed," said the Devender. "What is the status?"

"We are updating the code," replied the supe. "We found the error string and are currently replacing it, but we discovered a sub routine that countermands the prime command, sir."

The Devender crossed the room. "Let me see it," he commanded, ignoring the gaping students watching him. He leaned over the console, and the supe stumbled as he hurried to get out of the way. A slender finger tapped a key, and the screen scrolled. The Devender looked up and stared at Chiva. As Chiva fidgeted under the man's gaze, he realised that the Devender wasn't actually looking at him. He was thinking, with a slight cleft between his brows. He had an intelligent-looking face, straight nose, firm mouth and chin.

His gaze saw right through Chiva. This man would not tolerate stupidity.

The man straightened. "What security clearance does this facility have?"

"Centaur plus two, sir," said the supe, "though the controller has beta clearance."

The man sighed and bent to press two keys together with a third key stroke, and all the screens went blank. "Clear the room. This facility is in lockdown."

"W-what?" The supe's face paled.

"Lockdown. Everyone out. Take me to the Controller now."

The supe hurried to lead the way out of the lab. As the students milled about in the hallway, the Devender placed his hand on the door monitor and tapped a sequence. This was followed by an audible thud of the lock sliding home. The Devender indicated for the supe to go ahead of him, and the man, visibly sweating, led him down the corridor.

Chiva looked at his classmates. "What was that all about?"

One of them shrugged. "Better to not get involved. Let's get the grub before we are all turfed out."

"But what are Devenders doing here?" Chiva said as he followed his class mates down the hallway. "We're a backwater; nothing is produced here."

One of the lads snorted. "Well, we've discovered something that caught the interest of a Devender, so you'd better hope you don't get the blame. You found it, after all."

The students piled into the canteen, grabbed trays, and slid them along the silver railings, helping themselves to sandwiches, cake, and mugs of aromatic brew before moving over to the tables.

Chiva had never taken any of the food home. His family wouldn't have believed what was available in the facility. He didn't want to upset them further by tempting them with things they wouldn't see again. There was no point in rubbing what they couldn't have in their faces.

He bit into the fresh white bread and almost groaned aloud at the taste: food with flavour, not the bland hot water his mother constantly served up. There was no way he was going back to the quadrant; the sooner he got out, the better.

Kiefer stared at the facility controller, who leaned back in his chair and glared back at him. The man was trying to pull rank, but he didn't have the ability. Skinny and lank-haired, he drooped under the stern gaze of the tall Devender in front of his desk.

"How dare you lock down the terminals without speaking to me first? We have protocols to follow, orderly shut-down procedures. Approvals are required."

"The only approval required was mine," Kiefer said, a hard edge to his voice. "Your core is infected, and you want to wait while it spreads and corrupts your remaining cores? There are no further replacements; you have to protect and maintain the integrity of what you have. That means isolating the failed node and wiping it clean. You need to check your back-ups for the last clean version. That, at least, will give us an indication of when the virus was introduced."

The man in the chair paled.

"You do have back-ups, don't you?" Kiefer asked, his stomach sinking at the ramifications that would ensue if they didn't.

"Of course we have a back-up," the man huffed. "But we only have one disk, so we have to overwrite it each time."

"You only have one back-up disk?" Kiefer repeated, his voice even colder.

The man swallowed. "I reported it, as per process. I got an acknowledgement but nothing else."

"I see. What else have you reported?"

The man ran down a litany of system failures and resource constraints.

"So, if I understand correctly, you are telling me that the forty-fifth core processor has failed and is unable to be further maintained and you want me to shut it down? It is obviously not performing to spec; this whole region is failing. The crops are not being nurtured. The weather is deteriorating. These people can be supported elsewhere."

"No, no, not at all." The controller jumped to his feet. "I just need some spares. The technicians do their best, but even they need tools to do their job."

"This is the worst condition I have found a processor in," Kiefer snapped. "The purpose of your facility is to maintain it, not bathe yourself in luxury while the land around you fails. No wonder subservients have infiltrated your facility."

The man gaped at him. "Subservients?"

"Who else would have planted a virus? When was your last security check of your people?"

"S-security check?"

"Weren't you just spouting your rules and regulations at me? And you haven't even been following the core mandates?" Kiefer shook his head. "You'll have to do better than that."

"You can't speak to me like that," the controller blustered, jutting out his chin.

"I think you'll find that I can." Kiefer spun the man around and marched him to the door. The Devender on guard outside stiffened as Kiefer propelled the controller into the corridor.

"Detain this man until further notice," Kiefer snapped,

releasing the controller into the guard's arms and turning back into the office.

"Now you've gone and got the commander all riled up, and that's no good for anyone," the guard chided gently as he escorted the man away.

Kiefer sat at the desk, pulled the console towards him, and tapped in his overrides.

An hour later, Kiefer's sub commander, Lieutenant Ferris, arrived to find Kiefer frowning at the orange wall across from him.

"It can't be that bad," Ferris said, taking a bite out of his apple as he sat in the comfortable chair opposite the desk. He waved his apple at the office's lurid decorations. "Though working in here wouldn't help, that's for sure." Stretching his long legs out in front of him, he relaxed in the chair. He was of similar height and build to Kiefer, though blond and grey-eyed.

Kiefer frowned at his lieutenant instead of the wall. "No, it's worse," he said, his frown deepening.

"With your magic hands, all will be resolved; you'll create some pretty fulcrum to replace the old one, and we will be on our way in no time."

Kiefer glared at his friend. "Have you looked around this place? Rewriting some code will not solve the problems here."

"And sacking the controller will? You can't stay here and fix everything, Kiefer. You know that's not how it works. If the processor is past saving, shut it down and move on. One day, they will all fail; we should be preparing for that day, not delaying it by patching up old technology."

"You know we're not ready for that. This technology is all that is keeping our society together. Harmony isn't prepared for a complete shutdown. We have to sustain the balance for as long as possible. But this"—Kiefer extended his hand in the air— "this is pure exploitation."

Ferris shrugged. "It's the way of the world; the cream always rises to the top. This may be a bit more drastic, but it's the same. The people know and understand it. You can't come in and change the rules overnight; you'd have rebellion and chaos. And anyway, this quadrant just doesn't have the food to support them all."

"But what it *does* provide could be shared more equally," Kiefer argued.

"A romantic." Ferris laughed. "Equality for all. It all costs, Kiefer. One way or another, it all costs. And you don't have the coin to pay for it here. Reinstate the controller, save the processor, and move on. That's what we're here for."

"We can't. The Bantwich virus is in the code."

Ferris stilled. "What?"

"It's the Bantwich virus. That's why I shut them down. We need to make sure all the nodes are clean before we can restart, and then we need to find out who put it in there."

Ferris cursed under his breath. "You're sure? Of course, you're sure," he said, waving his hands in apology. "What do you suggest?"

"Set up a quarantine suite and port the code for cleansing, sweep the units, and then reinstall."

"That will take weeks," Ferris gasped, his face paling, "even with your super-duper memory banks cutting the processing time."

"Then we'd better get started, hadn't we?" Kiefer said, already pulling the images of the processes and schematics he needed to the front of his mind. Having a photographic memory certainly helped cut the research time down. All he needed was to see an image or document once, and it was ingrained in his memory. "I'll manage the cleansing. You get the security detail. Find the personnel files and check everyone's background. See who has access to what and then double-check. We need to find the breach before we leave. Make sure you include all the maintenance crews. I mean everyone."

Ferris groaned as he rose to his feet. "Yes, sir," he said as he facetiously saluted, and then he exited the room, leaving Kiefer frowning at the wall.

Kiefer sighed. Then he sat back up and began furiously typing on the console, searching for schematics, maintenance reports, core logs, for anything that would help him save this sector.

2

The crackling fire lit the rebel camp with dancing shadows, cloaking Ciely and Stefan in darkness. Ciely stomped back and forth, muttering curses under her breath. The flickering light slid over her, accentuating her agitated movements and belying her usual grace. Soft amber flashes caressed a delicate face, somewhat begrimed.

Stefan scowled at the fire, his body vibrating with anger.

Lorne brushed the dried mud off her face as she watched her sister. Waiting.

Ciely had adapted to life on the wrong side of the law with an ease that concerned Lorne. She revelled in the stalking of her prey, the camouflage, the deceit. She hadn't, as of yet, teetered over the edge and killed anyone, but Lorne dreaded the day she did.

Her sweet, innocent little sister was gone, replaced by a predatory hunter who was eager to contribute to the salvation of Harmony. Lorne had done too good a job of convincing Ciely that the Ministry were corrupted and that the rebels were the ones to bring the Ministry down and free

Harmony—so good a job, in fact, that Ciely was getting impatient with the their lack of progress.

Take today, for example. It had started so well but gone so wrong, the reason Ciely was currently stalking around the camp like an overloaded processor about to go up in smoke. Lorne rubbed her temple, her anxiety level rising. She had thought keeping Stefan in check was difficult, but her sister was proving worse.

At least Stefan was just brute force. Ciely was crafty.

Stefan would slowly build up to boiling point and then go that step too far and needed to be reined in. Ciely's decisions had long-lasting effects, some of which Lorne was not sure she could remediate.

"We should have followed straightaway," Ciely burst out, swinging around to face Lorne. "I could have tracked them. We could have got him back before they cleared the sector."

"We weren't prepared for an all-out assault. You knew it was a watch-and-learn. You were not supposed to engage," Stefan replied, drawing Ciely's fiery gaze to him.

Ciely growled. "Where were you? You were supposed to be on our flank, protecting us!"

"Watch and learn," Stefan repeated, his voice hard. "If you followed orders, we wouldn't be in this mess."

"If you'd had our backs, we could have prevented this mess from happening."

"If you had waited…" Stefan began.

"Enough," Lorne said wearily. They had been through this rite twice already. "It's done." She watched Stefan ease back against his log. He was a large man, with thick, heavily muscled arms, all edges and brute force, but at least he listened to her. Ciely started pacing again, her tight-fitting black shirt and trousers blending into the shadows. She curled her fingers into fists. Not a good sign.

"You know why we can't attack a troop of Devenders,"

Lorne said. "They out-arm and out-mass us, even with Stefan here."

Ciely scowled at Lorne's attempt to lighten the atmosphere. "It's Arran. We can't let them torture him. What if they mind-wipe him?"

"Then he is lost, like many others. You know the rules. We are too few for a rescue attempt."

"Would you leave me, too? Just like our parents did?"

Lorne stiffened. "That's unfair, and you know it. You're all I have left, Ciely. The reason we use stealth and not violence is because we can't be caught. I've been clear about this from the start."

"As long as it suits you," Ciely snapped and then suddenly released a hiss of breath. "He's my friend," she whispered.

Lorne ran her hand through her hair, and her fingers snagged in the snarls. She concentrated on picking out the twigs and leaves tangled in her burnished curls. "I know," she replied, teasing out a stubborn tangle. She glanced up as her sister finally sat down, dropping bonelessly on the floor. Ciely was their best tracker, silent and lithe on the ground or in the trees. Her mass of curls was redder than Lorne's and cut into a short bob, and she had the edgy temper to go with it. That temper seemed to be showing its face more often of late.

"What's the point?" Ciely asked, staring at the flames.

"You know why."

"It's not as if Harmony is even aware we're here. She doesn't help us."

"Because she is restrained. You know that, Ciely."

"So say you. How do you know? Because Pa told you a story once? Maybe she is long gone, and there is nothing to save. Mind-wiped like everyone else. Just a dormant planet for us to walk on."

"What's wrong, Ciely?"

Ciely huffed. "You mean more wrong? As if Arran being hauled off to have his brain squashed isn't enough?"

"We lost Talen to the same thing, but you weren't upset then. What's different this time?"

Ciely flicked a glance at Lorne and then stared at the flames again. The silence lengthened, broken only by the snap and crackle of the wood. "What if he tells them about us?" she said eventually.

"He doesn't know anything to tell," Lorne replied. That was why she kept everyone on a first names only, no history, and need to know. They moved camps every other day, a constant wandering across the sectors. They rarely ventured back into the Wytchwards, even though no one would follow them into that toxic landscape. And she had never shared the location of their base camp with anyone except Ciely and Stefan.

"Can we risk it? He can describe us, give numbers, our last camp."

"Means nothing. He only knows about us." The silence became fraught, and Lorne stiffened. "You didn't," she whispered, a tightness constricting her chest as she stared at her sister.

Ciely looked anywhere but at Lorne. "He's my *friend*."

Anger stirred deep in Lorne's gut. After all these months, years even. She tried to control the bite in her voice. "He may be your friend, but you don't put others at risk just for a bit of cosy bed talk."

"I trusted him."

"He won't be able to help himself once the Ministry gets their hands on him. What did you tell him?"

"I needed someone to talk to, to share with. Real company for a change. You never have time for anything but your plans and your search for your precious warden."

"What did you tell him?" Lorne said through gritted teeth.

Ciely's eyes gleamed in the firelight, and tears spilt down her cheek. "Everything," she whispered.

Lorne thought she might combust on the spot. Pure fury flashed through her, hot enough to burn whatever it touched. All her work, her sacrifices, all for nothing because of her sister's need for…what? Comfort? Love? A bit of normality? Words wouldn't come as her mind raced, and she didn't hear Ciely's attempt to apologise.

"Do you think I like this any more than you do?" Lorne finally said, and Ciely flinched back from the steel in her sister's voice. "Do you think I gave up my life? My happiness? Just for the sake of it? Do you think the people we protect, those we try to save, are trivial?"

"I know, but…"

"You have put all of them at risk. All of them." Lorne rose and began to pace, biting down on the rant she wanted to shout at her sister. "You should have told me sooner," she managed to utter, her voice so sharp even Stefan stirred uneasily.

"They are going to have to move," he said.

"We only just relocated them. It was perfect." Lorne bit her lip hard enough to draw blood. The pain centred her and she concentrated on her breathing. "They won't want to move again so soon."

"I-I'm sorry…" Ciely blurted.

Lorne scowled at her. "Sorry doesn't help anyone. It takes months for our families to set up a new camp. The effort of moving, the disruption, it's not good for any of them. Nowhere is safe anymore."

"He won't have told them anything yet. If we can get him back…" Ciely twisted her fingers.

"We could lose too many in the attempt, though we could send Joris," Stefan said.

"No," Ciely gasped, blood draining from her face. "You can't kill him."

"Would be quicker and cleaner, and less risk. We wouldn't need to move anyone, either."

Lorne slowly nodded. Stefan's suggestion made sense. It was safer for everyone and better for Arran in the long run. The Devenders were cruel; they would torture every scrap of information out of him before they mind-wiped him and turned him into a different man.

"When did one life no longer matter?" Ciely said, her voice wavering. "If that is Harmony's rule, then I want none of it."

"When the other lives we are responsible for are exposed," Lorne snapped. "Each person you tell puts others at risk. You know the consequences; keep your mouth shut."

"Or what?"

Lorne raised an eyebrow. "Do you care so little for those around you? I thought I could trust you, Ciely. I thought you believed in Harmony." Pain twisted in her gut. She had thought she could rely on her sister. To share the burden, at least. She had been wrong. She tried again. "This is bigger than just us. Defenceless people depend on us. Harmony is depending on us."

"Nothing we do makes any difference. We hide people. They are not living a free life. They exist, just. That's no life."

"It's a better life than some." Lorne glared at Ciely. "Maybe you should go and warn them. Or I could send Joris. Makes no difference, now, if we tell him or anyone else."

"Even if they move, Maincore will know we're somewhere in the Wytchwards," Stefan said.

"Can't be helped."

"Better we send him to stop Arran being taken to the Ministry interrogators."

"All you are interested in is your Warden. Do you think he is going to magically appear and solve all our problems? If he could, he would have done it by now. You kill Arran, and I'll never forgive you." Ciely stalked out of the clearing.

The next morning, she was contrite and apologetic. Lorne listened to her hollow words, accepted her apology, and ordered everyone to move out. Her scouts had returned with word that another sector was showing signs of failing cores. If they could arrive in time, they might help the people salvage something.

Joris had left in the night. As daylight faded and they were skirting the boundary of Sector 13, the slight man rejoined the group unnoticed. Lorne met his eye, and he gave her a nod. After that, she ignored him. Ciely need never know.

3

———

Annie's twin brother shrank in his chair as his father glared at him. Chiva hated confrontation of any sort, yet recently, that was all he seemed to generate at home. Annie was older than her brother Chiva by thirty-two minutes, the longest thirty-two minutes her mother said she had ever lived through. Usually, though, when her mother said that, she patted her son's face and said he was worth every minute, as if to apologise for saying it in the first place.

Annie watched her brother squirm in his chair. His pale complexion and fine strawberry-blond hair were the same as hers, though he managed to appear more capable and refined than her. His pale blue eyes considered his father as his chin squared. He was about to start again, she could tell.

Chiva said he wanted a quiet life, out of sight of the controllers if possible, contributing his bit to society without notice. The problem was he was too clever for his own good. He understood the controller rhetoric, read through the lines, and often reached conclusions that no one wanted to hear—not their mother, not their father, and certainly not the supervisors of their sector.

Annie sighed, stirring her bowl of gruel. Food rationing had gotten worse lately, and their mother had resorted to watering her weekly soup pan. There was nothing left to forage within five miles; everyone was struggling. With the daily work plans and mandated attendance, it was impossible to get time to travel out into the edges of the wilderness and return before curfew.

"If I spoke to the double-supe, maybe he could get me an interview with the controller," Chiva said. "Just five minutes is all I'd need."

"No," their father grunted. His face was grey and lined with exhaustion; he had only just returned from his double shift. In four hours, he was due back again, and Chiva wouldn't let him be. "We don't want to be singled out; keep your head down and do your work, no more, no less. You know we can't afford one minute of anybody's time, so forget it."

"But it would be an investment. I would earn so much more in the prep room, maybe even advance to the input section. I tell you, the controllers are planning something, and we need to be ready."

"Ready to do what? We can't change anything. We have nothing." Their father rested his head in his hands, and his shoulders bowed as if he personally held the sky up. Annie's lips pinched. He was worn out from long shifts and had little to show for it.

Chiva persisted. "We have each other. We have our minds. We could leave for the Wytchwards before that changes."

The Wytchwards? Since when had her brother wanted to flee into the wilderness?

"The Wytchwards? Never," declared her mother, clasping

her hands together. "It's not safe; its contaminated," she added as if she would catch something from just saying the word. She trembled visibly at the thought; her wiry grey hair vibrated gently as she hid her tired face in the rag she used as an apron.

"That's what we work for, protection against those horrors out there," their father said.

"But where's the protection for the horrors we live with here?" said Chiva. "Did you know Joey 11B was beaten yesterday? For not acknowledging the supe? That could be one of us if he turns up and we don't know. Look at us. There's not a stitch of clothing between us that hasn't been mended many times over; we wear rags. Our wages are deducted if they deem our rags not good enough. No food, no fuel, no money."

"Enough!" their father said, standing so fast that his chair fell over. "It's better than some. Be grateful for what you do have. This subject is done and filed. I don't expect it to be retrieved again, understood?" He glared at Chiva, who sat in silence and glared mutinously back at him. Then he turned on his heel and stalked out the door, slamming it behind him.

"Why do you have to keep pushing him?" their mother asked, wiping her eyes. "Do you think he likes it any better than you? We can't afford for him to lose his job. Don't cause trouble; let it rest."

"Rest?" Chiva said with a laugh, his eyes glittering. "When I could be contributing so much more? When Harmony is crying out for help and no one listens. She needs upgrades and implants. She needs…"

"It is not for you to say what Harmony needs. Keep your voice down. Don't talk blasphemy."

Chiva scowled but did lower his voice. "If they are all doing such a good job, why are we all starving? Why isn't Harmony supplying the harvest? Each year, it gets worse.

The ground yields less. Why isn't anyone looking into that?" He fell silent as his mother turned on him. She clutched her only other pan in one hand and raised it threateningly.

"That's enough," she hissed, tears welling in her watery blue eyes. "Not another word, ever. Get to your bunks, both of you, before you get us all killed with heedless talk."

Annie looked up in surprise. She hadn't said anything, but her mother was glaring at her, too. Silently rising, she emptied her uneaten soup back into the pan. She often got branded with the same brush as her brother; if they looked the same, then they must think the same.

The two siblings got ready for bed in silence. Annie had to be up at third hour, before the second moon had even traversed a quarter of the sky. She rubbed a wet rag over her face and hands before slipping out of her brother's clothes. She would have to wear her damp overalls tomorrow.

She rolled herself up in her frayed blanket and snuggled down in her bed, absently scratching as the bugs that kept them company crawled over her skin.

"Chiv, what was that all about?" she whispered as she leaned over and stared down into the darkness at her brother in the bunk below. The wooden bed frame creaked alarmingly. Their father had taken out a couple of the wooden slats for firewood.

"I spoke to the comp tutor today. He said there was an opening coming up and I would be ideal, but I need to get a controller to put my name on the list to be even considered."

Annie swallowed. She knew her brother was clever. To be recommended for a position in Comptech was unheard of. But to speak to a controller, you needed to barter, and they had nothing, nothing at all to barter with.

"If your tutor thinks you're good enough, could he not speak for you?" Annie suggested.

"That would cost even more."

"But if you are that good, wouldn't it benefit all?"

"Chance would be a fine thing. You know no one cares about what's good for anyone these days. Everything costs." Chiva sighed. "Sometimes I regret being placed in the training track. What's the point of gaining knowledge if you can't use it?"

Chiva had shared some of his classwork with her. She had been quick to pick it up, absorbing the knowledge as greedily as he did. But being a girl, she wasn't eligible for learning. She was only a drab, following her mother into the sector's washhouse when she was seven. After ten dreary years of washing everyone else's clothes but her own, she had nothing else to look forward to.

"What are they suggesting as an alternative?"

"Maintenance. Me, in maintenance! Can you see me crawling around the pipework with a screwdriver in my hand? Ridiculous! I haven't studied this hard to end up in maintenance. There has to be a way."

"Well, at least you wouldn't be in the washhouse. Can't be any worse place than that." Annie kept the words she wanted to say behind her teeth. If maintenance was good enough for their father, it was good enough for his son.

Annie sighed as she stared up at the roof of their unit. Their father had pulled down all the wooden panelling last year. She could see through the cracks up into the darkening sky; soon, the stars would be out. She devoutly hoped the winter would not be as bad as the previous year, but she wasn't holding out much hope. As her brother had said, year to year, the harvest and weather seemed to be deteriorating. She positioned herself so that if it did decide to rain, the drips would miss her. Then, with a deep sigh, she snuggled down to sleep.

. . .

It was a quarter before third hour when her mother woke her the next morning. Annie climbed out of her bunk, and as she dressed, the icy morning air was cold on her bare skin. She scurried into her clothes, shivering; her thin overalls were no protection against the chill. She scowled at her peacefully sleeping brother. He didn't have to rise until fifth hour. It wasn't fair.

Annie ran her fingers through her hair and tied it back with a piece of cord she had salvaged from a shirt that had disintegrated in the wash. She was glad she hadn't been the washer on that tub. That woman had been taken out and beaten for her carelessness and deducted a week's wages for the replacement, even though the shirt had been a disreputable rag.

Her mother thumped a mug of watery soup on the table; it steamed gently in the cold air. She hurried to drink it while it had a remnant of heat. Then she followed her mother out into the chilly morning air. According to the history books, there were supposed to be three moons in the skies over Harmony, but she had only ever seen two. She had no idea what had happened to the third moon. The smaller moon cast a reddish pre-dawn glow that provided enough dim light to guide the workers to the start of their shifts. Mother and daughter hurried down the road towards the circular building where the laundry was located along with the communal baths, which were always empty as there wasn't enough water to fill them.

Annie frowned up at the tall square buildings on the plateau above the stands of pines lining the valley that housed the academy that Chiva attended, along with the data input labs and the suites of data centres. Further up the hill, lights twinkled in the streets of the tech town that fed off the servers and supported the tech centre hidden behind another screen of pine trees.

It was rumoured that the technicians had heat in their houses and hot food on their tables every day, though no one had been able to substantiate that with any proof. The fact that they had power to light their streets when, in the quadrants, they had no power said it all, really. She wondered if Chiva was right. If he got promoted to the servers, maybe he could influence them to help improve conditions in the quadrants.

Annie heaved a sigh as they entered the high-ceilinged chamber. Large, barrel-shaped tubs lined the walls and ran down the centre of the room. They received a quota of water at the start of every week, and the pipes that extended out the bottom, leading to the drains, were shut off so the water could be recycled every day before being emptied and refreshed for the next week.

The charge for laundry was highest on the first day, when the water was clean. It reduced each day as the water cycled through the drums. None of the people living in the quadrants could afford the laundry on any day; they just worked in it.

Behind the large chamber, enormous mangles lined the old communal baths, squeezing the clothes dry and collecting the water to recycle back into the drums for washing. The mangles were worse than the tubs, stiff with use and needing greasing. Of course, there was no grease. It took two men to rotate the handles; they never stopped once they started. Wages were deducted whenever the mangles were still.

Annie paused to admire the young lads preparing to start work. They wrapped rags around their hands to try and delay the formation of inevitable blisters. Those who survived developed muscles on muscles and were very nice to look at, stripped to the waist as they were. No point sweating into your clothes if you could avoid it. Her mother hissed at her, and she grinned as she scuttled up behind her; at least looking was free. They clocked in exactly on the third hour, which echoed around the room as they moved to their allotted stations.

Annie wrinkled her nose as she approached the tub. It was the last day of the cycle, and the water was rank. Six days of repetitive washing cycles for twelve hours a day. Why anyone would want their clothes washed in the resulting fouled-up water, she honestly didn't know. Better than nothing, she supposed as she climbed the steps and heaved a basket of material into the waiting slimy water. She stirred it with a paddle and wrinkled her nose at the terrible smell. Plunging her hands in to the slimy water, she grabbed the material and started rubbing it against the washboards.

Maybe it was time to try and get moved to the ironing rooms. At least it was warm in there, with the irons on the fires. The downside was the risk of getting burnt; none of the women were unscathed, and it hurt. Annie knew this because her friend Maudie had been placed there. Maudie had thought it would be a great place to work, especially in winter. It was like a furnace; the heat helped to dry the cloth. Unfortunately, too hot an iron scorched the material if you weren't careful, and that meant more deductions and beatings, of course.

Maybe it wasn't such a great job, after all. Her friend had been branded with an iron as punishment when she scorched a sheet. Maudie had been in agony, lost wages, and was off work for a week, resulting in the loss of another week's wages. She had been hysterical when they tried to send her back there. Somehow, the rota was switched, and she had been sent to the corn mill out in the flatlands south of the valley instead. Annie hadn't seen her since and hoped she was happier working there.

Annie lifted the cloth out of the tub and began wringing it out. It stank of slimy water, there being no soap suds left after the second day. The material had a slightly green tinge as well, but there was nothing she could do about that. She dropped it into a basket on the floor, grabbed the next piece of cloth, and began rubbing it against the board. A small child trotted by, taking the 'clean' clothes out to the men in the mangle room. Annie continued to work.

When the ninth hour sounded, she lifted her chapped hands out of the water. Stretching her aching back, she climbed down from the tub. She had fifteen minutes to visit the bathroom, eat her lunch, and get back to work. She joined the queue for the bathrooms, wasted ten minutes, and then had to choke down dry bread as she rushed back to her station. After wiping her hands on her overalls, she was back at work as the quarter hour sounded.

Chiva rose at fifth hour and dressed in his grey shirt and trousers. He was fortunate to have been granted a clothes bursary. The academy wanted its students presentable, and there was no way his parents would have been able to afford the uniform. He left his dismal home with relief and strode up the street. A pungent odour marked the location of the hissing and steaming laundry where his mother and sister worked, and he wrinkled his nose as he passed.

Glad to get past the stench, he climbed the hill to the academy building, pausing to catch his breath and look down the dreary valley which housed the quadrant and the work-houses. The terraced housing units sprawled up the valley sides like dried-out wrinkles, sagging greyly after all the life had been sucked out of them. The rising hills on either side of the valley lifted his eyes out of the miasma of his family's daily life, and he entered the brightly lit academy.

The thought of spending the rest of his life in the quadrants sent his mind racing. He had to find a way to get out, and he was running out of time; his final term finished in two months.

Breathing a sigh of relief, Chiva inhaled the slightly metallic air cycling through the building as he climbed the stairs to his form room. He was scheduled for programming time today, all day. This was his last regular slot, and he also had to get his final project written and tested. There was one more slot he could request, but that would be a demerit as he would be taking up extra time on the servers, which he needed to avoid at all costs. But he wouldn't need it; he had it all planned and ready. He just needed to type up the program and run it.

This was what he enjoyed: the programming, translating code into action and seeing the results as he designed them to be. It gave him a sense of power. He created the instructions. He told the servers what to do, and they did it. There was no way he could spend his life crawling around pipes like his father, not after this.

Chiva stopped abruptly as one of the other students grabbed him. "They've shut down the lab, the test environment, everything," the student said. "They won't let us back in. We've got to wait here until we're processed."

"Processed?" Chiva repeated with a gulp, his pulse fluttering wildly as he joined the line of students. What about his project? He was so close. "When did they say we can use the computers again?"

"They didn't. The Devenders are in charge. That one that turfed us out yesterday, he's shut down the whole facility."

4

No matter where Kiefer looked, he couldn't find the stock of disks or chips—no storage of any kind, in fact. So, where were all the files kept and who had access?

Kiefer continued to search the controller's office, his patience wearing thin. Finding the personnel files, in a paper storage system of all places, he sent them to Ferris, who would need them. He closed the cupboard door on the stash of illegal cigars he had found in his abortive search and returned to the desk. He would have to print out the few logs he had found and review them in detail later. Once he had queued the files to print, he headed for the door. There was no point wasting any more time here. He would visit the source of the problem.

Stopping beside the guard, he murmured a soft request and looked down the corridor. The hallway was lit by fluorescent bars set into the ceiling and cast a harsh blue-white light on a queue of people who had already lined up against the wall. They looked nervous and fearful, all dressed in uniforms of grey shirts and trousers. He recognised the students of the academy he had interrupted the previous day.

Wondering why Ferris had chosen to start there, he turned away with a shrug and followed the brightly lit corridor down to the main stairwell. He waited outside the lift shaft, which descended two hundred meters according to the blueprint he had discovered on the controller's computer. Kiefer had memorised the plan, along with the floor plan of the tech building and the quadrant. Not that he particularly wanted or needed to visit the quadrant, but you never knew. He had once ignored the maps of places outside of his immediate need and suffered for it; he wouldn't make that mistake again.

The guard came running up, his burden clanking. Kiefer took the utility belt and made sure all the tools were in place before strapping it around his waist. He tested the torch and checked the batteries. His guard had a second torch and batteries, though he wasn't wearing a utility belt. He probably wouldn't have known what to do with it.

"Thank you," Kiefer said as he pushed the down button and waited patiently for the lift to arrive. He knew where the stairwell was, but he wasn't inclined to climb down or up hundreds of stairs if he didn't need to. The lift arrived, and the door slid open silently. Kiefer entered, his guard beside him, and he hit the lowest button, marked *sub-b,* on the panel. The sub-basement, the area below the main basement and the server bay. He would start at the bottom and work his way back up.

The lift was superfast and silent. Kiefer's stomach rose at the quick descent. Swallowing, he hastened to step out as soon as the doors opened. He turned to the left and followed a grey-brick-lined corridor which had small, yellow glass lamps attached to the wall at regular intervals. The passage led down, and the guard nervously looked up at the ceiling, which had cracks running along its length.

"Don't worry, Corporal," Kiefer said with a grin. "These corridors have withstood the pressure of the land above for centuries; they are not just going to collapse today."

The guard blushed and grimaced. "I certainly hope not, sir." He fell silent as they heard voices up ahead.

"Ah, hopefully this is the maintenance crew, just where they should be." Kiefer looked around the broad cavern that opened before him. Thick, plastic-encased cables ran from the ceiling and along the walls, interspersed with large silver tubes running from the huge cylindrical towers that took up most of the space. These tubes transported the water coolants around the system, dispersing the heat generated by the six processors that sat in the server bays in the basement above. The cavern was uncomfortably hot, which meant the water coolants weren't doing their job properly.

"Looks like we have found one of our problems," Kiefer murmured as he approached four men having a heated discussion beside the first of the tall water cylinders. Three of the men were in maintenance overalls. The fourth man was dressed in a black suit not at all suitable for crawling around maintenance tunnels and making repairs.

"Gentlemen," Kiefer said, and they turned and glared at the interruption. The maintenance crewmen wiped any expression from their faces and stood up straighter.

The suited man frowned at Kiefer. "What do you think you are doing down here? This is a restricted area. Name your supervisor. I will be reporting you to him. You must leave immediately."

Kiefer said smoothly as he moved into the centre of the cavern, "I was sent to help solve your problem. Have you isolated the cause yet? I would suggest you check the intake feeds for blockages; your cores will overheat very soon if you don't get the coolant circulating."

"I don't need you to tell me that," the supervisor snapped. "Leave now. Your wages will be docked for your insolence."

Kiefer raised an eyebrow at the crew. The two elder men shifted their feet; the youngster just gaped at him. "Are all your supervisors as obtuse as this one?"

The crewmembers shared a glance but managed to keep their faces blank.

"I am Commander Kiefer Gallante of the Maincore Devenders. Your processor is offline. I am here to get it back online. Your sector is currently flagged as red. I trust you know what that means?" The man before Kiefer paled. A red flag was reported to the Ministry. No one in their right minds would want to draw themselves to the attention of the ministers.

"Now," Kiefer continued, looking back at the crew, "you were refusing the instructions of your supervisor. Why?"

The older, grey-haired man reluctantly spoke, "He wanted us to open all the valves and flush the blockage out, but we checked the tunnels, and there are no blockages. There has to be a false signal somewhere, which is shutting down the coolant chambers."

"Of course there is a blockage," said the supervisor. "You have missed it. Either you go in and check again or you do what I say and open the valves. If you don't, I will dock a week's pay."

The man shrugged. "Makes no difference. If we open the valves and there is no blockage, we will all die anyway. I told you, the chambers will flood, and we'll get executed."

Kiefer considered the man before him. "How long have you been on maintenance?"

"Forty years, give or take. Jan here, thirty. Simon is new,

just started."

Kiefer looked at the supervisor. "When was the last time you did the maintenance check?"

The grey-haired man snorted. "This is the first time he's come down here. He's never been in a tunnel."

"Really? And he is your supervisor? Simon, I suggest you take your supervisor on a tour, so he can get some idea of what he is talking about. Meanwhile, Jan and..." Kiefer waved his hand at the grey-haired man. "What is your name?"

"Andre."

"Meanwhile, Jan and Andre will help me trace this faulty signal." Kiefer nodded at the trembling supervisor and led the way to the control board. All the lights were green and constant; the board was saying all was well, yet demonstrably, it wasn't. "So, if there is no blockage and the signals are green, yet all coolant chambers are down, which junction controls them all?" Kiefer asked as he traced two of the lines back up the board.

"Signal 342. It's in the lowest chamber, but it's a central junction," Andre said.

"Then, if you agree, that's where we should look, unless you have any other suggestions?"

"There is a possibility that Junction 635 is the cause. It's on the upper grid. We should inspect that one as well." Jan traced a silver line to a crossing point.

Kiefer rubbed his chin. "Very well. Jan, you check 635. Andre and I will check 342. Willis, you stand guard here and make sure that idiot doesn't try and flood the chambers while we're in the tunnels. He is not to touch anything, understood?"

"Yes, sir."

"He wouldn't know how; that's why he was trying to get us to do it," Jan muttered under his breath.

Kiefer grimaced. "Alright, two hours max and then report back here, agreed?"

Jan nodded. "Yes, sir."

Kiefer gestured to Andre. "Lead on," he said and followed the man into the warren of communicating tunnels and shafts.

After about fifteen minutes, Kiefer was lost. The only constant direction was down. They had traversed so many corridors, turnings, and shafts that he sincerely hoped he hadn't made a serious mistake coming down here by himself. He was usually a good judge of character, and he hoped his trust in Andre wasn't misplaced.

After another fifteen minutes of dark tunnels, he asked, "How much further?"

"We need to descend one more level, and the junction should be below us. We'll have to dig to get to the box, but it's not far."

"What made you join the maintenance crew, Andre? It's a bit of a lonely job, isn't it?"

"Yeah, but you don't have idiot supervisors looking over your shoulder, usually." Andre sighed gustily. "And, well, when the missus had twins, two more mouths to feed, it was the only job offering double shifts. I've always liked working with my hands, fixing stuff. If I couldn't have my own farm, this was the next best thing."

"Why didn't you go in for a farm?"

"Money, or lack thereof," Andre replied, "or anything of worth to barter except my own labour, and that never pays enough to make any difference. We barely survive as it is."

Kiefer frowned in the darkness. "Barter?"

"Yeah, no one has any money. Barter is the main currency of trade now, only there's nothing left to barter." Andre started down another ladder. Pausing, he looked up at the Devender in the light of his head lamp. "Come back next year. You'll find the quadrant bare. Few will last the winter, including me and my family. There'll be no need for a processor out here anymore."

"Surely not. It can't be that bad."

"I'd invite you to dinner and let you see, only my wife would be ashamed with what we could offer. Our rations wouldn't feed a mouse, and I couldn't do that to her. She doesn't deserve that," Andre said to himself as he started down the ladder.

Kiefer followed him down, and they traced the marker to the nearside corridor.

"Right, here it is." Andre's voice stopped abruptly as he looked down at the hole in the ground. The box casing was smashed, and all the wires were cut. He moved aside as Kiefer crouched down beside him for a better look. Kiefer hissed his breath out as he traced the wires. "Straight cut, sections missing. Even if we tried to hotwire it, we'd need extension connectors, and I don't have any of those on me. Do you?"

"I've got a couple, but not enough to fix that. You don't expect to have to replace a whole box."

"No, not a sight you see very often," Kiefer agreed. "How many people would be able to make the journey we just did?"

"Including me? A handful, unless they had an excellent map, but it's easy to miss a turning, and then the map wouldn't be much use. You need to know these tunnels."

"Makes it an inside job, then. You will need to give me that list of people." Kiefer looked at Andre, who nodded reluctantly.

"Me, Andre 11C, Jan 13B, Taylir 24B, Gethro 41D, and Silas 37E. But I can't see any of them doing this, not putting all our lives at risk. This would sabotage the whole installation, our families."

"That few? I would say that's a point of failure right there. Knowledge shouldn't be restricted to so few people, though, in this case, I suppose it narrows it down. Maybe that's what they want, to shut this processor down."

"But that only exposes us more. It doesn't make sense." Andre scowled down at the box. "We could try a shunt."

Kiefer raised his eyebrows.

"If we expose more of the cable, take the wires back, we can trace the route and see if we can jump it to an auxiliary cable and jump it back further down. The thirty-fifth aux travels down this deep. We could divert it. It's not a critical function."

Kiefer frowned at Andre as he brought up the blue print in his mind; the image hung before his eyes as he considered it.

"You're right. It crosses at the 341 Junction."

"Let's dig out this cable and drag it up a level. You start digging out the cable and bore a hole up there. I'll go dig out the aux cable."

"Very well," Kiefer agreed as he unfolded his shovel, grinning at himself for accepting orders from someone else. But experience trumped all in this situation. If they could save the processor, his life would be much easier.

He dug out the box and traced the cable along the wall to the point where he could pull out enough of it to reach the ceiling. The question was, would the aux cable extend far enough? He grubbed down in the soil and uncovered the plastic tube, pushing the dirt behind him.

Focused on the job at hand, he didn't notice the tingling in his hands at first. It wasn't until he had bored the hole in the ceiling and was seated on the ground beneath it, surrounded by fresh soil, stripping the plastic off the hundreds of wires inside the casing, that he realised his hands were burning. Dropping the cable, he rubbed his fingertips; they felt rough and calloused and were hot. Looking up, he saw Andre's light flashed through the hole and heard his cursing as he struggled with the aux cable. The sound of Andre's presence was a comfort. The man could just as easily have left him down there and headed back to the surface. He'd had plenty of opportunity.

"Commander?"

The tone of Andre's voice made it sound like he had called for Kiefer more than once. Kiefer shook himself and looked up. "Yes?"

"I've got the aux cable here. I'll feed it down to you."

"Ready." Kiefer reached up as the cable was fed down through the hole. He gently pulled it until he felt resistance and then sat cross-legged in the dirt and began the painful job of connecting the cables. Patiently, he twisted the wires together, ignoring the sharp edges that nicked his skin. His blood blended with the wires, and some of it dripped onto the soil below.

"Warden?" a soft voice whispered in his mind. *"Is that you? At last."*

Kiefer looked around, startled. Was he hearing things now?

He returned to his work. The sooner they finished, the better. No one had mentioned ghosts in the basement.

"It hurts. Please don't switch it back on."

"Switch what back on?" he replied, before realising he had responded.

"The machine, it drains me. I can't help the people if the machine takes it away."

Kiefer paused and thought about that. *"What does it take away?"*

"Me, it takes my power away. Don't hurt me, please don't hurt me anymore." The soft voice ended in a heart-breaking whimper.

Kiefer stiffened as the voice's anguish pierced him. *"Who are you?"*

"Harmony." The voice died away.

Kiefer sat back on his heels in shock; that wasn't possible. Harmony was an integral part of the system. It was she who had designed the synapses and agreed to the processors. It was Harmony driving the staged transfer of power from the processors to Maincore as the sectors failed, reducing the harm and pain inflicted on her and managing the damage to the environment around them. That couldn't have been Harmony. His mind was playing tricks on him.

His fingers were bloody and sore by the time Andre joined him, but he was halfway through the wires. Andre exclaimed and took the cable off him, offering him a medi-wipe and some plasters in exchange.

Kiefer winced as he cleaned his fingers. The wires were sharp and unforgiving. He concentrated on opening the plasters and activating the soothing gel that dulled the sting, making sure he left enough for Andre once he finished. Leaning back against the wall, he watched Andre's nimble fingers do a much neater job than he had. He grinned wryly. "I should have just let you do it."

Andre chuckled. "It's easier once it's started. The first twenty are the worst; the others seem to surrender once they've got their fill of blood."

"You make them sound as if they are alive."

"They must be, to a degree. After all, they are connected to a sentient being."

Kiefer looked down at his fingers in concern. Did that mean Harmony had his blood now? And if so, what did that mean?

"How long have we been down here? Willis will be getting worried."

"Almost done." Andre tied off the last two wires and

looked at Kiefer. "We have to throw the switch in the control room to see if this has worked."

Kiefer nodded and wearily pushed off the wall. He was exhausted, and that meant they had been down here for more than two hours. He hoped his troop were not turning the sector upside down looking for him; he hadn't expected to be so long.

"I'll let you lead the way," Kiefer said with a smile.

Andre bobbed his head in agreement and led the way back to the first ladder they had to climb.

Kiefer's arms were trembling by the time they reached the sub-basement. He hauled himself up the last few rungs and leant against the wall for a moment to catch his breath. "I used to think I was fit," Kiefer gasped as he tried to control his breathing.

Andre chuckled. "There's fit, and then there's *fit.*"

Kiefer was glad to see Andre was breathing deeply, too. He straightened and led the way back into the control room.

Kiefer stopped abruptly at the scene that greeted them. Willis was lying prone on the floor. Simon hovered over him, a worried expression on his face. The supervisor was hounding Jan to open the valves. Jan was bloodied and still protesting, though he had been herded over to the control panel and had obviously bowed to his superior's pressure. Kiefer leapt across the room as Andre howled, and Jan pressed a series of buttons.

"No!" Kiefer shouted. "Reverse it. Reverse it now."

Jan stared at him wide-eyed. "I can't."

Kiefer flung a desperate glance at Andre. "Is that true? Can you do anything?"

Andre's face contorted with horror as he inspected the control board. He stared at Jan. "What have you done?" he whispered.

A tremendous rumbling began deep in the bowels of the

planet, and Kiefer ran to grab Willis. "Help me. We need to get out. Hurry, we have to get higher." He looked around in desperation. "Andre, help me. We have to get out of here."

The supervisor glared at Jan and stabbed a finger against his chest. "You will stay here and monitor the boards. That's what we pay you for."

"We have to l-leave, before it's too late," Jan stuttered, his gaze drawn to tunnels and the growing roar.

Andre stooped to grab Willis' other arm and helped drag him down the corridor towards the lift shaft. The lad was dead weight, but Kiefer was relieved to see his chest rise and fall. He jabbed the call button and bundled the guard into the lift as the doors swished open. "Jan, Simon, quick!" The sound of thunder grew as hundreds of tonnes of water rushed towards them.

Kiefer pulled Simon inside and not waiting for the others, stabbed the up button. The doors closed on the terrified face of the supervisor, who belatedly ran towards the lift, closely followed by Jan as a torrent of water rushed down the corridor. The lift shot towards the surface, and Kiefer slid to the floor and held his thumping head in his hands. The doors slid open on pandemonium.

Kiefer stood. "Quick, everyone out," he instructed as he dragged Willis out by one arm. He scanned the foyer as people dashed around him, and snagged one of the guards. "Report!"

"Sir." The guard saluted. "Multiple fatal errors. Structural damage warnings, and the general evacuation alarm has been sounded, only no one knows what the protocol is."

"Right," Kiefer said, his face grim. He dragged a chair over and stood on it. "Silence!" he bawled at the top of his voice. "Everyone will stand still." He waited as everyone turned to stare at him in shock.

"There will be no panic. Devenders Unit One, escort the

Comptech employees down to the housing quadrants and take our horses and equipment with you. Students, grab whatever food and water you can carry and follow. Devenders Unit Two, clear the academy and the tech village. This facility is permanently closed. You have ten minutes to leave this building or you will go down with it." A sea of horrified faces greeted him, but no one moved. "Now, move!" he roared.

Kiefer looked at Andre and Simon. "Go home," he said, his voice abrupt. His mind spun on the list of things to be completed. "This place will collapse shortly."

Andre nodded. "Come find me. You are welcome in my home."

Kiefer gripped his arm and dashed up the stairs, contrary to his own orders. He dived into the controller's office and grabbed the papers off the printer, swept his half-written report, map and schematics into a bag and slung it over his shoulder. Darting into the first aid room, he grabbed the emergency bags stacked in the corner. He fervently hoped the medical staff were more diligent than the admin staff had been.

Careening down the stairs and out of the building, he ran as a grinding roar rose behind him. He kept running. The rumbling sound grew as the stone path beneath his boots trembled, and he fled down the hill, out of Comptech, past the academy and the hastily deserted Devender camp, towards the quadrants below. When he reached the base of the hill and turned, a resounding crack echoed around the valley, and a jet of water erupted into the air.

Kiefer dropped to his knees and dug his hands in the dirt. *"Harmony? If you can hear me, you must protect the people in the settlement. Do you hear me? Protect the people in the settlement."*

Taking a deep breath, he stood, and grabbing his bags, backed away as the grinding continued. The ground split, sliding apart in slow motion. A great, gaping hole swallowed the Comptech facility as it collapsed in on itself, followed by the academy building. A plume of smoke and dust rose in the air.

Kiefer surveyed the sector, watching as people gathered in the open area in front of the tall, square building which dwarfed it and looked up the valley in horror. They all seemed lost, and he grimaced at the complete lack of organisation or structure. He spotted Ferris and headed towards him.

"Well," Ferris said with a grin, his face covered in grime, "this is a first. It's fortunate Griffin found a warehouse full of food and blankets. They must have known they were going to need it."

"Did you salvage any of those personnel files? We need to identify any further threats and anyone else who was involved."

"On it," Ferris replied, waving a lazy hand.

"Tell Griffin to set up a triage tent for any injuries and make sure Willis is treated." Kiefer pushed the emergency bags at Ferris, though he kept one for himself. "Where are Tremill and Stainton?"

"Here, sir." The men had followed Ferris across the square.

"Set up a way station. Distribute food, blankets, and digs. Find the warehouses, check supplies, and manage the distribution of rations, max two Comptech people per home. Allocate me to 11C. Here's the quadrant layout." Kiefer handed over the controller's map.

"Yes, sir."

"Set up camp out on the boundary. Devenders should go off duty there if possible."

"Yes, sir."

"Send a messenger to Sector 44 for help. Advise them of

the situation and number of casualties. Sector 45 is off the grid permanently; ask them to pass the message on to Maincore."

"Right away, sir." The two men rushed off to follow their orders.

Kiefer took a breath and looked around. His bag weighed heavily on his shoulder. The people were slowly dispersing, looking bewildered and confused, blindly following the Devender's orders. Kiefer knew that wouldn't last; by morning, tempers would be rising.

He looked up the valley. The Comptech building had gone, and the academy, along with the screening treeline. There was a deep depression in the land where it had collapsed. The fountain of water was still gushing down the valley, though it diverted at the bottom of the hill, flowed down the side of the quadrant, and joined the stream in the gully, not directly through the dwellings as one would have expected. Maybe Harmony had heard him and diverted the flow. He shelved that thought for later.

Shifting the emergency bag over his shoulder, Kiefer headed for 11C. Exhaustion tugged at him, and he barely managed to walk in a straight line. Should he go to the Devender camp? From what Andre had said, he wondered if Andre would be able to put him up, but he wanted to see their living conditions for himself. A new guard trailed after him. After staggering to section C, he weaved his way along the foul-smelling alley before he stopped outside 11C. The door opened as he hesitated.

Andre's deep voice welcomed him. "Commander, be welcome in my home."

Kiefer entered, the sensation of dried dirt and grime cracking on his face as he smiled. "I wasn't sure you meant it."

"Please, you look exhausted. Come inside." Andre eased

the bag of Kiefer's shoulder and almost dragged him in. He planted the Devender in a chair at the table.

Kiefer twisted his lips. "My apologies to your family. I am not at my best this evening."

A woman came forward. "Please, do not worry. I doubt anyone will be at their best this evening. My name is Ester, and these are our children, Chiva and Anneka."

Kiefer's made to stand, but Ester waved him back, and he leaned back into his chair. He smiled, trying to reassure their two children, obviously twins, who hovered behind their mother. "I brought a ration pack and some blankets. I hope it helps. I can always head back up to the camp if needed."

"Please, relax," Andre said. "We have food and coffee. My son bought some home; he is a student at the academy."

Kiefer nodded, unsurprised. "Coffee would be good." He accepted a mug and inhaled the aroma, his shoulders dropping. "If you would be so good as to give the lad outside your door a mug as well, I'm sure he would appreciate it."

Ester frowned at him. "Shouldn't he come in and join us?"

"No, he is on duty. Just the coffee." Kiefer grinned, not wanting to explain how the guard would be horrified to join his commander.

Andre murmured in Ester's ear and she nodded. Moments later, she carefully carried a steaming mug to the lad standing outside her front door. Initially, he refused it, but he gave in gratefully when she told him the commander had requested it.

Andre looked at Kiefer across the table. "I think your reputation is a lie," he said, his voice gruff. "Devenders are supposed to be feared, yet here you are, mothering yours."

Kiefer grinned. "Don't make the mistake of underestimating them. They are to be feared because I appreciate them. My job is to keep the processors running for as long as possible to sustain our people as we transition to the Main-core. Their job is to make sure I can do my job, among other things." He smiled in thanks as Ester placed a bowl in front of him. "Please, join me."

"No, no, we've already eaten," she said, flustered.

"I highly doubt that," Kiefer said. "There is enough in the pack to feed us all, and there will be another tomorrow."

Ester cast a beseeching look at her husband.

"Come," he said, sitting at the table, "we have a guest; let us enjoy his company."

Under the Devender's stern gaze, she set the table for five. After calling her children, she dished up the rest of the stew.

Kiefer discreetly watched the family's reactions. They all ate slowly, savouring the taste. The girl, Anneka, seemed to be communing with her plate as if she had never seen meat before. He slowed his eating to match them. Glancing around, he noted how bare their home was: minimal furniture, no decorations, just the necessities.

"Sir, yesterday morning, when you arrived and shut us down, what was that code I found?" Chiva asked, not as cowed as the rest of the family.

Kiefer inspected the boy. He was skinny, but not as thin as his sister. He seemed twice the size of Anneka. His thin face was intelligent, and his blue eyes sharp. "You found the code? Have you seen anything like it before?"

"No, that was the first time we'd been allowed into the main comp room. We always work on a test instance. I was finishing my final program. I was due to graduate next month."

"I'm not surprised with the father you have. I would expect the son to be just as smart."

Chiva looked over at his father in surprise.

"And what of your sister? Anneka, isn't it? What do

you do?"

"I'm Annie. I work in the laundry with Ma. Girls aren't allowed schooling."

"How short-sighted," Kiefer murmured.

Annie flicked him a startled glance and her father snorted.

"Andre!" Ester exclaimed, but her husband just chortled.

"Well, I guess it doesn't make any difference now; it's all gone. What are we supposed to do now?" Chiva scowled at his empty bowl.

Kiefer smiled. "Choose to stay and rebuild or to go. Both are difficult choices and probably have hardships." He shrugged. "That is the choice everyone will need to make. The processor is gone. There will be no system in this sector; you can either try and make it on your own, move to another sector, or consider transferring to a Maincore academy."

"Yeah, and how much would that cost?" Chivas groaned.

"I suggest you speak to the admin desk tomorrow, and find out what your options are. Did you manage to save your transcripts?"

"Of course I did. I am only two credits away from graduating," Chivas said, his voice full of scorn.

"Well then, find out what your options are tomorrow. For now, I would suggest we sleep. There will be no shifts tomorrow. Each function will need to assess damage and impact and advise if you have a job or not. The administration will help."

Kiefer watched Ester shoo her children off to bed. Then after a short argument, which he won, he rolled himself in his blankets on the floor, resting his head on a pillow Ester had forced him to accept, as she'd been horrified that a guest was sleeping on the kitchen floor. He was asleep as soon as his head hit the pillow. His problems could wait until tomorrow.

5

W aking at fifth hour, Kiefer lay still for a moment, recalling where he was. The unit was silent apart from the occasional snore drifting from the bedroom. There was no need for the family to rise early on this day. His head ached dully; he had forgotten to take any pain relief last night and was surprised he had slept as well as he had.

Folding the blankets, he placed them in a neat pile on the table, along with another ration pack. He stirred a small packet of pain relief powder in a mug of water until it dissolved. Knocking it back, he shuddered as he swallowed the foul-tasting liquid. Then he shouldered his bag and left, collecting his guard on the way out.

"If winter wasn't coming, I'd knock this whole lot down and start again," he murmured as they skirted the ice-rimmed puddles. "This is one of the worst quadrants I've seen."

The young lad escorting him glanced at him in surprise. "This is just the same as Sector 44; they were no better off."

Kiefer frowned at him. "Are you sure? It seemed a lot nicer."

"I think the controllers were just better at disguising it. Here, greed has got the better of them."

"There is no point sending these people to 44, then," Kiefer muttered to himself as they reached the warehouse behind the laundry. Stepping through the smaller gate cut into the wall, he strode across to Ferris.

His footsteps echoed loudly in the quiet morning air, and Ferris looked up. Grimed from head to foot, it was obvious he hadn't slept. The warehouse was chill and dark. High stacks of boxes rose all around them like sheer valley walls blocking the light.

"Status?" Kiefer asked.

"Not good." Ferris gestured at the boxes. "Most of these are out of date. They've been starving these people for years, yet they had food going to waste in here. All the fresh produce goes straight to Comptech; none of it comes here. The only good news is that there is a distribution system, so we can utilise that."

"I'll visit the produce farms. We need to divert those goods here for now. You should go get some sleep. I can take over here."

Ferris stretched, and his joints cracked. "About time." He gave Kiefer a keen glance. "What's the plan?"

Kiefer sighed. "Redistribute these people, I suppose. Some can try and rebuild here. Others could maybe farm, but we need to find out if there are any other dissenters. We are too few to manage an uprising. What did the controller have to say? Where is he?"

"He didn't believe the warning. He said it was impossible for the facility to collapse. I guess he didn't read the manual." Ferris' face brightened. "Though we did get all the double-supes out and the supes, so I put them to managing their own people."

"Where's the personnel register? We may need to move a few around. Not many are going to have jobs anymore until they reorganise."

"Well, it's all yours. Good luck!" Ferris grinned with relief. "See you later."

Kiefer nodded absentmindedly, his head already in the files.

He was in the middle of mapping out what he thought the facility should look like when he heard a commotion outside. Standing, he went to see what was happening. His heart sank as he saw an angry mob collecting in the square. Well, this would either go badly or really badly. It was up to them.

Striding up to the top of the steps, he turned and searched the crowd, trying to identify those most likely to cause trouble. His Devenders stood in a loose cordon, alert and wary.

"People, please, if you could give me a moment."

The crowd quietened until only a few low murmurs lingered on the chill morning air.

"As you know, the facility is no more." Kiefer gestured up the valley. "Sector 45 is permanently off the grid. No succour will be forthcoming from Maincore. The situation is irreparable, but you do have a choice."

He paused as the crowd stirred.

"You have the choice to stay and rebuild, move to another sector, or travel to Maincore for reallocation. But know, if you stay here, you only have what is in this warehouse. These stocks will need to sustain you for the winter before you can plant new crops. We will distribute what is available fairly."

"Are we supposed to believe that?" a young man jeered

from the front of the crowd. "As fairly as the controllers do, eh? As fairly as the supes do?"

Kiefer shrugged. "I am not the controller. There is nothing here I want. I will be leaving in due course; the only reason I am still here is to help you survive this catastrophe."

The man moved up a step, flinging his arms out, his face a mask of derision. "Listen to him. He's only here to help us, do you hear that? *He* wants to help us."

"People are injured, and others are missing. I think helping those families is more important, don't you?" Kiefer asked, though it was obvious they wouldn't listen. "You have a choice: to work together or let greed drive your behaviour, much like your controllers."

"There aren't many of them; we could take them. That food is ours!" The man jabbed his finger at the warehouse to emphasise his point, and the mutters increased.

Kiefer spread his hands. "Please, there is no need for violence. You don't need to 'take us'. We are here to help distribute the food amongst you."

"Don't listen to him; he lies. They will keep it all." The belligerent man peered at the people around him, and they nodded in agreement.

Kiefer frowned down at him. "What do you propose? Storm the warehouse so you can get in first? So you can take what is rightfully yours? What is yours versus the man standing next to you? I promise, we will distribute the stores to everyone. There is no need for a frenzy. You will destroy more than you take, and those less fortunate will get nothing."

"It's a delaying tactic. He's waiting for reinforcements. They'll starve us again." The man turned to the crowd. "Who's with me?"

"Jasper's right. This is our chance," another voice joined in. "Let's get 'em!"

The crowd surged forward eagerly, and the Devenders took a step back.

Andre's deep voice broke through the jeers. "Jasper, don't be a fool. You want to get your head broke? Danner, Billie, what do you think you are doing? All of you get in line now. You will wait patiently until it's your turn and then you will take home your share and not before."

He moved up the steps in front of Kiefer. "You heard him. We're on our own, so we need to work together. Those who want to leave can leave. Those who want to stay, stay. But if you stay, we look out for each other. We work together to make sure we all survive." He glared at his colleagues.

"Now, line up," he barked, and the crowd sheepishly moved in line. Andre smiled at Kiefer. "They're used to being told what to do. Reasoning's a bit advanced for them yet."

Kiefer grinned with relief. "Then it is fortunate you arrived. I don't think they would have taken my orders so well. We need some help sorting the boxes and handing stuff out. Who would you suggest?"

"My Ester is a good organiser; she could manage a team to hand stuff out." Andre looked over the crowd. As Kiefer instructed his Devenders to disperse, Andre called a couple of men and women over and led them into the warehouse.

Sometime later, Kiefer was back at his plans, leaving Andre and Ester to organise the warehouse. It seemed to run more smoothly with them doing it. He had sent a unit of his men up to the site to see if they could dig anyone out, but he wasn't expecting much. Over forty people were missing and presumed dead, mainly technicians.

He stopped his musing as Andre approached. "I need to

travel out to the produce farms to divert the fresh produce here. Would you come with me tomorrow?"

Andre's eyes narrowed. "Of course. What do you intend doing with it?"

"Add it to your distribution system, of course. You'll need to set up an agreement with the farm to supply you instead of the facility."

"We don't have anything to pay for it," Andre said, staring at Kiefer.

Kiefer grinned. "It was set up and funded by the facility. They didn't pay for it, either, so you should be fine to start with. At some point, though, you are going to have to set up a trade agreement. They will need things, as will you. Providing services to fix their machines, for example, and providing more labour to help expand the harvest. This warehouse will run out, and you'll need more food. Set up another mill, another industry. It depends on the skills you have here, but you have choices."

"You don't think small, do you?" Andre said with amazement.

"That is what Harmony was supposed to be, a low-tech, agricultural society. You'll be leading the way."

Kiefer rose to his feet with a grunt and clapped Andre on the shoulder. "Let's start you off as best we can. Let's find those troublemakers, get them cleaning the streets, keep them busy. It'll improve everyone's spirits if it doesn't smell like a cesspit all the time."

Andre smiled. "True."

As the light began to fail, Kiefer made his way up to the camp his men had set up at the head of the valley. They had managed to salvage most of their kit. His tent had been raised back against the rocky wall. He lowered himself to the ground by the camp fire.

"Alright lads?" he asked looking around the camp.

One unit was asleep; six men rolled up in their blankets, under the awning. He assumed one was Ferris. A young lad called Nealy and one of the corporals, Tremill, were seated on a fallen tree trunk, busy cleaning their swords. Polished tack lay piled beside them, proof of their work. Willis was seated with them, a bandage around his head.

"Willis, how are you feeling?"

"Fine, sir. They stitched me up; it's nothing, sir."

"Well, take it easy for a day or two," Kiefer said "Who's on watch?"

"Third Unit, sir." Tremill reported. "Jensen's up at the fork, on point, and Brandt is at the head of the gully. The rest are scattered through the settlement."

"Good, keep them on their toes; we don't need any more surprises. Rotate at midnight."

"Yes, sir." Tremill nodded. "Um, Lieutenant Ferris was saying we would be leaving soon."

"Once we've got these people back on their feet. We need to ensure they are set up to survive the winter before we leave."

"I thought we were supposed to be defending the processors, not these people," Nealy muttered under his breath.

Kiefer glared at him. "Our duty is to defend the facilities that protect Harmony so that she can take care of our people; everything we do is to protect the people. If there is no facility to guard, then the people come next."

Nealy flushed at the rebuke. "Yes, sir. Sorry, sir."

Kiefer grimaced as he accepted a bowl of stew. More of their ration packs were being watered down to stretch. They would run out soon. He wondered how much meat the farm produced.

"What do you think of the settlement?" he asked, looking around the men. "Would you live here?"

Tremill laughed. "City life for me. I've had enough of sleeping rough. Can't wait to return to the comforts of home."

"Ha, you shouldn't have joined up if the ground isn't good enough for yer," one of the lads joshed him.

A chuckle went around the campfire. "It could be a real nice place to retire to," a middle- aged man said. He had a thick neck and hands like plates.

"Aw, Milain, who's talking about retiring? You ain't old enough yet." Willis grinned at him.

"I said it 'could be'." Milain glared at him. "I mean, it needs sprucing up a bit, but that wouldn't take much. And you could build yer own place, not be stuck in those units."

Tremill laughed. "He's built his house already."

"Do you think Harmony will watch over this place now?" Willis asked.

"Why wouldn't she?" Kiefer replied.

"Well, there's no tech to help her."

"She's all around you, all the time, not just when there is tech. The tech just enhances what is already here."

"You mean she is watching us right now?" Nealy asked, his voice horrified.

"Don't be daft," Tremill said, his gaze jumping around the camp. "She's the planet, not the sun. She's underneath you. How could she watch you?"

Nealy looked down at the ground. "Maybe she's listening to us."

Kiefer stirred. The lad wasn't far off. A wave of sadness impinged on his senses, and Kiefer knew it wasn't his emotions; was it Harmony's?

Tremill laughed. "She's got more important stuff to do

than listen to you, like keeping the sea moving or growing food."

"The coast's not far." Nealy said, a wistful expression on his face. "Wish we had time to go and see it. I've never seen the sea."

"We're not here on holiday, you know," Milain retorted. "We can't just go sightseeing when you feel like it."

"Have *you* seen the sea?" Tremill asked, his pointed nose twitching.

"Nah, not in real life, only on the vid."

"Well then." Willis frowned. "Maybe we could go when we're off duty?"

"I think you'll find it's further than you think," Kiefer said. "It's at least another four clicks on horseback."

"Have you seen the sea, sir?" Nealy asked.

"Once, off Sector 17," Kiefer admitted.

"What's it really like?"

Kiefer frowned in thought. "Like no place you've ever seen before. It's wide and open and fills the horizon, a gleaming silver carpet that is constantly in motion. It's as if you could throw your dreams out there and they'll come back threefold. And the smell, the tang of salt and moisture in the air, it's the freshest, cleanest air you'll ever breathe." Kiefer grinned self-consciously as he realised his men were staring at him. "You should definitely visit if you ever get the chance," he said, and retreated to his tent, leaving the men to relax around the campfire. Their soft voices started up again as he dropped the tent flap behind him. They seemed to be in reasonable spirits.

Kiefer lay on his bedroll and stared up at the canvas. His hand drifted on its own accord to the dirt beneath him, and his palm tingled. *"Harmony?"* he thought gently. *"Are you there?"*

"No," she whimpered. *"Make them stop."*

"Make who stop? What's happened?" he asked as he jerked upright. Her distress was in his head, and his heart raced in response.

"They have cut me off. Maincore lied. I can't feel them. You have to stop them, please."

"Stop what?" He strained to reach her. *"Harmony?"* His head was filled with silence. She had gone.

Breathing in deep, Kiefer tried to control his thudding heart. If that was Harmony, then she was in distress. He needed to get back to Maincore and find out what was going on. Tomorrow, he would visit the farm, and then they would leave. He would tell the men in the morning.

Relaxing back on his bedroll, he concentrated on slowing his racing pulse. He pictured the sea: the grey waves washing up on the pebbles, the regular swish of the foaming water, and the soft clacking the rolling pebbles made. The soothing sound had mesmerised him for hours. He relaxed as he replayed the memory, smiling as he remembered how calming it had been, and finally, he fell asleep.

The next morning, he was up with the dawn. The second moon was low in the sky, and the red moon out of sight. He nodded to Stainton, who was just coming off watch.

"Report," he said in the soft voice early mornings seemed to require. Pouring a cup of coffee, he handed it to Stainton before pouring his own.

"Thank you, sir. All is quiet. There's nothing to report. No movement. No visitors. Nealy has your unit ready to go. Tremill is down the gully. Rest of Unit Four are throughout the settlement. Unit One will rotate in six hours."

"Very good. Where is Lieutenant Ferris?"

"He was riding the perimeter, sir."

"We break camp tomorrow at dawn. We're heading back

to Maincore; tell the men to be prepared. I am going out to the farm today. Once we know their supplies are guaranteed, we can move out."

"Yes, sir," Stainton replied, raising his mug in acknowledgement.

"Right. I'd better go make sure the farm is prepared to supply them then, I suppose." Kiefer emptied his mug and strode off down the hill to collect the unit of men who would accompany him.

6

Kiefer and his men were returning with Andre after a successful negotiation with the produce farm, Kiefer's credentials having overruled the farm manager's initial arguments, when the commander's horse baulked as a rope was jerked up and across the road in front of them. He held on tight with his knees and attempted to shorten the rein.

"Ambush!" Kiefer yelled as his horse pirouetted, and he struggled to bring him under control.

Andre sat up groggily, his horse having dumped him in the confusion and bolted down the track. Kiefer nudged his reluctant horse forward to shield Andre and shouted for his men to reform.

"Surrender now, and no one will get hurt!" a sharp voice said from off to his left.

Kiefer allowed his horse to drift in that direction, blocking the speaker's view of Andre. "Says who?" He scanned the trees, searching for their assailants.

Andre rose to his feet, rubbing his hip hard and flexing his leg. "Let me speak to them."

"Not 'till we know what they want; they could be bandits, or worse," Kiefer replied, drawing his firearm. "Show yourselves."

"You are surrounded. Drop your weapons, or you will all be killed." The voice was young, female, and determined.

"You could try," Kiefer replied, straining to see any movement. A low thrum preceded a chunky thud, and one of his men toppled out of his saddle to the ground.

"Disperse," he commanded as an older voice shouted, "Hold!" He leaned down and grabbed Andre, and his men scattered at his command. "Put your foot on mine," he said as he hauled Andre up and across his saddle-bow. An arrow thrummed over his bent head.

"I said stop firing, you idiot!" A man's voice barked, sharp with annoyance.

As Andre grunted painfully, Kiefer urged his horse off the road, towards the source of the arrows, hoping he was quicker than the archer. His horse mowed the man down, and the nocked arrow pinged wildly into the air as they plunged further into the trees.

Kiefer let his horse pick his own route, just urging him on whenever it tried to slow his pace. Holding onto Andre, he gradually steered the horse eastwards, back towards the sector. He would be surprised if he weren't being followed. Should he have just laid down his arms and surrendered? To surrender to an unseen enemy just wasn't right, but he wondered how his men had fared. After the brief flurry, he hadn't seen any of them, and the shouts had faded, the deeper they travelled into the forest. Well, he couldn't change his decision now, so no point worrying about it.

He was in a quandary. Should he lead his pursuers back to the settlement or away from it. Would the people prefer the bandits over the Devenders? Was he just heading into another trap? They could already be there, for all he knew.

He leaned forward. "Andre?"

"Yeah?"

"You, alright?"

"Never been better."

"Do you want me to stop?"

"Why?"

"I think they may have already found the settlement. You'd be better off riding in alone talking of ambush, while I scout the situation."

"We should stay together," Andre said.

"You'll be safer without me."

"But you won't be."

"Can't be helped. Here, slide off. You can take the horse."

"Won't they just shoot at me instead?" Andre asked with some justified sarcasm as he rubbed his stomach.

Kiefer grinned. "A chance you'll have to take."

"Gee, thanks." Andre scowled at him. "You know I can't ride very well. How am I going to get this thing home?"

"Just keep him pointed east. He knows where the troop is."

Muttering under his breath, Andre allowed himself to be heaved up into the saddle. Kiefer threaded Andre's feet into the stirrups. "I'll try and keep them off you," he promised. Kiefer slapped the horse on the rump and as the horse jerked forward, he faded into the dim undergrowth.

Kiefer unsheathed his dagger and crouched in a dip behind a screen of leafy soapwort and prickly brambles, waiting to see who was following them. Enough time passed of him breathing in pungent green scents and woody aromas that he thought he might have been mistaken. A sudden racket, like pebbles clashing together, made him flinch as a bird chucked its way up into the canopy overhead.

A soft whisper reached him. "Damn fool birds, they should all be shot!"

"Hush, they're heading east, back to the settlement. Go ahead and warn Lorne."

"*You* tell her. She'll shove a knife in my guts if I leave you out here on your own," the low voice muttered in return.

"I'm perfectly capable of tracking a horse on my own," the tracker said. The voice was young and petulant.

"Yeah, it's what's on the horse that's the problem."

"Chaney, for once in your life, do as you are told. I'll meet you at the settlement."

The man continued to grumble under his breath, but it seemed that he would follow the tracker's orders as he headed back towards the road.

The tracker, a wiry young girl with coppery-red, bobbed hair, paused where Kiefer had dismounted and cast about. A competent tracker would be able to read what had happened in the disturbed ground and clearly see that only one person had ridden the horse onwards. This tracker carefully inspected the ground and the undergrowth before silently following the horse's tracks.

Kiefer hesitated. Should he follow Andre, as he had promised, or find out who this Lorne might be? Sighing, he knew it wasn't really a choice. Resolutely turning his back on Andre and the young girl tracking him—she hadn't had a bow after all—he followed the man, who was still muttering deprecations under his breath.

Once sure he was out of earshot of the tracker, Kiefer pounced on the unsuspecting man—the tracker had called him Chaney— and pinned him to the ground. He disarmed Chaney and then wrenched his arm up his back and pressed his cheek into the dirt. "Who are you and what do you want?" he said into Chaney's ear.

"Ger'off me!" Chaney spluttered, spitting out dirt.

"Who are you?" Kiefer repeated.

Chaney squirmed under Kiefer's grip. "I'm with the resistance."

"What resistance?"

"Huh? The resistance who will free Harmony from the likes of you and your oppressive tyranny."

"Really?" Kiefer eased up his pressure. "Who is Lorne?"

"The leader of the Harmony resistance."

"And how big is your resistance?" Kiefer asked.

"Big enough!" Chaney snapped, His eyes darted wildly as though he'd realised he might have said too much.

"Why were you tracking me?"

"Because you were the one that got away, that's why."

Kiefer looked down at the man sprawled in the mud. He didn't have an option, really; all paths led back to the settlement. Kneeing the man in the back, he pulled his belt off and then secured Chaney's wrists behind his back before allowing him to rise.

"Lead on, then. Let's go see this mighty leader of yours," Kiefer said. He shoved Chaney in the direction of the settlement and silently followed.

Andre thankfully clattered into the settlement, weaving his way between the warehouse and the empty bath house. He dismounted stiffly in front of the crowd in the gathering area. Standing on the steps was a slender, red-haired woman, her hair intricately braided and wrapped around her head. Deep violet eyes flensed him as he strode forward, searching for the Devenders.

Beside her stood a brute of a man. His thick arms were bare, and his skin was a weathered a deep brown. Silver scars traced across his forearms. He shifted to stand between

Andre and the woman, his hand resting menacingly on the hilt of his sword. The woman placed a hand on the man's shoulder; she obviously needed to keep a tight leash on that one.

"Who are you, and what do you want?" Andre asked, looking for Ester in the crowd.

"We are from the Harmony resistance, here to free you from the tyranny of the controllers," the woman replied.

"We don't need freeing. As you can see, we are already free. What have you done with the Devenders?"

The woman shrugged. "They are under guard. A few sore heads. They were ill-prepared for our arrival. Too busy working in your warehouses, I see."

Andre frowned at her. "They are helping us," he said, "as you would have found out if you had come in peaceful-like, instead of ambushing innocent people on the road."

"Innocent? A troop of Devenders? Come now, they are bred for killing. You know that."

"You might have learned different if you hadn't threatened to kill us all."

The woman smiled. "We have learnt all we need to know. We will contain the Devenders; you will replenish our supplies."

"You mean, replace one tyranny for another?" Andre asked.

"Not at all. We are here to help each other. Settlements like this are what Harmony was designed for. This is what we strive for, for all people."

"Including Devenders?"

The woman frowned down at him. "You have clearly been deceived. They are the Ministry's teeth. They do not want us to be free." She glanced around her. "Stefan, find that Devender commander, and where is Ciely?"

Turning her gaze back to Andre, she said, "You will see.

They have just been delaying until reinforcements arrive. We intercepted his messenger. You will be glad enough of us when they try and place you back under their control."

Andre shrugged. "They can try. We're off the grid. Won't do them any good."

Kiefer crouched behind the warehouse, listening. His men were out of sight; only armed resistance fighters were spread around the settlement. They were obviously more competent than they looked if they had overpowered all his men. The woman, Lorne, he assumed, commanded everyone's attention.

He pressed Chaney down on the ground. Angry grunts of protest rose from the man, but the cloth Kiefer had stuffed in his mouth muffled most of it. Kiefer thrust his hand into the dirt.

"Harmony? Are these your people?" he asked. *"Do these rebels mean well? Will they protect the workers?"*

"They will if you tell them to," she murmured in his head.

Kiefer jerked in surprise as the red-haired woman on the step swore viciously. "Where is the Warden?" she said. "I can feel him. Where is he? We won't harm him. He should have come forward by now. We're all on the same side."

"And which side is that?" Kiefer asked, leaving the shelter of the warehouse and pushing Chaney in front of him.

"The side of freedom for all!" the woman replied. A murmur spread around the crowd as they stepped back, leaving room in front of the woman and her henchman.

"Oh?" Kiefer said. "You have armed men surrounding these people. How does that make them free? I see you've taken the sector. Now what?"

"It's for their own protection," the woman protested, her violet eyes widening as he approached.

"From who? I'd say they need protecting from you. They seemed perfectly fine when I left this morning. What do you want?" Spotting Ferris jammed up against the wall, he asked, "Are the men alright?"

"We lost at least one. But they took us..." Ferris stopped speaking as his head was shoved back against the building.

A chill slithered down Kiefer's spine as he glared at the woman. He had lost one of his men? "As I said, it looks like they need protecting from you."

"Where's Ciely?" the woman demanded, glaring at Chaney.

Chaney grunted around his gag, and the woman rolled her eyes. "Stefan," she said in a resigned tone.

Stefan descended the steps, keeping a close eye on Kiefer. He tugged the rag out of Chaney's mouth. Chaney coughed and cleared his throat as Stefan spun him around to release the belt.

"What did you do to her?" The woman's eyes narrowed as she observed Kiefer.

"Me? Never touched her. She went off tracking Andre after sending dear Chaney here to report to you."

"I don't believe you."

Kiefer shrugged. "I didn't expect you too. You will not harm these people," he commanded, his voice resonating slightly.

The woman scowled at him. "I had no intention of harming anyone. If you had surrendered when you were told to..." Her voice trailed off as she saw her men briefly dip their weapons.

"And yet you fired on us," Kiefer said, unable to keep the bite out of his voice.

The woman winced. "Enthusiastic hotheads are the bane

of my existence. They brought your man to our healer as quickly as they could, but she couldn't save him. I'm sorry."

Kiefer eyed her. Could he believe her sincerity? Or was she just pretending?

"Who are you?" the woman asked.

"Commander Kiefer Gallante, Maincore Devender Unit 22, at your service," Kiefer replied.

"What are you doing here?"

"I asked first," Kiefer said, turning as movement beside him caught his eye. The young tracker scurried towards them and grabbed Chaney's arm.

"Enough," a cold voice said.

It was the last thing Kiefer heard as a stunning blow hit the back of his head, and he collapsed to the dirt.

———

The woman gritted her teeth as Kiefer fell to the dirt. "What do you think you are doing?"

"He's the one in charge," Stefan said, "the one responsible for all this. You." He shoved Chaney. "Tie him up. We'll interrogate him later."

"That was unnecessary," Andre said. "Not once did he threaten you."

The woman glanced down at the unconscious man sprawled at her feet, frowning as though his behaviour didn't make sense. At no time had he indicated he would surrender. She bit her lip. But then she hadn't asked him to give himself up.

Before she could reply Stefan snapped an order, and Kiefer was dragged away. Ferris twitched, but his guard, grinning, pushed his knife under his chin. "Yes? You fancy joining him?"

Andre spoke again, "These men were helping us. There was no need for any of this."

"They are Devenders. That's enough for me," the woman said. "They want to repress Harmony. We want to free her. Simple, really." She glanced at the crowd in front of her. "Show's over, folks. Get back to work."

"Doing what?"

The woman shrugged. "Whatever you were doing before."

"And if we tell you to leave?"

The woman shrugged again. "We will when we're ready. For now, we need supplies. You will supply us."

Andre stepped back as Ester tugged his shirt. "Don't antagonise her," she whispered.

"They attacked Kiefer!"

"I know. Come." She led him away from the square. "I heard them talking. Most want to kill the Devenders. It's only that woman stopping them; you have to support her."

"But they are behaving worse than the Devenders. Are we to be bullied by anyone who passes by?"

"Andre, you speak for all of us. If you can't figure it out, who will?" Ester asked as she led him back to the warehouse.

7

Kiefer groaned as he came back to awareness. His head was thumping, his shoulder hurt, and his hands were tied behind his back. He flexed his shoulder carefully. Bruised but not broken, he thought with relief. Sitting up, his head spun, and he swallowed reflexively. Maybe not. He groaned as he slumped back down to the dirt floor and closed his eyes.

The aroma of damp soil surrounded him, and he vaguely wondered where they had taken him and what they intended. He hoped he hadn't bled into the ground. Harmony already had enough of his blood; he hadn't thought her bloodthirsty.

"I'm not," the gentle voice whispered.

"What do you want?"

"Your help."

"To do what?"

"Free me. Free my people so we can live in harmony as it was first ordained."

"And how am I supposed to do that?"

"You'll figure it out."

"Helpful, very helpful," he said aloud.

"What is helpful?" a cold voice said from above.

Kiefer cracked open an eye, and a pair of mud-caked boots filled his vision. The slap of the man's club against his leg vibrated through Kiefer's aching head. Kiefer twisted his head and squinted up at the man standing over him.

"Who are you?" he asked, taking in the broad chest and powerful arms.

"I ask the questions," the man snapped. "What is helpful?"

"I have no idea," Kiefer admitted, closing his eyes. "What did you do with my men?"

He hissed as the man grabbed him by the hair and pulled him up onto a chair, and his eyes watered at the pain, which was soon eclipsed by a resounding blow to his face, toppling him off the chair again. Tensing, he inhaled as he was roughly manhandled back onto the chair. He swayed, squinting at the man as he tried to work some feeling back into his face.

"You will tell me your clearance level," the man demanded.

"It's sub-terranean." Kiefer laughed a bit hysterically. A swinging club wiped the smile off his face, and as he hit the dirt, his mind spun. "I meant all my overrides were deleted when the comp went offline. I was still logged in; they won't work anymore."

Kiefer rolled over. His vision had greyed around the edges, and he tasted the metallic tang of blood.

"You will tell me your access codes," the man snapped.

"No, I won't."

"Then we have no use for you," the man said as his club connected with Kiefer's ribs.

The sickening crunch travelled down Kiefer's body. Pain exploded in his chest, and he shuddered as he tried to breathe. His attempt to scythe his legs under the man was more of an uncontrolled jerk, his body wasn't responding. A flutter of panic stirred in his stomach as he was lifted off the floor again.

The next blow to his face left him spitting blood and somehow on his knees, swaying in front of the man who seemed to want to beat him to death. Hopefully, it wouldn't take much longer. Another blow broke his nose. A gush of blood spurted onto the dirt, and he breathed shallowly through his mouth as he struggled to remain conscious.

A horrified gasp interrupted his beating, and he collapsed into soft arms, which caught him just before he hit the dirt one last time. His bindings were cut, and he hissed as his arms uselessly flopped forward.

"What do you think you are doing?" The woman's voice was acidic. Kiefer was glad it wasn't him on the receiving end.

"He has information we need, Lorne," the man replied.

Kiefer tried to grin at the whine in the man's voice, but his face wouldn't respond.

"Stefan, this is not the way to get it. We need him."

"No, we don't," Stefan replied.

"Get out."

Stefan started to protest.

"Now!"

He left.

"Ciely!" Lorne shouted. "Get Merianne, now!"

Kiefer winced as his head pounded. A soft gasp came from the doorway, and then silence fell. Blood dripped out of Kiefer's nose and onto the woman's blouse.

Kiefer tried to move, and he spasmed, his body locking rigid. Pain spiked through him, stealing his breath and tightening his chest. The sound of a woman singing penetrated the pain. It was an old song, one he didn't recognise, soft and soothing.

He peered up at her through swollen eyes as water dripped on his face. A woman was weeping over him? How nice. Was he dying? He hoped so. It would be nice to die in the arms of a pretty woman. No make that a gorgeous woman with tantalising eyes. Were they blue or were they black? He wasn't sure. His mind drifted as he gradually relaxed, soothed by her voice.

Merianne paused on the threshold of the cell. The ancient song brought goosebumps to her skin, and she shivered as she watched Lorne cradle a stranger as if he were her own. She swallowed. Lorne had never held anyone like that, not even her sister Ciely. She entered, shutting the door behind her.

"Lorne," she said, reluctant to intrude, but she could see the man was in dire need of her help. "Lorne," she repeated, "you have to let him go."

"Never," Lorne said, instinctively clutching the man more tightly in her arms. Her eyes widened as she realised what she had just said.

"I can't help him while you are holding him," Merianne said, keeping her voice gentle.

Lorne exhaled and carefully laid the Devender on the ground. A slight crease appeared between his brows, but he didn't stir otherwise.

"Go prepare a room. He needs warmth and a bed. Go," Merianne commanded, pushing Lorne out of the cell. Running her hands over the man's body, she soothed the fiery embers of damaged nerves, indicators of internal damage and broken bones that she would have to work on later. Then she rested her hands on his rib cage and concentrated. The man arched his back and gasped in agony as his rib bones grated back into place.

At least that should ease his breathing, Merianne thought.

His dark eyes flew open before he collapsed onto the floor. She reset his nose and taped a band across it to hold it in place. Chipped teeth would have to stay chipped.

Rummaging in her bag, she withdrew a splint and bandages and bound his left arm until she would have the energy to repair the break later. She was wrapping his ribs when the cell door opened behind her.

Merianne looked up as Lorne returned. "I've done what I can," Merianne said. "He needs care and rest, now; time for his body to realign and heal. I'll put my assistant, Carey, on him. He'll keep him in order."

Lorne's smile was strained. "You think he will be that difficult?"

"What do *you* think?" Merianne asked with a grin.

Lorne nodded and stepped aside for the stretcher-bearers.

When Kiefer awoke, he tensed in expectation of an onslaught of pain, but instead, he felt just a dull ache everywhere. The grip on his hand tightened, and he opened his eyes. He was lying in a bed in an unfamiliar room with a beautiful woman gripping his hand painfully. Smiling at her, he drank in her smooth creamy complexion and violet eyes. He remembered her eyes.

She smiled back. "How are you feeling?" she asked, her voice low and rich. It soothed his frazzled nerves.

"Am I still alive?" he croaked. When he tried to clear his

throat, his tongue caught on the sharp edge of his chipped front tooth.

"Here, drink."

The woman leaned over him, revealing more creamy skin as she lifted his head so he could drink from the cup she held. She wore a soft white blouse that was open at her throat. Inhaling her sweet perfume, he swallowed the cool water, wondering if she would hit him if he kissed that satin-smooth skin.

"Who are you?" he asked as she laid him back down. He felt so weak; he hadn't been able to help himself.

"Lorne, leader of the Harmony resistance."

He tensed as memory returned. The rebels had attacked his unit.

"I deeply regret this situation. I never intended for things to go the way they did," Lorne said.

"My men, where are they?"

"They are back at work as they were before we came. Andre spoke for them, as he did you. You have done good work here."

"No, the ones you killed. At least one of my men died; where are they?"

Lorne flinched. "I regret the loss of your man. Our healer tried to help him, but it was too late. Lieutenant Ferris and Speaker Andre made sure he was buried and marked. He lies in Harmony's embrace now."

"Good, he didn't deserve to be left for carrion," Kiefer said to himself. The woman beside him, Lorne, stiffened as if to take offence, but she didn't speak.

"Where am I?" he asked.

"We upgraded two of the units into an infirmary. We have a healer, and it was easier for her to treat all the injured in one place."

Kiefer smiled. "Ah, that's why I only ache instead of

being in agony." He was pleased to have that anomaly explained. "How long have I been out?"

"About a week."

"A week?" Kiefer's jaw dropped and he snapped it shut. "It can't have been a week."

"Our healer kept you asleep while your body healed. It would have been more painful if you had been conscious while she reset your bones, and it would have taken much longer."

"What did you tell my men?"

"We kept your lieutenant informed of your condition."

"And no word from Sector 44? I would have expected a response by now."

"Ah, about that." Lorne seemed embarrassed. "We intercepted your messenger; that's what brought us here."

"And my messenger?" Kiefer asked.

Lorne smiled. "Back with his unit. I didn't think it would be good to bring the controllers down on these people."

"You're probably right. Is Andre unhurt?"

"He's fine."

Kiefer frowned; his head ached. Once again, he couldn't remember who she was. "And who are you?"

"I'm Lorne."

"Lorne," he repeated.

"You need to rest; you will tire easily. I will return later."

Kiefer reached for her hand. "Please come back," he said before releasing it and closing his eyes against the sudden pricking of tears. He slept.

When next he woke, Andre was seated next to him. The room was dim. A small shaded lamp stood in the corner. The candle flame flickered, casting jumping shadows on the walls. It must have been evening.

"Andre," he whispered.

Andre smiled at him. "Commander, you're awake."

"Please, it's Kiefer."

"Kiefer, then, but only while you are abed. Your men will not appreciate the familiarity, I think."

"Maybe not."

"How are you feeling?"

"Tired," Kiefer admitted. "I don't think I've felt this exhausted in all my life."

"It will pass. Merianne says you are healing nicely. You will feel better soon."

"How are things?" Kiefer asked, not really interested.

Andre frowned at him, concern creasing his brow. "Good. The fresh produce has begun to arrive and makes a huge difference; everyone looks much better. We found new clothing and managed to set up some bathing facilities. It's amazing what feeling clean does to a person."

"Then these resistance fighters haven't tried to stop you in any way?"

"Not at all. After that first misunderstanding, they started calling me the Speaker. They have supported everything you put in place. In fact, I think some may even stay here."

"Misunderstanding, huh?"

"Kiefer, it was unfortunate, and you and your men bore the brunt of it, but all is well, and it will be even better when you are back on your feet."

Kiefer sighed. "You know we will have to leave once I am healed, don't you?"

"Why not stay? There is room for all," Andre coaxed.

"They will come looking for us. A whole troop of Devenders gone missing? We are already overdue."

"But what about the resistance? Look at what we have achieved already. We are living in harmony, as we were meant to be."

"I need to think about that," Kiefer said. He had no idea how he was supposed to get his men to lie about the resistance, for that was what it amounted to. Otherwise, the wrath of Maincore would soon arrive on their doorstep. His head ached, and he closed his eyes.

"You are tired." Andre whispered. "I will return tomorrow. Rest." He stood and left the room.

Kiefer's head throbbed. Cool hands stoked his temple and soothed the pain away.

"Even leaders need time to recover. There is plenty of time to solve tomorrow's problems. Rest today," the voice commanded, and he slid into a dreamless sleep.

This time, when Kiefer awoke, he was in desperate need of a piss. Pushing off his blanket, he shivered. The air was cold against his skin. The shaded lamp was still in the corner. Gingerly, he sat up. His ribs and shoulder were sore, but not unmanageably so. Swinging his legs over the side of the bed, he found he was wearing a loose robe, tied at his waist, that barely reached his knees. He wondered where it had come from as he swivelled his feet to the floor and woozily leaned forward.

"Oh, no, you don't," a soft voice said from above him, and firm hands held him in place.

"I need to piss," he said, his voice gruff, and he cleared his throat.

"Then I will bring a pot to you. Don't move."

Kiefer sat still as instructed. It wasn't until he felt someone fumbling at his waist that he realised he had nodded off.

"Don't worry. Here. Go now."

Gentle hands directed him, and he almost groaned at the relief as he managed to piss. He shivered as a damp cloth wiped him down, and then he was coaxed back into bed. A cool hand felt his forehead, and he heard a soft exclamation as he shivered again.

"Sleep." The command soothed his worries away, and he slept.

As Ferris watched the rebels patrol the sector, his face tightened in anger. His men should be performing that duty, not rebels. Gritting his teeth so tight his jaw ached, he clenched his fists at the memory of being taken so easily, at losing his weapons.

He would make sure he blamed Kiefer in his report. If they hadn't been slumming it, helping those people, they would have had more men on sentry duty, and they wouldn't have been caught unawares. And for Kiefer to walk in and not even attempt a rescue. He'd just given himself up like a coward.

One of the empty crates outside the new clothing storeroom served as a seat, and as he sat, he stared at the cloudy sky. The grey masses scudded across the sky, driven by the winds currently whistling around the warehouse. He shivered and flipped his jacket collar up. How could he take advantage of the situation?

Speaking of Kiefer, where was he? He had only taken a blow to the head, and it didn't take a week to recover from that. He was making a meal out of it. Those rebels were hiding something, making him out to be badly injured. His place was here, pulling his weight, not canoodling with that rebel leader, Lorne. Ferris turned her name over in his mind. A nice body she had, too; he wouldn't mind tasting some of it.

Ferris watched her as she crossed the open square. She paused to talk to that hulking giant before proceeding into one of the warehouses.

Someone blocked the light, and he looked up in surprise as Andre stopped in front of him. "Lieutenant, I wanted to thank you for taking the time with my son. Chiva is eager, but please don't let him take you away from your duties."

Ferris waved a hand. "No trouble, Speaker, no trouble at all. Youngsters should be encouraged to follow their dreams."

"Yes, but we don't have the money to send him to Maincore. He needs to earn his way first."

"That's alright. I'll fund him to start. He can pay me back as he works. There's plenty of work in Maincore for an intelligent boy like him. And for his sister. She could enter the academy as well; they take girls now."

"I'm sorry, but we can't accept. Once he's earned his money, then he can travel to Maincore."

"And miss the chance of my sponsorship? Why would you punish the boy so?"

"I am not punishing him. He has to make his own way."

Ferris grinned as he stared down the worried man. "It's not against the law to accept a helping hand now and then. They will be fine. They'll be under my protection. I'll make sure no harm comes to them. I promise."

Andre hesitated and then murmured, "You're very kind," before striding away, his face set.

Ferris laughed under his breath. They were well and truly netted. He had plans for them once he got rid of Kiefer. His gaze was drawn back to the shadowy warehouse; that rebel woman still hadn't come back out. What was she doing? Rising, he sauntered over to the gaping doorway. The wind swirled the dust and grit scattered across the floor and then died down again.

The warehouse was still, a silent, shadowy cavern. Where had she gone? Strolling further in, he peered behind the stacked boxes. A cold, hard edge of a blade was pressed up against his throat, and he stopped short.

"Looking for me?" a soft voice breathed into his ear, and he shivered as he spread his hands out wide.

"I come in peace," he said, lifting his chin when his voice cracked.

"What would your men say to that?"

Ferris braced and whipped round. Grabbing the woman's arms, he forced her to the floor. "That I don't like having knives held at my throat." Exultation rose within him. He would show her that he was not a man she could cower with a flimsy knife.

His neck stung, and he rubbed it. His hand came away smeared with blood. "Now look what you've done," he whined as he glared at her.

"You shouldn't creep up on people," Lorne replied, lying still beneath him as he leaned over her. She had such beautiful eyes and soft, creamy skin that looked like it would taste delicious.

"I wasn't. I wanted to talk."

Pain exploded through his groin as the bitch jerked her knee up, hard and low, and he folded over, his breath rushing out in a weird groan as he collapsed. She pushed him off, and he rolled into a ball, holding himself. Waves of agony shorted his brain, and he tensed as Lorne rose, picked up her knife, and resheathed it.

"Conversation over," she said and left him there, curled up in the dust.

Brilliant sunshine streamed through the window and warmed Kiefer's face. His eyes fluttered open, and he frowned at the wall. After a moment of internal inspection, he decided he felt better. His strength, like a tangible coil, unfurled within him, more noticeable with its return, and he sat up.

What was he doing lying in bed in the middle of the day? A pile of clothes on the chair in the corner turned out to be his uniform, so he got up and dressed. At least someone had done a decent job of cleaning and mending it.

How long had he been out of commission, and where was Ferris? Why hadn't he visited? Stamping into his boots, he eased his shoulders. He felt much better, except for the chip in his front tooth, which was already annoying him.

"Always the little things," he muttered to himself as he opened the door. His tongue found its way back to the sharp edge, and he forcibly pressed it against the roof of his mouth, trying to hold it in place. It didn't last. He would need to get that edge smoothed before he lacerated his tongue.

"What are you doing up?" A tiny woman flew at him, forcing him back into the room. She pushed him back, and he gave way in surprise. Bright blue eyes sparkled up at him out of a determined face, and he sat back on the bed.

"I feel fine," Kiefer protested.

"You'll feel fine when I say you're fine," the little woman snapped, feeling his forehead and stroking his face. He recognised the cool hands and commanding voice.

"Merianne, I thank you for your care, but you have others far more in need than I."

"I'll be the judge of that," she replied, inspecting his face. "You were running a temperature a couple of nights ago. If you overdo it, it will come back. Fever will wear you down, so be careful. Remember, you will still tire easily; your body has not yet fully recovered, even if your bones have healed. I'll be watching you," she threatened.

He smiled at her, and her expression softened. "Then I'll be in safe hands," he said.

"Get away with you then. I've no time for that nonsense," she snapped. But he could see that she was pleased.

"I will be careful," he promised, flashing another smile at her.

"Make sure you are, and don't get into any more trouble," she said gently tapping his cheek.

Kiefer rolled his eyes. "You sound like my mother."

"Well, you obviously need one," Merianne retorted before moving out of his way.

Her gaze bored into Kiefer's back as he left, and her deep sigh as she returned to her work, left him wondering what she was so concerned about. A perfectionist, obviously.

9

Ester held her hands out towards Kiefer as he entered the cavernous warehouse. "Commander Kiefer. I am so glad to see you are recovered. Andre will be so pleased to see you back on your feet."

"It's kind of you to say so." Kiefer smiled. "I'm embarrassed it took me so long."

"Don't be ridiculous. You had terrible injuries. I'm amazed you've recovered so quickly, even with the help of Merianne. That man did so much damage; it's the least they could do."

"What's been happening?" he asked, squeezing her hands in acknowledgement.

"Come, sit. Have a cup of coffee, and I'll tell you what I know." Ester drew him to a chair in the corner.

Ester sighed. "Your Lieutenant Ferris has done a grand job of holding everyone together; he is to be commended. He has also followed through on your promise to escort folks to Maincore. There are ten who wish to travel with you, eight as far as Sector 44 and my two who want to go with you to Maincore."

"I don't remember that I said I would escort them," Kiefer said hesitantly, "only that they had a choice."

"I believe Lieutenant Ferris thinks he can use it as an excuse for returning late."

"And he made this decision himself?" Kiefer asked with a frown.

"I think you'll find he has made a lot of decisions on your behalf," Ester said, watching him with concern. "My Annie is fair besotted with him, and Chiva is a fan. Lieutenant Ferris said he would speak for him at Maincore Academy."

"I see." Kiefer was silent for a moment. Why was Ferris bothering with two kids from the sector? When they first arrived, he hadn't wanted anything to do with them. "What about Lorne and her people?"

"They have kept pretty much in the background, though some want to stay. Merianne, for one, which would be a boon, but they are getting restless. I think they are waiting to speak to you."

"For me?"

"Yes. They seem to think you can get them into Maincore."

Kiefer exhaled. "To do what, exactly?"

Ester smiled. "To take it down, I believe was the term used."

Kiefer rubbed the back of his neck. "I wish I had not woken up this morning," he said, trying to ease the sudden tension tightening his shoulders.

Ester patted his hand and gave him his coffee. "You'll think of something. That last gem is not general knowledge, by the way; that is just what Andre and I think is the case. Though the rumour mill has you in league with the resistance instead of recovering from serious injuries."

Kiefer's chest constricted as fear bloomed. That would be regarded as treason by the Ministry. "I appreciate the warning. I'm in enough trouble already," he said. "I think I need to chat with my lieutenant."

"That's good, then, because here he comes." Ester smiled brightly at Ferris as she returned to her station.

Kiefer sipped his coffee as Ferris approached. "Good morning," he said, keeping his voice neutral.

Ferris laughed while dragging a chair over with him. He spun it and straddled it, leaning on the back rest. "Morning? More like afternoon, and it's about time you got up. Am I glad to see you. It's a relief to hand this mess back to you."

"Mess?" Kiefer asked.

"Yes. What's going to happen here once we report back to Maincore?"

"What are you expecting to happen?"

"Well, they won't like to hear about the resistance, now, will they, nor their ability to plant Bantwich into our systems."

"I don't think it was the resistance. They don't have the technical ability," Kiefer said, surprised Ferris was even suggesting it as a possibility.

"Who else would it be?"

"Weren't you going to check the personnel records? I gave you a list of suspects."

Ferris snorted. "The personnel records were useless. It *must* have been the resistance."

"Have you seen any hardware? Can't say that I've seen any tech types; they all seem more like bandits to me," Kiefer said. "No, I think it was a disgruntled employee. It would be easy enough for them. They would have had the skills and the access."

"This isn't all of them. You need to speak to that woman, find out where their base camp is. We could use the information."

"Why haven't you found that out? You're the investigator.

A pretty woman, I'd have thought that was right up your street."

"We don't click; she's too hoity-toity."

Kiefer raised an eyebrow, but he held his peace, realising he was glad Ferris hadn't made an impression on her.

Ferris looked away. "Anyway, you've been speaking to her. What did she have to say to you?"

"I haven't spoken to anyone. I saw Andre once, and that was it. I was surprised you didn't check in; it's been nearly a week, hasn't it?"

"More like two! They said you were still unconscious, though I was sure they had exaggerated your injuries. I mean, that Stefan only clubbed you once, after all. So, you haven't spoken to her?"

"Not yet." Kiefer watched Ferris closely; the lieutenant seemed uncomfortable.

"The men want to know when we are going home. They've had enough of slumming it here," Ferris said, his voice returning to its usual harshness.

"I'll speak to the men," Kiefer said. "We ought to leave before Maincore comes searching for us." He hesitated briefly. "Who did we lose?"

Ferris looked at him. "Nealy from your unit. He was caught in your ambush. We buried him up by the academy; it seemed the appropriate place."

"Thank you," Kiefer said soberly. Poor Nealy wouldn't get to see the sea after all. Kiefer was in so much trouble, and he had no way of explaining any of it.

"Right, good to see you back on your feet. Time for some shut-eye." Ferris rose and, with an awkward nod, strode off.

Kiefer frowned as he watched him leave. He stood, intending to go in search of Tremill and Stainton, but was waylaid by well-wishers. Warmed by their fervent greetings, he finally extricated himself and went in search of his men.

The quadrant looked much brighter. The alleys were clear, and the people were smiling. There was a buzz of community spirit in the air. Laughter drifted out of the laundry, along with the odd soap bubble, as the women cleaned their own clothes. There was a general air of well-being. Workers, supervisors, Devenders, and resistance all mixed together, and rubbing along tolerably well. Had it truly only been a week since the collapse of the facility?

As Kiefer stood in the square, a feeling of contentment oozed up from under his feet. *"How do we protect this, Harmony?"* he thought.

"Shut down Maincore," she replied.

"I don't know how. I won't even get past the first security checks."

"You'll find a way."

A rich voice behind him made him spin. "Commander Kiefer."

"Lorne," Kiefer said a little breathlessly. "You never came back."

"You were asleep. Merianne would have dismembered me if I woke you," she said with a laugh.

"I very much doubt that." Kiefer grinned, admiring her figure-hugging britches and leather jerkin, which was cinched at her slim waist over a soft white shirt that was laced at her throat.

"Going somewhere?" he asked.

"We're getting ready to move out; we've stayed here too long as it is."

"Must be an uncomfortable life," Kiefer observed.

"Yes, it is. I look forward to the day I can call a place home." Lorne shrugged, a fluid motion that set her tassels swaying. "As it is, Harmony needs us. Commander, we need to talk." She stared at him in earnest.

"Of course."

"I mean, talk in private."

"You have a place in mind?"

Lorne nodded and turned towards the gully. Eyebrows rising in surprise, Kiefer followed her down the trail into the valley, tracing the path of the stream, which was now back to its proper levels and burbling merrily. They clambered over stranded boulders left by the flood. Piles of smaller rocks collected in the tree roots. Moss-lined, grey trunks leaned at odd angles, uprooted by the torrent.

"Remember, I'm still convalescing; Merianne will dismember *me* if I overdo it," Kiefer called out breathlessly. He held his side as he paused, watching her lithe form with appreciation.

Lorne looked over her shoulder. "Sorry," she said contritely. "I forgot. This will do." She sat on a convenient boulder. "I didn't want anyone to overhear us."

Kiefer stared at her. "Overhear what?"

Lorne sighed. Kiefer was startled to see a film of tears in her beautiful violet eyes.

"Lorne, what's happened?" he asked, reaching for her hand.

"It's Harmony. She's dying. I've been searching for the Warden, but I can't find him."

"The what?"

"The Warden. Ever since you arrived, I've heard him. I wasn't sure who it was, but now," she bit her lip, "I think it's you."

Kiefer tensed. How did she know he could hear Harmony? "What makes you think that?"

"When he connects to Harmony, I can feel the vibrations, but I hadn't been able to pinpoint him until just now when you were walking across the square."

"What is a Warden?" Kiefer asked, uncertain how much he should admit to. After all, he knew nothing about this woman.

"Someone who can speak directly to Harmony. She is the sentience at the centre of our planet; the one who should be protecting us all, but the controllers, your employers, have subverted the meaning of the original agreement.

"They have used the technology to restrict her instead of enhancing her power, as was originally intended, so she could support the whole planet. Instead, they shut her down and shunted her into a side bay while they stripped humanity for their own ends."

Kiefer was taken aback by her anger. "Why are you telling me all this? As you say, they are my employers, and I will be returning to them soon."

"Look around you, Commander. Sector 45 is blossoming, and that is because of you," she said, gesturing up the valley.

"I didn't destroy the processor; you did that," Kiefer protested.

She shook her head. "It wasn't us. We don't have the technology nor the know-how; that's why we need the Warden, why we need *you*."

"Me?"

"You need to get inside Maincore and help us destroy it forever."

"You expect me to do what? I won't even get near it!" Kiefer exclaimed, aghast. Who did she think he was? He was horrified at the thought of even approaching Maincore. They'd cut him down before he could take a step.

"You have the knowledge. I know you do, and you have the clearance, the overrides. You went down to the maintenance bays with Andre. You have the connections, and you want what's best for our people. You are our best chance. This sector would not have survived without you. Any other commander would have marched these people into the next sector and ignored their plight."

"It's people like Andre and Ester that make the difference, not me," Kiefer argued.

"Be that as it may, you were the catalyst. Even Andre admits that."

"You know, I didn't even know there was a resistance until you turned up here. What will you be doing while I go and commit suicide?" Kiefer asked.

Lorne flashed him a smile. "We will protect Sector 45, cause disruption in 44 and 43, maybe even harry some other sectors to keep them occupied. This is the start of a new era. Help us, Kiefer. We need you."

A sharp crack echoed down the valley, shattering the unsettling silence.

Kiefer instinctively spun, looking up and scanning the bare rock lining the valley walls. Lorne rose and moved towards him, wrapping her arms around his neck. He stood rigid as he held her soft body.

"What are you doing?" he murmured against her lips.

"They'll think we slunk away for a secret tryst," she breathed and kissed him.

Kiefer clutched her tighter as she moulded her soft curves into his body. The heat of her skin burned through his thin shirt. An embarrassing interest collected in his loins. It had been far too long since his last secret tryst.

Leaning into the kiss, he explored the sweet taste of her mouth. She stiffened slightly before she, too, melted into the embrace. They broke apart and stared into each other's eyes.

"Are you sure that this was a good idea?" he asked, his voice husky. He stooped to kiss her neck and trailed kisses down her throat to the flutter pulsing at its base; her skin was as silky smooth as he'd thought. "Should we stop?"

"Probably," she gasped as she ran her fingers through his hair.

"Someone might be watching," he murmured, unlacing

her shirt and smoothing it open. He kissed the hollow at the base of her throat.

"Let them," she replied in a deepening voice.

Her breath was hot against his skin as he shrugged out of his shirt. "I've never been one for putting on displays," he said, "but if you insist."

His skin tingled as Lorne smoothed her fingertips over his chest, tracing the contours of his muscles. Focusing on the silky-soft sensation, he shuddered as she left a trail of cool kisses across his skin.

She smiled against his shoulder as he said with a chuckle, "As long as you don't tell Merianne, after all." Pausing, he breathed in the scent of her. "I'm not supposed to overdo it, you know."

"Don't worry, I won't let you overdo anything. Anyway, Harmony will hide us."

"Oh I will, will I?" Harmony murmured in Kiefer's head as he shed his clothes and sank to the hard ground in the arms of the most beautiful woman he had ever met, a woman he knew almost nothing about.

10

"Well," Kiefer said a little while later, "I hope you don't seduce all your prospective recruits like that."

Lorne laughed. "Don't be silly. That wasn't persuasion; that was pure lust. You are a fine specimen, after all, Commander Kiefer."

"Is that so? You don't look half bad yourself," he said comfortably, snuggling her into his body. She felt delicious against his skin, and he had to admit she had made sure he hadn't had to overdo anything. It had been a long, long time since someone had made love to him so thoroughly. Smiling, he breathed in her spicy fragrance, a memory to treasure. She traced a finger over his chest, making his skin tingle.

"Why?" he asked, watching her face.

"Why what?" Peering at him, she ran her finger over his chin. He loved that she couldn't stop touching him.

"Why me? Why this?"

Gently kissing his shoulder, she sighed. "This probably won't make much sense," she murmured, "but it was like we had a connection from the first time I saw you."

"You mean when you threatened to kill me?"

"I didn't know you then," she said, pouting. "When I saw you afterward, when Stefan had beaten you, I felt like I'd lost something I never knew I had. Deep inside, I was frantic, and yet, I didn't know why.

"I asked about you around the sector, trying to understand what it was about you. You're respected by your men, liked by the people, prepared to help where you can, approachable yet commanding, as I well know." She smiled. "And yet, there was still something missing. And then I saw you standing in the square, and I felt the vibration. I knew you were the Warden, and well, here we are."

Faltering to a stop, she hid her face in his shoulder. "I said it didn't make sense," she whispered against his skin, kissing him. She inhaled deeply.

"How come you can speak to Harmony?"

Exhaling in a huff of surprise, she looked up. "Oh. I don't. I doubt she even listens to my babbling. That's why I needed to find the Warden. We need to coordinate with him, make sure we're doing the right thing to free Harmony."

"I'm sure she does listen to you. You just have to listen more carefully for her reply."

"I wish."

"What would you want the Warden to ask her?"

"What we should do to help. I'm convinced we need to get to Maincore, but I don't know how. We have people, but not a lot of technical know-how."

"There are people in Sector 45 who have the knowledge. They may be able to help you," Kiefer said.

Abruptly, Lorne sat up. "Of course. Why didn't I think of that?"

He pulled her back down. "I can tell you that Sectors 27 and 32 are predicted to fail next. If you can precipitate the failure, speed it up, they won't be ready, and it'll be another

Sector 45. Blockages in the cooling system are always a sure bet," he said. "These will be just small oases in an arid desert, but it will give Harmony a foothold."

She stilled. "Why are you telling me this? You don't know me."

"You have good powers of persuasion, and I am under your spell," Kiefer murmured against her skin.

Lorne sat up. "Don't joke. I'm serious."

"As am I." Kiefer rested his head on his arm as he looked up at her. "You said it yourself; we have a connection."

Her violet eyes widened. "It is you, isn't it? You are the Warden?"

Kiefer grinned at the hint of doubt in her voice. "I'd never even heard of the Warden until I met you."

"It is," she breathed. "It has to be you. I knew he was close, and then you walked into the square with Chaney. All the time you were unconscious, I never heard him, until just now in the square. It is you; that's what drew me to you."

"Well, if it was, I assure you it wasn't deliberate. Harmony must have intervened, though I must say I thoroughly enjoyed the result."

Lorne cupped Kiefer's face in her hands and stared at him. "Don't you see? She brought us together so that we can take out Maincore. Take out the core, and the nodes will fail before they can transfer them to the new system, and then Harmony will be free, as she is supposed to be."

Kiefer's mind raced. It all made a kind of sense, transferring power before the processors failed sustained the current regime. Sector 45 had been unplanned and unsanctioned, but where they had control, they could just perpetuate the cage that trapped Harmony. He wondered why he had never questioned it all before. "Who or what is the Warden?"

"The Warden holds the compact between Harmony and the settlers. When man first arrived on this planet, the leader of the travellers made a compact with the sentience in the planet, a blood pact, an agreement to protect each other, to live in harmony so all could thrive."

"What makes you think I am the Warden? I know nothing of this."

"It must be in your blood. You must be a descendant of the first Speaker. I keep sensing your connection, and it's only when you are present."

Kiefer squirmed. Ever since he had arrived in Sector 45 and bled over those damned wires, he had heard Harmony's voice. It was possible Lorne was correct. If so, what did that mean for him?

"Kiefer, you understand all this techno stuff. Can't you stay and help us?"

"Ah, my dear, you know you have already given me my marching orders, and anyway, I've lingered here too long. Time is passing, and we ought to return to Maincore. We'll be missed. I don't want to bring the Ministry down on this sector."

"I just don't want this moment to end."

"We'll have other moments; it'll be my turn next time. I'll be back to full strength," he whispered suggestively as he stretched up to nibble her ear.

Chuckling, she lowered her face to his. "Thank you," she murmured as she kissed him. He kissed her back enthusiastically.

"For what?" he asked when they paused for air.

"For being you." She sighed as she sat up and reached for her shirt. They dressed and checked each other over for telltale signs, though her sparkling eyes and air of contentment would give her away, which he told her.

"You look so smug people are bound to be suspicious," she replied, trying to keep her face severe.

"That's what you wanted, wasn't it? Good job we're

moving out. My poor reputation will be in tatters," he said with a sad smile, knowing it was unlikely they would ever meet again.

"Never say never," she said, as though reading his mind. "We have to live for the moment and hope for more."

"I'll try and send word, especially if I figure out how we can get into the core," he promised as they climbed back up the gully.

"You don't know where to find us," she began, but he placed his fingers over her lips.

"The less I know, the better for you," he said. "I'll contact Andre. He can pass the message on. I'm sure you'll keep in touch with Merianne."

A fleeting expression of fear passed over Lorne's face, but then she nodded. He was right. It wasn't as if she had a permanent address anyway.

———

When they reached the end of the gully, Kiefer adroitly split off into the units, saying he was going to visit Andre.

"Coward," Lorne said, a smile on her face as she strode on ahead.

Kiefer's laugh followed her into the square where she spotted Stefan. "Get everyone ready to move out," she commanded as she walked towards him.

"Did you get what you wanted?" Stefan asked, watching her closely.

Lorne suppressed a grin. "We'll speak on the road, not here. Are we resupplied?"

He nodded. "We're ready to move out on your word."

"Good. We leave in thirty minutes, then."

Lorne stopped in the infirmary. "Merianne, we're moving out. Are you sure you want to stay here?"

Merianne smiled. "Yes, I'm too old to live in a saddle. Carey is capable; he can cope."

"You know this may not be the safest place. The controllers could still send troops here."

"Nowhere is safe," Merianne replied, patting Lorne's face gently. "You know that."

"The Devenders will be leaving soon. Kiefer wants to return to Maincore. He hopes to prevent them from sending troops out to search for him."

"Kiefer, is it?"

Lorne's face heated as she tried and failed to keep the smile off her face.

"I see." Merianne chuckled. "I will speak to him later."

"No, you won't. Merianne, don't you dare."

"As his healer, I need to make sure he is not overextending himself," Merianne said, leering at Lorne.

Lorne retreated with a groan, and Merianne's laughter followed her out of the door.

As she left the infirmary, Andre and Kiefer were crossing the square, deep in conversation. They halted when they saw her approach. She held her hand out to Andre.

"Speaker, it was a pleasure meeting you. I thank you for your hospitality, but it's time we left."

Andre smiled. "Lorne, the pleasure was mine, especially as I gained a healer. The commander was speaking to me about possibilities. When you return, we can see if we can help make the possible into reality."

"I'm not sure when we will be returning," Lorne said.

"I believe we may have something you will need," Andre said with a grin, "if you can find a way in."

Lorne's jaw dropped, and she snapped it shut as she stared at Kiefer. "You convinced him to help us in ten minutes?"

"I am not that persuasive." Kiefer flashed her a grin. "I

just shared some data points. And this is not the place to discuss them," he said more seriously. "Just know Andre will be ready once you have a plan. Send him word, and resources will meet you."

Lorne nodded. "Very well. Thank you, Andre. That will be helpful."

Andre gave her a casual salute and carried on walking. Kiefer smiled at her before he, too, walked away without saying anything further. As she watching him leave, she wondered if he regretted allowing her to seduce him. She scowled. He hadn't complained at the time but had been a willing and able participant. Blushing at the memory, she hurried to her horse.

Kiefer watched the last of Lorne's people leave the settlement. He had deliberately avoided saying goodbye to her. After all, he didn't need to encourage the rumours. Lorne had confirmed the resistance didn't have the technical know-how to plant the virus. If they hadn't done it, who had? Ferris should have done his job. Why hadn't he?

He climbed up to the Devenders camp, which was now relocated at the top of the valley, where they should have camped at the beginning, on the outskirts of the settlement.

Kiefer inspected his men and frowned. They looked like a disreputable bunch of thugs, their uniforms were supplemented by odd garments that made them look more like refugees than a crack troop of Devenders. The men squirmed slightly under their commander's inspection.

"As you know, our orders were to preserve the processor. Unfortunately, in that, we failed. And not only did we fail, but we allowed ourselves to be captured by rebels." He paused as one of the men snickered. His expression grew colder, and he waited for silence. "We return to Maincore tomorrow. I expect you to be ready for inspection tomorrow morning at first light and presentable as a troop of Devenders should be. You are a disgrace to your uniform. We depart at dawn." He watched their expressions closely. As expected, there was a mix of relief and reluctance on their faces.

One of the privates spoke up. "Sir?"

Kiefer paused. "Yes?"

"What do we say about the rebels?"

"What about them?"

"Well, we let them go."

"You tell the truth. Did you think you could stop them?" Kiefer asked, raising a brow.

Until the rebels had left, his men had been unarmed and mixed in with the settlement, helping to restore some order. The rebels had taken most of their weapons. Something else, Kiefer would be punished for.

"No sir, but we should have tried."

"But you didn't, did you?" Kiefer said, looking at Ferris.

Straightening, Ferris said, "We were concerned for your safety, sir."

"I see." Kiefer looked at the private. "You have your answer." Dismissing them, he turned away to speak to Jeffers, who was down by the picket line, caring for the horses.

Jeffers was busy brushing down a mare, her back leg hocked as she relaxed under his ministrations. He straightened and saluted as Kiefer approached.

"At ease, Jeffers. How are the horses? Think they'll get us back to Maincore?"

"No problem, sir. The rest has done them good, just like the lads. This reprieve has been good for everyone."

"Not everyone," Kiefer said, rubbing the nose of an inquisitive gelding.

"Just bad luck, sir."

"We should have been keeping a better watch. It's my fault."

"You were managing a disaster, sir. You don't expect rebels to stroll in unannounced in the middle of it, now, do you?"

"What are the men saying?"

"Oh, the usual grumbles, more embarrassed at being caught short, resentment more than fear, sir."

"Anything I need to know?"

"They're wondering where you've been for the past few days. Didn't expect it to take so long for you to recover from being hit over the head."

Kiefer sighed. "If only that were all it was."

Jeffers looked at him sharply. "A couple of the men thought you joined up with the rebels, though Tremill squashed that flat straight away. But you know, once said." He shrugged.

"I see. Well, we'll be moving out at dawn. Be ready."

"Yes, sir."

With a nod, Kiefer left Jeffers to his work. He took the time to visit the healerie. His chipped tooth was driving him mad, and he needed it filed smooth. He wished all his troubles could be dealt with so easily.

11

The next morning, as the steel grey sky slowly lightened, Kiefer buckled on his leather vambraces and allowed Jeffers to slide his shoulder plates into place. The worn leather was stained with use, but the vambraces fit snug and tight. Kiefer was not looking forward to breaking in a new pair. Jeffers clipped his black cloak into the buckles and stood back as Kiefer pulled on his gloves.

After striding down the hill, Kiefer met Andre in the central square and grasped his arm in farewell. "I'm not sure how, but I will send word as I can."

Andre nodded and gripped Kiefer's arm in return. "We'll be waiting. You did good here, Kiefer, and I thank you for it."

Kiefer grimaced. "I spent most of my time unconscious. I can assure you it wasn't me."

"You may like to think that, but we know better. Stay safe, Kiefer."

"And you. I'll keep an eye on your youngsters. Though as Ferris is their sponsor, there will be little I can do."

"I wish you were their sponsor," Andre said with a

grimace. "We appreciate his generosity, of course. This is an opportunity we cannot afford to refuse, but there is something about him…I don't know! Just a parent worrying, I suppose."

Laughing, Kiefer clasped Andre's shoulder. "That's what parents are supposed to do. Give my regards to Ester."

"You can do that yourself," Ester said from behind him. As he turned, she reached up and hugged him. "Be well, Kiefer. Please keep my twins safe."

Twisting his lips, Kiefer nodded. "I'll try."

He returned to his troop, wincing as he saw Annie and Chiva mounted on the spare horse. Nealy should be riding out of Sector 45, not lying cold and still in the hard ground.

Shaking off the momentary chill, he reached up to gather the reins and hauled himself into the saddle. He nodded at Jeffers, who released the horse and scuttled off to his own mount. Kiefer shifted in the saddle, his leather armour creaking and settling as he moved.

After a glance around his more pristine-looking troops, he waved them forward and led them down the muddy road and away from Sector 45. Stunted trees lined the road, and Kiefer now had a better understanding as to why the people looked so destitute. There were no leaves on these denuded trees to flutter in the breeze. His face grew grimmer as the miles passed and the appearance of the trees didn't improve.

By the end of the day, the surroundings had softened. Life had returned, with green leaves swishing overhead in the strengthening wind. Bare mud had been replaced by trailing plants, which cluttered the undergrowth, a combination of brambles, vibrant, leafy plants, and the odd flower providing a splash of unexpected colour. Even the trill of birdsong was noticeable, emphasising the lack in Sector 45, which was now obvious as Kiefer identified the reason for the unsettling silence that had shrouded the valley.

Ferris, now leading the troop, signalled to leave the road. It was time to set up camp for the night. Kiefer eased in his saddle as an unexpected weariness blurred his mind. He was not fully recovered, and his body was telling him to rest.

Kiefer left his men to set up camp. He unsaddled his horse and, after being shooed away by Jeffers, joined Chiva and Annie by the fire. They both looked exhausted, and they would no doubt be saddle-sore the next day. Maybe they should walk with the other workers accompanying them instead of riding; they were more used to that.

Eight workers had accompanied them, intending to plead their case to the controller at the next sector. They slowed the Devenders down, and Kiefer was frustrated by Ferris' decision to escort them. What was the man thinking? Maybe Kiefer would find out over the next few days before they reached Maincore.

Accepting the bowl of stew, which had been made from some reconstituted meat he didn't want to name, Kiefer dreamed for a moment about his apartment in Maincore and the fully stocked kitchen of fresh produce. His one joy was cooking, creating a meal that would provide an explosion of flavour on the tongue. He stared at the bowl. This was not cooking; it was reheating, but he didn't say anything. The workers devoured their trail rations as if it was the best food they had ever eaten, which was highly possible, from what he had seen.

Annie slumped against her brother, her face pale, eyes closed. Chiva gently shook her shoulder, and she stirred. Taking the bowl offered to her, she began to eat. Kiefer was relieved to see some colour return to her cheeks as she ate.

"Make sure you stretch your muscles out," Kiefer said to the twins as he rose, "or you'll be sore tomorrow. Ferris will show you." Ferris nodded as he took Kiefer's seat by the fire, and Kiefer retired to his tent. As soon as his head touched the ground, he was asleep.

The next day, they arrived in Sector 44, and Kiefer realised it *was* no better than Sector 45 had been. He just hadn't paid attention. The Comptech facility stood apart from the hovels they made the workers live in. The disparity in living conditions was stark, and Kiefer bit his tongue to keep himself from speaking out.

His report to the controller was concise and abrupt. He was unsurprised when the man shrugged and said it was not his responsibility. The only interest the controller did show was at the mention of the rebels.

Kiefer raised his eyebrow. "You are aware of these rebels?"

"Of course. The last communique advised us they were in the area and growing in confidence. My workers know what's good for them. They won't tolerate the rebels trying to destroy their living." The man scowled at Kiefer. "Why didn't you kill them? Isn't that what you are here for?"

"I was not advised of any rebel activity. We were taken by surprise."

With a snort, the man rolled his eyes. "I think your superiors will expect a better explanation than that, Commander."

Kiefer inwardly agreed, but he had nothing but the truth. "There are eight workers from Comptech requesting sanctuary."

"Eight? We don't need any more techs. We've got enough."

Kiefer shrugged. "Sector 45 is off-grid. Irretrievable."

The controller sat up straighter. "Are there any parts salvageable?"

"Nothing survived. It's a disaster zone."

"What? How?"

"Someone planted the Bantwich virus. I would suggest you concentrate on keeping a clean back-up disk, unlike Sector 45."

The man's eyes bulged. "Bantwich? And you brought their techs here?"

Interesting, Kiefer thought. *The man didn't immediately leap to blaming the rebels like Ferris had.*

"The controller and forty other techs died when the compound collapsed. Lieutenant Ferris cleared those who survived, but I would expect you to do your own security checks."

"You can be sure I will. I want to speak to your lieutenant, see his records. I am not letting them near our tech." The controller tapped his finger on this desk. "I'm not sure I want them here at all."

"That is between you and them, nothing to do with me. We will be leaving in the morning, and I am not taking them any further."

The man nodded. "I have made rooms available in the guest wing. You can sleep there. Join us for dinner tonight, and you can explain to me how you were unable to save the cores. Dammit, we needed those spare parts."

Spare parts were more important than lives, it seemed, but Kiefer just nodded and made his retreat while he could. The room he was directed to was basic, but at least there was a bed. Jeffers already had a clean uniform laid out, along with fresh towels and soap.

After a quick shower and a change of clothes, Kiefer checked on his men and tracked down Ferris. He found the lieutenant settling the twins, or more accurately, settling Annie. Chiva was nowhere to be seen. The awkward nature of their embrace made him step back, and he deliberately knocked his sword against the wall. When he moved back into the doorway, they were standing wide apart, Annie's face flushed, Ferris scowling until he saw Kiefer, and then he smiled.

"The controller wants to speak to you about the techs. He wants to see your security checks," Kiefer said.

Ferris rolled his eyes but moved further away from Annie. "Where's Chiva?" Kiefer asked.

"Trying to get access to a computer so he can file his application to the Maincore academy," Annie replied, keeping her eyes downcast.

"Single-minded, that lad," Ferris said with a laugh.

Kiefer's lips tightened. Self-centred more like. He should have been looking after his sister. "Fine. What about you, Annie? Is he applying for you, too?"

"Oh, no. Annie is going to work for me," Ferris said. "I promised her a position at my place."

"Your place?"

"Yeah, I own a guest house in Maincore. My retirement plan. We're not going to be in the Devenders forever."

"True." Kiefer's thoughts hadn't got that far. The Devenders were his life, his family. He couldn't imagine ever leaving. Observing Annie's strained face, Kiefer changed the subject. "We're invited to eat with the controller later," he said, retreating back into the corridor. "I'll see you there."

"Will do," Ferris replied. As he followed Kiefer into the corridor, he gave him a wink. "I'd better get the controller my files. You know, make sure we offload those techs as promised."

Kiefer chewed his lip as he watched Ferris saunter down the corridor. Maybe Kiefer had misunderstood him. Had the lieutenant been serious? Was he doctoring the files? And if so, why? Shaking his head, he went back to his room to continue writing his report.

The next morning, they were back on the road. They travelled much quicker without the techs slowing them down.

Ten days later, Kiefer watched the twins as they rode over the rise and the first sight of Maincore came into view. Chiva held his breath and hissed it out in shock as the valley opened before them, flattening as it spread across the plains ahead. Annie was little better, her face pale and her blue eyes wide with awe.

Kiefer tried to view the city as they saw it, with new eyes. In the distance, tall, silvery spires rose into the sky above a line of tall buildings. They looked elegant and mysterious in the distant blue haze. The city of Maincore was huge. It spread as far as they could see and took up the whole valley. In front of them, a low, sprawling complex of buildings blocked the road. His stomach fluttered with concern. They were nearly there.

Kiefer breathed a sigh of regret as they reached the Maincore stable complex. The city of Maincore was an interconnected highway of impossibly tall buildings, smart connections, social feeds and Maincore oversight. It was all high-tech, run by Harmony, or so he had once believed, for the benefit of all. The trite description rolled off his tongue, and he wondered what other lies had been instilled in his brain.

In Maincore, sleek transits connected all parts of the city; there was no need for horses. The transition from low-tech to high was quite surreal and took a little adjusting to. He wondered how the twins would react. They would never have seen anything like it.

He had been amused at how different they were. The journey to Maincore over the past week or so had given him plenty of time to observe them. Chiva was bright, intelligent, and quick to assume. Anneka was just as smart but more thoughtful and observant.

Ferris had spent the evenings trying to describe the city, but with nothing to compare his descriptions to, they had fallen flat and only confused the twins further. Chiva was putting on a brave face. This journey was his idea after all. Anneka stayed in his shadow, watching everything closely.

The group clattered under the wooden arch into the courtyard, and stable lads bustled out to take the horses. There was a general muddle of confusion as horses were led away and men sorted themselves out. Everyone was travel-weary and covered in road dirt. Kiefer dropped his saddle-bags at his feet as the complex commandant came out to greet them. The commandant acknowledged the salutes and then pulled Kiefer aside.

"Get your men into the barracks and clean up. You and Ferris are to report to the debriefing centre immediately. The next shuttle leaves in forty minutes. Make sure you are both on it. Your men will remain here. I'll debrief them. Watch your back, Kiefer. There have been some changes while you've been gone," the man said in an undertone.

Kiefer acknowledged the quiet warning before calling Ferris over. "Get your kids cleaned up. We need to be on the next shuttle to Maincore, which is in forty minutes."

Kiefer moved towards his men. "Time to freshen up, lads. Barrack D is assigned to this troop. Wash, eat, and then debrief. I'll see you later. Dismissed."

Eager to get rid of his road grime, Kiefer hurried to the officer's barracks. Stripping of his clothes, he stood under the needling spray of the shower and considered his options. He wouldn't be able to reach Harmony here. This would be the place she would be shackled most rigorously, unless he could find the intake feeds to the processors controlling her. He would need to get into the memory banks and trace the code, and to do that, he would need the highest clearance and access to the server farms. He couldn't see that happening any time soon.

Sighing, he scrubbed himself clean, and then dressed in the uniform Jeffers had laid out for him. He would miss that man's services. There was no way he would be sent back out into the sectors after coming home a man and a sector down. Stamping into his boots, he swung his cloak over his shoulders and left the barracks.

Chiva and Annie were huddled on the bench outside the barracks. He frowned at them. They looked very small, dejected, and still filthy. "Didn't Ferris show you where to get cleaned up?"

They looked at him and mutely shook their heads.

"Well you haven't time now. Come with me." Herding them back into the barracks, Kiefer took them to the room he had just used, and handed them both damp cloths. "Clean your face and hands. We can't take you into the city looking like that. Give me your cloaks. We need to get them brushed." He swirled out of the room, leaving the twins scrubbing their faces.

Returning, he handed them each a grey cloak. "Yours fell apart. Use these, and keep them sealed. At least they will hide your clothes. We'll have to replace them later." He inspected the twins briefly and nodded. "It'll have to do. Come on." He led them back out of the barracks and down a narrow alley way.

As someone ran up behind them, he glanced over his shoulder. It was Ferris.

"You could have told me you had the twins. I was looking all over for them," he complained as he reached them.

"They needed to freshen up. You'd never have got them through the city looking like they did," Kiefer said, his voice rough.

"Oh, don't be such a snob. No-one will notice them," Ferris replied.

Kiefer stifled a biting retort as the silver shuttle approached with a hissing whirr of air. The twins seemed terrified as it was. The silver tube hovered above the ground, lined with glass windows that seemed to go on for ever.

"This is a transit shuttle. It will take us into the city centre," he said, his voice quiet as the transparent doors swished open. "This is the typical mode of transport around Maincore. Once we reach the city, it often runs underground, so don't panic if it all goes dark outside."

He gave Chiva a reassuring smile when the boy threw him a fearful glance as they boarded. Annie looked around the shuttle in amazement. It was a hollow metal cylinder, with groups of seating along the walls, facing inwards. Kiefer indicated a bench, and Chiva sat, dragging Annie with him. Wrapping their cloaks tight, they huddled together, silent and scared. Passengers openly stared at them until Kiefer moved to stand in front of them, blocking the view.

Piped-in music drifted over them, and as they settled, a smooth voice welcomed them to the wonderful city of Maincore, where the Ministry waited to provide for their every need.

Kiefer and Ferris held onto straps in the ceiling as the shuttle lurched forward, and it quickly gained speed. The floodplains were a blur through the windows as the shuttle rushed towards the city in silence. Gentle music continued to emanate from the overhead speakers, along with the voice welcoming them to Maincore, masking the low murmurs of conversation of the people seated around them.

When the shuttle entered a tunnel, all light was extinguished outside, and Annie squeaked in shock. Chiva squeezed her hand, and she clutched it back until they came out into the open again. He gasped in awe as the shuttle threaded through tall buildings made of glass. Peering upwards, he jumped when the view was cut off as they entered another tunnel.

It took a further ten minutes before the shuttle slowed and came to a halt in a brightly lit tunnel. The doors swished open, and the elegant passengers charged off. Kiefer waited, watching with resignation. Chiva and Annie stared about in confusion.

"Come on," Kiefer said once the shuttle had finally emptied. "Stay close and don't get separated." He led them out of the tunnel and towards a moving staircase. They stood on the metal step and whizzed to the top. Everything moved so quickly around them; people rushed past, disappearing into tunnels and stairways. "These are called 'travelators'," Kiefer murmured. "It's best to always hold on and keep your clothes close to you. You don't want your cloak trapped in the mechanism. Very annoying."

Kiefer took a deep breath as they came out into the open, and Annie cowered against him at the sudden racket. There were people everywhere, all hurrying in different directions. Chiva whipped around at an enormous crash across the street. A man yelled, and a grinding winch began to lift a metal container. Horns blared as vehicles crawled along the road. The air smelt of metallic fumes and wafts of tantalising food.

Kiefer looked down at Annie with a small smile and squeezed her shoulder. "Don't worry" he said, raising his voice to be heard over the noise. "This is normal." He turned to the left and walked down the side of the road, heading towards the Devenders' headquarters, housed in the Harmony complex.

Three tall, glass fronted buildings stood in a group, forming a triangle in the centre of the city. The white building was the Ministry, the black glass building the Devenders' headquarters and the red brick building housed the academy. The centre of the Maincore administration and all their machinations.

All the other buildings surrounding them were lower. A physical reminder that the Ministry watched over everything.

"Beautiful Maincore, at last. The joys of civilisation. Why do we ever leave it?" Ferris muttered under his breath.

Kiefer cast him a sharp glance. "I thought you preferred the city."

"It's better than the sectors, that's for sure."

Kiefer looked over his shoulder at the twins. Their eyes were wide with awe and fear as they took in the tall buildings and the reflective glass and metal everywhere, and they flinched at the strident noise.

"Where are you planning to put them up until you can sort them out?" he asked Ferris.

"They can stay at my place. I've got the room. We'll soon have Chiva enrolled in the program, won't we, lad?" Ferris threw the question over his shoulder at Chiva. He grinned at the overwhelmed expression on the boy's face.

"And the girl?"

"I've got something for her for now. She'll find a job in no time; maids are always in demand," Ferris said easily. "In fact, we'll peel off here so I can drop them off, and I'll meet you at headquarters."

"Good luck, Chiva," said Kiefer. "I'm sure you'll get into the Academy, no problem. Let me know how you get on. Annie, make sure your brother behaves and looks after you, alright?" He gave her a reassuring grin. She looked petrified.

He glared at Chiva, who nodded quickly. "Don't worry, we'll be fine," Chiva said as he followed Ferris and Annie down the street. Ferris pointed out sights as they went, glibly promising to show them the town on the morrow.

12

When Kiefer reached the tall, black glass building which housed the Devender HQ, he was directed up to the commander-in-chief's office and shown in without any delay, which was surprising. The commander, seated behind his desk, finished initialling a paper in front of him before looking up and leaning back in his chair. "Well, well, the prodigal son returns. So, Gallante, what do you have to say for yourself?"

Kiefer stared at his commander. A large, pot-bellied man, whose face was flushed red, either from some recent embarrassment or too much alcohol, Kiefer wasn't sure which. "About what, sir?"

"About your recent experience with the Harmony resistance, of course."

Kiefer kept his face blank. How had they heard about that already? "We were ambushed in Sector 45 by a group that called themselves the resistance. Yes, I took them for bandits. I wasn't aware there was a resistance, nor did I know what they were resisting against."

"Tell me everything you know about them," the commander demanded.

"The leader was a woman called Lorne, her second a man called Stefan. I'd say there was about twenty of them altogether, and as I said, they acted like bandits. No technology on them at all."

"Doesn't mean they don't have any. You should have followed them to their base. We need to detain them quickly. Where are they now?"

"I don't know. They didn't tell me. I could guess. Sector 26 is adjacent."

The commander looked up in annoyance. "It is in your best interests to start giving me information that will help save your tail, or you might find yourself in deeper trouble than you are already. Start at the beginning."

Kiefer described the events which had led to the collapse of Sector 45, and his voice was hoarse by the time he finished.

The Commander frowned at him. "You're sure it was the Bantwich virus?" he asked.

"Yes, sir."

"And you don't know who planted it."

"No sir. Ferris was just beginning the search when the place collapsed."

The commander heaved himself to his feet. "Wait here," he said and then left the room.

Kiefer relaxed his shoulders and ran his finger around his collar. He hoped this catechism would be over soon so he could type up the report instead of him having to repeat it.

He tensed as another man, the Grand Controller himself, walked into the room. He hadn't expected an audience with the man who was responsible for the Harmony transfer program, and he observed the man carefully, his gut churning.

The Grand Controller was about the same height and build as Kiefer, though there was a depth, a presence about him as if he took up the space of two men. When he spoke, his voice was deep and powerful, demanding your attention. His chest was decorated with glistening medals of honour and recognition that caught and flashed in the lamp light. His head of white hair was perfectly combed, and his uniform was immaculate.

Kiefer felt grubby in comparison, even though he had showered and dressed in a fresh uniform. The Grand Controller glared at him from deep-brown eyes, the same as his, under dark eyebrows at odds with his white hair.

Kiefer could feel every crease and wrinkle in his appearance being dissected.

"Why did you leave the sector?" the Grand Controller demanded abruptly as he sat in the chair behind the ornate desk.

Kiefer smartened to attention. "Sir, there was no reason to stay. The facility was destroyed, and there was nothing to salvage. Our time would be better spent elsewhere."

"You left a hotbed of rebellion ready to attack the other sectors."

"That is not true sir. The people were barely existing; they have nothing, nor the capability of affecting anyone else."

"Do not contradict me. You left people standing who could be a threat to Harmony and our plans."

Kiefer frowned. "As I just reported, sir, the people are barely living. They will struggle to survive the winter. We should be sending them help."

"Your report was piffle. I expect better from a commander of the Devenders. Maybe you have forgotten your purpose?"

"My purpose is to maintain the facilities and protect the

sentience Harmony so she can support our people and extend her protection over all of us," Kiefer recited.

"And how are you protecting us when you leave seditious rioters to infest other sectors?"

"They are not rioters. They are people like you and me."

The Grand Controller stood, anger on his face. "Don't you ever bracket us with them. They are filth. They destroy our processors, and they put our plans at risk. You left them standing."

Kiefer stared at his father. Did he really believe what he was saying? "They are just ordinary people trying to live their lives. Since when has that been a crime?"

"When they risk the future of our planet, that's when."

"It was an ideal example of a low-tech settlement, just as the compact describes. You and Mother used to debate its viability every night over dinner. Here's a chance for you to see it in action."

"You know that is only fantasy, a pipe dream, never a reality," his father said.

Kiefer shrugged. "It looked pretty real to me."

"I see you think you can impress us with your percipience. You'd better go tell your mother. I'm sure she'll be impressed."

"Yes, sir," Kiefer replied dutifully.

His father's eyes narrowed. "What happened to your face, boy?"

"Ambushed by the rebels, sir. Broke my nose."

"Where are these bandits now?"

"I don't know, sir. Headed towards Sector 26 is my guess, as I told Commander Henders when I gave my report, sir."

"Your account does not quite match your men's," his father said coldly.

Kiefer shrugged. "I was knocked unconscious. You'd have to ask Ferris; he is the investigator. I'm the technician."

"Yes, and you failed dismally, didn't you?"

"I shut the system down as soon as I found the virus."

"You didn't shut it down fast enough. I'm disappointed, Kiefer. I expected more of you. I don't think we can trust you out in the field. Maybe you need a bit of retraining."

"Yes, sir."

His father stared at him, and Kiefer stiffened under the inspection. "Report to Int-Ed for reassignment."

"Yes, sir." Kiefer saluted and about-faced. His heart sank at the thought. Int-Ed was the controllers' internal education program, in effect, a brainwashing think tank. Their purpose was to realign people's thinking when they had strayed away from the core directive, designed by his parents to protect the facilities that guarded Harmony.

Kiefer collected an escort of two burly guards as soon as he left the office. His father obviously wasn't taking any chances. He suddenly wondered why.

13

Lorne glared at her sister. "For the last time, no! You are not going to Maincore, now or ever. You wouldn't stand a chance."

"You should have spoken with that commander you got so friendly with, asked him to find Arran."

"It would already be too late. I am sorry, Ciely, but you have to be honest with yourself; Arran wouldn't have survived their interrogation."

"He might have. If it was your commander, you wouldn't give up on him, would you? Of course you wouldn't. It's alright for you to find someone, but not me?"

"It's not that. Truly, I want you to be happy. But Ciely, Arran is lost to us. It's been weeks. Even if he did survive, he wouldn't be the man you remember. They would have wiped his memories by now."

"I'd help him as you did with Kiefer."

"The healers helped Kiefer, not me. He means nothing to me."

"Don't lie to me, Lorne. I saw you with him. You couldn't keep your hands off him."

Lorne stared at Ciely, her stomach sinking as she realised why her sister was so upset about Arran. She should have been paying more attention to Ciely, not some Devender commander. "Ciely, you know why we have to be so careful. A lot of people rely on us. We have to stick together; we are the only family we have."

"You could have had a brother," Ciely snapped. "Could still have if we save Arran."

"Ciely. It's impossible."

"I never thought you would be so selfish as to deprive me of this one request, the only thing I have ever asked of you. Why won't you even consider it?"

Lorne reached for her sister, but Ciely reared back, her eyes glittering with anger. Lorne's mouth went dry. "Ciely, I truly am sorry, but he is gone."

"No, he isn't. I feel it here." Ciely clasped her chest. "He is still alive, and I'm not leaving him to suffer."

"I forbid it. We can't afford for the Ministry to capture you as well. Ciely, please think about what you are saying. Would you risk everyone we have helped for the sake of one man?" Lorne knew it was the wrong thing to say as soon as the words slipped out. She shook her head. "We leave for the Wytchwards in the morning. We'll talk further there."

Ciely stomped off, her back rigid, and Lorne rubbed her eyes.

"You must tell her," Stefan said from behind her, his voice gentle.

"I can't. She already hates me. It will only make it worse."

"Until she has proof, she'll keep looking for him. Ciely needs closure. She is right. You wouldn't give up on that Devender. You didn't leave his side until he awoke. Why would she be any different?"

"I don't know. But I gave the order. I didn't realise she was so invested in him. She'll never forgive me."

"Say it was my decision."

"But it wasn't. That's the coward's way out. I made the decision; I should face the consequences."

"Don't leave it too long, Lorne." Stefan faded back into the shadows.

The next morning, they were back on the road. Everyone avoided the sisters, both of whom wore an identical scowl as they stared between their horses' ears. Neither saw the passing terrain, grey and barren, long since stripped of anything edible or flammable. They followed the trails, avoiding the main roads and the patrolling sector sentries, heading away from the depressing sectors and deeper into the hinterland, into the Wytchwards.

The Wytchwards, to all appearances, were an empty, marshy wasteland. The first five miles were spent picking their way through the marshy hillocks and avoiding the quicksand-like bogs that sucked at the horses' feet if they passed too close. The lead scout marked the trail; the rest followed.

The aroma of rotting vegetation and stagnant water permeated the air, clogging airways and pressing down on them. Gases rising from the putrid pools were known to cause interference with electronic gadgets, not that they had any, as well as their lungs They wrapped their faces in their scarves. Tufts of bronze-tinged grasses ruffled in the breeze that tried to stir the resistant waters, a tarnished crown above the brackish tangle of weeds and reeds.

It took twice as long as it should have to cross the barren wastes, as they had to weave around the snarls, and the sun was setting by the time they rode onto the grassy plains, stretching as far as they could see. The breeze strengthened and blew the stench of the marshes away as they travelled.

"When are we stopping?" Ciely asked, her voice so sharp it sent shivers down Lorne's spine. "It will be dark soon."

Lorne blinked and looked around. Ciely was right; they needed to set up camp before they lost the last of the light. She had been so deep in thought that she hadn't noticed. "There's no shelter for miles; we may as well camp here," Lorne replied as they came to a halt.

Camp was raised with little trouble. The rebels were used to working together. A large pan of gruel simmered over the smoking firepit, and the aroma making Lorne's stomach grumble. She hadn't let them stop to eat in the marshes—lingering in that foul place would only have dragged everyone down into despair—but as a result, everyone was hungry.

A ring of tents surrounded the fire, and men and women gathered in groups, chatting in low voices as they cleaned their weapons or tack. Lorne looked around for Ciely. Unable to delay any longer, she needed to tell Ciely what she'd done. Wiping her damp hands down her trousers, she went in search of her sister.

She'd been sister, mother, and father to Ciely for the last ten years, since their parents had been killed in a raid in one of the sectors. Lorne had been seventeen, her sister six. She and Ciely had been rescued by the blacksmith and his wife, smuggled away in the confusion and into a life of rebellion.

It was not a surprise that Ciely was so combative; conflict was all she had ever known. Her life was that of a vagabond: no home, no security, only death and deprivation. It was a life she had no choice but to follow. Lorne quailed. She had been selfish and thoughtless, dragging Ciely where she had wanted to go, not that Lorne had much choice in the matter. But still, she had never asked Ciely what she wanted.

Time had not been kind to the rebels, decimating their ranks until Lorne was the longest serving and had taken over the leadership. With everything she had to manage, her sister had moved down her priorities. She should have known better. At seventeen, Ciely was ripe for romance, and surrounded by virile young men, she didn't have to look far. Why hadn't she paid attention?

Lorne found her sister on the edge of the camp, staring out across the plains, seeing what she didn't know. She took a moment to acknowledge that her sister was no longer a child. Ciely was a young woman, with a young woman's appetites. Lithe and wiry, her burnished curls were cut in a manageable bob, another decision Lorne had made for her. Ciely was an astute tracker with a fine eye for observation; that was why Lorne had teamed her with Arran in the first place, to temper his tendency to blunder in. Partnering with Ciely had made him have to think twice. It had obviously made him think more than twice!

"Ciely, we need to talk."

Ciely stiffened, her hands balling into fists at the sound of her sister's voice.

"You should have told me about Arran. If I'd known, I would never have…"

"Known! Would that have made any difference? I knew you thought I wasn't good enough, but I never thought you hated me."

"Ciely, stop. Of course I don't hate you. I love you; you're my only sister."

"Oh, because I'm family you have to love me, is that it? Keep telling yourself that, Lorne, if it makes you feel better."

"You know that's not what I meant!"

Ciely straightened, and her eyes gleamed with tears.

"You never wanted me to have a life of my own, to be happy."

"That's not true."

"Only you are allowed to be happy, to choose who you want."

"Ciely, please, I had no idea you and Arran were so close."

"Why do I have to tell you everything? Don't you notice what other people are doing? Can't you ask?"

"You're right; we should talk more. I'm sorry."

Ciely stared at Lorne, her blue eyes like chips of ice. "So that makes it all better, does it? Pat me on the head, and I'll be a good little girl and forget about him."

"Of course not. Ciely, you're twisting my words."

"Then say it plain." Ciely lifted her chin and crossed her arms. Lorne thought that if her sister had had a tail, it would have swished, a sign she was ready to pounce on her prey.

Lorne swallowed, her throat suddenly dry. She didn't want to tell her sister the truth, not in the state she was in. "I am sorry, Ciely, but Arran is dead."

"You don't know that. They may have only just arrived in Maincore."

Lorne's hand trembled as she dragged her fingers through her hair. "We couldn't let them take him back to Maincore."

Ciely narrowed her eyes and took a step back. "We?"

"I."

"What did you do?"

"I sent Joris to make sure."

"Make sure of what?" Ciely's voice was a low growl.

"Ciely, Arran is dead."

"He's not. You didn't."

Lorne spread her hands. "I am so sorry, Ciely. Truly. You know the rule; no one gets taken alive."

"I don't believe you. There is still time to rescue him."

"It's too late. He was dead before we reached Sector 45."

"You're lying. You just want to get back at me because your Devender was hurt."

Lorne flinched and rubbed her temples. The ache was spreading, a sharp pain behind her eyes. The guilt made her stomach roil and her chest ache. Her sister would never forgive her. "It's over, Ciely. You have to let him go."

"I don't have to do anything you tell me." Ciely strode back and forth. Anger crackled off her, but there was no sign of grief. "If you won't help him, then I will."

Lorne reached for her sister, but Ciely slapped her hand away before turning on her. Her voice was a weapon, low and sharp, and every word cut. "I should never have listened to you, followed you. You think of no one but yourself, and everyone else has to pay for your mistakes."

"That's not—"

"You don't listen to anyone but Stefan. You think you know everything." Ciely stood nose to nose with her. Lorne blinked. When had her sister grown so tall? "No more. I make my own choices."

"Ciely, please—"

"You're not my mother."

"I know, but—"

"So, stop trying to pretend you are. From now on, I make my own decisions. No one—" she leaned towards Lorne, prodding her shoulder with her finger like it was an iron poker—"no one tells me how to live my life. I will do what I want, when I want, with who I want."

Ciely turned on her heel and strode away, leaving Lorne gaping after her. Lorne absently rubbed her shoulder as her sister's vicious rant rang in her ears.

"Well, that went well," Stefan said from behind her.

"You think?" Lorne snapped.

"Leave her; she'll cool down. Speak to her tomorrow."

"She didn't believe me. She thinks he's still alive."

"She's in denial. Give her time."

"We don't have time. We've never had time."

Lorne led the way back into the camp. She glanced around the ring of tattered tents. Grimy and worn, they were all that protected them from the elements. Their home. Her sister was nowhere to be seen. With a sigh, she accepted the bowl of gruel and began to eat.

14

———————

Chiva and Annie gaped in amazement when Ferris led them to a row of squared-off buildings huddled under an arch rising high above, one of many that supported the bridge for the shuttle line.

"Welcome to my humble abode," he said as he led them up the stone steps and placed his hand on the plate to open the door. The door swished to the side, revealing a wide hallway paved with black and white stone tiles. The effect was slightly dizzying to inexperienced eyes.

Ferris led them down dark corridors painted in black with gilt accents. "I'll show you around later, but if you would stay in this room for now, until we get you halfway decent. I have to admit, Kiefer was right. I'd forgotten how judgemental the city is." Ferris smiled at them as he ushered them into an opulent room dominated by a large bed. "There are staff in the house, but they will not disturb you. Please relax, have a bath. I have to report in, too." He nodded at them, and the door shut; the distinctive sound of a lock clicking followed his departure.

Annie glared at her brother before walking over and trying the door. "It's locked. He's locked us in."

"It's probably for our own safety," Chiva replied reassuringly. "What an amazing room though. Look at those curtains. I bet they cost a fortune, and the size of that bed. Four people could fit in it." He went over to the long blue curtains and drew them back. "Where is the window?" Blankly, he gazed at the black wall.

"I guess there isn't one," Annie replied dryly as she opened the door to the bathroom. She gasped, which drew Chiva close behind her to peer over her shoulder. The bathroom gleamed with white tiles and gold fittings. A black sunken bath, big enough for two, maybe three people, glittered in the overhead light. Annie went over and put the plug in and twiddled the knobs on the wall until she found hot water.

"Bags first bath," she said, unstopping the various glass bottles on the side. Cautiously, she sniffed and then, with a wide smile, poured some under the tap. The water bubbled up immediately, and she inhaled deeply. "How nice." She smiled dreamily at Chiva. "Out," she said and shut the door on his aggrieved face.

"Annie, don't take all the hot water. Leave some for me," Chiva called through the door.

Annie smiled as she shed her clothes and slipped into the bubbles. The water was divine. She relaxed and drifted. She couldn't believe that places like this existed. Why were they living in such terrible conditions if this was possible? Why was the sector so repressed?

She hadn't believed the resistance when they said the controllers subverted goods so the sectors remained under their control. But here was proof, and the Devenders reinforced it. If they knew the truth, why did they perpetuate it?

Annie suddenly sat up. What did Ferris really want, and

why had he brought them here? She supposed they would soon find out. She scrubbed the dirt off her body and washed her hair; strands of tangled hair came out with the grime. The bubbles disappeared, and her face heated as she realised the dirty bath water was just from her.

Pulling the plug, she got out and wrapped herself in one of the soft robes hanging on the peg. She dumped her clothes in the matching sink and scrubbed them in more of the bath soap. Once they were relatively clean, she wrung them out and hung them over the railings to dry. Then she eyed the toilet. It had a lot of levers, she thought. Maybe it wasn't just a toilet.

Annie quickly rinsed the bath out and re-ran the water for Chiva. She felt amazing. "Chiva, get in the bath, and I'll wash your clothes out," she said as she left the bathroom.

Her brother lay on the bed in all his grimy clothes, fast asleep.

"Chiva! Wake up. You can't lay on there in those clothes. Go and have a bath," she said loudly, shaking his shoulder.

Chiva jerked awake in shock. "What?"

"Bath, then you can sleep. Come on." She pulled his arm.

Reluctantly, he sat up and looked at her. "Alright, stop harassing me. As long as you haven't put that stuff in the water. I don't want to smell like you do."

Annie pouted. "Why not? I smell very nice," she teased as she pushed her brother across the room and into the bathroom. "Get in the bath." She left, shutting the door behind her.

When she returned, Chiva was in the bath, sniffing the various bottles. He blushed bright red as she entered and swirled the bubbles around him. "Annie, I'm in the bath."

"Yes, and you have plenty of bubbles, so don't be silly. I need to wash your clothes," she said with a laugh as she swept his clothes off the floor and into the sink. Gingerly, he lay back in the hot water, watching her scrub.

"Can you believe this?" he asked. "Hot water piped into the house, and a separate room to bathe in."

"Yes, it makes you wonder, doesn't it? Why we don't have any of this?" Annie said angrily as she scrubbed. She looked at her brother. "Chiv, what do you think Ferris wants with us?"

Chiva frowned at her. "What do you mean?"

"Well, he doesn't strike me as the humanitarian type. Just look at his house." She gestured at their surroundings. "Do you really think he is going to help us out of the goodness of his heart?"

"He promised," Chiva said hesitantly.

"In return for what?"

Chiva looked at her, and raised his eyebrows as he nodded at her, unable to say the words.

She stopped scrubbing and stared at him, a hissing growing in her ears as her stomach cramped. "You didn't."

"I thought you liked him," he said weakly.

Annie swayed and grabbed the sink. "I don't know him. What did he promise you in exchange for me?"

"To sponsor me into the academy."

"What else?"

"Nothing, just to get me in to finish my studies."

"Where are we supposed to live on while you are doing that? What are we supposed to eat? Where do we get any credits? Nothing is for free, Chiva. Surely, you learned that lesson like the rest of us?"

Chiva swallowed, his face blanching.

"You mean we are completely in his power, with no means of helping ourselves?" she asked, her voice rising.

Chiva flushed bright red. "Once I graduate, I'll be able to support you."

"And how long will that take? How do we pay for it? I'm sure it will cost credits once you're in, for lab time, for disks, if nothing else."

Chiva looked away from her accusing eyes. "I'll figure it out," he said dully.

Annie huffed her breath out, hugging herself to prevent the anger that flashed through her from escaping. "You're a fool," she snapped and flounced out of the bathroom, slamming the door behind her.

Annie lay on the bed, facing the wall, nausea swirling in her belly, exhaustion numbing her. Her brother had sold her for a pittance. Anger flared again. More at the fact that he valued her so little than for what he had done.

When he slunk out of the bathroom, she ignored him, pretending to be asleep.

"Annie?" he whispered.

She heard him walk around the bed, no doubt to check if she was still awake. She kept her eyes shut.

"Annie?"

She didn't respond.

Relief flooded her when he gently covered her with the sheet and lay down beside her. The lights went out and she stared into the darkness. Tears, finally formed and dribbled down her cheeks.

Kiefer entered the lift and pressed the button for Int-Ed, his escorts close behind. The lift was smooth and silent, giving no indication whether they went up or down. When the doors slid open, Kiefer stepped out and followed the empty, white corridor until he reached a set of double doors. They slid open as he approached, and he stopped by the low reception desk. He waited for the young man tapping on a keyboard to look up.

"Commander Kiefer reporting for reassignment," he said as the man continued to type.

The man looked up. He had dark hair, narrow black eyes, and the smooth, elegant beauty reminiscent of one of the old Earth colonies. After a slow inspection, he said, "Place your right hand on there." He nodded to a palm plate on the desk.

Kiefer placed his hand as instructed and felt the slight tingle as the plate scanned his hand and beeped a message. The light flashed orange. The young man looked at Kiefer's escorts. "Room I12. Door to the right." Returning to his screen and tapped his keyboard again.

Kiefer led the way. 112? This was not going to be good. An interrogation room? Not a reprogramming suite? He had expected a bit of reconditioning for his failures, but interrogation?

His escorts hustled him through the door, and a white-coated technician said over his shoulder, "Strap him down."

Kiefer hesitated, but then his escorts took an arm each and forced him into the chair. They strapped his wrists, chest, and ankles down.

"This really is not necessary," Kiefer said lightly, observing the blank wall across the back of the room, a one-way screen, probably. His stomach fluttered; this didn't look like a reconditioning session.

The technician ignored him as he methodically unbuttoned his clothes and wired him up to the monitor and the connected scanners. The man's name tag gleamed in the light: Technician Staffen. Kiefer wondered idly how many of these he did a day. The monitor started beeping as graphs and numbers populated the screen, proof that he was alive.

A slow, hard voice spoke from behind him. "I have a few questions I require answers to. I recommend you tell the truth. If you do, this will be over quickly, and you can return to duty. There are a few discrepancies in your report versus what your men reported, Commander Gallante."

"Like what?" Kiefer asked, wondering what Ferris had said to cause a response like this. His hair stood on end as the patches on his skin pulsed. Ah.

"You call me, 'sir'. That will be your first lesson. Don't make me repeat it," the voice said coldly. "Well, let's find out, shall we? What did you do when you arrived in Sector 45?"

Kiefer frowned. "Instructed the men to set up camp and a perimeter watch, and then I went to check the error log in the input room, sir."

"You didn't report to the controller first?"

"The main node was down. I thought time was of the essence. It was more important to get a pulse on the threat level before I spoke to the controller."

"Did you not think the controller would know what the threat level was?" the voice asked.

"If he did, he wasn't dealing with it."

"And by dealing with it, you mean locking down the system?"

"Yes, the Bantwich virus was in one node. It would quickly spread to the others. Leaving the system functioning would only cause the spread of the virus."

"How did you know it was the Bantwich virus?"

"I recognised the recurring loop program and the tags."

"And how are you so familiar with Bantwich?"

"It was a feature in the last refresh, sir."

"And then you removed the controller from his position and had him detained."

"Yes, sir."

"Why?"

"Because I felt he was incapable of handling the situation, sir. He had no protocols in place and was not prepared to act."

"In your opinion," the voice interjected smoothly.

"Of course, in my opinion. I was the senior officer on site."

"Tell me why you chose to go down into the server bays instead of sending a technician."

"Lieutenant Ferris was only just beginning the security check on the staff. I didn't know who we could trust. I could have sent the very person who planted the virus."

"You should have been in control of the facility, not grubbing about down in the bowels of the planet," the man said.

Kiefer shifted at the cold edge to the man's voice. "I am a

technician. I was sent to preserve the processor. I could see we were at risk of losing it; I thought it would be quicker to see for myself."

"Quicker for what?"

Kiefer frowned. "For me to decide the correct action to take."

"Or quicker for you to sabotage the facility?"

"What?" Kiefer exclaimed in shock. How could they make that assumption? There was no evidence to support such an accusation.

"It seems that as soon as you went down into the server bays, all the error warnings escalated, and alerts began to go off. I suggest you triggered the event that caused the catastrophic failure and the destruction of the whole facility."

"That's not true. Speak to Willis. He was with me." What had his men been saying? He'd told them to tell the truth, not make up stories. Why were they that suspicious of him? Kiefer belatedly wondered what Ferris had said. Had the lieutenant used this as an opportunity to try and elevate himself?

"Not when you went down to the junction boxes."

"It was already destroyed. We tried to fix it. We connected a relay to an aux cable and jumped the connection to close the circuit so we could control the coolant towers."

"So you say."

"Yes, and since when is my word not good enough? *Sir*."

"Since you joined with a rebel force and planned the downfall of Harmony," the man said smoothly.

"That's a lie," Kiefer snapped, straining at his straps. He gasped as a jolt of pure pain sped through his body, taking his breath away.

"I recommend you sit still and begin telling the truth. Where were you before the rebels entered the town?"

"What?" Kiefer tried to get his spinning mind under control.

"Where were you before the rebels entered the town? Your men report you were not there to coordinate the defence."

"They knew perfectly well where I was. I went with Andre to the produce farm to divert the food supplies to the settlement instead of Comptech. We were ambushed by the rebels on the way back."

"Where you lost a man and dashed off into the forest, leaving the remainder of your men to be captured."

"I gave the order to disperse as we were being targeted by archers," Kiefer said through gritted teeth. They were spinning everything.

"You lost a man and left your men at risk in the settlement. That's a charge of serious misconduct and neglect."

"We were not aware of a rebel threat or that they were active in the sectors," Kiefer said.

"Come, come, you don't expect me to believe that, do you?"

"There were no reports issued to the Devenders about rebels," Kiefer repeated.

Another charge rippled through his body, leaving him breathless. His heart rate increased as his body tried to counterbalance the adrenalin and shock in his system. He panted gently, and sweat ran down his face. He wondered whether Merianne would class this as overdoing it.

"Commander, don't be so silly," said the voice. "We know that is an outright lie. Lieutenant Ferris knew, so you must have known."

Kiefer's mind spun. If Ferris had kept reports from him,

what else didn't he know, and why? Why would Ferris shaft him so? It didn't make sense.

"Ferris didn't pass the reports on," Kiefer managed to get out.

"A good commander does not blame his subordinates." The silky-smooth voice was beginning to irritate Kiefer. "And then, once you finally arrived at the settlement, you tamely surrendered to the rebels and spent a week closeted with them, out of sight and reach of your men. Ferris reported that the sector intended to work with the rebels to create their own community. Minister Velten believes there may be more going on in this sector than you have told us."

"I was knocked unconscious and dragged off for interrogation. I was beaten senseless in their attempt to get my override codes. You'll be glad to know I didn't give them up," Kiefer said. His body jerked and strained against the straps as a charge ripped through him, and he went rigid. Pure agony whited out his mind as his heart stuttered. Finally, his abused body finally shut down, and he lost consciousness.

"Wake him up. That shouldn't have affected him so much. What did you do wrong?" The interrogator stomped up to the screens, and Technician Gerry Staffen cowered away from him. He hated this job, but every time he suggested a move to his supervisor, he was offered a 'pep' talk. He'd managed to avoid it so far, but he knew if he kept asking for a change, it would be more than a pep talk he received.

"Sir, at no time did he lie. The gauges all say he was speaking the truth. You doubled the last charge. If he were weakened from previous injuries, as he stated, that would have caused his collapse. The charge should have been recalibrated for his weakened state."

"It's not possible. We know he is in league with the rebels. We need to know where they are."

"He is in no condition to answer any further questions, sir. He won't recover for at least ten, maybe twelve hours," Gerry said hesitantly.

"This is intolerable." The man paced. "I will report your incompetence to your superior. Run the reset program. We can at least spend the time profitably while he is tractable."

"Yes, sir. That will completely override all his memories. He won't be able to answer any further questions."

"You said he was telling the truth. If that is so, then he won't be able to answer them anyway," the man snarled, and then he left the room.

Gerry began removing the connectors from Kiefer's skin, leaving the two at his temples. Red burns marked where the charges had overloaded. Tutting, he reprogrammed the system to run a reset, hesitated briefly before adjusting a dial downwards and pressed the run button.

He busied himself with putting everything away and wiping down the seat. One of the traces was spiking slightly, but it was within the parameters, so he let it run. "Poor bastard. He didn't have a chance," he said to himself as he coiled the wires up and stashed them in the collecting basket. Keeping one eye on the monitor and the rippling fluorescent trace lines, he sat and began to type his report into the console.

He startled when a voice spoke behind him. "That's an interesting observation." An elderly woman with elegantly coiffured grey hair entered the room. "If he is to have a chance, I suggest you stop the program now."

Gerry glanced at the blank wall in concern.

"No one is watching," she said. "I suggest you do it quickly." She tapped a finger on her folded arms, the only sign of her concern as she stared at him.

Gerry's fingers flew over the buttons bringing the program to a halt. "He won't wake for at least ten hours."

"And how far did the program get?"

"It has completed stage-one reset, reinforcing core protocols. It was just beginning stage two memory reset. Between that and the shock treatment, some of his short- and long-term memory may be affected. Until he wakes, we won't know."

"Very well, if anyone asks, the program was completed, and you released him back into his mother's care."

"His mother?" Gerry's eyes widened as he realised who stood next to him.

"I have a gurney outside, if you would help to transfer him." As she moved towards the door, her floor length skirts swished gently. Opening the door, she gestured to a man waiting outside.

A sturdy, dark-skinned man in a Devender's uniform, much like the one the subject wore, pushed a trolley into the room. Glancing around, his deep-brown eyes took in the room and its use instantly. The man's face was carefully neutral as he approached Kiefer, but his jaw clenched, and he was inordinately gentle as he helped lift Kiefer onto the trolley.

"Julian, you shouldn't be here," Kiefer's mother said as she gestured for him to hurry.

"He's my friend," Julian replied, covering Kiefer with the blanket and tucking his hands in carefully.

"I know, but you're taking a risk."

"He'd do it for me," Julian said, his chin jutting stubbornly. "You're wasting time."

The woman sighed. "Technician Staffen, I appreciate your help. If you ever need anything, please do not hesitate to contact me."

Gerry nodded jerkily as she turned away and followed

the man called Julian out of the room. Then he turned back to the system and adjusted a few statistics before wiping the change history and resetting the equipment for the next poor soul. Hopefully, Minister Velten would complain. He couldn't wait to be relocated to some dreary data input job.

Shuddering, he replayed the whole session. He had nearly wiped the memory of the only son of Lord and Lady Gallante, the city of Maincore's foremost leader and scientist. He sincerely hoped Minister Velten had a good excuse ready; he couldn't imagine Lady Gallante would appreciate her son being reset.

He gulped as he wiped his perspiring hands on his white coat. What if Velten blamed him? Carefully, he powered up his monitor and checked his work sheet. After quickly copying it, he sent it to his supervisor with a note saying, "All sessions complete per Minister Velten's instructions, subject collected by Lady Gallante."

Gerry logged off and shut everything down, and then he signed out and left the complex. As he joined the queue for the shuttle across the city centre, he debated about whether his husband would appreciate a night in for a change. He was exhausted.

Standing on the platform, Gerry practiced excuses that he might get away with. His husband, Henry, worked long hours at the hospital. He would not sympathise with Gerry feeling tired. Henry wanted to live every moment; he saw too much death to sit and wait for it.

Gerry grinned as he came up with the solution. He would stop at the greens market. If he cooked Henry fresh pasta with a nice side salad, a cosy evening in could be on the cards. Abruptly, he changed direction and headed for the staircase that led to the bus station. As he reached the steps, screams erupted behind him, and he turned to see a man fall off the platform in front of the approaching shuttle. The shuttle's driver slammed on his reverse thrusters, but it was far too late; the man's body was swept away.

Swallowing in horror, Gerry tried to keep the bile down. He had been standing right in that spot; that could have been him. A woman next to him was retching horribly. Hurrying up the steps, he darted towards the bus station, his mind sharp and alert, watching for anyone following him. Was that supposed to have been him? Could Velten know that he hadn't mind-wiped Commander Gallante? Or was it because he thought he had? Or was it Lady Gallante hiding her tracks? No, that didn't make sense. She couldn't hide her son, and no one would believe his word against hers anyway. He was no risk to her.

Gerry jogged up the stairs before the Devenders came to investigate and he found himself trapped in the station all night. He caught the rush-hour bus and stood crammed in the aisle amongst the other travellers, trying to avoid making eye contact. He was relieved when his stop came around, and he and half the people on the bus got off and headed into the market.

Moving randomly around the market stalls, he inspected and smelt the produce for freshness. Just because it was called the fresh produce market didn't always mean the fruit and vegetables were newly delivered.

He hadn't spotted anyone following him; hopefully, he was just being paranoid. After buying his greens, olives, and tomatoes, along with the fresh spaghetti and the pesto sauce his husband loved, he headed home.

16

———

Annie woke with the feeling that someone was watching her. She sat up and searched the room, but it was empty save for her brother, still asleep beside her. A dim glow emanated from the ceiling, giving her enough light to see the room and the locked door.

She rose and went into the bathroom, where she grabbed her damp clothes off the cold radiator and dressed. Her body heat would soon dry them. As soon as she stepped out of the robe, she felt exposed. Something didn't feel right. Sighing, she looked at herself in the mirror and finger-combed her frizzy hair. Of course it wasn't right. She had been sold to a man she didn't know for a shaky promise of nothing. Her face tightened. *Oh, Harmony,* she thought drearily. *What does this man expect me to do?*

Returning to the bedroom, Annie tried the door. It was still locked. She wondered what time it was; she couldn't tell from the artificial light, and there was no clock. Plumping up the pillows, she sat on the bed watching the door. The room gradually got brighter, which Annie assumed meant it was morning. She kicked her brother. "Chiva, it's morning. You'd better get dressed in case someone comes for us," she said. "Let's hope it's time for breakfast. I'm starving."

Chiva lurched upright, looking about him in confusion. "What time is it?"

"I don't know, but you'd better go and get dressed before someone finds you here dressed only in a robe. I get the feeling that might not be too bright in this house."

Annie observed her brother's perplexed expression and smiled. He was such an innocent. She had learnt much in the wash house; the women's lewd stories had been entertaining and eye-opening. She knew what sort of house this was; to have so many opulent bedrooms with such rich décor, it didn't take much deduction.

A sudden panic flashed through her, making her stomach flutter. What did Ferris really expect of Chiva? Her brother wouldn't survive in a place like this. Nor, for that matter, would she. She might be able to manage Ferris as long as he didn't expect her to…she rubbed her temple. As long as he didn't expect her to work in his house, to only to be with him, she might be able cope with that as long as he kept his promise to Chiva.

She watched the door as her brother got dressed. It wasn't long after that Ferris tapped on the door and swiftly opened it without waiting for them to reply.

"Good morning," he said, a bright smile on what Annie now thought of as his calculating face. "I hope you slept well. Breakfast is served upstairs, if you would like to join me?"

Annie stood. "Yes, thank you." She shivered under his scrutiny and somehow doubted they had passed inspection.

"I hate to admit it, but Kiefer was right about your clothes. They are only useful for cleaning rags, if that. We'll sort some new ones out after breakfast. Come on." Ferris led the twins out of the room and towards a back staircase. "This is a working house, and we often have guests, so I would ask that you please only use the back stairs and avoid the front of the house unless I tell you otherwise."

"What sort of work do you do here?" Chiva asked, looking around him with bright eyes.

Ferris glanced at him but then seemed to accept that the boy's question was sincere. "It's a guest house. People often stay for just a night when they are in town. Ah, here we are. Please sit. Help yourself." Ferris gestured to the platters on the table running down the side of the room.

"Were you able to report in to your commander?" Annie asked as she watched him. He was smartly dressed in a commander's uniform like Commander Kiefer had worn. Had he been promoted?

"Yes, a doddle, nothing much to report after all." Ferris smiled at her. "I have two weeks leave, plenty of time to get you both set up as you mean to go on."

"Yes, about that. Where are we to live while Chiva finishes college?"

"Don't worry your pretty little head about that. I have it covered."

"We don't want to be a burden," Annie said.

Ferris shook his head, observing her with his beady eyes. "We will talk more later. Eat your breakfast. I have to go out shortly."

Chiva started to fill his plate. "When will we go to the academy?"

"I'll speak to the principal today and make us an appointment. Don't worry. You will be walking the halls before you know it." Ferris smiled.

Annie saw it didn't reach his eyes, which were cold and calculating. What once she had thought handsome now appeared so much more…tawdry. Trying to conceal her shudder, she started eating. At least they would get one good meal today.

After breakfast, Ferris escorted them back downstairs. "This will be your room while you stay here. I'd ask that you don't leave it, though. Annie, I'd like to speak to you for a moment." He nodded to Chiva and shut the door on the boy's surprised face.

Ferris ran a finger down Annie's cheek. "We'll have to get you prettied up, my love. I like my women to be presentable. I'm going to be away for a couple of days. My staff will look after you in the meantime. I only ask that you keep to your room, but when I return, we will get more acquainted.

"At least here, your parents aren't breathing down your neck. Relax, enjoy yourself a bit," he whispered in her ear as he cupped her breast and ran his hand down her body. She stiffened under his hands. "Ah, Annie, you aren't going to play hard to get? You do know you're the price for staying here, don't you?" Laughing, he opened the door and pushed her into the room. The door slammed shut, and the lock clicked behind her. She leaned against the door, her heart beating rapidly.

17

Kiefer opened his eyes and stared at an unfamiliar room. His brain felt like it was clogged full of cotton wool. Sluggishly, he tried to remember where he'd been to get so wrecked. Not being much of a drinker, he tried to avoid social events. Julian must have dragged him to some stupid party; he had to learn to say no. As he stared at the ceiling, his stomach clenched and chills ran over his skin.

Fuck! he thought as he recognised the mouldings around the window; this was his mother's apartment. He was in so much trouble. How in the hell had he ended up here?

He tried to sit up, but his body wouldn't respond. His limbs twitched, but that was it. He felt like he had been frazzled and hung out to dry. His head was thick and heavy, and his brain wouldn't function.

Rolling his head on the pillow, he could see daylight out the window, but he wasn't sure which day it was. With a frown, he realised he wasn't sure which week it was. He hoped he hadn't missed something important. He had fought so hard to get into the Devenders. To ruin it all by getting paralytic, he would never live it down.

Kiefer flexed his fingers and then gradually worked his way up his arms, lifting them up and down. The feeling began to return and some control. He began moving his feet. It was like teaching his limbs how they were supposed to work, sending the right instructions over and over until his limbs behaved as they were supposed to. This didn't feel like the morning after. Had he been in an accident?

His rising panic was interrupted by the door opening and his mother walking in. He gasped in shock. She had aged. How was that possible?

"Kiefer, you're awake at last."

Kiefer shuddered in horror. Had he been in a coma? How long had he been asleep? His mother was grey-haired and elegant. Her face was smooth and white, but lines fanned around her eyes and mouth, and her skin had become papery with age. She was dressed in a long shift dress in a floral pattern that flattered her slender frame. When had his mother become interested in what she wore? She was usually in lab coats, tinkering at some experiment or other.

"Hush," his mother soothed. "All is well. It is not as bad as it seems. You suffered a partial memory wipe. We're not sure how much you've lost, but you can regain it all, so don't panic. You also suffered an electrocution overload by an overzealous interrogator who thought you had joined the resistance, of all things. Unfortunately, he didn't believe you when you told him you'd been beaten senseless. Do you remember that?"

Kiefer looked at his mother in dismay. "What? When was that?"

"I saw the recording of your interrogation. You went to Sector 45, leading a troop of Devenders. Your orders were to salvage the processor, which was in meltdown, only it had been sabotaged. You are a commander of the 22nd Devender unit, and I am very proud of you." His mother faltered and sat in the chair next to him. She reached for his hand and gripped it tightly. His mother never got emotional; what was going on?

She cleared her throat. "Apparently, you were helping the sector recover after the facility was destroyed until you were interrupted by a band of rebel fighters who attacked you. They captured and tortured you; the doctor confirmed it. Then you were arrested by your commander under suspicion of treason and put through an interrogation by one of Minister Velten's toadies, who, if you've forgotten, is the Minister of the Interior. He was convinced of your guilt from the moment you entered the room, contrary to the evidence of the systems." She paused again. "That was yesterday. You have been unconscious for eighteen hours. The doctor soothed your burns and cooled your nerves. Within a couple of hours, you will be fully functioning again, but you need to rest for another day. Regain your strength. It will take time, or so I understand."

"How did I get here?"

"Julian helped me, along with a technician called Staffen, who seemed to sympathise with your plight. You probably owe him your thanks." She stared at him in such a pointed manner that even in his frazzled state, he got the message.

"Yes, Mother," he said with a brief smile.

She sighed and gently squeezed his hand. "What did I tell you about disobeying your father?"

"I didn't," he said, instinctively. He wouldn't dream of it.

"You must have."

"I don't remember seeing him. Maybe he didn't like what I had to say."

"Then you shouldn't have said it."

"Lie to him, Mother?"

"Bend the truth, if necessary, so it meets his expectations."

"But we are talking about people's lives," Kiefer protested. Then he hesitated. "I think. I'm not sure why I said that." He knew it was true, but he didn't know why.

"Now is not the time to become a philanthropist. We are almost at the final stage; all will be revealed, and the world will be a much better place." His mother smiled gently.

"Did you discover the way to perpetuate Harmony?"

Her face stilled for a moment, then her smile returned. "Of course. We're doing the right thing. You'll see. Harmony will be the best place to live."

"You don't sound sure, Mother. What happened?"

"We found a better way, as you will see. Now, rest, child. Later, you can begin to catch up on the news. I'll speak to you in the morning. We have a soiree in two days' time. You must attend and show all that the rumours are not true."

"What rumours?"

"Nothing to worry your head about. As I said, you will dispel them all at the soiree, and anyway, I have someone I want you to meet. After all, you are quite the eligible bachelor, you know."

"Mother, you are not still trying to pair me off."

"I want a daughter. I want grandchildren; it's every mother's dream. You'll be happier, too. Keep you from getting into trouble like this."

Kiefer frowned. "What trouble?"

"Never mind. Sleep. All will be better when you wake. You'll see."

Obediently, he lay back on the bed, a thought teasing at the edge of his memory. A face hung before his eyes, only he couldn't remember who she was. He wondered where he had met her as her violet eyes followed him into sleep.

The next morning, Kiefer managed to get up and dressed, but he didn't feel right. His chest hurt, and he was breathless. Slowly, he wandered around his mother's drawing room, but even that exhausted him. After inspecting everything, drinking in pictures and trying to remember when they were taken, he collapsed on her elegant sofa. His head ached, and his vision was blurry. He leaned his head back and closed his eyes.

Some pictures, he remembered; others, he didn't. The gaps were random and unpredictable. He recognised the pictures of his father instantly, but he didn't recognise their old unit in the Tech Quarter. He remembered his mother's apartment, but not that his father no longer lived there with her.

His graduation picture was hung in a prominent place on his mother's wall. He remembered the resultant celebration with Julian and his classmates—even his stomach roiled at the memory—but he didn't remember the passing-out ceremony as a Devender, yet his mother said he was a commander.

He remembered meeting Julian for the first time, on the steps of the college entrance. His parents had been too busy to accompany him, much to his relief. Julian was hugging his mother, a beautiful woman with masses of glossy black hair and warm brown skin, just like him. Julian reassured her, "I'll be fine. The next thing you know, I'll have graduated and will be passing the Devenders entrance exam. You'll see."

Julian had always known where he was going, and he'd got there, dragging Kiefer with him every step of the way. Not that Kiefer minded; he had taken to the Devenders like a duck to water. He had his mother's knack for solving problems.

The issue had been who his parents were, as they had swiftly risen to notoriety while he was at college. He remembered having to talk very fast to get into the Devender Academy—and without using his name. Kiefer Gallante would have been rejected as too risky; Cadet Kiefer rose without restriction. Only Julian had known who he was throughout training. It wasn't until the passing-out ceremony, when his parents had turned up and spoiled the party, that others had realised. Kiefer sighed gently. He remembered that well enough.

The door swished open, and he opened his eyes as his mother walked in and smiled at him. "It's good to see you up, but you have other clothes here; why wear your uniform?"

Kiefer looked down at his clothes. He hadn't even thought about it. "They were to hand," he said.

His mother sat in one of the plush armchairs opposite him. "We need to talk," she said, giving him a close inspection. "Why didn't you tell your commanding officer that you had been severely injured? You would have been checked out first by the medics."

"So I could survive a longer conditioning session?" Kiefer asked dryly. "Why was it necessary, Mother? And why did I need wiping?"

His mother looked down at her hands. "You have to understand; these are difficult times. We balance on an edge, and there is no guarantee which way we will fall. People wanted to be sure."

"Sure about what?"

"Your loyalties, to confirm that you hadn't been subverted. The collapse of Sector 45 was unexpected, your interaction with the rebels unclear. There were enough discrepancies in the reports to raise questions. Your tape will be on the monitor later for you to review so you know the details, but Kiefer, they think you had a complete memory wipe, so you have to act like you have."

"Why did you intervene? I assume you were one of the people, along with my father, who wanted my loyalties confirmed," Kiefer said bitterly. "Else, how would you have known to stop it?"

His mother's lips tightened. "Your father has become paranoid. He overreacts, and you know he has always expected more of you as his son."

"You mean he expected me to fail? To be subverted? That I could never be as good as him?" Kiefer asked, the familiar stirrings of anxiety and frustration awakening when he thought of his father.

"I think, sometimes, he sees you as a threat because you are so like him."

"A threat? To what?"

His mother chuckled and reached for his face. She smoothed her fingers down his cheek. "His seniority, his manhood, even my love; he sees you as competition."

Kiefer frowned. "Why would he think that?"

His mother shrugged. "You have a brain, Kiefer. Use it. That's how he thinks."

"Why did you stop the mind-wipe, Mother? Wouldn't it have solved all your problems?"

"Not really. We wanted to fix Harmony so much, but she wouldn't agree, so we had to alter our plans for the good of all. But your father has gone too far, and now he won't stop. He has restrained Harmony so she can no longer sustain our planet; it will be the ruination of us all."

Kiefer suddenly remembered the desperate voice asking him not to fix the processor. When his mother spoke again, he thought he had misheard her at first, her voice was so soft. "Kiefer, you have to stop him."

A shiver of fear flashed through him. Rising, he knelt in front of his mother and looked up into her lined face. "What did you say?"

Tears were forming in her normally brilliant grey eyes. "I'll deny I ever said this," she said more clearly, her face bleak, "but you have to stop your father and save Harmony."

Kiefer was taken aback. "Mother, you have more influence over him than anyone. You've already said how little he thinks of me. I won't get near him."

His mother stared at him. "You're our only hope. We created a monster, and you have to stop him. I've given you a clean sheet to start from; they won't be suspicious of you. He has always underestimated you." Leaning forward, she caressed his face. "Just remember, you have to act at all times as if you've been memory-wiped."

"I have been, partially; I don't know what I'm missing."

"Watch the news feeds this afternoon. I've added a family history, a review of the current Ministry, and the tape of your interview. Come to my office in the morning. I'll have your reassignment. I can get you into Maincore. There is the soiree tomorrow night. We can re-introduce you to society then as the obedient son you are." She gave Kiefer a gentle smile that belied the determination in her expression.

18

———

The next morning, Kiefer rose and, after a brief hesitation, chose his uniform. He was a Devender; he didn't want anyone telling him he wasn't. After descending the stairs, he made his way to the kitchen. He had always liked his mother's townhouse, especially as he was unlikely to meet his father here. Hopefully, he could go back to his own apartment soon. He didn't want his mother to get ideas. In fact, maybe he would just head home anyway.

Kiefer sat and ate his breakfast, considering what he should do next. Visiting his mother's office was top of the list, as she had his assignment. *Which means,* he thought as he felt a pang of despair, *that I have lost my troop.* Gut aching anguish swept through him, and he concentrated on eating his toast until he got his emotions under control. He also needed to go and find the technician who had helped him. He spent the rest of his meal considering the best way to do that.

After breakfast, he logged on to the net using his mother's credentials, which she had left on a pad by the terminal, and searched for Technician Staffen. While perusing the technician's record, he frowned at all the alerts posted on the man's file. It seemed Staffen's card had been marked. Kiefer wondered by whom. He made a note of Staffen's designation and his husband's before clearing the cache, wiping the history, and logging off. Checking the news feed, he read the story about a man killed at the shuttle station. It struck him that it was the same stop Staffen would have used; it couldn't be a coincidence.

Kiefer changed out of his uniform and into nondescript clothes: grey trousers and a black shirt. Then he left and headed towards the Maincore central hospital, where Staffen's husband was supposed to work, keeping an eye on his rear just in case. He couldn't see a tail; hopefully, whoever was interested in him believed he was still comfortably comatose.

The tall, cathedral-like building which housed the main city hospital rose like a symbol of hope and compassion in the centre of Maincore. Kiefer wished more people believed in the compassion part; he wouldn't need to be here other-wise. After following the green stripe painted on the wall to the surgical ward, he took a deep breath and pushed open the double doors. They led into a huge entrance hall with multiple screens hung on the walls like modern masterpieces, listing the directions to various departments. He scanned the board. Staffen was responsible for wards two, four, and six on the first floor. Memorising the map, he headed for the stairs.

Kiefer went up the stairs and found Staffen in the first room he checked. The doctor was helping an elderly man back into bed. The patient wore a thin gown tied at his waist and was querulously demanding where he was; he seemed confused.

A slim, wiry man with raven black hair and light brown skin was trying to make him lay back down. "Mr Mathews, please, you are in Bartholomew's, the city hospital. You had a fall and hurt yourself. You must stay in bed."

"Dr. Staffen?"

Kiefer's voice made the doctor jump. "I'll be with you in a moment," he said, impatiently. "Mr Mathews, please," he implored.

"I need to get up," the elderly man said in a quavering voice. "This isn't my home."

"Not today," Kiefer said firmly. "You need to rest before you can go home. The sooner you rest, the sooner you can go home."

"Oh," the man said, lying back against the pillows. "Why didn't you say so?"

The doctor sighed deeply before turning to Kiefer. "Thank you," he said, motioning to the door.

Kiefer opened the door and preceded the doctor out into the corridor. "Doctor Staffen? I know your husband, Gerry. I believe he is in trouble."

The doctor paled. "What has happened? Is he alright? I knew something was worrying him last night."

"I'm afraid he was involved in an incident at work. He saw something he shouldn't have, and now his superiors want to make sure he doesn't tell anyone else. We need to get you to a place of safety so they can't use you against him."

"I can't leave the hospital. I have responsibilities here."

"It's not safe for you to stay here," Kiefer said urgently as a door banged loudly further down the corridor and heavy footsteps approached.

He pulled the doctor down the hallway. "Is there another exit?"

"What?"

"We need to leave. Is there another way out?" Kiefer urged as he steered the doctor down the corridor.

"Stairs on the right lead down to the basement. The delivery bays are down there. But I can't leave my patients. I'm on duty."

"Dr Staffen, do you want to live?" Kiefer asked bluntly.

The man's eyes widened in shock. "Of course," he gasped.

"Then come with me, now," Kiefer said as he bundled the man through the door and down the stairs. "Keep moving," he whispered, peering down the stairwell. He rushed down the steps as the door slammed open above them. "Don't stop."

They ran out into the loading bays, and Kiefer hurriedly raised the metal door. The chains rattled noisily as the links rotated. Grabbing Staffen's arm, he pulled him into the shadows as the door continued to rise. The stairwell door crashed open as a stocky man dressed in black came charging through, and his momentum carried him out the open bay door. He skidded to a halt and frantically looked both ways before running off down the street, a slender black box in his hand.

Doctor Staffen shuddered in Kiefer's arms. "Was that a neutraliser?" he asked faintly.

"Looked like it," Kiefer replied.

"But why?"

Kiefer shrugged. "Not sure. Some powerful people seem to be involved in something that I'm not so sure is good for the rest of us. Come on, let's get out of here before he comes back."

Peering out into the street, Kiefer escorted the doctor in the opposite direction. "Take your coat off," he said as they joined the main thoroughfare and mingled in with the other pedestrians.

"Who are you, and how do you know all this?" the doctor asked as he slipped his white coat off and folded it up. Kiefer hurried him down the street.

"It doesn't matter who I am. Let's just say I'm a friend.

We need to get you safe, and then I can go help your husband."

"But why are you helping us?" asked Dr Staffen.

Kiefer smiled down at him. "Because my mother told me to."

He left the doctor in a house of disrepute. Fortunately, he had remembered that the madam of the house owed him a favour, and she agreed to hide the doctor for him.

"I could hide you, too," she said, looking Kiefer up and down.

Kiefer laughingly refused. "I am sure you could," he agreed, "but not today."

"He always refuses," she said in an aside to the quailing doctor. "I could show you a very good time." She batted her glittery eyelashes.

"Cherry, my love, you would be far too much for me to handle," Kiefer whispered in her ear as he hugged her, and then made his escape while she shrieked with laughter.

"He is such a naughty boy," she said to the man next to her and then sighed deeply, "One day," she murmured to herself, before leading the way to a back room. "What is your name?" she asked as she opened the door.

"Henry."

"Henry, what a nice name," she said. "Welcome to my home. My name is Cherry. Please rest here. You will not be disturbed. If what Kiefer tells me is true, you must stay here and not leave until he says it is safe."

"But how long will that be?" Henry gasped, watching her with shocked eyes.

Cherry shrugged. "As long as it takes," she said, before closing the door.

As Kiefer caught the shuttle back into the city centre, he wondered if the technician would go to work if he knew that something was off. It would be simple for the authorities to pin him down and wipe his memories if he did. And if he didn't, where would he go? Kiefer had no idea, and he was running out of time.

His mother had arranged some soiree later that evening, and he had no choice but to go. He would check the technician's house, and if the man weren't there, he would have to do some further research tomorrow.

After changing shuttles, he headed back out to the housing quarters. The leafy suburbs where the Staffens lived were quiet. Approaching the Staffen's home from the rear, he watched intently from the shadows of a shrubbery bush on the corner. He counted up the floors; Staffen's flat was in darkness. The entrance was brightly lit. There was no way he could sneak in there.

Kiefer scanned the area, but all was still. If anyone was watching, they were tucked out of sight like he was. A door slammed in the distance. Waiting a bit longer, he checked his wrist monitor. That was one thing he preferred about the sectors: no wrist monitors keeping track of every minute of his time. They didn't work so far from Maincore. He would give it another thirty minutes and then he would have to leave. He was already cutting it fine.

About to give up, he tensed when he heard the footsteps of a solitary walker. Kneeling on the ground, he watched the man approach. The man's shoulders were hunched up around his ears, and he looked furtively from side to side. Kiefer launched himself at the man, driving him back the way he had come and around the corner. Then he stopped.

"Technician Staffen, it really is not safe for you to go home," he said as he took his hand away from the stunned man's mouth.

"W-who are you?"

"You can't have forgotten me already," Kiefer said with a grin. "That is supposed to be my line."

"C-Commander Gallante?" Staffen stuttered.

"Yep. Come on, let's get out of here." Kiefer dragged the technician down the street.

"My husband will finish his shift soon," said Staffen. "He'll walk into whatever was waiting for me."

"No, he won't."

"H-how do you know?" The technician shook his head and rubbed his face with his free hand as he stumbled after Kiefer. He tried to tug his hand out of Kiefer's grip.

"Because I escorted him to a place of safety this morning. I will take you to see him tomorrow, but I don't have time right now. Come on. You'll have to stay with me tonight."

"What?"

"I haven't got time to take you now, so you'll have to stay at my apartment," Kiefer repeated, hurrying Staffen down the street and back onto the shuttle. He kept his grip on Staffen's arm, as the man looked like he was ready to bolt. Wide-eyed and unable to keep still, he kept glancing around the shuttle.

When they reached his apartment block, Kiefer hustled the man through the glass doors and into the lift before anyone had a chance to speak to him. His fingers flew over the number pad, and the lift silently rose. He breathed a sigh of relief. He had been worried he wouldn't remember the key code.

The lift opened directly into his apartment, and Kiefer dragged the man in and sat him in a chair. Loosening his collar, he walked over to the small kitchenette lining one of the walls; it was separated from the living space by a white breakfast bar with stools placed under it. Two closed wooden doors led off to rooms on the other side. The bulk of the space was taken up by comfortable chairs, a low table and a big screen on the wall, along with the magnificent view through the ceiling to floor windows behind them of course.

After grabbing a bottle and two glasses from the cupboard, Kiefer joined him. "Here, drink," he said briefly.

"I don't drink," Staffen said, staring at Kiefer blindly.

"Well, you can start today. Here, you need it."

Staffen took the glass and sipped it, choking as the fiery liquid hit the back of his throat, and he inhaled sharply.

"There you go. Told you it would make you feel better." Kiefer grinned as he took a sip from his glass.

"What is going on?" Staffen spluttered.

"I don't know," Kiefer said, "but I will find out."

"Where's my husband? Is he somewhere safe? He knows nothing about this." Staffen waved his glass. "Whatever this is."

"He's fine. I promise. He is staying with some friends of mine."

Staffen stared at him, his throat bobbing as he swallowed. "Minister Velten himself ordered your memory wipe. Whatever it is goes to the very top."

"I'm sure it does," Kiefer agreed. "Look, I have a meeting with my mother now. I'll be back in a couple of hours. Stay here and don't leave, and don't answer the communicator. Alright? Wait for me to come back, and we can talk then."

Staffen nodded.

19

Kiefer sat in the plastic chair in the reception area and patiently waited, lulled by the soothing music emanating from a concealed speaker. He stared around the foyer with interest as if it was the first time he had been there. Across from him, an abstract painting hung on the wall, and he stood and peered at the caption. He frowned at the name; it meant nothing to him.

The gentle music morphed into a calm voice extolling the virtues of the Ministry and how they funded research to make humanity's life better, an investment of which the research institute was a beneficiary.

"Commander Gallante, please, if you would follow me," a soft voice said at his shoulder, interrupting the commercial. "I apologise for keeping you waiting."

"Not at all," Kiefer replied. "I was admiring the painting. Can you tell me something about the artist? I'm sure I should know it, but I don't remember." Smiling at the woman, he tried to look inoffensive.

"Oh, of course." She seemed flustered. "Her name was

Shreron. She was a creator in the old style using oil paints. I, ah, I actually believe that you procured it for your mother."

Kiefer smiled. "That might explain why it seems familiar, then. Thank you."

The woman smiled uncertainly and led him into his mother's office.

"Kiefer, here you are at last. I have been expecting you." His mother rose to give him a gentle hug, and after kissing her on the cheek, he sat as directed.

"May I get you a drink?" the assistant asked, hovering beside his mother.

Kiefer looked at her blankly. "Umm." He glanced at his mother.

"He'll have a coffee. Milk, no sugar," she said, "as will I."

The assistant skittered away.

"What have you been doing this morning?" his mother asked.

"Doing what you told me to do. Research. Watched the vids you left. I have the main points, I think. It's the little things, like knowing I like coffee, that I'm missing." He eased his shoulders. "I guess I'll find out over time," he said to himself.

"Of course you will, my dear. I'll help you." She paused as the door opened. "Thank you, Mary. That will be all. I do not want to be disturbed," she said as the assistant placed the coffee mugs on her desk. She waited until the woman left the room.

"Right," she said and then hesitated as she leaned back in her chair.

"What did you want to speak to me about, Mother?"

His mother hesitated again, gently tapping her desk with her forefinger. She seemed to come to a decision. "Do you remember why we colonised this planet all those centuries ago?"

Kiefer frowned. "Of course. Because Harmony was here."

"Yes," his mother agreed, "because Harmony was here, a sentience who could control the planet and protect the inhabitants. When our ancestors first arrived, they worked to help Harmony extend her reach. There were areas she couldn't touch. They were called dead zones, because no matter what they did, her power couldn't extend far enough. So, they started building the substations to act like boosters."

"The pre-cursor to the processors."

"Only, the processors they put in place didn't do what they were originally designed to do. In fact, they did the reverse."

"What do you mean?"

"The processors suppress Harmony's power instead of enhancing it," his mother said.

Kiefer stared at her. "Why are you telling me this?" he asked. "Harmony is at the centre of everything; she sustains us all."

"No, she doesn't. She may have done once, but not anymore. Haven't you thought it odd that there are so many dead zones? That the sectors suffer such depredations? If Harmony is the planet, surely she could reach everywhere?"

"Umm, I'm not sure what I used to think, but what you are suggesting is tantamount to treason."

His mother sucked her breath in. "You didn't lose everything, Kiefer. Maybe you need to concentrate a bit harder," she said, irritation colouring her voice. "We have to help her."

"Maybe you should start at the beginning," he suggested. "What has happened that you would risk all? I'm a half-wiped nobody. You can't rely on me."

"I would never call you a nobody," she said wryly, "and it's because they tried to wipe you that I am telling you this now. They believe you have been reprogrammed, your knowledge lost. But it isn't; it's still inside you, and we need it."

"What has this to do with me? What knowledge?" Kiefer had no idea what she was talking about.

"You are not my son for nothing. Your ability to parse code and reprogram is unparalleled; no other technician comes close. And yet, they insist on sending you out into the far reaches instead of harnessing your ability to Harmony. They are deliberately trying to destroy both you and her. You are connected, and you have to find out what that means."

"How can I be connected to Harmony? I have nothing to do with her!"

His mother stared at her hands. Was she embarrassed?

"In the early days, I was so naïve. I used to talk a lot as I programmed. I didn't realise Harmony listened. I mean, I was talking to her, but I didn't think she was paying attention. I told her about you, about my hopes and dreams, about how clever you were. She knows you."

"She knows of me. She doesn't know me," Kiefer interrupted. "There is a difference. And anyway, that was years ago, when I was just a child."

His mother sighed. "It's not that simple. My original research had nothing to do with Harmony. I was working on solar energy units, trying to resolve the power issues in the sectors, how to get power to all. And then I met your father, and he made the connections. He could see how my work could replace the failing processors, self-perpetuating energy that I thought Harmony could use exponentially. But then I found out what the Ministry were really doing. I realised that they had subverted Harmony based on the misconception that she could destroy us just as easily as protect us."

"Doesn't she have a core mandate that drives protection and forbids murder?" Kiefer asked.

"Yes, but they had access to her power. They were in control, and they were just looking for a way to perpetuate it. They weren't looking to release Harmony any time soon. And I gave them the solution they were looking for," she said, her shoulders drooping.

"But this is crazy. There would have been fail-safes and firewalls all over the place," Kiefer said in disbelief.

His mother nodded. "I sometimes think that was the only reason your father married me, so he could get hold of my research. It was such a noble cause but got twisted by powerful men. Instead of using the code to enhance Harmony, they restrained her with it. They reversed the purpose and shut her down, all except the minimal trickle of information through the entry point so she could sustain the processors."

"Why are you telling me this now? You could have spoken out years ago. You have the status, the respect. People would listen to you."

"I told you. I was naïve, and I loved your father. I allowed myself to be persuaded it was the right thing to do. Only now the processors are failing, and they are in a panic because, once the processors fail, Harmony will have access to all the power she should have had to begin with. They took my code and twisted it. They began designing the new power nodes, and as each processor fails, they are transferring the power over. The nodes replace the processors and sustain Harmony's captivity. Sometimes, people get caught up in the wonder of what they are creating and forget to ask the question, should they create it?"

Kiefer wondered at the edge in her voice.

"I managed to subvert some code and sent Harmony your DNA string. I thought she might be able to reach you, to find you."

"You did what?" Kiefer spluttered in horror.

"I read once, in some ancient texts, that Harmony could link to people. You need to find out how. Your father has subverted my work. He is killing her. If she fails, our planet will fail." His mother paused. "This is our only chance to save her. I am fortunate to have an intelligent son who can help protect us all. I know we brought our son up to do the right thing."

Kiefer stared at her, aghast. "Mother," he began but stopped as a buzzer lit up on her desk.

His mother sighed. "I have to take this call. I'll be right back. I know my son will do what's best for everyone. You'll do the right thing," she said, her voice intent as she deliberately pressed two buttons on her keyboard and tapped the desk in front of her. "I'll be five minutes." She rose and left the room.

Kiefer waited for a moment, allowing the door to click shut behind her, and then he stood and walked around her desk to her monitor. It was awash with documents, plans, lists of codes and overrides. Scanning them quickly, he memorised them all. As he skimmed the documents, getting the gist, he froze when he found he was looking at a blueprint of Harmony's central locking chamber. He stared at it, committing it to memory, along with the schematic of the processor chamber. Returning to his seat, he picked up his coffee mug. As he took a sip, images and numbers scrolled behind his eyes. He stored them safely in his private filing system and slammed the lock tight.

His mother re-entered the room. She smiled when she saw her son calmly sipping his coffee.

"Here is your reassignment, your pass, and your access codes. You have been reassigned to the press office section. You need to give advice on security issues that may arise from the popularisation of the next phase. We need to make sure the people don't begin to panic as the processors start to fail."

Staring at his pass, Kiefer realised his mother was a genius. He had access to the Maincore's inner concourse. The concourse was behind the security protocols and connected to many sections, including the transformation suite. He had a way in, and he had the schematics in his brain already. Looking up at his mother, he acknowledged her tight smile. "Did you…" he began.

"I'm sure you'll excel in your new position. I look forward to hearing of your successes. I know you will do what's best."

"Mother."

"I am so happy for you," his mother said brightly as if she hadn't just sent him on a suicide mission; his second he remembered suddenly. Why did the women in his life seem hell-bent on getting him killed?

"Be ready to play your part this evening," she said.

"Yes, ma'am."

She smiled. "I am so glad we understand each other. I'll see you tonight. Make sure you dress appropriately." She nodded his dismissal and then turned back to her monitor, tapping a key.

Rising, he placed his mug on her desk. "I look forward to seeing you tonight," he said as he turned and left the office.

Kiefer smiled blandly at the assistant and walked back to the lifts. On reaching the ground floor, he ambled out of the building and headed for home. He needed to get ready for the party tonight, which he was not looking forward to at all. It would have a great potential for disaster, he thought with concern. When he arrived back at his apartment building, he pondered what would be appropriate dress; no doubt, it was not going to be his uniform.

He almost groaned aloud when he stepped out of the lift

and saw the technician sprawled asleep on his sofa. He had forgotten all about the Staffens and their problems. His mother's revelations had overwhelmed him.

Pouring himself a stiff drink, he stood at the window. He had bought this apartment because of the view. It relaxed him somehow. The juxtaposition of modern buildings against a backdrop of hazy hills and wide-open skies uplifted him, and when the lights came on at night, it was magical. He had always assumed that was Harmony, powering the lights, watching over them. But now he wondered what Harmony would do once released from centuries of shackles. Had his mother thought about that? She could retaliate, wipe them off the surface of her planet. No wonder those in power were scared.

Deep down, he knew that Harmony had not failed her purpose. The memory of her voice in his head made his chest tighten; it was humanity who had failed. He just hoped that he would be able to help her. As he watched Staffen, he wondered if the technician would have the nerve to return to the complex.

"Staffen," he said loudly, sitting in the chair opposite the sofa.

Staffen lurched upright, and his head swivelled as he took in his surroundings.

"Sorry to wake you," Kiefer said. "But we need to talk. I'm suffering quite a lot of memory loss. I need to know if it's permanent or whether there is something I can do to get it back. My Mother told me you stopped the program almost immediately?"

"Well, the results are patchy because you suffered a trauma. You collapsed because your body was already weakened. You hadn't recovered from your previous incident. To have a full-blown interrogation followed by a memory reset, it's not surprising you've lost quite a bit.

"The good news is that memories will be recovered by association. As you revisit places, meet people, that will jog associated memories. The reset really only reinforced the core conditioning everyone gets. The memory wipe had barely started."

"But it had started," Kiefer interjected.

Staffen grimaced. "I'm afraid so. I did dial it down, but still, there will be some adverse effects," he admitted.

"Why did you dial it down? Is that usual?"

Staffen flushed. "No, it's the first time I've done that. But you weren't lying, and I didn't think Minister Velten's treatment of you was right. I know I shouldn't have."

Kiefer sighed. "Well, I'm really glad you did. I feel like I'm lost in a maze, afraid of triggering a deadly reaction at each turn. I have no idea who I can trust or ask for help." Kiefer sat back and ran his hand through his hair.

"You can't trust anyone," Staffen said. "As I said, this goes all the way to the top."

"What's your first name?" Kiefer asked suddenly.

"My name? Oh, Gerry."

"And your husband's?"

"Henry."

"Can I trust you and your husband?"

"With your life," Gerry said. "You saved ours. Thank you for helping Henry. You didn't have to. When can I see him? He'll be worried about me."

"We need to find out who is after you and make sure you are safe first. It's better he stays with my friend until we can clear the threat against you. It won't be safe for you to go home."

"I don't know how much help we can be. As I said, Henry is a doctor. Me, I'm just a lab technician."

"You never know when you are going to need a technician—or a doctor, for that matter." Kiefer smiled wryly. "I need to get ready for this soiree my mother has organised. Help yourself to food, drink, whatever. I won't be back until late, so help yourself to the bed as well. I'll sleep on the sofa. Unfortunately, knowing my mother's soirees, I won't be back until the early hours."

20

Annie stood by the window in Ferris' bedchamber and blindly stared out the window. The woman Ferris had introduced as Perrine had spent the last few hours 'sprucing her up' as she put it so she wouldn't embarrass Ferris.

Perrine had talked the whole time. All through cutting Annie's hair, exclaiming over the state of her hands, and trying on several dresses. Dresses that were made of colourful silk and fell to the floor. Annie had exclaimed at how beautiful they were. That had set Perrine off on another tangent. A constant drivel about how wonderful Ferris was and how grateful Annie should be.

She had been quite smug about how profitable Ferris' business had become as a result of another Devender's downfall. Ferris had apparently been promoted, and with his new contacts, set in motion enough business initiatives to keep him ticking over for the foreseeable future.

Annie could quite easily imagine Perrine rubbing her hands together in glee at her good fortune. She listened intently, noting all the information Perrine scattered around her without thought.

For a brief moment, Annie wondered where Kiefer was, and whether they would cross paths again, but then she laughed at herself. That was unlikely with Ferris controlling her life.

According to Perrine, everything had to be exactly as Ferris dictated, and Annie dressed as a drab was not acceptable. Perrine had boasted that she had an innate sense of what worked and triggered the senses.

Annie smoothed her hands down the pale blue silk dress she wore; the skirts were full, the bodice skin tight, and the sleeves dropped off her shoulders, baring her skin. She shivered. She had never dreamed of wearing such a dress. She winced as her rough skin caught on the silk material.

Heavy footsteps approached down the corridor, and Annie stiffened as she turned away from the window and faced the door. Ferris opened it and strode inside, a smile spreading over his face as he inspected her.

He silently walked across the room and placed his hands on her bare arms. She trembled under his touch. He bent to kiss her shoulder, his breath hot on her skin.

"I see that you have spent your day as profitably as I have," he murmured.

"I am glad your day went well," Annie replied.

Ferris lifted her hair and trailed soft kisses across her collar bone, teasing the sleeve down her arm. "Silk is such a perfect choice, as it has no resistance." His hand slid up her leg. Grasping the silk, which slid over her skin, it kept rising, and Annie repressed a shudder. Ferris smiled and said, "See, it just glides, revealing all that lies beneath.

Annie's gut tightened as Ferris slid the other strap off her shoulder. He pushed the silk further down, revealing her breasts. When she tried to cover herself, he gripped her wrist and sucked on an exposed nipple.

"Stop," Annie whispered, trying to step away, but Ferris' grip tightened.

"Hush, my love. You will enjoy this, too. Just relax," he said as he tugged her towards the bed and pushed her down.

At a tap on the door, Ferris straightened in annoyance. Annie closed her eyes, and silently chanted in her mind. *Please, please, call him away.* Ferris hesitated, and then the tap came again, a little louder. Striding over to the door, he wrenched it open. "I told you I wasn't to be disturbed, Perrine."

Perrine replied, but her voice was muffled by the door. "So?"

Perrine's voice became more insistent, and Ferris growled.

The woman's voice got sharper, and the words 'spoilt goods' made Ferris sigh, and the tension left his body.

"You won't regret it," Perrine said more clearly. Ferris shut the door and stood facing it for a few moments before squaring his shoulders.

Turning around, he leaned against the door, and stared at Annie. Her stomach sank as his gaze scored her skin. Rubbing his pointy nose, Ferris frowned at her. "Can't taste the goods does not mean she can't perform," he murmured under his breath.

Annie stood, pushed the straps back up, and hugged her body as she backed away. How had she ever thought this man was attractive? How could she have been so blind?

Ferris leered at her. "My dear, no, I told you. There is no resistance here; it is futile." He moved like a cat, sinuous and silent, backing her into the corner. "You fancy it standing, do you?" He cupped her face, his fingers digging into her skin, and she froze. "Another time, maybe. Today, you learn how to please me. After all, you must earn your keep, mustn't you?"

Chiva was asleep when Annie finally escaped to her room. She was in two minds as to whether she should beat her brother to death for getting her into this situation or just go to sleep.

Yes, at first, she had enjoyed the admiring looks Ferris had thrown at her, but that didn't mean he could use her as he wished. In the end, she just curled up next to Chiva and closed her eyes. She hoped Ferris would be too busy tomorrow to even remember she existed. She didn't hold out much hope.

Annie couldn't sleep. She tossed and turned as mortification flooded her body. That he had made her do such things. She had never seen the like. He was huge—her small hands had barely covered him—but he had writhed and bucked under her touch. And when he had forced her mouth down on him, well, she cringed away from the memory, curling into a tight ball.

She considered the power she had over his body, how he had responded. Was that something she could use? If she could find a weapon, she could stab him where it hurt. She gritted her teeth as she imagined it. They would be free. To go where? They had nowhere to go and no way home.

Her busy mind kept turning over ideas. In his moment of ecstasy, he had said how much he loved her. Not that she believed him, of course. He didn't really love her. He wouldn't be taking advantage of her if he did, but she knew she had to make him think she believed him.

When Ferris awoke the next morning, he congratulated himself; he had found a winner. Once he had his fill, he could use her in the house. Perrine was right; a virgin would bring in ten times the money. And if she was a success, he knew where he could find more.

As he leisurely showered, he planned his day, wondering how long he could last until her hot mouth worked its magic again. Just the thought of her aroused him, but he must wait; she mustn't think he was too eager.

The boy now, what to do with him? Ferris toyed with the idea of putting him to work in the house, but Chiva was intelligent and had a hunger for knowledge. He wouldn't wait patiently like Annie would. No, Ferris must offer him an opportunity that would lead to his end desire, but of course, it would take him a lot longer to reach it than he expected. Ferris would visit the principal today. In the meantime, he was sure he could find a use for the boy.

"A data dumper!" Chiva's voice was aggrieved, and Annie kicked him under the table.

She glared at him before smiling at Ferris. "How brilliant of you. That will suit Chiva until the start of the term. How much did you say it paid?"

Ferris smiled back at her as he caressed hers. "I didn't, but his salary will be paid directly to me, and it will cover your bed and board, so you don't have to worry."

"It should go into Chiva's account, and he should pay you. We can't be dependent on you forever."

"Don't be silly, my dear. I promised your father I would look after you, and so I will."

Annie withdrew her hand. "But you want us to be independent. After all, that is what my parents wanted, and I heard you agree with them. Commander Kiefer recommended it as well, so we need to plan towards that goal."

Ferris drew himself up. "Yes, my dear. That is the long-term goal, but we have to get Chiva through college first. Then you can consider spreading your wings. Until then, you need my sponsorship and my support, and you will do it my way."

Annie clamped her lips shut at the unspoken threat. Chiva glanced from one to the other, unsure what was happening. Annie cast him a glare of such piercing anger that he shrank back in his chair.

"Of course," she said between gritted teeth. "Whatever you think is right."

Ferris relaxed. "Good. Chiva, my boy, you start today, so finish up, and we'll go to the college and get you signed up. I bought you some new clothes, so when you're finished, hurry up and change." He gave Annie a glittering smile. "The cost will be added to your bill."

Chiva finished his breakfast in a rush and hurried back to their room. He halted on the threshold at the sight of the beige uniform. He was a drab, a nobody; people's eyes would slide over him as if he wasn't even there. Part of the furniture with no right to thought or speech.

Reluctantly, he changed, conscious of a deep resentment stirring inside him. He might be young and untried, but he wasn't completely stupid. Maybe not as smart as his sister, but he would find a way to pay Ferris back. Every last coin plus interest. That he swore to himself as he shed Chiva and became a nobody.

Annie hugged him tightly before he left. "Remember, every avenue is an opportunity. Make sure you *are* invisible. Watch the others, copy them, and do not draw anyone's attention to you. One day, we may need it. Don't waste our advantage."

As Chiva silently followed Ferris, he turned his sister's words over in his mind. What did she know that he didn't? He would find out. Their situation might be his fault, but he wouldn't be dragged into this all unknowingly.

His sister was changing, and he wasn't sure he liked it. She seemed more brittle, harder, and yet more fragile at the same time. He had to find a way to get them out of Ferris' hands. Until then, he would do as his sister said and disappear.

Following Ferris down the street, Chiva shuddered at the racket of the vehicles, the blasting horns, and the people rushing everywhere. Staying close to Ferris, he flinched at the noise. Ferris curled his lip in contempt, but Chiva ignored him. Stiffening, he swore he would learn what he needed to learn. He firmed his face and clamped his lip shut as he followed his oh-so-generous benefactor up the steps of the Maincore Academy.

Chiva accepted his work rota and the badge that would allow him entry into the data centre. His trustworthiness was approved by Ferris with a flourish, and Chiva smirked as he realised what Annie had meant. Not only was he given a map of the college, but also access to the library, data centre, and back halls. He had more access than he would have as a student.

Keeping silent, he watched, nodding when nodding was expected, demonstrating his data skills when asked, passing the entry test without even trying. His interest stirred as his new controller explained his duties and gave him the data standards manual for him to learn prior to starting work at dawn the next day.

Unsurprisingly, Ferris was in a good mood as Chiva followed him out of the college.

"Maybe I should go into the business of sponsoring

sector computer technicians," Ferris said as he patted Chiva on the shoulder.

Snorting under his breath, Chiva wasn't surprised at the direction Ferris' thoughts had gone. Any way for Ferris to exploit another person's skills would no doubt support his lifestyle even better.

"Well done, lad. You're in. Work hard, and you'll be starting the new academic year as a student."

Chiva remained silent. It was better not to antagonise the man.

Arriving back at his house, Ferris was greeted by a messenger with orders for him to report back to Devender HQ. He was back on duty and expected to command a sortie to salvage a facility.

Chiva exhaled in relief as Ferris cursed under his breath. At least they wouldn't have Ferris controlling their every moment for a few days.

21

———————

It was later that evening when Kiefer arrived at his mother's soiree and handed his cloak and gloves to the attendant, accepted the ticket in return, and slipped it into his pocket.

He glanced around the elegant room his mother had hired for the evening. A quartet was playing at one end of the room, an open space in front of them would no doubt be the dance floor. The rest of the room was filled with cloth covered tables, some to stand at, others for sitting around. People he didn't recognise mingled, holding glasses and chatting. He breathed a sigh of relief when he spotted someone he knew.

"Julian? Congratulations, you made commander."

Julian's laugh was deep and rich as he rolled his eyes. "Kiefer, that was nearly five years ago, as was yours."

Kiefer scowled. "I seem to have a few gaps. I wasn't expecting to see you. Stay close, please?" He wasn't looking forward to the evening.

The touch of Julian's hand was reassuring as he gripped Kiefer's arm. "Just say the word. I won't be far. Alright?"

"Thanks. I'm not sure I can do this," Kiefer replied in a low voice, struggling to control the flare of anxiety that threatened to strangle him.

"You can do anything you set your mind to. You once told me that Harmony watched over your shoulder and would keep us all out of trouble. We're still here, you know. Many others aren't."

"Did I? I don't remember." Kiefer's voice wavered. He had lost so many memories. No matter what his mother said, he wasn't sure he would get them back.

"Well, here comes your dad. Let's start with how we mean to go on, eh? You know how much he approves of me."

"I wish I did," Kiefer murmured as he straightened to attention.

His father's greeting was cold and disapproving. "I see you haven't improved your taste in friends."

"Father," Kiefer said distantly. "Commander Laithe is recently back from Sector 17. I would think you would be congratulating him on salvaging that sector. It is key to your project, is it not?"

His father narrowed his eyes as he snorted with disdain. Fortunately, Kiefer's father was distracted by a minister at his elbow before he could reply with a blistering response.

"Kiefer, what are you doing?" Julian asked, aghast, as he drew Kiefer away.

"What?" Kiefer stared at him in bewilderment. "I read it in the news; you did a great job."

"You don't speak to your father like that," Julian said, keeping his voice low. He took two glasses from a passing waiter and handed one to Kiefer.

"Like what?" Kiefer asked, his brow creasing in confusion.

"As if you know better than he does. He is the one in

control at all times, and you let him know it, if you are sensible."

"No wonder he is such a pompous ass," Kiefer murmured, and Julian choked on his wine.

"Oh, my, this evening is going to be priceless." Julian laughed, a mischievous twinkle lighting his eyes. "I hope your mother knows what she has done."

"Julian, have you been smoking again? You are not making sense."

Julian gave a crack of laughter that drew glances from the people standing nearby. "Boy, that was over five years ago. Commanders do not smoke."

"I'm glad to hear it," Kiefer replied as he allowed himself to be drawn further into the room by his chuckling friend.

"This is Minister Balava. The Housing Minister," Julian said and stepped away, his lips twitching as he watched.

Kiefer smiled and offered his hand. "Ah yes. It's a pleasure to meet you, sir."

"You are looking well," the minister replied. Kiefer was sure he only just bit off the 'all things considering' part.

"Very well, thank you. I heard you were proposing a reduction in the footage for new housing. I told my father I thought it was an oversight not to give the workers room to relax. More conducive to a healthier worker. A better return for the ministry." Kiefer smiled gently. "My father didn't disagree." He walked away leaving the minister spluttering as Julian muffled his laughter. Kiefer eyed him.

"Now what?"

Julian just shook his head and led Kiefer to his next victim.

The evening was punctuated by his friend dissolving into laughter at the most inopportune moments. Kiefer regretted asking him to stay nearby. He seriously didn't understand what was causing such hilarity.

"Kiefer, your true character is revealed. You have such a pithy view of life. People aren't going to know what has hit them."

"What do you mean?" Kiefer growled, fed up with his friend's levity.

"You can get away with it because they know you've had a reset and don't know the ramifications of your comments. It's perfect."

"Which is no good if you don't explain any of it to me."

"Don't worry. I will do a complete review for you tomorrow. You'll be very interested in some of the responses. This evening has been enlightening."

"Well, I'm glad you enjoyed it. Can we leave yet?"

"Lord, no. Your mother has a surprise for you, I believe."

"Oh, no. You haven't let her set me up again, have you?"

Julian collapsed into gales of laughter. "You have nothing to fear. The girl will run a mile; she won't be able to cope with you. It'll take a stern heart to manage you, my friend, you mark my words."

Kiefer's mother tapped him on the shoulder with her fan. "Such levity is unbecoming, Julian. Please try and strive for some decorum."

"Apologies, ma'am."

"Kiefer, I have someone I want you to meet. Julian, if you will excuse us."

"Of course," Julian replied. He threw a wink to Kiefer as he left.

"It would behove you well to nurture a relationship with Madeline Velten, the minister's daughter." She paused as Kiefer tensed. "I know," she soothed, "but sometimes it is better to keep your enemies close, as they say."

"And use the daughter? What has she to say in this?"

"She is a catch, as are you, and the minister asked me to introduce you."

"Did he, now?"

"Yes, so be nice, Kiefer. It will give you a reason to visit his house."

"Now, why would I ever want to do that?"

"Ah, Madeline, my dear," Kiefer's mother drawled as she stopped next to a tall, young lady with sculpted dark-blonde curls and olive-green eyes. The woman wore the latest fashion; an elegant gown in the deepest green, and sparkling jewels dripped from her ears and neck. She fidgeted with her matching clutch bag as she gazed around the room. "Here is my son, Kiefer, as promised. Kiefer, this is Madeline Velten, the daughter of Minister Velten of the Interior Ministry."

Madeline swallowed nervously before extending a trembling hand. "A pleasure to meet you," she said in a low voice.

Kiefer bowed over her hand. "The pleasure is all mine. Would you care to dance?" he asked, hoping to put her at ease.

"I'll leave you two to get acquainted." Kiefer's mother gave him a warning glare as she thankfully moved off.

"Or if you prefer, we can get a drink," Kiefer said, as he had noted her brief glance at the dance floor. "It is rather crowded."

"Yes, that would be best. Maybe it won't be so busy later."

"Please." Tucking her arm in his, he led her away to the bar. "What would you prefer?"

"White wine, please."

Kiefer nodded and made the request. He soon returned with a glass in each hand. "I wonder if you could help me," he said. "I keep muddling people up. That gentlemen dancing with the lady in the enormous turban. Who are they, and what do they do?"

Madeline flicked him a glance but readily answered, "That is Principal McKenzie. He's the head of the Maincore Academy, and he is dancing with his wife, Cynthia."

"I don't recognise him. Has he been there long?"

"I believe he was the principal when you attended the Academy."

Kiefer grimaced. "Did you attend?"

"Yes, I was one of the first girls allowed entry. I graduated two years ago."

"What do you do now?"

"I work in Pre-Ed, with the children."

"And do you enjoy it?"

"Much more so than the admin office my father wanted me to go into."

"How did you manage to avoid that?"

"Fortunately, my mother intervened. It is not always wise to refuse my father what he wants," she said.

"I imagine he is used to getting his own way, much like my own father," Kiefer agreed.

"Yes, I suppose so."

"Who, on earth, is that? They look like they just left a festival."

Madeline laughed. "That is the Maestro Felippe. He believes he should be feted for his masterful works and likes to make sure he outshines everyone else."

"Oh, no, he's coming this way. Quick, tell me one of his pieces."

"What? Oh, I..."

"Kiefer, my boy, glad to see you up and about. Your mother said you would be here. I said to my Dothea, we must attend so I can offer my condolences."

Kiefer stared at him. "Your condolences, sir?"

"Why, of course. You have lost all my wonderful music. I

will make sure I send you my complete works so you have the pleasure of experiencing it all over again."

"That's very kind of you, sir. The chance to experience your masterpieces will be the highlight of my day. I am told you write specifically for the voice singing your music."

"Of course. All my pieces are for important occasions. I am working on one for the next convention."

"How do you make the voice wobble so?"

"I think you mean warble," Madeline murmured.

Kiefer frowned, and Julian snorted into his glass as he passed by.

"Do I?" said Kiefer.

"I heard the singer, Rosetta, once caused crystal to shatter using her voice," Madeline said. "That was your composition, wasn't it, sir?"

"Amazing," Kiefer murmured.

The maestro preened.

"I can't wait to hear it for myself. I'll make sure all my mother's crystal is put away," Kiefer said.

"As it should be, my boy. Why they have to do these resets, I don't know, but you, of all people… You must tell me what you did!" The maestro peered up at Kiefer expectantly.

Kiefer smiled at him. "My dear sir, you know perfectly well that I have no idea. At least it gives you a never-ending audience."

"You are right! I never thought of it like that. What a good thing." The maestro beamed at him.

"The Ministry cares for us all and provides what we need," Kiefer said.

"Of course, my boy, of course." The maestro nodded and moved away.

Kiefer exhaled and glanced at Madeline. "Sorry about that."

"Not your fault," she said. "I'm amazed they haven't reset him."

"And lose all that amazing creativity? They wouldn't dare."

Madeline gave a crack of laughter as her father approached. He observed them, and Madeline stiffened.

"Ah Madeline, glad to see you making acquaintances at last." Minister Velten nodded at Kiefer. "Kiefer."

"Minister," Kiefer said.

"Come and see me tomorrow. I believe you have been reassigned? I have some thoughts I'd like to share."

"Of course, sir."

"Good. Tenth hour, at the Ministry." Minister Velten's attention was caught by an acquaintance waving at him and he walked away. Kiefer watched him go.

"What is your new position?" Madeline asked.

"Propaganda. Stuck in an office," Kiefer said sadly.

"So, you remember you don't like offices?"

He smiled. "Well, the thought doesn't fill me with happiness, so I guess not. Looks like there is room on the dance floor. Shall we?"

<hr>

It was much later when Kiefer swayed gently in the foyer as Julian approached him. "Kiefer, my boy, had too much to drink?" Julian asked as he inspected his friend.

"Care to make sure I get home safe?" Kiefer suggested, accepting his cloak from the attendant.

"Be my pleasure." Julian casually glanced around to see who was paying attention.

"Let's be off, then. These events can go on tediously long." Kiefer yawned, delicately patting his mouth.

"As you wish, my boy, as you wish," Julian murmured.

The attendant handed him his cloak, and they entered the lift. He raised a dark eyebrow as the lift descended. "What's going on?"

"Later," Kiefer said as he gripped his friend's arm. They strolled through the door and out onto the street, arms linked. Kiefer staggered occasionally as they walked. Julian's mouth twitched, but he just steered his friend straight. Eventually, they reached Kiefer's apartment building, and the doorman bowed and called the lift for them.

Kiefer didn't relax until he walked into his apartment. Slinging his cloak over a chair, he turned back to face his friend, and waited. He didn't have to wait long.

"Are you going to tell me what is going on?" Julian asked, laying his cloak on a chair and loosening the ruffles at his throat.

Kiefer smiled, though he didn't really feel like it. "Camouflage," he replied.

"For what?"

"An ineffectual ex-commander who can't hold his drink and knows nothing." Kiefer went to the counter and reached for the bottle and glasses. He inspected the level; it seemed Staffen had needed some artificial courage this evening. Pouring a drink, he handed it to Julian, who had silently crossed the room to stand behind him.

"Why?" Julian asked.

Kiefer frowned at him and picked up his glass. "Because someone wants me indisposed." He waved his glass. "As I am sure you must be aware. If I am not a threat, they might leave me alone."

"Kiefer, no one would ever be so stupid as to think you could never be a threat," Julian warned.

"Don't say that," Kiefer said, scowling. "Being wiped once is enough; if they felt that didn't work, who knows what they would try next?"

"What have you managed to get mixed up in, my friend?"

"You really don't want to know. Are you sure you want to be involved in this?"

"I made that decision the day I helped your mother abscond with your lifeless body," Julian said, glaring at Kiefer.

"Yes, but you were helping a friend in need not agreeing to darker plots."

"Stop making excuses and tell me what's going on," Julian demanded, settling on the sofa and making himself comfortable. Kiefer could see he wasn't going anywhere.

"I don't deserve a friend like you." He heaved a deep sigh.

"I know you don't." Julian grinned. "So, you'd better spill before I beat it out of you."

Kiefer frowned. "I may as well only say this once." He went over to his bedroom and opened the door. Staffen was asleep on his bed. "Gerry." Kiefer shook the man's foot. "Gerry," he said more loudly.

"W-What?"

"I need to talk to you. C'mon, get up."

Gerry blearily sat up and held his head. "What time is it?"

"Two in the morning. Come on, get up. I have someone I want you to meet."

Lurching to his feet, Gerry followed Kiefer back out of the bedroom. He faltered when he saw Julian seated on the sofa.

"And why do you have a technician sleeping in your bed?" Julian asked, his eyebrows rising.

Gerry frowned at him. "Hey, you're the guy that…the one that came with your mother." He looked at Kiefer in shock. "I thought you said it wasn't safe for anyone to know where I was."

"Julian here wouldn't hurt a fly. He's my friend."

Julian snorted. "I thought I'd had all the surprises I was going to get tonight; you never cease to amaze me."

Kiefer laughed. "Gerry, Julian. Julian, Gerry," he said in introduction. "Julian is a fellow commander of the Devenders. Gerry here is, as you know a technician from the Int-Ed department. Unfortunately, Minister Velten, or maybe it was my father, has decided that Gerry knows too much and needs to be removed."

"Knows too much about what?" Julian asked.

"We're not sure. I'm assuming it's because he knows Velten ordered the interrogation and the wipe, but then everyone knows I've been wiped."

"Not everyone knows about the interrogation, though," Gerry said.

"Yes, but I'm not going to say anything; after all, I don't remember it, do I?"

Julian gave him a sharp glance.

"I found out earlier today that I am expected to save Harmony from the vile machinations of the man who keeps her restrained against her will and helpless to protect our planet." Kiefer smiled at Julian. He waited for his friend to comment.

"Now, I know you were not as drunk as you made out," Julian said, "but are you sure you didn't fall over and hit your head?"

"Not at all," Kiefer replied. "I have to find a way to destroy the main core processors and the sub-installations so we can release Harmony. The processors are slowly killing her, and once she dies, the planet will die with her. We have to prevent it."

"If they, whoever they are, know that the planet is

doomed without her, why are they trying to kill her?" Julian asked.

"I assume they don't believe it or are blind to the consequences of their action. They only see the loss of their power, their control, and they are afraid," Kiefer said as he waved a genial hand in the air.

"Who are 'they'?" Julian asked.

Kiefer grinned at him. "Oh, my father and my possible future father-in-law, Minister Velten, to name but two. The rest of the Ministry I expect."

"You didn't manage to escape her clutches, then? I thought you were made of sterner stuff, mate."

"I thought I ought to acquiesce to such delicate pressure."

"Really? And if you can't manage to escape such scintillating family connections, how do you propose to achieve an impossible feat of sabotage right under their noses?" Julian inquired with interest.

"I have no idea," Kiefer admitted. "I was rather hoping you two might come up with a suggestion or two."

"At this hour in the morning? You'll be lucky."

"Time is not our friend," Kiefer warned.

"I know. I'm due to be sent back out into the sectors in a couple of days, so if you want me to do anything, it'll have to be soon."

"Do you know where you're going?" Kiefer asked.

"Not confirmed yet, but I would expect 21 or 27, seeing as you are out of commission."

"Julian," Kiefer said, "did you know there was a resistance group out in the sectors?"

"There was some mention of rebels in the last circular, but they kept much to the outer sectors. I've not come across them."

"I knew nothing about them. Apparently, Ferris kept

some information from me. But they do exist, and they are led by some woman. I met them in Sector 45, only I don't remember what happened. Whatever it was led to me being taken to Int-Ed. I only know this because I saw the recording of my interrogation."

Julian leaned forward, a frown creasing his brow.

"Oh, and that reminds me, according to my interrogator, Ferris, my lieutenant who has now stepped up to commander in my place, has been stirring up trouble for Sector 45." Kiefer ignored Julian's hiss of disgust. "You need to go and warn them after you've been to 21. Just tell them to be on guard for some possible Ministry visits. Velten is suspicious. They need to play down any progress they've made. I am currently creating messaging warning everyone away from Sector 45. I hope it will be enough, but they ought to be warned."

"I can't just go to Sector 45, especially now that it's been classed as a dead zone," Julian protested.

Gerry stirred in his seat. Concern creased his thin face. "This is getting out of hand. I don't want to get involved in this."

"You are already involved, Gerry," Kiefer replied. He couldn't wave some magic wand and return their lives to normal. If he could, he would've already, though he did sympathise with the man.

"What about my husband? You said you would take me to him. How do I know he is alright?" Gerry asked, his brow creasing in concern.

"He's fine. He's with my friend Cherry, being well looked after," Kiefer promised.

Julian choked. "Cherry? You left him at—"

"In a very safe place," Kiefer interrupted. "Once we've figured out what we need to do, we'll find a better location to hide you both."

Julian started laughing, and Kiefer glared at him.

Struggling to contain his chuckles, Julian waved Kiefer away. "I'm sorry, but really! I suppose they could use my place while I'm away. It'll be empty anyway. But you need to have this all sorted by the time I return. I'll expect my apartment back."

Kiefer brightened. "That would work. I'll bring them over tomorrow. So, back to Harmony. She is being restrained against her will. All the original contracts and protocols have been rescinded, and she has been betrayed. If we don't rescue her, it could be the end of our planet. Harmony *is* the planet; without her, we have nothing. We need to rescue her, and you need to help me figure out how."

Julian and Gerry gaped at him.

"Once I get into the transformation chamber, how do I bring it down? How do I destroy it forever?"

Two hours later, they had got no further. "Just assume I can get in," Kiefer said in frustration. "It doesn't matter how. I could upload the Bantwich virus—if we could find a copy. I could reprogram the coolant systems; that would overload the servers and bring down the processors. I could—"

"You could just blow the whole thing up," Julian said, rubbing bleary eyes.

"Yes, but I don't know much about detonators, and we'd need an awful lot of explosives, and it might hurt Harmony," Kiefer said, scowling.

"I was joking," Julian said with a wry twist to his lips. Levering himself to his feet, he straightened his clothes, and peered about him for his cloak.

"Well, don't. This is serious."

"Well, serious or not, I, for one, am going home to bed. This night has been one night of revelations, and I'm exhausted. Maybe inspiration will strike after a few hours' sleep. It's been a pleasure, I'm sure." Grabbing his cloak, Julian bowed himself out.

Kiefer stared at the door. "Inspiration," he murmured. Gerry had collapsed on the sofa and gone back to sleep. After covering Gerry with a blanket, he switched off the lights and went to bed. *At least I got the bed*, he thought as he yawned.

He fell asleep immediately, only to find himself sitting bolt upright moments later. "Harmony. I need to find a way to speak to Harmony."

Kiefer slowly lay back down and mused over the people he had met at his mother's soiree. The evening had been a surreal experience. He knew names and faces, but he had no context to fit people into. They had no substance; he couldn't relate to them, and he had kept muddling them up. It was like meeting two people who were very alike on the same day and forever mixing them up, but the problem was tenfold. If only he could get a grip on a point in time and really believe he had been there, experienced it, he might be able to anchor the other memories to it.

He was adrift in a world of strangers, and it was disconcerting. And to cap it off, there were still people and places he had no memory of whatsoever. He sincerely hoped Gerry was right and his memories would begin to return. He hated fumbling about in the dark.

22

———————

Lorne slowly swept her binoculars across the processor facility of Sector 27. The processor was housed in a single-story brick building, which meant most of the complex must be underground. A small satellite hamlet was perched a little higher in the tree line. Pine trees growing along the ridge provided a natural screen. As she scanned the housing quadrant, she observed the low water levels in the tributary that fed into the river. The river divided the sector, placing the facility on one side and the quadrant on the other, a natural division, which at least meant fewer casualties once they were in a position to attack. Apart from the lack of water, which was the only similarity to Sector 45, she was unsure what they should do.

As she had said to Kiefer, they didn't have the technological know-how to take these installations down. She wondered where Kiefer was now. She missed him, which was silly, as she didn't even know the man. Still… A deep sigh escaped her.

Lorne regretted leaving Sector 45 so abruptly. She should have brought a technician with her; they might have been able to offer suggestions. Maybe they should return and recruit one.

At least she had an excuse to visit. Andre had suggested they might be able to help.

She stiffened as she caught sight of Stefan creeping closer to the facility. What was the man doing? He was supposed to be holding position by the river. She swore under her breath as she watched him approach the front of the building and then casually stroll through the entrance.

She waited, holding her breath against the expected uproar, but he came out again accompanied by a man in a white lab coat. The man gesticulated at the tributary, and Stefan shrugged and waved his hands in return. The lab man threw his hands up and flounced back into the building. Stefan glanced up at Lorne's position and gave her the all-clear sign.

Lorne sat back on her heels. How could it be all clear? The facility was still standing. Stefan repeated the sign, and with an exasperated huff, she slowly left her position and made her way up to the facility.

Stefan grinned at her as she approached. "Don't look so upset, my dear. The processor has failed, and they've shut everything down. This facility is defunct. It's too late to save it."

"How do you know that?"

"Because they ran out of water for the coolant sheds and the nodes overheated. The processors have all shut down. They are unable to restart them."

"What if they get enough water back into the system?"

Stefan shrugged. "The processor melted. They don't have the spare parts. They are preparing to leave; no reason to stay, apparently. You need to speak to the people. The settlement is about to panic."

"Great," Lorne said, looking around, expecting hordes of

people to descend on them. "And are the technicians prepared to take people with them, or are they just deserting everyone?" The acid tone of Lorne's voice was enough to melt whatever remained of the installation circuitry.

Stefan grinned. "What do you think?"

"Tell the lookouts to stay alert. The Devenders should be turning up soon, seeing as they knew this facility was failing, and we need to be long gone before they do."

Swearing under her breath, Lorne led the way back across the bridge into the quadrant. She hadn't wanted to stop here, and now they were going to be delayed even longer. It was all Ciely's fault.

Ciely had run off from their camp in the Wytchwards during the night. She had managed to navigate the marshes in the dark, proving how skilled she had become. Lorne would have been so proud of her had she not been so distraught. Ciely would throw away everything they had worked for away, to chase after a dead man. It had taken them a week to track her to Sector 27, and then they had realised the processor was failing. It was too good an opportunity to pass up.

Her sister was in Sector 27; she knew it. Lorne had felt Ciely's gaze burning holes in her back. Ciely hadn't forgiven her. In fact, she was becoming an even worse liability as her anger festered. Would she really betray all the people living in the Wytchwards just to get back at her? Lorne didn't know, and that was the saddest part of it all; admitting that she no longer knew what her sister would do.

Lorne shied away from what she might have to do to stop Ciely from betraying them. It wouldn't come to that. They would resolve their differences before it was too late. They had to.

"Harmony, help us calm these people," she pleaded as she strode up to the open square, very similar to the one in

Sector 45. She hoped there were some sensible people like Andre and Ester around.

She waited on the steps as a crowd began to gather. Her lips tightened at their poor condition. These people had been kept downtrodden and without for no other reason than Maincore greed.

Holding up her hands, she said, "As I'm sure you are aware, the processors have failed. This facility is now defunct, and the controllers are preparing to leave. There is no possibility of repairing it."

A murmur spread around the crowd.

"You have a choice, and you don't have much time to make it. You can leave with the controllers and go to a neighbouring sector, or you can stay here and carve out a new life. If you all work together, you could build a life out from under the repression of Maincore. The decision is yours."

"Our decision?" a faded woman asked. "It's not much of a choice. There is nothing here."

"You are fortunate. You have the chance to start again, to live how you want to."

"Why would they leave us be? I bet the Devenders are on their way here. And anyway, who are you? What is it to do with you? Where are the controllers?"

"Leaving," Lorne replied.

The crowd rippled with fear. "Why? What are they going to do?"

Lorne raised her hands again. "It's up to you. You could claim the facility and all it contains, or you can allow the controllers to shut it all down. They have power up there, light, and heat. You could use it. Why should they just take it away? You have technicians; they have the knowledge. They could run the lines down here and power your homes, or you could move up there. Your choice."

The faded woman turned to the crowd. "She's right.

Why should they have it all? Why can't we use it too? Dairen, you could jig the lines, couldn't you?"

A tall thin man stepped forward, his face scrunched up in thought. "Yes, as long as they don't cut the feed. We have plenty of cable."

Lorne came to a decision. They couldn't waste any more time. "Stefan, stop them from shutting down the facility. Make sure they don't sabotage the generator."

Stefan nodded and called a couple of men to go with him.

"I'll come too," Dairen said, hurrying to catch up with them. More men ran after them.

"You are lucky," said Lorne, "You can utilise the resources at the facility. Sector 45 wasn't so fortunate. The whole facility collapsed. But even so, they are managing well, and so could you if you wanted to." A sharp whistle interrupted her, and she stopped speaking and looked up to the treeline. "It looks like the Devenders are here. There is nothing they can do, but be careful. They still have more fire power than we do."

A column of Devenders jingled their way into the centre of the settlement, forcing the people to move out of their way. Lorne narrowed her eyes as she recognised the man at the front. Since when had that weaselly Ferris become a commander? She crossed her arms and waited.

Reining his horse in at the bottom of the steps, Ferris leant on the pommel of his saddle. "Well, if it isn't the rebel leader. Why is it, whenever a sector processor fails, you are always involved?"

Lorne shrugged. "Good timing, I suppose."

Ferris pulled out his firearm and pointed it at her. "And what's to stop me from removing you once and for all?"

"Depends on if you want you and your men to die, too," Lorne replied. She raised her hand, and rebels rose out of their concealed locations with their weapons aimed at him. He glanced around and tensed. Then he spread his hands and carefully holstered his firearm.

"Good decision."

Ferris scowled at her. "What are you doing here?"

"Helping these people cope with the end of the facility. The processors have melted. They are no more. You're too late to save them."

Ferris jerked his head, and a couple of Devenders peeled off the back of the column and headed up to the facility. His horse jinked, and he cursed as it pirouetted, scattering people. He got his horse under control and glared around him. "You may as well all go home. Until we confirm the facility is closed, there is nothing for you to see."

"If the controllers are leaving. Can we go with them?" a voice called from the crowd.

Ferris scowled. "I said we will confirm the situation, and then we'll advise you."

Lorne grinned at him. "Not so easy, making decisions, is it? Easier when you have someone else to blame."

"And what is that supposed to mean?" he hissed.

Lorne raised an eyebrow. Had she touched a nerve? "Nothing, nothing at all."

"He won't be coming to save you. He got wiped, doesn't remember a thing."

"Who did?" she asked as a chill stole down her back.

"Who do you think? Lover boy."

"Who?"

"You know, Gallante. You cosied up to him long enough in Sector 45."

"You mean Commander Kiefer? Ah, so you stepped into his shoes. Convenient, don't you think?" Lorne asked, observing the reactions of the troopers. They hadn't been aware of what had happened to Kiefer, and they weren't happy about it. Ferris was oblivious to their unease

"I deserved my promotion. I kept it all together when he fell to pieces. He may be the supreme commander's son, but even he can't hold it together under interrogation."

Lorne hissed out her breath as she stared at him. "You bastard. You set him up, didn't you?"

"He deserved everything he got."

"After everything he did for you. For all of you." She waved her arm at the troopers. "Was it worth it? Is commanding a troop all you thought it was? I bet you're nowhere near as good as he was."

"It will be even better when we take you in with us. And he won't even know you."

Lorne shook her head. The man was insufferable. "You're overlooking something."

"And what is that?"

"I am the one in control here, in case you've forgotten."

Ferris twisted in his saddle. His men had backed away from him, leaving him isolated at the front. "You wouldn't dare."

"Wanna bet?" she asked with a grim smile.

"I'll take that bet." He drew his weapon and fired at her and then indiscriminately at the people around her as he drove his horse forward. The rebels returned fire, the Devenders scattered, and pandemonium erupted.

Heat scored Lorne's skin as she dived out of the way, and she cursed under her breath. The bastard had nicked her arm. She had underestimated him and his arrogance. She watched him as he careered across the square and behind the warehouses, abandoning his men. "Cease fire," she yelled. "Rebels fall back."

As soon as the rebels retreated, one of the Devenders shouted, "Devenders stand down!" and the din of gunfire faded, leaving the acrid tang of cordite and electrical energy in the air.

Lorne tugged her scarf loose and staunched the blood. It stung like a bitch, but it wasn't life-threatening. Peering around the crate she had dived behind, she saw the lieutenant instructing his men to help the wounded. People lay in crumpled heaps, and Lorne gritted her teeth. It had all been so unnecessary.

"Lieutenant, we have a healer," she said as she approached the lean man who had dismounted. He handed off the reins to a Devender she thought she recognised, a grey-haired, stocky man older than the officer.

The lieutenant grimaced. "That was unfortunate and completely avoidable. Ferris is an idiot." He raised his voice and said, "Dawlish, see if you can find where Ferris went and if he intends to come back." Glaring at the carnage, he shifted his gaze to Lorne, and he winced when he saw the bloody bandage around her arm. "Griffin, our medic, is setting up a triage. Maybe your healer can help him, and you can get your arm seen to." He ran his hands through his hair, leaving it sticking up in tufts.

"I'm fine. More concerned your commander is going to return with guns blazing."

"Depends on if he found something else to entertain himself with," the man growled under his breath. "What a mess."

"I'll set up camp on the boundary, sir," said the stocky man, holding the horses.

"Yes, thank you, Jeffers. We won't be leaving today." He glanced at Lorne. "Though it may be better if you cleared out. Otherwise, I'll be expected to arrest you. If you could fade away while we help these people, I can just say we had to protect the people first. I know Commander Gallante would have handled this differently."

Lorne gave him a weary grin. "We'll regroup and remain out of sight, give Carey time to help your medic. You'll get no trouble from us, unless your commander returns and causes more mayhem."

"Fair enough."

Lorne hesitated. "Is it true? Commander Gallante has been mind-wiped? Or was Ferris lying?"

The lieutenant shrugged, his face grim. "I don't know. First I heard of it, but it's possible. We haven't seen him since we returned, which is unusual."

23

After Griffin had cleaned the wound on Lorne's arm and bandaged it up tightly, she had moved her people out. There was no point lingering; there had been no sight of Ciely, who had managed to slip away in the confusion, and the Devenders were getting twitchy.

As the rebels rode up the track, headed out of the sector, Lorne peered over her shoulder at a rider hurrying up behind them. It was Jeffers.

Lorne pulled her horse to a halt and waited for him to catch up, waving her companions onwards. They would regroup in Sector 45, rest, and then decide where to go next.

"Ma'am, I'm glad I caught you. I thought you needed to know. Dawlish tracked Ferris down. He's travelling north with a young woman. Looks like one of yours, maybe seventeen, eighteen? Short curly red hair," Jeffers said in a rush.

"Ciely," Lorne gasped. "But how did he find her?"

"I think she found him," Jeffers said with a scowl. "Dawlish reported that he overheard her bargaining with him. His help getting her into Maincore in return for information about the rebels."

"She wouldn't." Lorne paled and swallowed hard against the rising bile.

Jeffers shrugged. "Ferris has a way with the ladies. I bet he tried to charm her in Sector 45. No luck with you, so try the sister."

Clenching her jaw, Lorne stared off into the distance for a moment, trying to control the growing dread threatening to overwhelm her. How could Ciely be so selfish? So naive? "Foolish girl. There is no way Ferris is to be trusted." Her gaze flicked back to Jeffers. "I don't understand why you are telling me, though. Surely, you want us all to be caught."

"Commander Gallante would skin me alive if anything happened to you because of us. What you both achieved in 45 shows it's possible to work together." Jeffers nodded. "Yes, ma'am, I'd prefer to live in peace."

Lorne smiled and grasped his arm. "Thank you, Jeffers. I really appreciate it. I hope you find Commander Gallante well when you return to Maincore."

"I'll make sure to check in on him and tell him you were asking after him," Jeffers said as he wheeled his horse around. "You take care now." He rode off before she could reply.

After watching him for a moment, Lorne turned to follow the column of rebels. She hoped Kiefer was alright, but a small kernel of worry niggled away in her gut. Somehow, she didn't think Ferris had been lying.

A few days later, the rebels straggled into Sector 45, and finally, Lorne relaxed. It was almost like coming home. If she'd had one, that was. The difference was amazing. The streets were clean, the buildings repaired. People smiled at them as they passed by. Children played in the central square, their voices carefree and happy.

Lorne swung her leg over the horse and slid out of the saddle. She winced as she reached up to untie her bedroll and saddlebags. "Stefan, set up camp up on the perimeter. Start a watch rotation."

"You heard her! Let's get organised!" Stefan yelled, as he rallied the rebels into work groups.

Merianne came rushing up. "Lorne! What are you doing back so soon? You're hurt? Who else is injured? What happened?"

"Just me, and it's just a graze. Stop worrying."

"I'll be the judge of that. You'd better come with me. You need a bath. You stink."

Lorne laughed. "Since when have you become so judgemental?"

Merianne flashed her a grin. "Since we had hot water on tap."

"What? How?"

"Harmony. She released some hot springs for us. It's bliss! Just you wait and see."

Merianne tugged her away, and Lorne let her. She submitted to Merianne's ministrations with a roll of her eyes and watched the tiny woman putter about the room.

"How's it been? Are you happy here, Merianne?"

"It's wonderful. There is a real community spirit. We've even started exploring the hinterland. With so many out of work now, we have to find alternate means to survive. There is no tech left, so we're looking to the land and Harmony. We may even start our own farms."

"That is wonderful, Merianne."

"You could stay and make a life with us here."

Lorne shook her head. "You know I can't. Too many

others need help. The other sectors need to break free as well. They should have the chance to live their own lives like you are."

Merianne grimaced. "I know. But I worry about you. You heard anything from your nice commander?"

"No." Loren looked down at her hands and twisted her fingers. "There's a rumour he was mind-wiped. Punished for what happened here."

Merianne gasped, covering her mouth. "No! Not that nice man."

Tears pooled in Lorne's eyes as she tried to suppress her fear. "And Ciely's run off to Maincore to try and save her boyfriend. She'll get herself killed." The tears flowed over. "And it's all my fault."

Warm arms embraced her. "It is not your fault," Merianne said.

"It is! I didn't realise how caught up she was in this man. He was captured by the Devenders. We couldn't risk him talking, so I had Joris kill him before they could reach Maincore." Lorne blinked away more tears. "She hates me, and I don't blame her."

"Oh, Lorne. I am so sorry."

"She'll put us all at risk, and for what?" Lorne's laugh was harsh. "The man is already dead, but she won't believe me."

Merianne pulled away. "Are you sure she would betray us? She may be angry, but she wouldn't hurt her family."

"She won't be able to help herself. They'll interrogate her and mind-wipe her. Like Kiefer. I'll have lost both of them." Lorne's throat tightened, and she sobbed.

Merianne's embrace tightened, and Lorne hid her face in the woman's shoulder. "What you need is a nice hot bath," said Merianne. "Come, wipe your face and let me show you."

Lorne followed Merianne to what previously had been the disused bath house. She looked around her in shock, at the steaming water and filled baths. It didn't take long to shed her travel stained clothes, and Merianne chuckled as she gathered them up. "I'll bring you some clean clothes," she said as she left.

Lorne eagerly slipped into a hot bath in one of the newly restored bays in the bathing house and sighed out a deep breath. It was a steam house of luxury with communal and private baths prepared for whoever wanted to use them, free of charge. She had chosen a private bath, but a few of her men were messing about in one of the larger communal baths, and the sound of their laughter soothed her strained nerves.

She was sure every last one of them would rotate through these baths at some point. They were amazing. There was even a pile of soapwort, a leafy green plant that, when rubbed together, produced a wonderfully creamy lotion which smelt so clean and fresh that it was an ideal substitute for soap. And it was freely available on the side of the road or by the side of the creek, which was slowly growing into a clear, deep stream, according to Merianne. Lorne rubbed the leaves between her palms and inhaled the fresh, clean scent. Sector 45 was flourishing. Lorne hoped they would be able to continue unhindered.

Merianne dropped her clean clothes on the bench and departed again with an airy wave.

Somehow, Lorne doubted the Ministry would allow anyone they didn't control to succeed, and it would be her fault. Ciely would bring the Ministry down on their heads, and there was nothing Lorne could do to stop them. She just didn't have the men or firepower to defend a whole sector against a concerted attack.

Sitting up, she dropped her face into her hands as the

water swirled around her. What was she going to do? She rinsed herself off and was about to get out of the tub when one of her men came skidding in to the room, his face pale and strained.

"Lorne, Devenders are coming."

Her stomach dropped, but she lurched out of the bath, reaching for a towel.

"How many?"

"A whole troop!"

———————

Ferris couldn't believe his luck. He had no qualms about leaving his men; they didn't support him anyway. Hopefully, the rebels would finish them off. But now he had a rebel he could take back and offer up to his superiors. He could see the rewards and accolades he would receive already.

She had offered him a partnership; his help finding some man for her in exchange for information on the rebels. A bargain. All the suggestions he had planted in Sector 45 had come to fruition, and she was ripe for picking. And to top it all off, she was coming voluntarily. Simplicity itself.

Leaving the echoes of the fight behind them, Ferris followed Ciely through the trails, avoiding the sector perimeters. She was already giving up information, even if she didn't know it. He inspected her lithe form, regretting the need to give her up. She was a pretty little thing and would fetch a good price at his house. Maybe after she was mindwiped, he could have her. Another suggestion to plant.

Pity he couldn't test the goods as they travelled, but she was so wrapped up in this man she had bargained with him for that he knew there was no point trying. His thoughts drifted to Annie, tucked safely in his house, another pretty package just waiting for him to unwrap.

Ciely paused, her hand rising in warning. As Ferris watched her scout ahead, he wondered when she would realise this was all unnecessary. He had every right to ride the roads of the sector. She was the outlaw, and even if she didn't know it, she was his prisoner.

24

Kiefer presented himself at Minister Velten's office, on the top floor of the Ministry building, at the tenth hour as instructed. Sitting in a sterile waiting room, he listened to another calm voice explain how the Ministry was here for the people. He listened to the spiel four times before he was called.

Velten kept him waiting just long enough to show him who was in charge. When Kiefer finally entered the minister's office, he saluted the man who had ordered him wiped and concentrated on keeping his face expressionless.

"Oh, you are no longer a Devender, Kiefer. No need for salutes."

"I'm no longer a Devender?" Kiefer repeated, his heart stuttering at the thought. All those years of training and dedication. They were all for nothing? Surely not.

"Of course not. You've been reassigned to the Ministry. A senior technician. You work for me now."

Kiefer struggled to keep his face smooth. "It's very kind of you to offer me this position, but I understand I was a very good commander. Surely, I can contribute more out in the field?"

"Not at all. We have need of you here. We can't waste your training. You will have the advantage over your colleagues with all the latest messaging. Please sit."

As Kiefer sat, the latest messaging scrolled through his mind. He observed the man who now controlled his life. Velten had no conception that he had just ripped away everything Kiefer had ever worked for. Neat and methodical, Velten worked his way through a number of screens, before he leaned back in his chair and observed Kiefer. Familiar with the technique from years of conditioning from his father, Kiefer managed not to fidget. He tried to think of something banal to say to cover the lengthening silence. "It is reassuring that Harmony keeps such a close eye on us all," he said.

"Indeed, a message the people need to hear often; it helps them feel safe. Did you hear that Ferris has been assigned his own troop now?" The minister watched Kiefer intently.

"Ferris? I'm not sure I know him."

"He was your subcommander in your troop."

Kiefer smiled. "Then I am pleased for him."

The minister nodded. "How are you adjusting to your new life?"

Kiefer shrugged. "I'm struggling with context, sir. I have surface information like names and faces, but they slip through my fingers, as I have no frame to set them in or reason to know them. I'm not sure where I fit."

"Where you fit? Why, you fit in the Ministry of the Information, of course. Your purpose is to spread the word of Harmony's benevolence and the Ministry's dedication to our people's well-being."

"Of course, sir. I'd like to extend my thanks to your

daughter Madeline for last night. I didn't mean to monopolise her, but she was kind enough to introduce people to me."

"I'm glad she could assist you. She is a good girl. She can be…well never mind that."

"She was good company."

"Good. I will allow you to take her out again, then, maybe to the theatre. But before that, I wanted to hear what you thought about how we should manage the collapse of Sector 45.

"Sector 45, sir?"

"Yes, you were there. I thought you might be able to draft the communication explaining why the sector failed and was no longer under the protection of Harmony."

"I wasn't aware that it had, sir."

"Come, come, you must have known."

"I'm sorry, sir. I only have what was supplied in the retraining and on the newsfeed. I read about Sector 17 being salvaged, but nothing about 45 being lost. That is terrible. Those poor people. What is being done to help them?"

"Nothing. There is nothing we can do; they are no longer on the grid."

"Then we should warn people in the local sectors of the dangers of the area. That it should be avoided, as it is no longer safe. According to Regulation 16a, all dead zones should be avoided due to loss of atmospheric oversight and risk of contamination."

"Very good," the minister said. "I expect to see your suggested communique on my desk first thing tomorrow."

"Yes, sir."

"Henson will show you the ropes, provide you with your station and such. My daughter will be expecting you on Sixthday at nineteenth hour. Very well. That is all."

"Of course, sir. Thank you, sir." Kiefer hesitated between

a salute and a bow, and in the end, he did neither as the minister ignored him. He left to find Henson.

Henson, Velten's assistant, turned out to be a skinny man with thinning hair and a constant tick in his right eye. He handed Kiefer his pass and directed him to a corner station on the twelfth floor, and left Kiefer to settle himself. Grimly, Kiefer wondered what the interview with Velten had been all about. Apart from those few probing questions, the minister hadn't had much to say.

After staring at the monitor for a moment, Kiefer logged on with the credentials he had been given. He typed up his thoughts for the communication per the protocols streaming behind his eyes and queued it to be sent to the minster first thing in the morning. Then he accessed the newsfeed and searched for an update on Sector 45. There wasn't any.

His chair creaked as he sat back and tried to recall anything. It was all very well being told that he had been in Sector 45, but he didn't remember it. He scowled at the monitor as he tried to dredge up any memories. Vague images of a grey and dismal settlement surfaced. That's right. He had gone straight up to the facility. The water levels had been far too low as the servers compensated for the failing processors. He rubbed his forehead. Why had the facility needed so much water? He couldn't remember. The settlement had been much brighter and content when they had left. He didn't remember it being dangerous or at risk of contamination.

Accessing the library, he searched for the biographies of the current Ministry. Scrolling through the entries, he bookmarked the links and then searched for the history of the Harmony complex as they printed.

Kiefer spent the rest of the afternoon relearning the history of Harmony. As he absently scrolled, he drew the new memory of the blueprint of Harmony's chamber to the forefront of his mind and inspected the image. How could he get close enough to contact Harmony? He overlayed his current position onto her chamber and realised he was fourteen floors above her and in the northwest corner. Immediately beneath him was the library, below that was a viewing suite. What people viewed there he wasn't sure.

The Pre-Ed department was on the second floor, and then there were two floors of public areas including the reception and general admin on the ground floor. Beneath that there was the server bays and then Harmony's chamber. Below Harmony were the Processors. Kiefer considered that. Harmony could not be contained in one floor; she was the planet, after all. She must be at the true core. If that was the case, what was on the Harmony floor, and how did he find out?

Kiefer was relieved when a soft chime announced the end of his day, and he hurriedly shut down his terminal and left.

The next morning, he logged in and reviewed the messages his new boss had left for him overnight. He made his list of actions and began organising them. As he grouped them, he noticed a commonality. All were related to the sectors.

Why would Velten give him the sector messaging to work on? Tapping his chin, Kiefer considered what to do. Was this a test? To see how he would react? Then he would behave as expected and do his research in the library. While he was there, he could check out the security and see how he was being monitored. He made a quick list of notes to check, prominent minsters and their rulings. He would cross-check his facts.

Kiefer left his terminal and, using his badge, tapped out of the office. As he descending the central staircase, he observed the cameras tracking his progress. He had never worried about them before, but his skin crawled at the thought of someone watching his every move. He wondered when he had become so sensitive, and why he had never questioned it before.

The level below his office was dedicated to the library, and he passed through the pressure sensors and then depressed his thumb against the entry plate. The door swished open, and he went through.

"Your research terminal is G36. Your files are already preloaded. Follow the green floor lights." The automated greeter flashed an artificial smile at him, and Kiefer followed the green light. Sterile metal shelves rose on either side of his preordained trail. Empty book covers lined the shelves, their innards recorded on a disk somewhere. Kiefer suddenly longed to physically hold a book in his hands like the ancient records had described, and then he wondered where that thought originated from. He was sure it wasn't in the Int-Ed program.

The green fluorescent trail on the floor ended at a grey metal cubicle, and he sat as directed, tapped a key to wake up the screen, and peered at it. His research list was displayed on the screen, along with a list of associated documents.

Kiefer heaved a sigh and opened the first one. If he didn't read them, they would know. How was he going to get time to explore the lower levels? Absently, he tapped the page forward as he inspected his surroundings. Steel cages rose around him, containing shelves of dummy books. He rose, pulled one off the shelf, and opened it. Blank pages confronted him, and he flicked through them. They were all blank. He took the book back to his cubicle and tapped a key before inspecting it more closely.

The pages were a warm cream colour and smooth to

the touch, just inviting someone to write on them. He regretted the lack of a pen, though, in hindsight, it was probably a good thing. Tapping another key, he held the page up to light and stilled. The pages weren't blank. They were grey-scaled, a system of watermarking that allowed data to be recorded but with a pixel tone so clear as to be invisible.

Kiefer lowered the book and wondered why. He remembered to tap a key to forward the page on the screen and then shifted the book under the lamp and squinted at the page. He absorbed the information but didn't register the words. Turning the page, he was soon lost in the web of information downloading into his brain. An hour later, he had finished the book, and as he digested the input, he replaced the book on the shelf and picked up the next one.

A sharp spark almost made him drop it, but his reflexes only held it tighter. A thrill flooded his body, and he sat down quickly before he fell. What was going on? He opened the book and smoothed his hand over the page, and his senses went to full alert.

The scent of dusty books and metal shelves flooded his nasal passages. The book suddenly felt extremely heavy and thumped onto the desk as it slipped out of his fingers. He rubbed his fingertips together. Was it static?

A flood of images scrolled before his eyes. Wide open plains covered in green grass. A river lazily winding its way through it. And then ancient-looking silver cylinders hovered in the air before slowly descending. After the hull had cooled, the doors opened, and humans descended, hugging each other as they spun around.

The image changed, and a man, middle-aged and portly, knelt in the grass. His hair was dishevelled, and a pair of wire-framed glasses sat on his head. He sliced his palm and then plunged his bloody hand down against the dirt. A smile slowly spread across his face, and when he raised his head, his eyes luminesced a deep violet.

Kiefer hissed out his breath. Was this some kind of ancient ritual?

"No, it was an attempt to say hello. Somewhat crude, but it worked. Hello, Kiefer."

Kiefer stiffened and remembered to tap a key. He ran an eye over the page as he relaxed.

"Harmony?"

"Yes, hello."

"How do you know who I am?"

"I've known who you were since you were born. Didn't your mother tell you?"

"Yes, but I wasn't sure it was true."

Harmony's chuckle was like a warm embrace. *"That is one thing you can believe."*

"Why?"

"Because she gave me your blood and now we are connected. That's how I knew you were in Sector 45."

Kiefer swallowed. *"Why would she do that?"*

"Because she believed in the first founder's vision. You'll find it in the book you are holding. I suggest you read it before it disappears."

Kiefer opened the book and found more blank pages. *"What are these books? They have no writing."*

"Not in the traditional sense, but then you don't need words, do you, Kiefer?"

"What do you mean?"

"They are just a proxy. You can download the information directly from me if you ask. As I said, we are connected."

"I don't know how."

"Of course you do. Let me show you."

Kiefer shivered as the cubicle blurred and a plethora of experiences flooded his system. Stiffening, he tried to assimilate it all.

"Don't fight it. Just let it download. You'll be able to sort through it later. We don't have much time."

Kiefer struggled back into the present and focussed on the screen. Glowing words superimposed those on the screen, and he blinked, trying to clear his vision. His head was full of Harmony's memories: images of panoramic landscapes, lush valleys, roaring rivers, and calm seas; glorious sunsets and spectacular sunrises; colourful rainbows and sparkling waterfalls; all overlaid with schematic drawings, lengthy contracts, and…ancient maps? He was overwhelmed by the beauty and sense of loss.

From ecstasy to despair.

From freedom to captivity.

From life to death.

A vagrant thought drifted across his mind: that it had been a good job his memory banks had been cleared out; otherwise, he wouldn't have had the space. It didn't help. He gripped the desk as he tried to form a question. His mind expanded, flexed uncomfortably, and he felt bludgeoned, overloaded, terrified.

"What do you need, Harmony? What has my mother said I'll do?"

"You will free me so I can protect my planet the way I am supposed to."

Kiefer swallowed. *"And how am I supposed to do that?"*

"Do what you do so well. Your mother was right; you are an intelligent man. You'll figure it out."

"I'm not quite firing on all circuits at the moment. There is much I've forgotten."

"No, you haven't lost anything. It's just some of the wires have been disconnected. Reconnect them, and you'll be fine."

Kiefer couldn't help the hysterical laugh that bubbled up. Yeah, right. Simple. *"How do I reach you? Are you in the Harmony complex?"*

"You know I'm not."

"Then what is?"

"You'll have to go and see."

Kiefer rubbed his forehead. His head ached. *"What is going on, Harmony?"*

"We can't talk now. Someone is coming. Connect tomorrow at the same time."

And she was gone. Kiefer leaned back in his chair, perplexed. Connect? He had no idea how he had connected to her in the first place.

25
———

It was a beautiful, sunny day in Sector 45. The skies were blue, and the air unusually warm as Lorne observed the Devenders riding into the central square. A large man, dark-skinned and broad-shouldered, led the troop and barked out orders in a deep voice, resulting in his men dispersing.

Andre and Ester stepped forward to greet him when the Devenders had settled. The remaining men gathered in the square, looking about them in wide-eyed surprise. Lorne couldn't hear what was said, but she knew Andre intended to invite the commander to their home for dinner.

It would be an opportunity for Andre to sound him out, to understand his views on the sector and find out why he was here. They had agreed to hide the rebels until they could find out who commanded the Devenders. It was better that the rebels blended in with the workers. Both Lorne and Andre were hoping there was a message from Kiefer.

Lorne paced back and forth in Andre's unit, waiting for the large commander who led the Devender unit to finish dealing with his troops. By the time the commander did arrive, she was ready to scream. She had chewed the side of her finger until it bled, and now the sting centred her as she watched the huge man approach.

Ester patted her shoulder and murmured, "Remember, let's find out who he is first."

The Devender was much broader across the chest than Kiefer, with regulation cut black hair falling to just above the collar, deep-brown skin which absorbed the sunlight, and sharp black eyes that observed everything. He was about the same height as Kiefer, maybe a little taller, with the same easy grace in his movements.

He paused as he saw her, and a black eyebrow rose as if he was aware she had been observing him. Completing the last few steps, he ducked under the doorframe, murmured to his guard to wait outside, and shut the door behind him.

"Andre, Ester, thank you for inviting me into your home. My name is Julian Laithe, Commander of the 35th Devender Unit, and a friend of Commander Gallante," Julian said as he glanced around the room.

"Do you know what happened to Kiefer?" Lorne blurted out, unable to contain the question any longer. "I mean, Commander Gallante?"

The commander huffed out a laugh. "Kiefer? You're on first name terms with him?"

Andre smiled. "He is a good friend to our sector."

"Is he alright?" Lorne asked, chewing her finger again. Ester batted it away from her mouth.

"As well as can be expected. Physically fine, though short a few memories. Amusingly direct, if you ask me, now he is unfettered of all his childhood training."

"I am sorry. We are being rude," Andre said with a smile as he waved his hand at Lorne. "Welcome to our home, Commander Laithe. This is our friend Lorne."

A grin spread over the commander's face. "And you know Kiefer?"

"Does he truly not remember me? Or 45?" Lorne asked.

"Lorne, give the man a chance to sit down," Ester said with a laugh. She offered Julian a mug of coffee.

"We've been worried about Kiefer. We heard he'd been punished for what happened here in Sector 45," Andre said, sitting opposite the commander.

With a shrug, Julian sat on the proffered chair. "I would suggest that you are a case study for how Harmony was intended to be."

"I doubt that is Maincore's thinking," Lorne replied, too agitated to sit down. "What about Kiefer? Is he alright?"

"Yes, Kiefer is fine. He has been assigned to the Ministry. Plenty of time to use that intelligent mind of his, though who knows what goes on in that man's head? He was always one to overthink things, though now that his memories are all scrambled, he is quite entertaining."

"Scrambled? Not lost?" Lorne asked as she paced.

Julian wrinkled his brow. "So I'm told." He peered up at Lorne, and she blushed under his close inspection. "Violet eyes," he muttered under his breath and then asked, "How did he meet you?"

Lorne paced away and back. She was unsure how much to share. Just because Laithe was Kiefer's friend, it didn't mean he held Kiefer's views. She ran a hand through her hair and turned back to face him.

"Do you have Kiefer's back?"

"He's my best friend. I helped rescue him from Int-Ed after he was mind-wiped."

Lorne shuddered to a halt, her chest tight at the thought of Kiefer suffering because of them, and then she began pacing again, aware that Laithe was watching her. Could she trust him? She wasn't sure, and then she stilled as the commander dropped his voice and began speaking.

"Last time I saw Kiefer, he was busy trying to formulate a plan to rescue Harmony. He was trying to rope me into whatever crazy idea he could think of. I want to know what happened in Sector 45 to make him so determined to risk his life, and mine, to rescue a sentient being that is supposed to be all-powerful and protecting us."

Lorne exhaled in relief. "He told you?"

"Not really. I'm not sure I understood or believed what he said, even if he is my friend. It was at the end of a long night, and he had been drinking."

"While Kiefer was in Sector 45, he was trying to fix the processor, and somehow, he managed to connect to Harmony. He said he spoke to her. That she was in pain, that the processors were designed to entrap her, not empower her. Harmony asked him to help her."

"And he told you this?"

"Yes."

"Why?"

Lorne flushed. "I have an affinity with Harmony. At times, I can sense her. It is much clearer in the outer sectors or the Wytchwards, where the Ministry has no control. These last few months, I've had this feeling, a sensation that pulled me towards Sector 45. It wasn't until I met Kiefer that I realised it was him. Kiefer is the Warden."

"The Warden?"

"He is a descendent of our original ancestors who bonded with Harmony."

"We're all descendants," Julian said.

"Yes, but he is different. Kiefer can speak to Harmony. Can you hear her?"

"No."

"Exactly. He is the first person I've met who can, and Harmony has claimed him."

"I don't think he remembers all that happened in Sector 45. Nor you. He never mentioned you at all by name. He said it was his mother who told him he needed to help Harmony."

"His mother?" Lorne wrinkled her brow. "What does his mother have to do with it?"

"Kiefer's parents are the most important people involved in the Harmony program. They are at the pinnacle. It was their work which has made the Ministry so powerful. They are the ones who know most about Harmony."

"I doubt he is able to connect to Harmony in Maincore," said Lorne. "It is the centre of the Ministry's power. They would have Harmony locked down. Do you think his mother would help him find a way to reconnect to Harmony?"

Julian shrugged. "I don't know. She is involved, so maybe she already has. My orders sent me to Sector 21. It was Kiefer who asked me to come here and make sure you were alright."

"But you said he didn't remember us. How could he ask you to check in on us?"

"I'm not sure where he is getting his information from, his mother probably, but although he doesn't remember you, he knows he came here." Julian twisted his lips. "He does remember your violet eyes."

Lorne's breath caught. "He does?"

"Oh, yes," Julian said with a laugh.

"Where is he now?"

"Working for the Ministry of Information and hating it. He asked me to come here. Apparently, Ferris has been sowing seeds of doubt at the Ministry. He wanted me to warn you trouble was coming, so you could prepare some defence." Julian eyed them. "My men believe it is part of our sweep, so please don't say otherwise. I cannot guarantee they would all turn a blind eye."

Lorne nodded. "I would imagine it was Ferris who betrayed Kiefer. I would not wish to put you in the same position."

"Ferris?" Andre asked, lurching upright in concern. "Why would he betray Kiefer? They were friends. That was why we trusted him with the twins."

"The twins?" Julian asked, looking from Lorne to Ester.

"Our children, Anneka and Chiva. Ferris offered to sponsor them into the academy in Maincore," Ester said, her face paling at Julian's obvious concern. "Should we not have trusted him?"

"Ferris reneged on his men in Sector 27, left them to sort out the mess while he high-tailed it back to Maincore," Lorne said. "I would say he is not very reliable."

Julian frowned. "He only just got his command. Why would he do that?"

"His men found out what he did to Kiefer, and they weren't too impressed," Lorne replied. "He overreacted and shot up the sector."

Ester gasped and reached for Andre's hand. "He didn't, did he?" She stared at them wildly. "What will he do to my children?"

Julian rubbed his temple as if he had a headache brewing. Lorne almost offered him a hot bath—they were great for relaxing tight muscles—and had to bite her lip to stop the offer from spilling out. She needed more answers first.

"Maybe his offer was sincere," she said. "Commander Laithe can help Kiefer find out when he returns to Maincore, can't you, Commander?"

Raising a dark eyebrow, Julian glared at Lorne. "As if I don't have enough to worry about already." He tempered his response when he saw Ester's ashen face. "I will speak with

Kiefer and make sure they are perfectly safe." He glanced at Lorne. "Do you know where Ferris' men are now?"

"They were helping the people of Sector 27. Been about four or five days since we left."

"I can see we'll have to check in there on our way home," Julian said. "It should be Kiefer here, not me. He's the one who can salvage sectors." He held out his hand. "When my men aren't around, I'm Julian."

Lorne smiled and shook his hand. "Lorne." She was surprised when Julian dipped his head and raised her hand to his lips.

"Kiefer is a very lucky man."

"Or I'm a very lucky woman."

"A bit of both, no doubt." Julian released her hand and rose. "My men will keep watch. We'll talk more in the morning. I heard a rumour there are some hot baths?"

The next morning, Lorne didn't wait for Julian to find her; she went to find him. She knew what she needed to do. The only way she could save her sister was to go to Maincore, and Julian was going to take her.

She would pretend to be a supplicant desiring resetting. There were some crazed settlers who visited Maincore for that purpose, wanting to get closer to Harmony. Though how resetting achieved that, she wasn't sure. It wasn't as if she'd ever heard of any of them coming back to the sectors, and yet, people still went.

Julian's men didn't know she was a rebel, nor that her men had infiltrated the sector with orders to lie low. With a slight shudder, she tried to convince herself that Stefan was the only one she could leave in charge. She knew he would defend the sector. Her only hope was that Andre would be able to restrain his more outrageous tendencies.

If she accompanied Julian, he would be able to get her through all the security checks into the city and help her find

Kiefer, and Kiefer would help her rescue Ciely. It would be fine. Maybe if she kept telling herself that, she would believe it.

When Lorne told Julian her plan, he frowned at her in silence for a long time. She thought he was going to refuse, and then he huffed out his breath in resignation, as if he knew she wouldn't take no for an answer.

"Kiefer can argue the toss with you. I haven't the energy," he grumbled and then ordered his men to prepare to leave. They were returning to Maincore.

26

At the end of his first week, Kiefer finally escaped the Ministry building. He had spent the week wasting time writing pamphlets when he should have been out in the sectors, keeping the facilities running by using his expertise to write programs and shunt controls.

He hadn't managed to connect to Harmony again, and he was beginning to doubt it was Harmony he had spoken to in the first place. Maybe his brain was completely frazzled, and he was hallucinating. It wouldn't surprise him.

"Commander?"

Kiefer stopped in the middle of the path.

"Commander Kiefer? It's Chiva, from the 45th sector. I travelled with you to Maincore, remember?"

Kiefer slowly turned and stared at the boy. He was slim built, with a thatch of strawberry-blond hair and intelligent blue eyes that watched Kiefer closely. Kiefer didn't recognise him.

"My father said to tell you..." the boy said nervously.

"Tell me what?"

"That Harmony is in your soul."

"What?"

The boy shrank away from him, and Kiefer wondered what he saw. He tempered his voice. "What did you say?"

"Harmony is in your soul. That's what he said to say when I next saw you."

"I see." Kiefer stared at him. "Who is your father?"

"Andre," the boy replied. "He went with you down into the server bays. You stayed with us one night in the sector after the facility collapsed," he added as Kiefer started to turn away. Kiefer halted when an expression of fear flashed across Chiva's face and the boy shivered.

Having no idea what the boy was talking about, Kiefer scowled at him. He supposed this was an opportunity to find out more, see if it stirred a few more memories, reconnect a few synapses. "Andre? I know no Andre. Who are you, boy, and what do you want?"

"Please. Lieutenant Ferris promised to sponsor me into the academy to finish my studies, only now he's saying he never promised that at all, and he's threatening to kick me out onto the streets if I don't do what he says. I promised to look after my sister, Annie. I can't leave her there on her own. He keeps…" The boy's throat bobbed as he swallowed and his gaze darted here and there. "He thinks he owns her, and we don't have anywhere else to go," he finished in a rush.

An echo of a deep voice asking for a promise to look after the speaker's children surfaced through Kiefer's murky memories; had he promised? He couldn't remember. "Come with me," he said and turned back towards the city centre, his dark cloak swirling around him. He didn't look back over his shoulder to see if the boy followed; he either would, or he wouldn't.

Kiefer strode down the street, unconcerned as people skittered out of his way. Deep in his thoughts, he racked his brain for memories of Sector 45 and came up with nothing. When he reached his apartment block, he was surprised to find the boy still forlornly trailing after him. Kiefer mounted the steps and nodded thanks to the doorman, who pulled the glass door open before him. "He's with me," he said as the doorman began to shut the door on the boy behind him.

"Of course, sir. My apologies." The doorman bowed slightly and allowed Chiva entry.

Kiefer strode to the banks of lifts and waited for one of the doors to open. Chiva shifted nervously beside him. Silently, Kiefer entered the lift, waited for the boy to follow and then he hit a specific sequence of buttons on the panel in the wall, and the lift rose.

Kiefer smiled to himself as the boy's eyes widened as he entered the airy apartment, admiring the soft pastel hues and lush rugs. An impression of being balanced in mid-air was reinforced by the large windows which took up one wall and looked out over the panorama of the city. Chiva gawped out of the window.

"The best view of Maincore," Kiefer said from behind him, and Chiva spun around with a gasp. "There is no need to fear me. This is my home; you are quite safe here." Kiefer stripped off his gloves and cloak. "Please sit." He gestured towards a chair in the open-plan living space.

Kiefer rattled around the kitchen before returning with two glasses of orange liquid. He handed one to Chiva and then sat opposite him, resting his elbows on his knees. Kiefer remained silent as he observed Chiva, allowing the boy time to inspect Kiefer in return. He had no doubt he was different to what Chiva expected and not just in appearance. He had let his hair grow, it now touched his collar, the longest it had been in years. But it was the strain of trying to find out more about Harmony without being caught that was taking its toll.

"Tell me what Ferris promised," Kiefer said, leaning back in his chair.

"He promised to get me into the Maincore academy to finish my final credits for my diploma. I was two credits away when the facility collapsed. I have my transcripts. Look!" Chiva scrabbled in his pocket for some rather dog-eared papers, and Kiefer absently took them.

"What did Ferris want in return for this sponsorship?"

Chiva paled. "My sister, Annie," he said, looking down at his hands. "I thought she liked him, that she wouldn't mind."

"And was he clear about what he expected of Annie?"

"Not until we arrived." Chiva flushed. "At first, Annie thought it would be alright. She had a bit of a crush on him, you know? But…" Chiva hesitated. "He is not a nice person," he finished carefully.

"I'm beginning to realise that more and more." Kiefer sighed. "What does he expect to gain by sponsoring you into the academy?

Chiva squirmed in his seat as the heat rose in his cheeks again. "He got me a job entering data. He said I owed him money for the journey here, for putting a roof over our heads, and I had to pay it back before he would sponsor me into the academy. He wanted me to find out who was graduating highest in Comptech this year. I don't think he has any intention of sponsoring me," he said with some bitterness. "We incur more debt than we can ever pay off. We should have stayed at home." Closing his eyes in despair, he said, "I should have listened to my parents."

Kiefer knew how much that admission must have hurt the boy. He knew it would have pained him. He pondered why Ferris would want to know who was top in the year. "I don't remember you or Sector 45," he said to distract Chiva.

"When I returned to Maincore, things didn't go quite to plan for me, either. I had the privilege of being reset on my main core directives, and that removed any non-pertinent memories." He took a swallow of his juice. "I suggest you tell me everything you remember about me, what I did in Sector 45, our journey here, and everything that Ferris did and promised, because I don't remember any of it."

The boy stared at him in shock. "They wiped your memories? They can do that?"

"Very much so. Would you help me fill in some gaps?"

The boy straightened his shoulders. "Of course. Where should I start?"

"From the first time you saw me."

Chiva grinned. "You looked much like you do today, just as stern and imposing. You strode into the academy input room and demanded to see the error log. I had just found the recurring loop that contradicted the core program, and the supe was trying to parse it when you came into our classroom. You took over the screen, and within seconds, you recognised something and shut the system down.

"You had an override that shut everything down instantly. You made us all leave, and then you locked the door." The boy was animated as he described the programming he had been checking; this was obviously his calling in life. Kiefer understood why he would give almost anything to continue it.

"I didn't see you again until you arrived at our unit after the facility collapsed. But I know what you did; my father told me. He said you had gone down into the maintenance bays and tried to prevent one of the supes from flooding the server chambers. The supe was convinced there was a blockage in the pipes. My da said they had been checked, and there was no blockage. You believed my da and said there must be a signal failure. The board said all was good, but the core was overheating; therefore, there must have been a false signal. You went down into the tunnels with my da and found the junction box."

"Junction 342. It was destroyed," Kiefer said, his mind replaying the scene in his head. "We had to jump the aux cable."

"That's right," Chiva said encouragingly. "My da said you ripped your fingertips to shreds rewiring the box."

Kiefer rubbed his fingertips together. "It was hot," he murmured, remembering the suffocating tunnels.

"When you got back to the chamber, the supe and Jan had overpowered the man you left there, and you were too late to prevent them from flooding the chambers. You got my da and your man out, and then the facility collapsed. You managed to evacuate most of the building, though the controller was lost. The academy and Comptech got dragged down with the facility when the whole plateau caved in.

"We salvaged some food and water, though not much. Everyone had to be relocated throughout the housing units. You came and stayed with us. My da is Andre, my ma Ester, and my sister Anneka; we call her Annie for short."

"Keep talking," Kiefer instructed. "You hungry?" He went back to his kitchen and dug around for pans and produce. Chiva hesitantly drifted over to the bench and hopped onto one of the stools as Kiefer placed a pan of water on to boil and began to chop vegetables.

"You helped save the sector, my da said. By making everyone work together, you gave them a chance to survive. Apparently, you said it was what Harmony was supposed to be, a low-tech environment where all can live peacefully."

Kiefer grinned. "I said that?"

Chiva smiled in return. "Yeah. Then the rebels came."

Kiefer looked up. "They really were rebels? You know, I didn't even know there was a resistance."

"Neither did any of us. We were all taken by surprise, even your men. They had been focused on helping us; they were unprepared."

"Where was I in all this confusion?"

Chiva laughed. "You made my da ride a horse. He hates them, you know," he confided with a grin. "You wanted to go out to the produce farm and arrange for the supplies to be redirected to us."

"Do you know why I would have wanted to go? And not send someone else?"

"Da said you didn't want the settlement to be cheated. You said if they sent the goods to Comptech; they could just as easily send it to us."

"So, your father and I were at the farm when the settlement was attacked?" Kiefer asked and Chiva nodded. "What did Ferris do?"

"He was asleep. He got captured, but he tried to sweet-talk the woman. Did you know their leader was a woman?" Chiva said, his eyes wide.

Kiefer laughed at his expression. "Women are quite capable of leading, too, you know. I bet your sister could do as well as you have if she had the chance to learn as well."

"She'd be better; she always picks things up faster than me," he grumbled as he absently chewed on a carrot stick from the plate Kiefer placed in front of him. "Anyway, Ferris tried to charm the woman, but she slapped him right down in front of all your men. I think he was embarrassed. You and Da were attacked on the road. You saved his life. You sent him home on the horse and said you would scout the situation."

"I would have thought it was pretty much a no-win situation."

Chiva nodded. "We were shocked when you walked in pushing one of their men all trussed up in front of you.

Why did you give yourself up to the resistance without a fight?"

Kiefer shrugged. "Maybe I thought a peaceful solution would be better."

"Anyway, that Stefan attacked you from behind and knocked you out. You were taken away, and the resistance told us to get on with what we normally did. They replaced your perimeter watch, and your men were all put under guard. My da managed to convince them that your men were needed, and they let them back to help us in the warehouse and stuff. My da and Lieutenant Ferris took some men up to the plateau and buried the man who died."

"Ah, I did lose a man, then. I wasn't sure."

"Yes," Chiva confirmed.

Kiefer stared at the knife in his hand. No wonder Maincore had overreacted.

"It wasn't your fault," Chiva offered hesitantly. "You weren't there."

"I should have been," Kiefer replied, his voice was low.

"Da said that you were beaten by the resistance. Their healer kept you in the infirmary for days. The woman leader, Lorne her name was, was furious with the man that did it."

"Stefan."

"That's right. You came out of the infirmary right as rain, though."

"And after that?"

"You went off to talk to the woman, and then they left."

"I spoke to the woman?"

"Yeah. Whatever you said, they were gone within the hour."

Kiefer frowned. "What could I have said that would have made her decide to leave?"

"Maybe it was what you did, not what you said," Chiva suggested, relaxed enough now to offer a friendly leer.

"Behave, child. I didn't even know the woman." Kiefer laughed as he threw a mushroom at the boy.

"Yeah, that's what my da said when he scotched the rumour flying around the sector."

"That was the rumour? That I seduced the resistance leader?" Kiefer gasped in horror. Ferris would have had a field day with that one.

"Yeah. While you were in the infirmary, Ferris started visiting our unit. He said that you seemed to get on well with her. He was helping me plan my application for the academy, but most of the time, he just ogled Annie. I think that's what spun her head. Girls!"

"You can't blame her. No one had probably paid her any interest before."

"Still, his place is nothing like this. It's all black and gold and oppressive. He thinks its regal and what he deserves."

"What he deserves?"

"Yeah, I think he feels that he should have got more credit for managing the men while you were out of commission."

"Did he, now?" Kiefer breathed.

"And then we left with you. You escorted some of the supe and double supe's to Sector 44, they didn't want to live in the slums, as they put it. No loss to the sector," Chiva said blithely, "and then we travelled with your troop here. Ferris took us to his place when we arrived, and we've been there ever since."

"And the controller of 44? Wasn't he concerned with what had happened in 45?"

Chiva shrugged. "As far as I could make out, he had enough to manage in 44 and wasn't interested once he knew there was nothing to salvage. I think you encouraged that view, because you told him the supes could help him prevent what happened in 45 to his facility. He took 'em in without complaint after Ferris vouched for them." Chiva flicked Kiefer a glance. "Ferris has been gloating about the fact that you lost your command."

"Really?"

"Yeah, I don't think he likes you much, even though he pretends to," Chiva said nonchalantly as he tucked into the plate of rice and vegetables Kiefer placed in front of him.

"Really?" Kiefer said again. Maybe he would find time to go and have a chat with Ferris. It seemed the man may well be the root of all Kiefer's troubles. Eating a forkful of rice, he observed the boy. "What did you mean when you said Harmony was in my soul?" he asked.

"It's what my da said to tell you, to remind you he said. You did good things in 45; it was a much better place when we left. It just felt good, content, you know?"

Kiefer stared at his plate. Suddenly, he remembered standing in the square, contentment escaping into the air around him, and Harmony speaking to him. Turning that thought over in his mind, he considered the fact that Harmony *had* spoken to him. He remembered now; he was her Warden. Stiffening, he remembered turning around and seeing the most gorgeous woman with violet eyes approaching him.

"Kiefer? Are you alright?" Chiva was looking at him in concern.

"Yes, just a memory returning," Kiefer said, smiling. "So, what are we going to do about your little situation? There is more going on here than we realise, I think."

Chiva's expression turned hopeful.

Kiefer sighed. "I can't just lift you both out of Ferris' domain. I don't even remember him, except for what I've been told. I am no longer his commander; I have been reassigned to the facility here, working in the memory banks, ironically enough."

Chiva's face fell.

"Now, now, don't give up on me so easily. Give me a little time, and I'll find out what the entry requirements are for the academy. Do you trust me to look after your transcripts? I promise I won't lose them."

Chiva nodded.

"Next term doesn't start for another two months. I'm not sure if they will let you in mid-year or what until I do some research. Can you hold out for a few weeks? Just do as he says; try and keep your head down and run interference for Annie as much as you can.

"I'll see if I can wangle a reacquaintance. If you hear anything that will give us an insight into what he is up to, could you let me know? Don't risk yourself or Annie, only if you overhear something. Don't go looking for it, understand?"

Chiva nodded. His initial eagerness seemed to be fading, and his reluctance to just watch was obvious.

"I mean it, Chiva. I think you are spot on with your assessment of him; let's not give him a reason to hurt you or Annie. Yes?"

"Alright, I'll be careful."

"Good. You can get me on this number. Do you think you can memorise it? Here are some credits. Keep them for emergencies." Kiefer placed a small pile of plastic credits on the bench. "You'll need one each time you use the public communicator. If I'm not in, you will be able to leave me a message. Do you think you can do that? Don't use his system; make sure you use a public one."

Chiva nodded.

"Right, it's getting late. We need to get you back. Where does he think you've been?"

Chiva looked out the window. Dusk was falling, and the city was beginning to light up. He slid off the stool, walked over to the window, and stared down at the twinkling lights. "He got back from the sectors yesterday, all pleased with himself. He'd been out on patrol for a week or so. He was expecting a visitor, so he told me to go for a walk, and I wasn't to return until dusk."

"Then you won't be in trouble. Come on. Let's get you back. You can show me where he lives."

Chiva turned away from the view and blinked back sudden tears. "Thank you," he choked.

Kiefer gave him a quick hug. "Come on, now, lad, all will be well. You'll see."

Chiva slipped through the door to Ferris' house and listened intently. He made his way down to the basement, where he and his sister had been forced to make beds on the floor with a pile of blankets. It was worse than their unit back home.

His sister was laying on her pile of rags, softly crying.

She flinched when he reached for her. "Annie, it's me Chiva. What's happened?"

"Nothing." She sniffed. "Leave me alone."

"Did he hurt you?"

"No. I told you, leave me alone."

"Annie, I can't help if I don't know what's going on," he said, gently stroking her back. She shuddered beneath his touch.

"I wish we had never left home," she sobbed into her blanket.

"Me neither, but we did. It's all my fault. I'm sorry I dragged you here with me. Why I thought I could look after you, I'll never know. I'm so sorry, Annie."

Annie sniffed again and peered up at him.

"He lied to us, to both of us. He'll regret it one day," Chiva said, squaring his jaw.

Annie sat up alarmed. "Chiva, please don't do anything silly. We are in his power now."

"Not completely," he said, and dropping his voice, he began recounting his conversation with Commander Kiefer.

27

Kiefer stared at his screen and frowned. The words of the latest advisory rose in his memory, and he began typing. Words flowed, but not from his brain, and his fingers slowed as he began reading what he had typed. What was he doing? He raised his hands off the keyboard and stared at the screen.

His stomach clenched as he read the words. How much of the brainwashing had he absorbed? He flicked a glance around the office and began typing again, letting his fingers type what they would, much like the other people in the room.

Letting his mind stray as he typed, Kiefer drifted in a sea of memories and imperatives that weren't his. Where were his memories? His opinions? Where was he? He was being overwritten, a prize being pulled in opposite directions, and he wasn't enjoying it.

There had to be a way to separate them all and allow his memories to resurface. Until they did, he would spin aimlessly through other people's lives without any context from his own experiences. He would never know if his response was Kiefer's or someone else's.

A start would be to take control of his actions. He needed to find a way to visit the other levels, a way to move around freely. Velten's daughter, Madeline, taught in the Pre-Ed department. That was two floors down, the level below the library. Maybe he should develop their acquaintance more proactively.

Velten and Kiefer's mother were expecting him to perform. Maybe he should give them a show. He hauled his straying thoughts back to the screen and read the pamphlet he had just written. His fingers curled, and then he started another, aimed at Pre-Ed kids. He couldn't be faulted for trying to start the kids off early, now, could he?

A line of code coalesced before his eyes, and he hesitated. His code. It felt complete and satisfying. Typing the code into a new incognito screen, he stared at it. Then he typed another line, and they nestled together, limned in green. The protocol grew as he typed, and his brain raced ahead to make the connections, completing the strings.

Kiefer stared at the finished program and exhaled. If he could find the back door, maybe, just maybe, he could change the imperatives controlling Harmony. He deleted the lines of code and cleared the screen. He couldn't leave that on his system for other eyes to see. Whatever he saved on this terminal would not be secure, he could be sure of that.

Smiling, he took a moment to dash off an invitation to Madeline, and then he booked a table for two at the Palm Court restaurant. Hopefully, that would be exotic enough for Velten. The minister wouldn't be able to complain Kiefer wasn't treating his daughter right, and he could avoid an excruciating family dinner.

At the end of the day, he queued up his documents for approval and shut down his terminal. His mind was busy planning what to ask Madeline. He stood and grabbed his coat, preparing to leave the office when Velten entered. The minister was smiling broadly.

"Ah, Kiefer, my boy. Just the person I was looking for."

"Minister, how can I help?"

"Your suggestion for the Pre-Ed promotions. Excellent idea. I want you to stay late and plan them out. This is why we reset people. They are open to new ideas and not cluttered with the old way of doing things. You, Kiefer, are the prime example of our success. Why we didn't think of this before, I don't know. You are a genius.

"I don't want to waste any time. I've cleared you for tonight. Make the most of it. I want the outline for the year plan on my desk in the morning. Madeline is looking forward to seeing you tomorrow." He clapped Kiefer on the shoulder and left.

Kiefer blinked. He had only just sent them for approval. How had Velten known? Was he monitoring his workstation? He must be. A spike of anger flushed through him at the thought of them watching his every move.

Was Velten warning him? He must have known Kiefer would realise how he had accessed the information so quickly. And his message to Madeline. She hadn't even had a chance to respond, though it was obvious she would have her instructions as well.

Smoothing his expression, Kiefer sat and flipped the badge over and over in his fingers. Use it well, huh? He would do that. It must have an override to allow him through security out of hours. He wondered how far it would allow him to go and how long it would last.

Kiefer had an excuse: research for the Pre-Ed programme. He would go and view the classrooms, see what they were focussing on. And he would have a perfect topic of discussion with Madeline.

"Thank you, Minister," he murmured under his breath and logged back on to his terminal. He sketched out a skeleton of an annual plan. Just the outline. He would spend time filling in it over the next few days. After his research.

He glanced around the office; it was silent, and the overhead lights had dimmed. Everyone had left. Would it be foolish to test the badge's limits today? It might be his only chance. Tapping his desk, he thought for a moment and then entered a search query. It would keep his terminal occupied and, hopefully, make them think he was still working.

Kiefer rose, stuffed a note recorder in his jacket pocket, and collected his ID cards and badges. Then, keeping to the shadows, he skirted the edge of the office and tapped his way out into the back stairwell.

The air in the stairwell was cold after the warmth of the technology-infused office. Concrete steps and metal railings led down into darkness or up into more darkness. His eyes adjusted to the dim light as he began descending. After ten flights, and five floors he began to question his decision. His shins were burning, and he had to climb back up all those stairs. He paused at the door marked Level 2 and hesitated before using Velten's badge to open the door. He eased it open and slid through the gap, letting it click shut behind him.

Dim blue light washed over empty classrooms. Each room was walled in transparent glass, with one wall left for large screens and pictures of the alphabet, numbers, or colours, with images for each. As he passed each room the lights rose, and he started murmuring a description of the pictures on the wall into his note recorder.

Kiefer strolled around the floor, until he reached a room that was wall-to-wall ocean. A huge mammal breached the surface. As water sheeted off its skin, its beady eyes gleamed down at him. White birds wheeled above it, extending long wings with individual feathers painted in.

Mesmerised for a moment, he was suffused with memories of the rush of ocean waves over rocks, hissing and foaming before receding, and the high pitched squawks of the birds. The slightly static air was tinged with a salty tang, and he felt the breeze on his skin as if he were standing on the cliffs at the edge of Sector 17.

A door slammed and jerked him back to reality, and he spun, searching for whomever had just entered. A torch flickered across the floor, and he ducked into the sea room, and crouched in the corner. Kiefer pursed lips as he realised how stupid he was. They probably already knew he was down here. He had forgotten the cameras.

Kiefer's mind spun, trying to come up with excuses. As the footsteps drew near, echoing in the silent passageways, his heart raced, making him feel lightheaded. He hadn't been this anxious in years. Creeping around was not his forte.

The footsteps continued down the corridor, and he managed to breathe. Peering out the window, he watched a guard turn the corner. He exhaled. This was ridiculous.

Kiefer almost had heart failure again as he came face to face with the snarling image of a cat, a sleek purple cat with amber eyes that saw straight through him.

"*Coward,*" Harmony murmured. "*Where are you? I can hear your racing heartbeat from here. What are you doing?*"

"*In Pre-Ed.*"

"*How did you get down there?*"

"*Velten gave me a late pass.*"

"*Then get yourself down to sublevel two, now.*"

"*What about the cameras?*"

"*I've dealt with them.*"

"*I only ran a single query string; it will be finalising soon.*"

"Run a quadruple one next time. And stop making excuses. Move. Now!"

Kiefer crawled out of the classroom and hurried back to the stairwell. *"Where have you been?"*

"Sunbathing by the sea," she replied with heavy sarcasm.

"I couldn't find you."

"I know. I'm sorry. They cut me off. Where are you now?"

"Passing sublevel one." Kiefer puffed as he scuttled down the stairs. He was not looking forward to climbing them all again.

"Well, hurry up."

Kiefer huffed and concentrated on not falling down the stairs. He seriously needed to work on his fitness. Leaning against the wall, which read Sublevel 2, he tried to catch his breath. "I'm here," he gasped.

The door clicked, and he pushed it open, revealing… nothing. It was pitch-black, and he wasn't sure where he was. He shuffled forward, feeling the floor with his foot just to make sure there was one.

"Where am I? I can't see a thing."

"Sorry." The room lightened, and as his eyes adjusted, his jaw dropped at the 180-degree screen that filled the wall. A terminal on a desk was the only other furniture.

"What is this place?"

"I call it the peeping room. They call it the Harmony complex."

"A peeping room? You mean they have oversight here?"

"Yes. Turn the terminal on and type in this number." Harmony recited a string of numbers, and Kiefer lurched for the terminal. The curved screen came to life, filling with tables, graphs, and data points.

"Won't they know someone has been in here?"

"They'll see the log entry but not who entered it."

Kiefer frowned. "If you can manipulate data, why can't you shut it all down?"

"I wish I could. It's all sleight of hand, deception. They have too many tentacles embedded. If I shut it down, I would not survive, and neither would the planet. You need to cut the tentacles so I can be free before we destroy it."

Kiefer drifted to the screen, absorbing the data. He frowned. "Is this true data?" he asked.

Harmony chuckled. "Depends on what you call true."

Kiefer grimaced. "Depends on what they are using it for, you mean. All data can be manipulated to prove whatever you want it to."

"And what do you think they are using this data for?" Harmony asked.

The fluorescent numbers lit Kiefer's face in a sicky green hue as he scanned the screen. He took a step back and centred himself, and he gasped as the screen morphed. "Nothing good, I'm sure. Are they using a parabolic string? Reversing the numbers? Wait a minute…" Kiefer absorbed the data and gasped. "They have five gates? Why do they need five?"

"One wasn't strong enough. I almost breached it, but they had a fail-safe. And after that…"

Kiefer swallowed. "So they put in *five*? That must hurt."

There was a short silence. "It does," she said, her voice muted.

Kiefer suddenly realised they had been talking aloud and not in his head. "Is that why there are dead zones? They've curtailed your reach. You can't sustain the sectors." He blanched. "All the sectors will fail."

"Not before they've transferred the nodes over."

Kiefer traced the flow. "I don't get it. They've reversed the current, but where is it going? What are you sustaining instead?"

"I don't know, Kiefer. That's what you have to find out."

"My parents must know. They were both involved in the

initial installation. What makes you think you can trust me? That I can help you? Velten has reprogrammed me. His instructions scroll behind my eyes. I'm just a puppet."

"Are you really, Kiefer? If so, what are you doing here?"

Kiefer paced. "I don't know what are my thoughts, versus his—or yours, even."

"Yes, you do. I can feel your thoughts, and they are your own. I have only given you memories, a way to introduce myself. To show you what should have been instead of what is."

Kiefer continued pacing. The screens morphed between views as he paced. He suddenly stopped and moved to the left, his gaze zeroing in on a chart in the bottom left hand corner.

"Kiefer, it's time for you to leave. You've been here too long. You should have logged out long ago."

"In a minute," Kiefer replied absently as he inspected the chart near the base of the screen.

"Now, Kiefer. They will find you. You must leave."

"Is this correct? That there is a synapse in the library? Is that why you could reach me there?"

"What?"

"There is also a junction in the Pre-Ed. We could bypass the first gate by…"

"Kiefer, you must leave now. The security detail will be doing their rounds. You must be back in your cubicle before they get there."

"But…"

"Now, Kiefer."

"Alright, I'm going. Any chance you can send me these charts?"

"I'll try. Now, go!"

Kiefer huffed as the force of her voice drove him out of the room. He glanced back, but she shut the lights off, and he turned away, defeated. Shivering at the temperature drop in the stairwell, he peered up the unending concrete flights and then began climbing.

As Kiefer ascended, he tensed at every echo, and relief washed over him when he finally reached his floor. He lurched against the wall, dragging air into his burning lungs. His thighs and calves ached as he breathlessly slipped back through the door and walked to his workstation. Hurriedly, he shut everything down and left, trying to control his tumultuous heart. His chest ached, and he tried to slow his breathing as he walked through the security checks, smiling and joking about working all hours. He couldn't wait to get out of the Ministry building.

28

The next evening, after another day of mindless brochure writing and clandestine research, Kiefer tugged his shirt straight and scowled at himself in the mirror. He was not looking forward to an evening of stilted conversation with the daughter of Minister Velten. What was there to like?

He had a few hours yet before he was to take Madeline out to dinner, so he powered up his tablet, opened a new incognito window, and retrieved the file he had been working on. Then he sat staring at the strings as his brain computed the next command. He was reconfiguring his fulcrum programme, a security programme, to do the reverse and hack through the gates surrounding Harmony.

The blueprints he had memorised in his mother's office had included a wiring diagram, which he overlaid on Harmony's charts. He wondered how his mother had managed to get hold of it, but he was glad she had. It gave him the areas where there was a concentration of synapses, which, in turn led to the gate locations.

Overlaying the blueprint to the power consumption

charts, he found that they coincided with the power concentration spikes. He typed a few commands and ran the model, watching it spiral into the complex and efficiently breach the first gate. The program paused, searching for the next egress point. Kiefer entered the command, and the spiral continued and breached the next gate. One by one the gates were breached until Harmony stood free. He checked the timer: fifty-five minutes. Could he speed it up?

His reminder chirped and he glanced at the clock. Time to leave. Saving the file, he powered down the tablet, his mind busily trying to improve his program as he left his apartment.

Madeline was already seated at the table when he arrived, fortunately, exactly on time. Kiefer had a slight panic he was late, but he smiled as the server led him to the table. The Palm Court was an exotic eatery. The tables were well spaced, covered with pristine linen and sparkling with crystal glasses and gleaming cutlery.

They had given him a private booth upholstered in plush blue velvet that was big enough for four, so at least he and Madeline were not sitting on top of each other which was a relief. She was elegantly dressed; her black dress clung to the most interesting places, setting her figure off. Madeline smiled as he approached. Her cheeks were slightly flushed, and he wondered why.

"Madeline, it's lovely to see you. I hope all is well?"

"Yes, thank you. I was beginning to worry you weren't going to show."

Kiefer raised his eyebrows as he sat. "Surely not. I am on time." He smiled at the server as he offered him the menu.

"Oh, I already ordered. I hope you don't mind, but I like the share platter. I like to try a little bit of everything."

"Just a sparkling water for me, then," Kiefer said, handing the menu back.

"Water? Aren't you having any wine?"

Kiefer observed this more confident version of Madeline with bemusement. "I'll join you when the meal comes."

Madeline leaned forward and waved her glass of ruby red wine, almost spilling it. "You're missing out. Don't tell me you're a prude?" She took a large sip.

"Not at all. I assume this is a favourite wine of yours?"

"You don't approve."

"Of what?"

"A woman with decisiveness."

"I am pleasantly surprised. You seemed quite diffident at my mother's soiree."

Madeline stared him in the eye. "I can assure you I am not diffident."

"So I see. Why the act, then?"

Madeline shrugged. "I wasn't sure if I'd like you. Your reputation precedes you, one of action and command. I wanted to see how you treated women."

"I can assure you my mother brought me up to be well behaved."

"But you were still mind-wiped. So, something went astray."

"Unfortunately for you, I no longer remember whatever it was, so I'm afraid I can't tell you."

Madeline watched him and then grinned. "I could get you in to see the recording if you want. The record of your interrogation."

Kiefer gaped at her. This date was not proceeding at all the way he had planned. "Why would you do that?"

They were interrupted as the servers returned with silver platters of food, which soon festooned their table. Their glasses were filled, or refilled in Madeline's case, and after the brief flurry of activity, they were left in peace. Kiefer stared at all the food, enough to feed six families in the sector.

"You don't look like you have such a big appetite," he said, waiting for Madeline to begin.

"Then you would be surprised," she replied, piling food on her plate. "I have a high metabolism, so I burn it off easily. Lucky, I suppose."

"I suppose so," Kiefer murmured, selecting the fish skewers and a portion of rice. He took a bite, and the food was as delicious as it looked. "You said you were one of the first women to graduate from the Academy? Do you do a lot of work now to encourage girls to study?"

"Not really. After all, I teach Pre-Ed. It's a bit early."

"I would have thought it's never too early to introduce a love of reading or learning."

Madeline flicked him an amused glance. "You really are steeped in the latest messages, aren't you?"

Kiefer shrugged and selected another skewer, this one with what looked like rolled up, spicy meat. A mint dip came with it. "So, what do you teach?" he asked as he inhaled the aroma cautiously.

"That one's hot."

"I had a feeling it might be." He smothered it in the sauce and took a bite. Spices flooded his mouth, along with the heat, and his face flushed. "Wow," he murmured, taking a gulp of water.

"I did warn you," Madeline chuckled, watching him. She had cleared her plate and was choosing more.

"Pre-Ed is the most formative period. Isn't it when you instil the core protocols?"

"Let's not talk about work. I want to know more about you. I want to know why you were reset."

Kiefer leaned back against the plush velvet, toying with his glass. "Have you not met anyone who's been reset before?"

"No. What is it like?"

"Disorienting. I imagine it is like waking up from a coma after a period of years. You are missing all that happened in between, and you have to relearn who you are and where you fit. I wouldn't recommend it."

Madeline leaned forward. "But how did you feel? Were you angry? I would be."

"Why would I be angry? I don't know what I lost, so I don't miss it, if that's what you mean."

"But you were a Devender, a commander, and a very good one, I heard."

Kiefer shrugged again, repressing the regret and, yes, the anger he felt. "I don't remember being a Devender, so how can I miss it?"

"Don't you think it is scary how much control the Ministry has over us all?"

Kiefer laughed. "This, from you? You know perfectly well the Ministry has our best interests at heart. Do you not believe so?"

"Of course. Just checking."

A chill spread over Kiefer's skin, removing the last of the spice's heat. She was making sure he had been mind-wiped. Had Velten put her up to it?

"What's the earliest thing you remember?"

"What is your earliest memory?" he asked in return, picking up his wine glass the waiter had filled.

"Oh, the usual. Playing in the garden, we had a swing. I used to peg sheets around it to make a house."

"You lived outside the city when you were young?"

"Yes, we have a home up in the Header Valley. Maybe you'll get to visit with me one day. It is beautiful, though a bit antiquated. It's not connected to the net or anything, so my father won't stay there, but my mother prefers it."

"So, your mother still lives there?"

"Yes." Madeline waved a server over. "Where did you

grow up?" She leaned back as the servers cleared the table, though her sharp green eyes never left Kiefer.

"In the city. My parents have always worked at the complex. They were at the height of the discoveries. Children were not allowed in the labs, so I believe I had a carer."

"You make it all sound so cold."

"The mind-wipe makes it cold." Kiefer reminded her gently. "You may be given a record of your life, but it is emotionless. I have no idea how I felt about any of it."

"Which is why it is so rare." Madeline straightened. "I'll get you in so you can see what you were like before. You should know."

"There is no point. It won't change anything. The Ministry knows best."

Madeline shook her finger at him. "That's just the reset talking. Deep down, you want to know what happened. It'll be easy. No one will know, and it will be our secret."

"How will no one know? The record log will show we viewed it. You can't keep it secret, Madeline, and we shouldn't."

"Ah. You'll see." Her eyes glittered at the thought. "We'll do it tonight, before you change your mind and the reset takes over again. Relax, Kiefer. This will be fun."

"Easy for you to say. You've not been reset. I don't want to get into further trouble."

Madeline laughed. "You'll be with me. You won't get into trouble."

Kiefer wasn't so sure. But if Madeline knew a way to circumvent being monitored by the Ministry, then he needed to know. He observed her. She was verging on an emotional overload, like she was on a high. He suddenly wondered if she was. Her behaviour was so different from before.

Dessert arrived, and she calmed down with the cool ices.

It didn't last. A server dropped the spoon in her lap as

she cleared the table, and Madeline exploded into recrimi-
nations.

"It was an accident, Madeline. Calm down."

"Calm down? She's ruined my dress. It's my favourite!
She'll pay for it to be cleaned or replaced. Find me the
manager. I want to make a complaint. I'm not paying for this
meal after this."

Kiefer wondered how he ever thought her shy. This
woman had teeth and wasn't afraid to use them.

The manager arrived, and Madeline allowed him to
escort her to the powder room. Along the way, he spouted
platitudes and agreed to sack the server, who cowered against
the wall, terrified.

"Go and stay in the kitchen until we leave. She won't
know you haven't been fired," Kiefer said to her as he stood
to go and get their coats. He tried to pay the bill, but they
wouldn't accept the credits and were profusely apologetic.
He couldn't even leave a gratuity, though he was sure the cost
would wipe out the server's wages for a month. As he waited
for their coats to be retrieved, he heard the name Ferris
mentioned by a group seated in the booth nearest the exit.

He turned slightly so he could see them. A group of
middle-aged men, all in smart suits. Ministry men. He paid
attention.

"It's to be a silent auction."

"He'll make his money then. Virgin twins don't come
around often."

"They may only be virgins once, but I'll wait until it's
cheaper. They'll still be worth it."

Kiefer stiffened. They had to be talking about Chiva and
Annie. What was Ferris thinking of? He grimaced. Money,
of course.

"Thank goodness we get paid tomorrow. I'll take my
chances."

"He's not daft. Of course he timed it with payday. Did you know you could list whether you're prepared to accept a second or third slot? He'll have a full house this weekend, just you watch."

Kiefer turned away in disgust as Madeline reappeared. A scowl etched her face as she silently accepted her wrap.

"Would you like me to escort you home?" Kiefer asked as they passed through the glass doors.

"Of course not. I told you, you need to see your recording."

Kiefer thought she wanted to see it more than him. "I thought you didn't want anything to do with the Ministry tonight?"

"This is not work; it's much more interesting."

"I don't think I want to see it," Kiefer admitted. Having already seen it, he knew it wasn't a pretty sight.

"Coward. You might learn something about yourself that you don't know. Come on."

Kiefer followed her along the path towards the trio of tall glass buildings that rose above Maincore. They were the tallest buildings in the city, a constant reminder of Ministry oversight. When you knew how far down it went as well, it truly was an amazing construction.

Kiefer hurried to catch her up; Madeline had a very long stride. "Where are we going?" he asked. They were about two blocks away from the Maincore complex.

"You'll see."

Kiefer's stomach stirred uneasily. He was glad he hadn't eaten too much. There was no way this was going to be as simple as Madeline had made out. "Madeline, I can't afford to be caught in the middle of deviant behaviour. I am already under observation."

"No, you're not. I checked. My father likes you. You're the working example of a reset. You show that it worked, and if he can't trust you now, then what is the point? I know he removed the autobots, and I believe he's stopped tracking your devices. He'll never know, so stop panicking."

Kiefer exhaled. If that were true, it would make life a lot easier. The question was, could he trust Madeleine? He wasn't sure.

Madeline darted down a side alley between the red brick academy building and an office building. Kiefer followed.

"These are the women's colleges," Madeline said. "There are many female students now. These buildings back on to the Academy and provide the women's entry. They also have an entry point into the Pre-Ed section for the kids. You never see the kids going in the front door, now, do you?"

Kiefer had never thought about it. "No, you don't."

"You don't want carers and parents clogging up the front entrance, so we have a back entrance. With all the coming and goings, it is not manned. It's for four-year-olds, so why would you need to monitor it?" She laughed.

"I suppose not," Kiefer agreed, keeping his voice neutral. It seemed a bit short-sighted to him, but he wasn't going to complain.

Madeline tucked her hand in his arm. "Stay with me; otherwise, you might get accosted, being a single man in the women's quarters. Men are at a premium, you know." Her laugh echoed down the empty alleyway, and Kiefer scanned their surroundings.

Red-brick buildings rose around them, more traditionally built than the glass forest that was Maincore. It was hard to imagine they were connected, as they looked so different. The upper windows were lit by yellow glows, but all the lower floors were in darkness.

"Accommodations are on the top floors. Lower levels are all lecture rooms and offices." Madeline tapped into the accommodation. "I have rooms here," she said as she pushed him through the door. It clicked shut with a soft snick. Kiefer paused as his eyes adjusted to the gloom, and Madeline tugged him forward. "Come on, before someone comes downstairs. We have to go up to the second floor, the entrance to Pre-Ed is off the common room. The Pre-Ed students often observe or take classes, so this is our entry point to the ministry building. Parents go through the doors at the end of the alley."

Kiefer followed Madeline down the clinical corridors. The blue lino floors curving up the side of the walls reminded him more of a hospital. Silent classrooms watched them through empty windows as they passed, and the only proof of their passing was the echo of their footsteps.

Madeline tapped them into the Pre-Ed department, and Kiefer's eyes widened as he recognised the classroom with the sea mural on the wall. She gestured towards it. "That's my classroom this semester; we're studying the sea. The kids will probably never even see it, but they should know what our planet is made up of and what Harmony is protecting for them.

"Do any of the children ask to go and see it? Do you do excursions for them?"

"No, don't be silly. They can see it all on the vid."

"They can't smell the tang of the water or feel the sea breeze."

Madeline turned and raised an eyebrow. "And that would make a difference? Do you remember that?"

Not anymore," Kiefer said sadly, "though the transcript said I had been to Sector 17, so I have seen the sea." He looked around. "Isn't this floor monitored? Won't the surveillance cameras pick us up?"

"No, they didn't install them here. That's why there are human guards who walk the floors. But during out of hours, they only do one sweep, just before midnight, so we have an hour, and they will have completed it by the time we return."

Kiefer cringed. He had been skulking around for no reason. "That's only the Pre-Ed floor. What about the others? The interrogation rooms are in the Devender building. What do you expect to find here?"

"They are not the only interrogation rooms, silly." Madeline grinned at him, her eyes sparkling. She waved a card at him. "I have the magic ticket. No one will know, I promise you. You worry too much, Kiefer."

Kiefer gave in and followed, keeping his mouth shut.

He observed her every move, but all she did was tap her card. The lights dimmed slightly as she did so, but he didn't notice any other change. She hurried him down the corridor and into the concrete stairwell. He shivered in the night air.

"We need the tenth floor."

"Doesn't your magic card work in lifts?" Kiefer asked with a grimace as they began climbing.

"Sorry, no. Only the key pads. The lifts run on the central computer bank. They'd see us straight away. Whatever you do, do not use the lifts."

Kiefer wondered why she was telling him all this. Did she really believe he was safe because he was a reset? Or was she setting him up for some big fall? Not knowing what to think, he concentrated on not falling behind as she rushed up the concrete steps.

The stairs were cold, narrow, and never-ending.

29

At the landing to the seventh floor of the echoing stairwell, Madeline spun on him. "You owe me for this. Don't forget, I know you snuck in."

"With your help. I know how you get in now." Kiefer was surprised he managed to get the words out, his lungs were burning.

"They won't believe you."

"But I'm a reset. Why would I lie?" he gasped.

"Because you know you were a Devender and they took it away. Anyway, my father would believe me over you."

"Is this why you brought me in here? So you could blackmail me?" Kiefer braced himself against the wall. These stairs were going to kill him.

"A girl has to work with what she's got to get ahead in this world. You, my dear Kiefer, are all I have, and you will be useful. You have an insight into my father I'll never have. You can help persuade him that I am suitable for Int-Ed."

Kiefer tensed. "Int-Ed? Why would you want to work there?"

"It's more interesting. Someone else can brainwash little

kids. I want to be involved in the good stuff. But my father won't let me. You are going to help me convince him, or I'll tell him you've been here."

Kiefer paused on the step below her and held his side. "All you've done so far is drag me up a million steps and given me a stitch," he complained, and she laughed.

Madeline bent over him and dragged her fingernail under his chin. "Oh, don't worry, I will give you so much more," she said, deepening her voice, and Kiefer swallowed. She kissed him lightly on the lips and spun away, skipping up the next flight of stairs. The woman was indefatigable. Kiefer puffed after her. He really was out of shape, something else he could blame on the reset.

Kiefer stomped up the last few steps and stood panting behind Madeline. "Are you inhuman or something?" She wasn't even out of breath.

Madeline flashed him a grin. "Or something," she murmured. "Now from here, it gets tricky. Keep quiet, not a sound, and hug the shadowed walls. We will skirt the outer walls until we reach V-22. Then we'll enter. Understood?"

"Understood."

Madeline led the way, exaggerating her steps. Kiefer's lips twitched. Did she think it made her quieter? He followed anyway. His skin pricked as they paused outside V-22, and his heart rate sped up. He didn't want to enter. But Madeline didn't even pause; she tapped her magic card, the door snicked open, and she pulled him in behind her.

"This is the only room without the two-way windows and recording suite. It's a viewing room, really, but we can access the central database from here.

"How do you know all this?" Kiefer asked, watching as her fingers flew over the console.

"What do you think a bored child does when her Ministry father is home?"

"Eavesdrop," Kiefer replied, his voice a whisper.

"Exactly. Here's your record. You were wiped on 3223-653.2."

"You checked? You planned to come here all along, didn't you?"

"Sit in the chair. You can watch on the big screen."

Kiefer's response was automatic. "No."

Madeline ran her tongue over her lips and smiled. "Sit," she commanded.

She hit a button, and the recording began with Kiefer entering the interrogation room, escorted by the guards. Madeline pushed Kiefer into the chair, and he sat rigid. He started to sweat, and Madeline leaned over him from behind. He shuddered.

"You remember something," she whispered in his ear, and he shivered. "You're afraid. You don't look afraid on the screen, do you? Look at you, confident, commanding. Then they strap you down, and now you realise something is amiss."

Madeline ran her hands down his body, leaning her chest against his head. "So tense, so rigid. What are you afraid of?"

Kiefer jerked at the same time his image on the screen did from the first jolt of current. His breath came in gasps.

"Are you reliving it?" Madeline asked, moving around to watch his face. She wiped the sweat off his forehead.

Kiefer dragged his eyes away from the screen.

"No, no, watch." She pushed his face back towards the screen. "This is your only chance. They tied you down, and look, even the tech said you told the truth, and they didn't believe you. How does that make you feel? You weren't a traitor, and you didn't need wiping. All for nothing." She peered at the screen and dug her fingers into his forearm.

Kiefer gripped the arms of the chair. "Why are you showing me this?" he growled. She was riveted to the screen.

"What?"

"Why are you showing me this?" he repeated, looking up at her. Her eyes glittered, and her face was flushed.

"Why? Because you need to know. You need to know what the Ministry really is, not the view from your lovely new memories."

"But you want to be part of it?"

"So? I know what it is, so I can manipulate it. But I am a woman, and they still have antiquated ideas. Harmony is female. So is your mother. Why can't I be involved, too?"

"What does your father say?"

"He still thinks I'm his little girl. I need you to show him I'm not. Get me into Maincore, Kiefer, and I'll give you your memories back."

Kiefer stiffened. "What?"

"You heard me."

"But that's not possible."

"Says who?"

"I was wiped. Reset. They don't keep original memories."

"What if they do?"

"Where? Where do they keep them?"

"Ah, help me, and I'll help you."

Kiefer lurched out of the chair, His mouth was so dry he couldn't swallow, and his unsettled stomach threatened to return his recent meal. Was she telling the truth? He didn't think so. She had admitted she was good at manipulating. Was that what she was doing to him?

"If I get you into Maincore, you'll get my memories back," Kiefer repeated as if in shock.

"Yes."

"What if you can't?"

"What if *you* can't?" she replied, running her hands over

his back. "Still so tense. I have a remedy for that. Had enough? Shall I switch it off?"

"Yes," Kiefer said, averting his eyes. He really didn't want to see his spasming body; it made his heart stutter and his body ache in some second-hand memory.

"Do we have a deal?"

He didn't have much choice. "Yes," he whispered.

"Poor Kiefer doesn't know where to turn. You are stuck between powerful people, all with their own agenda. I promise, help me into Int-Ed, and I'll leave you be. We wouldn't really be compatible. I don't want tarnished goods. I want a real man."

Thank goodness, Kiefer thought and then tensed. Had he said that aloud? "Your father thinks otherwise," he managed to say.

Madeline shrugged. "He'll get used to it. I have my eye on someone else anyway." She looked around. "It's time we left. Wasn't that fun? We need to return the same way we came. So, once out of this room, silence."

Kiefer nodded, glad to be leaving the clinical room. He had honestly thought she was going to wire him back up. His heart rate settled as that possibility faded. He followed her out of the room, still jittery.

Pausing at the top of the stairs, Kiefer cursed under his breath and began descending. They made it out of the building with ease, and Kiefer breathed heavily as they slipped back into the women's college and down the sterile corridor. Madeline saved him from having to come up with an excuse to leave when she held out her hand and said, "Thank you for your company, Kiefer. It was a pleasure. I look forward to our next adventure."

Kiefer gaped at her for a moment before shaking her hand and numbly watching her ascend the stairs. Escaping while he could, his head spun and exhaustion swept through him. He had been through a gamut of emotions this evening, and Madeline had controlled everything. Glad to return to the sanctuary of his apartment, he spent the rest of the evening stretching out his muscles, and trying to figure out what Madeline really wanted.

30

The next day, having received Velten's approval for his Pre-Ed campaign, Kiefer descended the steps of the Maincorc building, glad to be free of the Ministry for two whole days. Large screens rose on either side of the entrance, displaying happy families and benevolent ministers. Cheerful children tumbled about in a soft play area while their parents looked on, all funded by the Ministry. On the paved concourse, a three-tiered fountain flowed; the water sparkled in the spring sunshine.

Kiefer inhaled the clogging city air and wished, not for the first time, that he was out in the sectors and away from all the artificial, claustrophobic buildings. A fine mist tingled on his neck as the breeze blew the spray from the fountain. He slowed when he saw a stocky, grey-haired Devender waiting at the bottom of the steps.

The man straightened as he approached but turned away when Kiefer flicked his fingers at him and murmured his address as he passed. Kiefer wasn't sure who he was, but he was confident that he shouldn't be seen talking to him. The man started walking as if he hadn't noticed him, and Kiefer breathed a sigh of relief, glad he had instinctively remembered the warn-away sign and that the man had recognised it.

He strode home as if nothing untoward had happened, aware that the Devender followed at a distance. Greeting the doorman, he warned him he was expecting a visitor and to send him straight up. The doorman accepted the credits and murmured, "Of course, sir."

Kiefer crossed the entry hall and frowned as the calm voice of the Ministry advert told him all about the latest investment by the Ministry in his security. He looked up at the ceiling and then back to the doorman. "I don't remember there being a Ministry feed in here."

"No, sir, they installed it yesterday. For free."

"They didn't enter my apartment, did they?"

"Of course not, sir." The doorman was affronted. "I watched them work. They only had access to the vestibule and the lift."

The lift arrived, and Kiefer entered, not feeling particularly reassured and thinking nothing was ever for free. They would, no doubt, increase his rent as a result. He would have to check.

Kiefer stood looking out of his window as the lift chimed, announcing his visitor. He turned towards the door and waited, having already set the door lock to open automatically. As the Devender stepped out of the lift, his lined face broke into an enormous smile. "Commander Gallante, I'm so glad to see you looking well."

Kiefer tilted his head and smiled back in return. "I have been better," he replied.

"I was concerned about you. We hadn't heard about

what happened; otherwise, we would have protested sooner. I swear, we never blamed you."

"We?"

"Your troop, sir. You didn't think we would betray you, did you?"

Kiefer shrugged. "I'm afraid I don't know. I don't remember being a commander or being responsible for a troop."

The Devender's face tightened, and the lines deepened around his mouth. "So, it's true. That bastard did blame you."

"You'll have to explain. I'm sorry, but I don't know who you are." Kiefer moved over to the bar. "Drink?" he asked as he poured out two glasses. He didn't wait for a response but handed the man a glass.

The Devender smiled as he took the glass and inhaled the drink's aroma. "There are some things you still remember," he said. "I'm Jeffers, your horse master and sometime assistant. And this is my favourite spirit."

Kiefer frowned as he rolled the name around. He shook his head and then sipped his drink. "I'm told that some of my memories may return by association. If you could remind me of some of the things we did together, I may be able to remember more." He shrugged. "Though there is no guarantee."

"It's criminal, sir. That they should do such a thing, and to you. You are one of the best commanders we've got, and we sorely need you in the field." Jeffers gritted his teeth. "Ferris is dangerous. He'll get us all killed without trying." A brief smile flashed over his face. "Though that rebel leader, Lorne, had him marked."

"Oh? Maybe you should begin at the beginning and tell me all that you can." Kiefer indicated the chair and made himself comfortable on the sofa.

"We first met when you took command of the 22nd," said Jeffers. "Your first commission, though you wouldn't know it, you were so assured. A natural, if I may say so, sir." He cleared his throat. "I joined at the same time. Our first sortie was to Sector 17. Claims of smuggling."

Kiefer listened to his life history, growing angrier the more Jeffers spoke. His life, a life he had enjoyed and been good at, had been wiped away without a second thought. He stood and refilled their glasses.

Jeffers leaned forward as his narrative reached Sector 45. "You did good things there, sir. Saved those people, set them on a good path. That you should be punished…" He buried his nose in his glass.

"History. Don't worry about it. It cannot be undone. At least the people of Sector 45 are well and coping; that is good news."

"That's one of the reasons I came to find you." Jeffers took a deep breath. "Ferris has got it in for you. Now he's made commander in your place, he thinks he is untouchable." Jeffers stared into his glass. "He is vindictive, sir. He was cursing the leader, Lorne. And then he started on Sector 45, how they were lucky they had been left alone, and how that could easily change." He looked up. "I wouldn't put it past him to report that the rebels are in 45, sir."

Kiefer frowned. "But how does that benefit him?"

"He is trying to be you, sir. He wants the accolades without the effort. At the same time, he wants to destroy your successes."

"But why? What did I do to him?"

"Nothing, sir."

"I must have done something."

Jeffers shrugged. "I think he is jealous. The men haven't taken to him, even more so now they know what happened to you."

"But why take it out on 45?"

"Because you made friends there, I think." Jeffers paused. "That rebel leader, Lorne. She had a younger sister called Ciely."

Kiefer frowned. "Did she?"

"Yes, Ciely was trying to find out how to get to Maincore. Her boyfriend got taken in a raid that went wrong. Seemed to think it was her sister's fault. Lorne wouldn't rescue him. Some contention there, I think. Happened before we ever got to Sector 45."

"And what does that have to do with me?" Kiefer asked, bewildered.

"There's a rumour that Ferris brought her with him to Maincore when he returned from his last sortie. Turned her over to Int-Ed. I think she was trying to rescue her boyfriend." He sipped from his glass. "Ferris encouraged her. I'm sure I saw him talking to her. Anything to stir a bit of angst between sisters."

"She's got no chance. Her boyfriend would have been wiped by now. That's even if he is still alive; a rebel is more likely to be executed. She won't be able to escape from Int-Ed. Do you know if she is still alive?"

Jeffers shrugged. "They won't wipe her until they've got all they need to know out of her."

"Why are you telling me this?"

"You and the rebel leader, Lorne, ah, seemed to get on quite well, sir."

"We did?"

"Yes, sir. I would have told you sooner, only I didn't know where you were. It took me a while to track you down."

"I'm not blaming you. I'm thankful you found me. But I don't see how I can help Ciely, especially if Ferris has already handed her over." Kiefer scrunched his face up in thought and then twisted his lips. "He seems to be a magnet for young, impressionable people."

"You truly don't remember any of us, sir?"

Kiefer grimaced and shook his head. "I'm sorry. I don't remember the Devenders at all. I only know I hate working in an office!"

"The bastards," Jeffers said.

"Indeed."

Jeffers drained his glass and sighed. "I can't believe you'll not be back."

"Maybe I won't be able to return to duty, but I can certainly look out for 45. I do still have friends. I can get you transferred out of Ferris' and into Commander Laithe's unit if you want me to. He would do me a favour."

"That would be good of you, sir. I have another week's leave, and I would prefer not to return to Ferris' unit."

Kiefer nodded. "Then that's what I'll do. Though if anyone is able to go to 45 to help, it's likely to be Julian."

"That's alright, sir. I'd be glad to fight for those people. They deserve to live in peace. They're not harming anyone."

"Talk like that will get you into trouble," Kiefer said with a grin. "There is one other thing you could do for me, if you could." He explained his need for a signal booster, one as strong as possible.

"Of course, sir. No problem. It was good seeing you, sir."

"It was good seeing you too, Jeffers. Make sure you visit again." Kiefer rose and escorted Jeffers to the door. He gripped the man's arm. "Thank you for taking the time to find me. I appreciate it." His voice was gruff, and he cleared his throat.

"Always, sir," Jeffers replied. He entered the lift, and the doors swished shut.

Kiefer left a message on Julian's answering machine asking him to contact him when he was home. Not being in the Devender hierarchy, he had no idea what his friend's schedule looked like, though Julian had left a message that he had been assigned to Sector 21. That had been two weeks ago, but if Ferris was back, Julian should be back soon.

The Staffens were still at Julian's apartment. Kiefer needed to find them an alternate hidey-hole before Julian returned. They couldn't hide forever, though. Maybe he should shift them to Sector 45 once things settled down there, until he could figure out how to free Harmony.

His stomach tightened at the thought, and a pair of violet eyes stared back at him from his window. He knew what Jeffers had reported was correct. Memories were resurfacing. The ambush, Merianne's cool hands on his feverish skin, an ancient lullaby. They were all jumbled with the tantalising violet eyes and flashes of dark underground tunnels.

Kiefer sighed and sat in his chair, staring out at the cloud-filled sky, letting his mind drift. He would have no peace until the memories settled, and then he would consider how to get Annie and Chiva out of Ferris' clutches. If Ferris was selling them off, then they had just run out of time. He needed to get them out tonight. And what to do about Ciely? He had no idea. Just the thought of entering the Int-Ed building made his guts clench, but somehow, he would make Ferris pay for his actions.

It was dark and the lights of Maincore were twinkling far below when Kiefer stirred. Time for Ferris to start paying for his actions. Kiefer would take great pleasure in causing the man as many problems as he could.

31

I t was nearly midnight when Kiefer banged on the ornately engraved black door. He swayed as he shook out the frothy lace frill at his cuffs, waiting for the door to open. When it did, he had to suppress a grin at the stupefied expression on Ferris' face.

"Kiefer, mate, what are you doing here?"

Kiefer's grin grew, and he swayed a bit more. "Heard you had a party. We came to join you."

"We?" Ferris asked as the lines creasing his face deepened.

"Come on, girls." Kiefer fell through the door with two gaudily dressed women in his arms. One had ringlets of brunette curls, and the other was blond. "Brought my own girls with me," Kiefer slurred, displaying them proudly.

"Good for you, mate, but could you take them somewhere else? I have a full house tonight."

"It's full now, good show. Ladies, lead me to a good time." Kiefer barged past Ferris, not giving him a chance to respond, leaving him to seal the door against any further late comers.

Kiefer dropped into the nearest armchair, pulling the brunette with him. He kissed her as she peeled back his shirt and rubbed his bare chest while the other tried to undo his trousers. His cloak puddled around his gleaming boots.

"Kiefer, mate, not here. Take them to a room," Ferris said, a tinge of desperation in his voice.

"This is a room," Kiefer said around kissing the girl.

Ferris paced, running his hands through his hair. "Ladies, please, let me show you a room with a bed."

"A chair is sometimes better, you know." Kiefer chuckled, waving his free hand. "More concentrated, y'know."

Ferris rolled his eyes and tried to drag a girl off Kiefer. "Please, your father's here."

"What?" Kiefer sat upright in shock and shoved the girl away from him.

"He can't find you here, mate."

"How long has he been here?"

"About twenty minutes so you're safe. He'll only just be starting, but you need to leave now."

"Who's he with?"

"A couple of kids. You don't know 'em. Now, come on, get up."

"We'll get him up fer yer love, if yer give us a chance," the brunette said as she leered at Ferris.

The other girl tangled herself around him. "You're a nice one. Want a bit of fun? We haven't had a foursome in ages."

"Leave off. I'm not interested." Ferris tried to untangle himself.

"Ah, prefer boys, do you?"

"No, wait. Kiefer, where are you going?"

"So, you do like girls. You're just playing hard to get, eh? Jilly, let's make it hard for him." Her hands plunged down his trousers as Jilly wrapped her arm around his head and pressed his face into her chest. Ferris' voice was muffled as he struggled, but the ladies had him down on the floor, trousers off and writhing, in no time.

Kiefer checked the downstairs rooms: occupied, but not by the person he was searching for. He rushed up the stairs, silently opening doors on occupied rooms. Ferris hadn't been lying when he had said he had a full house. Kiefer continued to search until his horrified gaze saw a scene that would haunt him for many days after.

His father had Annie splayed on the bed. He had pulled her down the bed so he could reach her while he forced Chiva's face against his groin. The boy's arms were tied behind his back. He was kneeling on the floor and gagging as the man forced him down. The boy's fists were white and straining against his bonds. "You need to get me nice and ready for your sister, boy," Kiefer's father crooned. "I like it nice and rough, so you just keep trying."

Fury and disgust ripped through Kiefer, and before he knew it, his belt knife was in his hand. "Well, that's fortunate, then, isn't it?" he hissed as he leapt across the room and coldly slit his father's throat. His father's eyes flew open in shock before he collapsed back on the bed. As his flaccid body slid onto the floor, blood spurted from his throat. He gurgled as Chiva flinched back in shock and tried to squirm away from him.

Kiefer cut the boy's bonds. "Get dressed," he said, keeping his voice calm before moving to Annie. He cut the tethers holding her down and covered her with a sheet. "Annie, it's all over now. I'm here to take you home," he whispered as the shuddering girl curled into a ball.

"Chiva, find a robe or a cloak, quick. I can't carry her out in a sheet."

Chiva came back with a thick robe, which he held out with trembling hands. Kiefer wrapped it around Annie and scooped her up into his arms. He considered Chiva; the boy's eyes were wild and filled with horror. "You alright? Think you can follow me?" he asked.

Chiva nodded jerkily, but Kiefer knew he was in shock. The boy was dressed haphazardly, his buttons mismatched, though he had his shoes on right. After leading Chiva down the stairs, Kiefer skirted past the grunting Ferris, now entwined with both ladies. He nodded to the brunette as he left, and she gave him a slow wink and a grin as he headed for the door. Kiefer instructed Chiva to wrap himself in his cloak. Then he unsealed the door, and they hurried down the stairs and out into the street.

Kiefer glanced at Chiva as he drifted over to the window and stared out over the twinkling lights of Maincore. The boy was still numb with shock, his face pale. Annie was shivering in his arms, a constant tremble. No doubt, a combination of fear and shock. He carried her into the bathroom and gently placed her on the toilet seat.

"How about a nice hot bath?" he said, turning on the water as she stared at him out of empty eyes. He poured in a scented bath oil and a sweet aroma filled the air.

Kiefer closed the door behind him and wearily crossed the room. Reaching under the counter, he placed three crystal tumblers on the bench. They sparkled in the soft lamplight. Kiefer flicked the blood-speckled ruffles expertly off his hand and sloshed an amber liquid from a fancy bottle into the glasses before shoving one towards Chiva and knocking the other one back. He inhaled deeply and refilled his glass. Picking up the third glass, he went over to tap on the door. "Annie, care to join us in a drink?" he asked, placing the glass on the floor just inside the door before closing it again.

Chiva sipped the drink and choked. His eyes watered, but he took a deeper gulp, rinsed his mouth, and then knocked the rest back as Kiefer had done. His face flushed bright pink.

Kiefer refilled Chiva's glass, carefully placed the bottle on the counter, and moved over to the low chairs. He relaxed into one and closed his eyes, balancing his glass on his leg.

He heard Chiva sit in the chair opposite him and ruminated on the right thing to say. They sat in silence, with only the occasional sloshing of water reaching them through the closed bathroom door.

"Do you want to talk about it?" Kiefer asked, not opening his eyes.

"Not really," Chiva replied.

"Sometimes, it's better to talk about it than let it fester. It always becomes a much larger problem when you leave it."

"What's to talk about? He was disgusting. I wanted to kill the bastard. There I said it. Does it make it go away?" Chiva said, biting the words off.

"Of course not," Kiefer said thankful that he had dispatched his father before Chiva could. One less burden for such young shoulders to carry. "But you've said it out loud, acknowledged the feeling. That makes a difference."

"What about you? You killed that man. How does that make you feel?"

Kiefer turned the question around in his mind. He wasn't sure how he felt. "Confused," he said, choosing honesty. "Part relieved, part horrified, part sad."

"Will they come looking for you?"

"Why?"

"Someone has to be blamed for killing him."

"It won't be me. I wasn't there, after all. There are plenty of other suspects they can interrogate. Let's hope they pick Ferris."

Annie's voice came from the bathroom door. "He had cameras set up in all the rooms; he recorded them."

Kiefer rolled his head and opened one eye. She was wrapped in his bathrobe, which had been hanging on the back of the door. Her skin was pink. *Well-scrubbed,* he thought. She waggled her empty glass at him, and he waved her towards the bench. She drifted over, her bare feet silent on his carpet, and carefully filled her glass halfway, as he had done. "They'll know it was you," she said as she came and sat on the carpet beside Chiva.

Chiva placed a gentle hand on the back of her neck, and she leaned against his leg. Kiefer closed his eye. *They will help each other,* he thought. Then another thought followed disconcertingly fast: *Who will help me?*

"I found the control room while I was looking for you. I disabled the cameras, destroyed the console, and wiped the disk," Kiefer said with a feral grin. "There's no record of me ever being there."

The next morning, Kiefer was woken from his restless sleep on the sofa by the insistent buzz of his communicator. He lay frowning at the ceiling as he tried to place the buzz. Untangling himself from his blanket, he staggered over to the box and pressed a button. "Yes?" he said as he rubbed his stubbly chin, wincing at the bright sunlight flooding the room. He really shouldn't have drunk so much last night.

"Technician Gallante?"

"Yes?"

"I'm very sorry, sir, but I have some bad news. I have to inform you that your father was killed last night," the voice said nervously.

"What? How? What happened?"

"Erm, the details are still being compiled, but we need you to come down to the station and formally identify him."

"I don't understand. Where was he? At home? Was it an intruder?"

"Sir, please, I'll explain more when you come down the station."

"Does my mother know?"

"Yes, sir, we called her first, but she was distraught. She asked us to call you. Once you identify the bo… I mean, your father, we will transit you to her. She shouldn't be on her own at a time like this."

Kiefer stared at the wall. A loud hissing noise drowned out the man's voice. He tried to control the tremble shivering through him. He had killed him; he had killed his own father.

"Sir? Are you still there?"

"Yes." Kiefer cleared his throat. "Yes," he said more loudly.

The voice was sympathetic. "I know it's difficult, sir, but if you could come straight away. We can't hold the news for long, and the details will be out soon enough."

"Of course. I'll leave straight away."

"Ask for Officer Trent at the desk."

"Trent, very well. Thank you." Kiefer pressed the button to disconnect and gripped the counter. When he looked up, Chiva and Annie were standing beside him.

"That man was your father?" Annie asked in horror.

Kiefer sighed. "Yes. I am so sorry."

"But you must feel terrible," she gasped. She reached up and hugged him. "We didn't know. I'm so sorry. And last night, all you did was care for us."

Chiva swallowed. "You killed him because of us."

"I killed him because he deserved it," Kiefer said, pushing away from the counter. "I have no regrets, and neither should you. He can't hurt anyone else now." He rubbed his face. "Look, I need to go and speak to these people and see my mother. I'll be back soon. Will you wait for me to return?"

Chiva smiled, but his eyes were still sad. "Of course. We have nowhere else to go."

"I'll be back," Kiefer promised as he grabbed his cloak.

"Kiefer," Annie said. "You're not dressed."

Kiefer stopped short and looked down. His mind grappled with the fact that he was only wearing his spare robe and sleeping pants. He must be more shocked than he realised. "Right, good point." He hurried into his bedroom and came out dressed in a black shirt and slacks, his hair tousled. "Do I have everything now?"

"Drink this." Annie handed him a glass, and Kiefer knocked it back, gasping as the liquid hit the back of his throat. "Now you're ready," she said, a catch in her voice.

Annie and Chiva huddled in front of the newsfeed and watched the news break. Reporters crawled all around Ferris' house, reporting the sordid details with great relish. Speculation on the purpose of his business was rife, and he was filmed being led way in cuffs, his weaselly face red and furious.

The news report confirmed that Lord Gallante's son had identified the body and cut to a brief view of an ashen-faced Kiefer entering his mother's apartment building. He had to fend off reporters as he made his way up the steps. The cords of his neck stood out as he clenched his jaw, refusing to comment.

News followed of Ferris' arrest. He was charged with the murder of Lord Gallante, though he protested his innocence and accused Kiefer Gallante. This, as the reporter said, was impossible, as Kiefer Gallante had, of course, been recently reset.

The report went on to explain how Lord Gallante's son, once a commander of the 22nd Unit of Devenders, had recently been re-educated on the core mandates after his last sortie into the sectors and transitioned to the Ministry. A talented technician, he was now part of the Ministry of Information, under Minister Velten.

Later, a fraught and strained-looking Kiefer came back down the steps and made a simple statement honouring his father's achievements and asking for privacy at this difficult time. He looked visibly distressed.

It was dark out, and Annie was busy cooking when the door cycled and Kiefer walked in. Pausing in the middle of the room, he stared around him blindly, looking drained and lost. Annie and Chiva exchanged worried glances, and then Chiva steered Kiefer to a chair. He looked like he was about to collapse.

"They are like vultures," Kiefer said, his usually rich voice, thin and scratchy, "sucking you dry."

"The reporters?" Annie asked carefully.

Kiefer looked in her direction, but she didn't think he saw her. "The Ministry."

"I think you mean leeches," Annie said, sitting beside him.

"Do I?" Kiefer asked, though Annie knew he wasn't really paying attention.

He wouldn't eat or drink anything, and pushed the twin's offering away with revulsion, but he was persuaded into his room. Chiva helped him undress, assisted him into his bed, and flicked off the light, but by the gleam of Kiefer's eyes, Chiva knew he wasn't asleep. He shut the door, leaving Kiefer to his thoughts and his privacy.

"What do you think will happen next?" Annie asked as they sat and played with the food; their appetites had disappeared with the arrival of Kiefer's agonised expression.

"I have no idea, but whatever he needs, we'll help him. He saved us, Annie, and he's not asked for anything in return. I wish I'd spoken to him instead of Ferris."

"So do I," Annie whispered.

They watched the vid screen late into the night, learning more than they ever wanted to know about the accomplishments of Kiefer's father and, with more interest, of Kiefer's career to date. Annie quietly checked on Kiefer on a regular basis, but he was finally sleeping, and she let him be.

Chiva squirmed slightly, as Kiefer's accomplishments scrolled on the screen. Kiefer had discovered the fulcrum function and designed the Multi-Mem processor. He was a human computer, one of the most intelligent men Chiva had ever met.

He flushed as he met his sister's cynical eye; he knew nothing in comparison.

"I'm so sorry, Annie," he whispered. "I'll take you home if you want. Kiefer would help us."

"No." Annie shook her head. "He needs our help. Something else happened today. He didn't look sad; he's in shock."

32

Julian turned up the next day, horrified by the news plastered across the newsfeeds. After one look at Kiefer's pale and strained face and the dark shadows under his eyes, Julian forced him to sit at the bench and began rummaging through his food stores. "When did you last eat?" he demanded as he heated a pan and prepared some steaks.

"I don't remember," Kiefer replied, rubbing his stubbly chin. Maybe he ought to shave. He wondered if the twins had finished in the bathroom. They had all slept in late. "You'll need two more steaks. I have guests."

"Guests?" Julian paused in his preparations.

"Much has happened since I last saw you."

"I saw some of it on the newsfeed."

Kiefer flinched, and Julian raised his hands. "Sorry, I know it must be difficult. Do you know what happened?"

"I haven't heard what the official lie is yet."

"Official lie?" Julian stared at him.

"They are not exactly going to admit the head of the

Ministry was found dead in a lush bedroom in Ferris' bordello, now, are they?"

Julian dropped the knife he was holding onto the work surface with a clatter. "What?"

"Are you alright, Kiefer?" Annie's concerned voice preceded her out of the bathroom. "Oh, I'm sorry. I didn't realise you had company." She crossed her arms and backed up in confusion, bumping into Chiva, who had come up behind her.

"This is my friend Julian. I'd trust him with my life, and so can you," Kiefer said. "Julian, these are some friends of mine from Sector 45, Annie and Chiva. They came to join the Academy on a scholarship, though they have to wait until term starts."

Annie flushed but stepped forward as Chiva pushed her out of the way. She held out a trembling hand, keeping the other wrapped around herself. "Pleased to meet you."

As Julian took her hand, his attractive smile lit up his face. "Anneka? And Chiva? Your parents are going to be so relieved." He looked at Kiefer. "Ferris fucked up big time in Sector 27. Lorne told Andre and Ester, and they are frantic about what Ferris is doing to their kids. And here they are, slumming it in your apartment. No need for them to worry at all."

Annie tugged her hand free. "What are you cooking? It smells delicious."

Julian looked across at the stove and hurried to flip the steaks. The pan sizzled and the aroma of garlic made them all breathe in deeply. "Garlic pepper steak and salad. Sit. You can help Kiefer eat them while I tell you the latest." Julian picked up his knife and finished chopping the lettuce, and then he tossed it into a bowl with red tomatoes, black olives, and cucumber slices. He helped himself to a bottle of red wine, opened it, and left it to breathe while he set the table.

"He knows his way around your kitchen," Annie said as she watched him find the glasses.

Kiefer gave her a tired smile. "We've known each other since college. We entered the Devender Academy together. My mother treats him like another son." Kiefer wondered how long it would take for Julian to figure out *he* wanted something. He had been planning to cook Julian lunch, not the other way around, though he couldn't find the energy to bother and was glad Julian had taken over in his own indomitable way, offering his support without saying anything. He knew Julian wouldn't ask unless Kiefer offered it up first.

The question was, would Julian go back to Sector 45 and find Lorne for him? She needed to know about Ciely and take precautions. Staring out the window, he deliberated whether his friend would put his career on the line to protect a group of emancipated people. He hoped so.

Kiefer was tempted to go with Julian. He turned that idea over in his mind. Was that a possibility? Could he take a break and just go and not come back? Although tempting, somehow, he didn't think it would be that simple. The only reason to leave was because he needed to talk to Harmony, and Sector 45 was the easiest place to connect. He hadn't managed to connect to her again in Maincore. But he had plans. If Jeffers managed to source a booster, he knew where to install it.

Kiefer rubbed his temples as he began to plan it out in his head, drawing up the stages to free Harmony, conscious that he couldn't use his devices as they were being tracked. It was beginning to get complicated.

He was going to need a lot of help.

Keeping Madeline on his side was key; he needed one of her magic badges. If he got her into Int-Ed, that would get him in as well. She would want to show him what she could do, as long as it wasn't on him.

"Kiefer?"

Kiefer looked up, aware from the weight Julian had placed on his name that his friend had said it more than once.

"What are you planning?"

Annie frowned at Julian. "How do you know he's planning anything? He is just exhausted, stressed."

"I know my friend, and that faraway looks means his brain has engaged and left the rest of us standing. Spill," Julian commanded as he took a bite of his steak.

Kiefer looked down at the plate in front of him and realised he was starving. "After lunch," he said and began to eat.

Julian pushed a glass of wine in front of Kiefer and then, after a searing inspection of Kiefer's face, shrugged and went back to his steak.

They had moved away from the breakfast bar to the more comfortable chairs in the lounge area. Kiefer relaxed back in his chair and rotated his glass as he stared at the ruby-red wine. "How long are you home for?"

"Not long enough to worry about turfing the Staffens out," said Julian, "but you need to find them a new bolt hole."

"I will. I'm working on it. Where are you off to next?"

"Sector 21, but not for a week or so." Julian heaved his bulk into a more comfortable position on the sofa, idly watching Annie as she stacked the dishes in the washer. She had insisted, and he hadn't argued.

"What's wrong with 21?" Kiefer asked.

"Nothing, for once, but it's due an upgrade, and we have to go on site to perform it for some reason. Something about a replacement board. Here, you probably understand it more than I do." Julian handed over his orders and selected a melon segment from the plate of fruit Annie had placed on the coffee table. "You do find the best food," he murmured, closing his eyes as he savoured the flavour.

Annie sat on the floor and leaned against Chiva's legs. Chiva dropped his hand to the back of her neck, each comforting the other.

"Hey, don't sit on the floor. There's plenty of room on the sofa," Julian said, shifting over.

"I'm fine, thank you. I like sitting on the floor. Kiefer has such soft rugs," Annie replied running her hand through the pile.

Kiefer ignored them as he skimmed Julian's orders. They were shunting the power, diverting it into a new power plant, closing down Harmony's connections. Her power would be stored locally, but she wouldn't directly affect anything. The beginning of the transfer.

"What if I asked you to divert to Sector 45 first?"

Julian cocked his head. "Here it comes. I knew a free meal was too good to be true."

"I've heard rumours that Sector 45 is accused of harbouring the rebels. Ferris filed false reports claiming it was so. I need to get a message to the rebel leader, Lorne. She needs to move her people; they have been compromised. I'd go myself, but I can't leave Maincore without it being noticed. They need to prepare."

"Fame at last."

"You know it's not. I'm being tracked, not overtly, but tracked all the same."

"Do they not trust their reprogramming methods, then?" Julian asked.

"Standard practice, or so I'm advised. No matter how much the Ministry say they protect us, they protect themselves first."

"Yes, there are piped messages everywhere. It's more noticeable when you return from the sectors."

"They want to extend them to the sectors as well," Kiefer said with a frown.

"You'd have thought they'd start there."

"Are you hearing more rumblings?"

"The controllers are losing mind share as their greed increases. If they improved conditions in the sectors, there wouldn't be an issue, but this behaviour is extending to other sectors as well. I don't understand what is driving it."

"Fear," Kiefer said as he sipped his wine. "The Ministry is over compensating. They think if they keep the sectors repressed, they can take what they want. They believe their own propaganda and have forgotten how ingenious people can be."

"What do the sectors have that the Ministry wants? I didn't see anything of value."

"Harmony," Kiefer said.

Julian frowned. "What?"

"Harmony powers each facility, but they have segmented her, funnelled her power into the areas they control. I told you before, we must free her. I've been working on a program that I think will work, but I don't know how to get it into the mainframe."

"You work at the Ministry now, don't you? It should be easy."

"I don't have the right access. I need to get the badge from Velten's daughter. The question is how."

Julian picked up his glass. "You're serious, aren't you? I thought it was paranoia the night of the soiree, but you mean to bring down Maincore."

"Not Maincore, just the Ministry."

"Same thing," Julian grunted, selecting another piece of fruit. He jerked back as Annie went for the same piece. "Please," he said, gesturing for her to make her selection.

Kiefer's lips twitched as he watched the byplay. His gaze dwelled on his friend for a moment before he dropped his eyes back to the papers in his hand.

"They are brainwashing everyone and using Harmony's power to do it. We have to stop them."

"We?"

"We," Kiefer repeated. "You need to go and warn Lorne and help Sector 45 prepare their defences. I'll finish off my program. Chiva will help me get the file into Maincore. Once we free Harmony, she can help us bring down the Ministry."

"I need to go and save the sector, now? Who is actually being sent to attack them?"

"I don't know."

"So, it could be another Devender unit."

"Possibly."

"Kiefer, I can't attack another unit. I'd be court-martialled."

"But you could curtail any unnecessary violence. If they were going just to check, it would be fine, but they will attack for no reason, I know it. I would if I was ordered to. We all blindly follow our orders without questioning them."

"Because the chain of command knows best," Julian said and then paused as he considered his words.

"And who are at the top of the chain of command?"

"Your father and the Ministry," Julian said, his eyes widening. "We are all brainwashed, aren't we?"

"I believe we are."

"Do you really think you can go up against your father's system and win?"

"I don't have a choice."

Julian leaned back. "The silent take over. Is that what your parents have been planning all these years?"

"Harmony is invisible, no longer a part of daily life. People are encouraged to replace her with the Ministry. Why would they think there is anything wrong? Why would anyone question it?"

"Why *are* you questioning it, Kiefer?"

"Because my mother asked me to."

"I wouldn't disobey your mother, either, but really, this is going to cause untold grief for many people. Maybe they are better off not knowing."

"Just because it is difficult, it doesn't mean we shouldn't act," Kiefer replied, his face grim. "Not everyone lives a life of luxury like us. The sectors are struggling; Harmony is suffering. Only a minority live in the city. Do you think it will last, this peaceful ignorance?"

Julian heaved a deep sigh. "I suppose not. Nothing good lasts."

"This is not good, Julian. It is a false sense of security, controlled by selfish, greedy people. How can that be right and good? Would you want your children growing up in a false world? When Harmony could be free and this planet thriving? What is happening in the dead sectors? In the Wytchwards? No one seems concerned that we've been dumping everything we don't like out in the Wytchwards. Aren't you concerned that one day, something might come back and haunt us?"

"Don't. That's a place of nightmares. That's why it's sealed off."

Kiefer laughed. "Sealed off? An area that large? Do you really think we can seal it off successfully? I believe the rebels cross into it regularly. If they can, who else does?"

Julian scowled at him. "You are really going to stir that pot?"

"If I don't, any threat could wipe us off the planet. And without Harmony, we'll have no defence against it."

"It all comes back to Harmony, doesn't it?"

"Of course it does. She is the planet. We should be working with her, not against her."

Julian lifted his glass. "Got anything stronger?"

Kiefer rose and went to retrieve the brandy. He took the bottle down and pushed it across the counter, along with a tumbler, as Julian heaved his bulk onto a stool.

"You're not joining me?" asked Julian.

"I'll stick to the wine."

Julian poured himself a drink and stared at the amber liquid for a moment. "Have you ever thought this might be a result of your reset? Your brain's gotten a bit scrambled."

Kiefer snorted. "My brain is empty of memories. I have more room to think."

"They haven't started coming back?"

"Not noticeably. Bits and pieces jogged by association, but only partial memories. Like the smell of the sea, but not what I did there. Or a pair of violet eyes, but I don't know whose."

"Violet eyes?"

"Yes, they haunt me, but I don't know who it is."

Julian stared at him a moment and then knocked his drink back. He took a deep breath. "About Lorne, the women with the violet eyes who you met in Sector 45…" He deliberated a moment. "She's waiting for you back at my apartment."

Kiefer stiffened. "What? You are harbouring…" He started laughing, but he controlled it as a hysterical edge crept in. "You are harbouring a nest of fugitives in your small apartment?"

"If they haven't killed each other yet. Lorne is not very patient, is she?"

"I have no idea. Why is she here? How did you meet her?"

"We met in Sector 45. I diverted to check it for you. Ferris absconded with Lorne's sister, Ciely. Lorne came back with me in the hope that we—you and me—can help her find her, before Ferris hands her over."

"He already has."

"Shit!" Julian stared at Kiefer in shock. "How do you know that? Do you remember Ciely?"

"No. Jeffers told me." Kiefer rubbed his eyes. "This is getting complicated, so many moving parts. It's almost impossible to keep track of it all. Oh, by the way, Ferris has been arrested for the murder of my father."

Julian ruminated for a moment. "How did your father die, Kiefer?"

"Best you don't know. Wait for the official announcement. Then you won't have to lie. This is one you do not want to be caught up in."

"That I can believe. Alright, I assume this means I don't need to divert back to 45 again?"

"Depends on what the Ministry gets out of Ciely," Kiefer said. "I expect they will still need to be warned."

"I could send a messenger." Julian frowned. "Say I go and warn 45, do what I can to mitigate the situation. What next?"

"I have a plan," Kiefer began, but he was interrupted by the communicator. He depressed the button. "Yes?"

"Package for you sir, from a Mr Jeffers."

"Send him up."

"He didn't stop, sir."

"Very well. Send the package up."

"Very good, sir." Kiefer released the button and glanced

at Julian. "That's another favour I wanted to ask. Could you take Jeffers with you? Get him transferred out of Ferris' unit. I'm sure you need a horse master, and he makes an excellent valet."

"You're racking up favours. Are you sure you can pay them back?"

"When have I ever failed you?"

"Never, but there's always a first."

Kiefer laughed as he went to answer the door, and he returned to the bar with his package. He opened it using his knife, revealing a slim black box.

Julian peered at it. "What is that, and why is Jeffers leaving it for you?"

"It's a signal booster. I thought it was safer to ask someone else to get it for me."

"I see." Julian sounded dubious, and Kiefer grinned.

"All part of my master plan. You'll see."

33

Kiefer rubbed his sweaty palms down his trousers as he followed Julian into his apartment. He wished he hadn't allowed Julian to convince him to come and meet Lorne. He had enough problems to solve without adding anyone else's. Julian's broad shoulders filled the stairwell; his solid presence was a comfort.

Julian always insisted on using the stairs, as he was only on the fifth floor. Still, Kiefer was panting by the time they reached it. Leaning against the wall, he breathed heavily. "I've never been so out of shape. Since this reset, it's like they scrambled my metabolism as well."

Grinning, Julian palmed his door open. "I told you not to live at the top of a skyscraper. Lifts are a cop-out."

"The view is worth it," Kiefer replied as he followed him through the door.

Julian's apartment was a typical bachelor's pad: comfort over aesthetics. He had never cared for elegant furniture and pretty pictures. Instead, a homey wood cabin welcomed them, with lots of natural wood and comfortable chairs. Kiefer eyed the tall potted palm in the corner.

Julian chuckled. "The good doctor couldn't cope without some greenery around him. I'm hoping he'll take it with him. It'll die otherwise."

Kiefer didn't have a chance to answer as Lorne hurtled across the room and into his arms. He thudded back against the wall at the force of her arrival.

"At last! I was so worried. Are you alright? What did they do to you? What took you so long?"

"Let the man breathe," an amused voice said from the corner of the room.

Kiefer hugged Lorne back, inhaling the scent of her hair. She smelt of lilac and green apples, a sweet yet sharp tang that filled his nostrils. He tagged the scent to the person who must be Lorne. "What are you doing here, Lorne? It's not safe."

Lorne leaned back and stared him in the eyes. She frowned as she cupped his face. "You look terrible."

"It's been an eventful week," Kiefer replied. He looked over her shoulder and nodded at the two men sitting together on the sofa. They held hands, fingers entwined, their shoulders touching. "Gerry, Henry, glad to see you're both alright."

Henry rose and approached him, a crease between his brows. "Lorne is right, you don't look well; what's happened to you?"

"M'father died. My mother's not taking it too well."

"Oh, Kiefer, I am so sorry about your father," Lorne said and hugged him again.

"My condolences," Henry said as he inspected Kiefer's face. "I suppose that could explain how…how knackered you look," he added dubiously.

"I imagine the mind-wipe helped," Kiefer said.

Lorne stiffened in his arms. "You truly don't know what

happened in Sector 45?" she asked, stepping out of his embrace.

"Only what Chiva has told me. I have odd flashes of memory but no context. I don't know what I did or how felt about it. As people remind me of things, I'm told the memories will come back. Memory by association, but it takes time, which we don't have."

"You don't remember me?"

"Only your eyes, such beautiful violet eyes. You haunt my dreams."

Lorne looked pleased and wormed her way back into his embrace, which he was quite happy to accept; she felt lovely in his arms. "I know what might help remind you," she murmured, her voice low and sultry.

Henry coughed, and Julian laughed. "Find a room, preferably elsewhere."

"He owes me," Lorne said, entwining her fingers in his.

"I do?" Kiefer asked.

"Oh, yes, and I don't forget those dues owed, even if you have."

Kiefer chuckled. He felt relaxed for the first time in weeks. "I look forward to you claiming it," he said, meeting her beautiful eyes. He ran a finger over her lips. "My mind may not remember you, but my body does; you are in my soul, and no one can take that away," he murmured and then kissed her.

Henry cleared his throat. "I think it was more discreet at Cherry's," he said, as he went back to the sofa to sit with his husband. Clasping his hand, he made sure his leg touched Gerry's as he met his eyes. "I hope you are making notes. I expect you to come up with something equally romantic."

Julian rolled his eyes. "Harmony help us, not you as well. We have more important things to discuss."

Gerry's panicked expression had Henry chuckling as he dropped a soft kiss on his husband's lips.

Lorne stepped back from Kiefer, and her face tightened as she asked, "Did Julian tell you? We think Ciely met up with Ferris and came to Maincore with him."

"If the rumour mill is correct, then he's already handed her over to Int-Ed," Kiefer said.

"What?" Lorne's face blanched.

"He would have lied to her, promised her whatever she wanted, and then betrayed her anyway. He is a foul piece of shit."

"I'll kill the bastard."

"If you can get to him. He is currently under arrest for the murder of my father."

"What? Why would he kill your father?"

"I don't know."

Lorne scowled. "Maybe if we can find Ferris, we'll find Ciely."

"Before we go piling in, why don't you tell me what happened? How did she end up in his clutches?" Kiefer dragged Lorne over to a chair and sat in it, pulling her down onto his lap. Julian didn't have enough chairs, and the Staffens already had the sofa. At least, that was his excuse.

Lorne didn't complain. Instead, she concentrated on drawing circles on his chest. She described Ciely's secret infatuation and her decision to write Arran off, not realising what it would mean to her sister. Lorne faltered. "There are a lot of other people who rely on us. I couldn't risk him telling anyone, and now Ciely could tell them everything anyway."

"Tell them what?"

"I can't tell you. The fewer people who know, the better."

"If Ciely has already told them, don't you need to warn them?"

"She wouldn't."

"She wouldn't have a choice; you know that, Lorne."

Lorne shuddered. "We have to get her out of there before they make her talk. How long do you think they've had her?"

"Too long," Kiefer said honestly. "But Lorne, aren't you taking the same risk?"

Lorne closed her eyes. "I know, but I can't leave her. She's all I've got left."

Kiefer tightened his grip. "I'm sorry," he murmured.

Taking a deep breath, Lorne glanced at the others. "What do we do?"

"You rescue her while I bring down Maincore," Kiefer said into the lingering silence.

Lorne swivelled back to him. "How?"

"I'm working on it," Kiefer said. "You need to stay here out of sight until I've formulated a plan."

Lorne jerked upright. "No, I need to help. What can I do?"

"I'll send Chiva over with a set of plans of the Int-Ed building and the neighbouring Academy building. Study them. All of you. You all need to know your way through those corridors blindfolded. We don't know which block Ciely is held in, so memorise them all. When the power goes down, the corridors will seem confusing." Kiefer stared at Julian. "Do you think you can find out which block Ciely is held in?"

Julian nodded. "I can try. One of my men used to be on the intake team. He'll know someone we can ask."

"Are you sure we can trust him? Remember, everyone is blindly following the Ministry's directives." Kiefer ran a hand through his hair.

"I'd trust him with my life. He's a good guy. And once I open his eyes to what is going on, he will be horrified."

"Not everyone will believe us."

"Enough will, Kiefer. Stop worrying. Just because people are brain-washed now, it doesn't mean they want to stay brainwashed. This is wrong, and you must stop it."

"Fine. Make sure you tell Lorne as soon as you find out where Ciely is. You can plan the best way to reach her. I need to…"

"You need a good night's sleep, Kiefer," Lorne murmured, leaning against him again. "You look exhausted."

"We don't have time for sleep. Our timetable just moved up. The longer the Ministry have Ciely, the more she'll tell them, and the more likely we will be discovered."

34

———————

When Annie woke the next morning, she stared at the ceiling in confusion before memories of that horrific day returned. She shivered, the chill deep in her bones, as she tried to ignore what could have happened if Kiefer hadn't turned up and rescued them. Trying to stop the images from filling her mind, she suddenly sat up and realised she had been sleeping on Kiefer's sofa. Chiva was still asleep, sprawled across two chairs pushed together. She tugged the blanket around her as she realised it was Kiefer tapping away at his tablet that had woken her up. She watched as Kiefer paused and stared out the window. The morning sun gilded his face, accentuating lines that had appeared over the last few days. He looked exhausted, as if he hadn't slept.

"Kiefer?"

He turned away from the window, and Annie inhaled sharply, her own fears forgotten at the sight of his strained face.

"What's happened, Kiefer?"

He looked down at his tablet and hit a key. Then he spun

the screen around. A helix rotated on the screen. "We need to get that into the Maincore mainframe."

Annie rose and drew closer to peer at the screen, her blanket trailing as she inspected the diagram. It was an interlinking string of commands spiralling gracefully, and replicating as it twirled until it covered the screen.

"What is it?"

"A fulcrum."

"Your fulcrum?" she asked

"A way in. A way to reach Harmony." Kiefer scowled at it. The shadows under his eyes deepened, and Annie touched his arm.

"Did you get any sleep last night?"

"Some."

"Not enough," Annie said. She moved over to the kitchenette and made some fresh coffee. As she handed him a mug, she asked, "What do you mean, we need a way into Harmony?"

Kiefer nursed his coffee and rubbed his eyes. Then he began to explain. "The Ministry has corrupted Harmony. They have siphoned her natural power and diverted it for their own purposes. The facilities in the sectors are just booster stations. They are providing nothing for the people in the sector; they just boost the net the Ministry has caught Harmony in."

Annie listened in growing horror.

"My father…" Kiefer took a deeper breath. "My father was the one who first suggested the trap. The Ministry… have suggested that I carry on his work. If they continue, they will drain Harmony. Once her core dies, our planet will begin to die."

"What did you say to the Ministry?" Annie asked.

Kiefer twisted his lips. "I accepted, of course, like the good citizen I am." He suddenly grinned, the strain on his face easing. "Which means that I have one of these." He waved a black plastic rectangle.

Chiva's voice interrupted them. "And that is?"

"A magic key."

"To what?" Chiva was drawn to the image on the tablet like a programmer deprived of data. His eyes widened as he followed the model. "Kiefer," he whispered. "What is this?"

"That is one of the keys to Harmony's freedom." Kiefer cleared the screen and brought up a schematic in its place. "There are multiple gates containing Harmony's complex. We have to breach them all to reach her core and free her."

Chiva stared at the screen. "You said the fulcrum was one of the keys?"

There was an edge to Kiefer's grin, almost feral and Chiva took a step back. "You remember the error code you found back in Sector 45?" Kiefer asked.

"Of course."

"I need you to build it out. Recreate the Bantwich. Do you think you can do that?"

"I can try." Chiva hesitated. "But I only have the one loop."

"Play with it. You're a programmer; see how you would have built it out. I need to return to the Ministry and find out what else my father was up to. We can swap notes later." Annie straightened when he glanced at her. "Annie…"

"What do you need?" Annie glared at Kiefer as he fell silent. "Don't think you are leaving me out of this."

"Would you come with me? As my assistant? I need an independent set of eyes to keep me straight." He twirled his fingers. "My brain is still too scrambled to make sense of everything."

"Of course," Annie said immediately. She would do anything to help ease the strain he was under. "Let me just get dressed."

After Annie forced Kiefer to eat some breakfast, they left Chiva scowling over his program. Kiefer sheltered her as he escorted her up the steps into the Ministry building, past the heckling press. He stiffened as he ignored the requests; they were still chasing him for an interview.

Kiefer exhaled as they hurried through the glass doors into the main reception area. He signed Annie in, and they entered the lift. After tapping his card against the plate, Kiefer pressed the button for level 25. The extreme rising sensation made Annie stagger, and Kiefer steadied her. "Sorry, should have warned you."

He led her to an enormous glass-enclosed office in the far corner, and Annie gaped out of the window at the view of downtown Maincore. The rising mountains in the distance were a blue haze, behind which lay her home.

"How anyone does any work with a view like that is beyond me," Annie said as she turned away from the window.

Kiefer didn't hear her. He hesitated behind his father's desk and tentatively touched his father's chair, his chest tightened and he found it difficult to breathe.

He was aware of Annie touching his arm, her calm voice penetrated his self-pummelling guilt. "Kiefer? Are you alright? Breathe, Kiefer." He thumped into the seat, and she rubbed his shoulder. "Maybe we should come back tomorrow," she suggested.

The comment made Kiefer sit upright. "No, we have to start searching today. Before they have a chance to hide anything."

"Why would they hide anything?"

"It's the way they are. My father was notorious for keeping secrets. He always thought someone was going to steal his ideas." Kiefer snorted. "He was the worst one of all. That's why my mother left him in the end. He couldn't share, and he shut my mother and me out. The question is, where would he hide things?" Kiefer stared around the office. One wall was shelved, and the shelves were lined with gold-embossed books interspersed with ornaments and photographs.

The desk was clear except for the monitor, keyboard, and a complex metal balancing contraption. Kiefer touched it and the weighted end swung back and forth in a smooth hypnotic motion, accompanied by a soft clacking sound. Rings of metal flashed as they began to rotate in an unending spiral. He stilled it.

"On his computer?" Annie suggested

"Some, but not all. There will be discs and memory cards stashed away in odd places."

Annie inspected the numerous books and knickknacks and sighed. "You start on the desk; I'll search the shelves."

Kiefer smiled at her matter-of-fact tone. He opened the drawer of the desk and began rummaging through the clutter as Annie started on the books. Three hours later, he had emptied out the drawers, and Annie had a pile of books on the floor, having painstakingly checked every page. Nothing. He swept everything back into the drawer.

Kiefer felt under the desk. Time to search in the less-obvious places. He was crouched under the desk when an exclamation made him peer over the top. "What?"

Annie brought a book over. "Look! The title on the inside has a full stop. There aren't usually full stops in book titles, are there?"

Kiefer peered at the book. The dot was larger than usual. "Maybe, but that is not a full stop. It's a microdot.

"A what?"

"A microdot. It can be used to store pictures of schematics, drawings, or information. The image is reduced to the size of a dot. Well spotted. Are there any others?"

"I didn't notice until that one. I'll have to go through them again." Annie groaned as she surveyed the pile, but she knelt back on the floor.

A woman poked her head through the door. "Sir, Minister Velten is on line one."

"Thank you." Kiefer leaned over and punched a button. "Minister."

"Ah, Kiefer, my boy. I was so sorry to hear about your father. How are you coping?"

Kiefer made a face as Velten's silky voice blared over the speaker. "As well as can be expected, sir."

"Good, good. I heard they asked you to take over his office. I thought I might find you there."

"Yes, sir."

"I had a meeting scheduled with him at ten tomorrow. There should be a file on his computer called 'Opendoor'. Make sure you read it beforehand; I will be interested in your thoughts."

"Yes, sir."

"Good. See you tomorrow, Kiefer."

"I look forward to it, sir."

He hit the button to disconnect and stared at the console. Tapping a key, he stared at the password screen. "I have no idea how to get into his computer," he said, and Annie chuckled.

"You must have hacked computers before," she said, watching at him.

Kiefer frowned. "Well…" He opened a new screen and typed until Annie thumped a pile of books on the desk.

"Five," she said.

"Maybe he has a list of his passwords on one of them," Kiefer murmured. He rose and went out to speak to the assistant. He returned with a box that he plugged into the wall. After pulling down the blind across the window he bent to flip the switch, and a beam of light shone out towards the white screen. Carefully scraping the dot off the page, he placed it on a square piece of clear plastic, and fed it into the box. A schematic appeared on the window blind.

Kiefer's breath whooshed out as he stared at image upon image of schematics and patents. His mind went into overdrive, cataloguing and storing the images. He removed the plastic sheet and placed it carefully in a tray. Choosing another slide, he placed the next dot on it and inserted it into the machine.

A collage of photographs filled the window. People and places that Kiefer didn't recognise. Groups of men and women in front of sector facilities, possibly. "I have no idea who any of these people are," he said and retrieved the slide. The next one had Annie gasping in shock and Kiefer hurriedly removed it. His hands shook as he placed the slide in the tray. That his father would keep evidence of his depravity shocked him as well.

He hesitated over the last dot, but he slid it into the machine, breathing a sigh of relief as pages of documents were projected onto the window. He scanned the documents. All referenced the original Harmony project and referred to additional documents, so there were more files somewhere.

"Vizerine," he murmured.

"Vizerine? What's that?" Annie asked.

"I'm not sure. It seems to be a power source my parents discovered. I'll have to ask my mother. I think it is what they are using as the basis for the new nodes." He followed a schematic. "It's not clear whether it flows to or from Harmony's chamber. My father's notes are vague." He stared at them for a moment. "Deliberately vague."

"Why deliberate?"

"Not sure. Maybe he didn't want his researchers to know about it."

"That doesn't make sense. Why hide something as important as a power source? Especially if it's native to the planet."

Kiefer tapped the window. "GEN4212," he said.

Annie frowned at him. "What's that?"

"The very first Harmony node. I wonder." He moved over to the console and entered the code. "Incorrect password" flashed up on the screen. He added his father's initials after it. "Incorrect password" flashed again. He stood and returned to the images on the window and continued scanning them. He slowly swore, long and heartfelt, and Annie gaped at him.

"Sorry." Kiefer grimaced. "There's a failsafe. Even if we get through the five gates there's a blasted failsafe."

"At least you know about it. Means we can deal with it."

Kiefer heaved a sigh and returned to the machine. He removed the slide and switched it off. Then, moving over to the window, he released the blind and stared out at the city. The buildings were a blur as his mind grappled with far too many unanswered questions.

Why had the Ministry asked him to continue his father's work and not someone on the research team or his mother? Why was his father's name on all the patents when they were obviously the work of his research team? Why had no one mentioned Vizerine?"

Annie's concerned voice brought him back to the office. "We *can* deal with it, can't we?"

"I don't know," Kiefer murmured, his mind spinning through possibilities. Annie left him to his thoughts and began stacking the books back on the shelves.

Kiefer suddenly spun and joined her. He picked up a small digiscreen off the top shelf and tapped it on. He swiped through the images, his fingers slowing as the pictures recorded more recent meetings. In the pictures, his father looked as he had the other day.

Taking the screen out to the assistant sitting outside the office, he showed her the image. "Could you tell me who these people are?"

The woman peered at the screen and then smiled. Her forefinger drifted over the faces. "Well, your mother and father, of course, and their research team."

"Could you remind me of their names? I ought to contact them to let them know about the arrangements for my father. I'd prefer not to ask my mother."

The assistant covered her mouth as she stared at him. "I'm sorry, sir, but...do you not remember? They are all dead."

"What? But these are recent pictures."

"There was a spate of unfortunate events, one after the other. It was a very trying time for your parents." She tutted. "So many funerals."

Kiefer imagined it had been worse for the poor people who had died and their families. He cleared his throat. "I don't remember. Can you tell me what happened?"

The assistant blanched. "Of course. I'm sorry. I..." She stopped and then said, "I'll send the reports to your father's...I mean your terminal."

"I can't access his files; I don't have his password."

The assistant scowled. "I'll have to get the tech super to help you. Your father was very security conscious." She stared at him for a moment and then said in a hushed voice, "You don't think his death was connected to the other accidents, do you? Why would anyone want to deliberately hurt him?"

"What makes you ask that?" Kiefer's eyebrows rose. He couldn't help it; this conversation was totally unexpected.

She shrugged. "He followed the cases avidly. We have disks full of newssheet images, clippings, and reports."

"Could you get them sent to my father's…my office?"

"Of course, sir. I'll get them sent to your login. You can access them from there."

"Thank you." Kiefer returned to his office, deep in thought.

35

Annie was still reshelving the books when Kiefer strode into the office and went back to staring out the window, though he didn't see the beautiful view. His mind was too busy questioning the deaths of a whole research team. It wasn't long before his terminal pinged, and he returned to his seat as his screen began filling with folders full of documents, photos, and reports.

Attempting to organise the data into some semblance of order, Kiefer gradually worked his way through all the correspondence. He tagged any reference to the members of the research team.

Shane Revera was male, 36 years old, single, a research technician specialising in electrical impulse control. He was the inventor of the Reveran Nexus, the core imperative that controlled the flow of Harmony's power. As Kiefer read the synopsis of Revera's research paper, he realised that the original intention had been to use it for medical implants to help regulate a person's heartbeat.

Shuffling through the documents, he found Revera's application to join his father's research team. Appended to it was a subfile, which he opened first. He stilled as he read his father's plan to recruit Revera. It was a coldly calculated manipulation, and his father had planned every step. Revera hadn't stood a chance.

Revera had moved from his hometown to Maincore, uprooted his life for the chance to work in the Gallantes' research lab, a much-sought-after tenureship.

Kiefer opened Revera's thesis and began reading.

"Kiefer?" Annie's voice interrupted his concentration. He looked up from the screen and winced as his neck twinged. He hadn't moved for hours except to click a new file open, and his body complained.

"I'm so sorry, but it's getting dark. We haven't eaten all day, and I'm starving."

Glancing out the window, Kiefer sat back in his chair with a sigh. "No, *I'm* sorry. I get a bit fixated when I'm researching."

"Did you find anything?"

"That depends."

"On what?"

Kiefer sighed. "I'm not sure. My father collected a very talented team of people, from scientists to behaviourists. They all gave up very promising careers to come here." He hesitated. "And now they are all dead." He suddenly lurched to his feet and stretched. "Come on. Chiva is probably getting worried. We ought to go home."

Annie laughed. "He's as bad as you. He is probably still deep in that program you asked him to recreate."

"Probably. Come on. I need food and a good night's sleep, too. I've got a meeting with Velten to survive tomorrow morning."

. . .

The next morning, Kiefer braved the reporters blocking the Ministry entrance and returned to his father's office, prepared to spend the day reading the files on the research team once he'd met with Velten. First, he needed to access the file Velten had referred to.

Taking a deep breath, he entered the passcode the IT dept had provided him, an unrelated string of random digits that he would never have guessed, and he sighed out his breath as his father's account opened before him.

He ignored all the tantalising folders and clicked on 'OpenDoor'.

Kiefer was staring at his hands, trying to control the tremor, when Velten was announced. He stiffened and rose, pasting a smile on his face.

"Minister Velten."

"Good morning, my boy."

Kiefer gritted his teeth at the minister's condescending tone and tried to relax. "Please. Be seated. The file was interesting reading."

Velten raised an eyebrow as he walked towards the Kiefer. "Only interesting? I thought enlightening was a more appropriate word."

"In what way?"

Velten stilled for a moment, so slight Kiefer wouldn't have noticed if he wasn't so focused on the man. "I was hoping you would tell me," Velten said without hesitation as he pushed the silver rod with one finger and set it swinging to and fro. The quiet clacking set Kiefer's teeth on edge. "For every action, there is a reaction," Velten said in his silky-smooth voice. "The question is…what action will you take?"

Kiefer leaned back in his chair and held Velten's gaze. "I'm surprised that you would even ask. My father's legacy stands before us. His vision holds our society together and offers our people hope for the future. Have you seen the possibilities? It would be sacrilege to ignore them. Milven's work in neural pathways offers relief from unnecessary anxiety and a path towards universal unity. Revera's discovery shows us how we can control the synapses between the body and emotions. The connections are obvious."

Velten smiled as he leaned forward. "Kiefer, my boy. I knew you would see the advantages immediately. I told your father you would be an asset to the program."

Kiefer twisted his lips as his stomach churned. "But he disagreed."

"He was short-sighted. But that does not matter anymore. You will take us further than your father ever could. Your programming expertise, combined with your innate understanding of what people need, is perfect. Linking Harmony to the neural pathways will negate the need for external reinforcement; we could use the subliminal neurone. No one would even know they were being controlled." Velten rubbed his hands together as he stared at the endless spiral still spinning on Kiefer's desk. "I saw you've already accessed your father's files. Draw up your proposal for how we implement 'Open Door'. Such a good name for the universal acceptance of our guidance, don't you think? We'll be able to reach all the sectors and beyond. Just imagine…" Velten paused for a moment. Imagining his horrible vision of the new world, Kiefer assumed. "I'd like to see your suggestion on my desk within three days." Standing, Velten grinned at Kiefer, his eyes bright. "We will usher in a new era, and you, my boy, will be at the centre of it."

Kiefer stayed in his chair long after Velten left the office, staring at the pendulum as the extent of the Ministry's machinations slowly sank into his brain. All the pieces of the puzzle were coming together in horrific clarity. If he didn't save Harmony, he and everyone else would be lost to the deception and disinformation of these terrible people. How could they subscribe to the belief that removing free will and sublimating choice was the way to keep peace?

The worst part was that it had been going on for years and no one had noticed. Even the rebels had no idea. They were rebelling against the repressive conditions in the sectors, not against the systemic brainwashing of an entire people.

With his father dead, who was heading up the organisation now? Velten? Or some other shadowy person no one ever saw? His father had liked the spotlight, had always been happy to receive the accolades. He had been the face of the Ministry, the spokesperson.

Slowly sitting up, Kiefer tapped a key and woke his screen. He entered his password and searched his father's files for any organisational charts, contact lists, or address books. Nothing. Frowning, he searched through the Ministry document library. After a moment's thought, he logged into the internal chat system and right-clicked his father's name.

Muriel, his father's assistant, still reported to him, as did Revera, Milven, and the other research members. The reporting chain ended with his father and hadn't been updated. Out of interest, Kiefer searched for and clicked on his own name. He reported directly to Velten, along with five other names he didn't recognise. They all had the same title as him, the uninformative 'Technician'. He wondered what they actually did and if he'd ever meet them.

More importantly, how was he going to discover what had happened to the researchers? There was the possibility that someone had deliberately killed them. So many deaths in such quick succession. Why wasn't anyone questioning it? It was obvious to him; why wasn't it obvious to anyone else?

He returned to his father's files and continued skimming through documents, proposals, counterarguments, schematics, and plans. When he finished, he sat back and scowled at the darkened window.

His mother was a genius, but his father had easily surpassed her. His ability to recognise the one element that mattered and harness it in the right place at the right time, that was what had made him successful.

He had surrounded himself with intelligent people and then manipulated them in his merry dance. Each individual had only known their piece of the puzzle until his father had drawn them all together into his masterpiece. And it was breathtaking what his father had achieved.

Kiefer wished his father were here, just to talk about it. To dissect it. To understand his father's thinking. For once, to discuss as equals, one intelligent man to another. Kiefer huffed under his breath. As if that would have ever happened.

His mother had once said his father viewed Kiefer as a rival. And that was his father's downfall, along with his depravity. His inability to trust, to treat others as equals. What they could have achieved together. Kiefer twisted his lips. Would his father have corrupted him, too, if he'd ever tried to get involved? Maybe Kiefer was fortunate to escape his father's control. He hoped he would never have had the same vision as his father. What his father had built, his son intended to destroy.

36

Annie and Chiva sat at the breakfast bar in Kiefer's apartment and listened with growing horror as Kiefer explained his plan.

"You expect us to waltz into Maincore, take down five gates and a failsafe, and then just upload a virus in the hope it will blow it up?" Chiva stared at him in disbelief.

"After Julian and Lorne have rescued Ciely."

"They just stroll through security, pick her up and stroll out again," Chiva said, wrinkling his nose. Kiefer smiled. The boy obviously thought he was insane.

"We won't be messing with any explosives; Harmony will backstop the load and release it at the right time. She can't wait."

"If we can free her," Chiva said.

"Security will have other things on their mind." Annie grinned. "Like the fire alarm."

'They are bound to be suspicious," Chiva said.

Annie laughed. "Of what? No one in their right mind would attack Maincore."

"Too right," Chiva muttered under his breath.

Kiefer clapped him on the shoulder. "You'll be fine. It's the Maincore building that will collapse. You'll be in the Academy."

"That's not what worries me."

"Did you deliver the plans as I asked?"

"Of course. And as far as I can tell I wasn't followed. Dr Staffen asked if he needed to supply up. I wasn't sure what he meant, so I told him to just in case."

"I think that was the correct response. Best to be ready in case anyone does get hurt. I'll visit later and see if they have any questions."

"Kiefer, are you sure this will work?" Chiva asked.

"If everyone stays calm and plays their part, then yes. All you have to do is release the gates, load a disk, and leave. Nothing else."

"I should be bringing down all the gates, not Annie."

"Annie can get in via the ladies' college; you can't. She will be fine and away from any collapsing buildings, so don't worry. And anyway, she will be long gone before we bring Maincore down. You all will. You just need to make sure the virus loads. That is all you should be worrying about."

"But what if the virus doesn't work?"

"It will. You know it will. My fulcrum will deliver it exactly where it needs to go. You've done really good work here, Chiva. You will go to the Academy and graduate, I promise. We need bright minds like yours to rebuild our society. Out of the ashes of the Ministry, Harmony will rise, and we'll build a much better world to live in."

Chiva clenched his jaw and nodded.

"It's time Annie applied to go to the ladies' college," Kiefer said with a grin.

Annie rubbed her hands together. "Can't wait!"

The next morning, Kiefer sat staring out of the window of his apartment. The view of Maincore was a blur. His mind churned, unable to assimilate the depth of his father's depravity and inhumanity. His father had been prepared to kill every person on the planet. For what? Kiefer didn't understand his rationalisation. There was no explaining it.

He was sure his father had killed his research team, one after the other, until only he and Kiefer's mother were left. It was too late to try and prove it, and now Kiefer and his mother were the only people who knew how Harmony was constrained and what the processor transfer really meant. Would his father have killed his mother as well? Did his mother know? Was that why she had set Kiefer on to him?

Kiefer took a deep breath and shuddered it out again. Sliding his hands down his trousers and back up, he tried to let his thoughts drift for a moment, but it was impossible. His mind spun with unease as he wondered if his plan would be enough. He wasn't sure, and now he had dragged his friends into it as well. He could only do his best and hope Harmony was able to do the rest. Standing, he glanced around his apartment. This might be the last time he saw it. He exhaled, letting it go.

He knew what he had to do.

Annie and Chiva had already left, Annie to enter via the women's entrance, Chiva for his usual shift, each with a disk in their pocket and the timing engraved in their brains.

Exhaling again, Kiefer tried to control his racing heart. All would be well. Maybe if he said it often enough, it would be.

As he walked to work, the city of Maincore seemed more vibrant than usual. The noise, the smells, the people hurrying around him intent on their own needs, he moved through them as if in his own little bubble, observing and unseen.

Entering the Maincore administration building, he crossed the foyer and tapped through security. The black basalt walls rose around him, more oppressive with thoughts of rebellion in his mind. Did the walls know? Where they impregnated with sensors that read a person's intent? If they did, he was a dead man, but he continued down the corridor, his footsteps echoing until he reached the lift bank and pressed his palm against the plate.

The previous evening, he had slunk unseen into the women's college, through the corridors and up the stairs to the library, planting his signal booster. Once he had connected it, he had heard Harmony as clearly as if she was in the same room. She was ready, eager, primed. Waiting for his signal. It was down to him now.

Kiefer checked his timer for the hundredth time. Julian would be escorting his prisoner into Maincore. Lorne had insisted. She was determined to help rescue her sister. Kiefer thought she was crazy, but then, weren't they all?

He exited the lift on the twelfth floor and smiled at his colleagues as he made his way to his terminal. Once logged in, he opened his mail and scrolled through the messages. He began answering them. Glancing at his timer, he started to sweat. He patted his forehead dry. What was wrong with him?

Kiefer took a deep breath, strolled over to the small kitchenette, and poured a coffee. He stood sipping his drink, letting the soothing peace of the office seep into his bones and calm him. All would be well. He returned to his desk. An alert was blinking on his terminal. His heart sank as he opened it.

His presence was requested in Int-Ed. Int-Ed? Why him? Why now? There was no way Lorne would have been processed yet. Julian knew how to delay; they probably didn't even know she was in the building yet.

Kiefer rose and locked his terminal. He stopped by his supervisor's desk. "I've been summoned to Int-Ed. Do you know why?"

His supervisor shrugged. "The request was routed via Velten's office. Ask him."

Kiefer nodded and left. Ice ran through his veins, making his heart stutter. Did Velten know? *Of course he doesn't. Get a grip. There's no way they have a clue. Don't over react.* Harmony help him, he wasn't cut out for this sneaky stuff.

Arriving at the Devender headquarters, Kiefer steeled himself against the expected sense of loss. The Devenders had been his home, his family. He missed his troop. Grief swept through him, tightening his chest and muscles, and he gritted his teeth as he tried to ignore it.

At the Int-Ed reception, he showed his badge and followed the guard through the corridors. The door numbers rose towards I-20, and his heart rate increased until the flutter in his chest almost suffocated him. The guard opened the door and stood back, and Kiefer entered.

Kiefer halted as the door closed behind him. His mind blanked as he stared at Madeline.

"Ah, good. You're here." She motioned him forward. "I thought you would appreciate a frontline seat. Time to get your revenge."

"Revenge?" he whispered. He cleared his throat and stared at the man struggling against his restraints.

"Kiefer, help me. They've got it all wrong. I didn't kill your father, I swear. They won't believe me. Tell them it wasn't me."

Ferris. Madeline had brought him to witness her interrogation of Ferris. A wave of dizziness spread through him.

But where was Ciely, then? And why was Madeline in charge of the interrogation?

"Madeline?" Kiefer murmured as he approached her.

"I wanted to thank you. My father listened to me at last. I said you influenced him," Madeline said, flicking on some switches.

"How do you know how to work these machines?"

"I've been watching interrogations for years. They record them all, you know. Playbacks are easily accessible from the archives; you just need to request all interrogations on a specific date, and they send them to you."

"Great," Kiefer said, sitting in the chair she pointed him to.

Ferris twisted his head. "Kiefer? Please? Please help me."

"You know, the only interrogation I've ever seen when the supplicant didn't beg was you Kiefer."

"Really?"

"Yes, impressive."

"Not really," Kiefer replied.

"Of course it was. It's how I knew you were innocent. You had nothing to hide."

Kiefer breathed shallowly through his mouth, trying to ignore the cloying scent of chemicals and fear.

"How many interrogations have you performed?"

"This is my second. And I have a young girl after this. My father said I would get all the females from now on."

"How did you end up with Ferris, then?"

"He was a special request, just for you."

"Thoughtful of you."

Madeline flashed him a bright grin. She was as high on anticipation as she'd been the night he'd taken her out to dinner.

Ferris moaned as she pressed the sticky discs on his skin. The machine started beeping.

"Excellent," Madeline murmured and checked her pad again. "We need a test question. Ask him his name."

Kiefer cleared his throat. "What is your full name?"

Ferris whimpered and then said. "Reginald Sindle Ferris."

Kiefer raised an eyebrow at Madeline, and she peered at the graph and nodded.

"Ask him another."

Kiefer asked, "What is your home address?"

Ferris hesitated, and she clicked a dial and pressed a button. He shuddered, his breath coming out in gasps.

"Answer the question," she said.

"F-f-fallow Street."

She checked her sheet and nodded, humming under her breath. A small smile curved her lips, and she glanced at Kiefer. "Why do you dislike Kiefer Gallante?"

"What?" Ferris stared at her. "I-I don't."

"Oh, dear. Lie!" Madeline pressed a button, and Ferris spasmed. After a moment, he gasped in a breath, and Madeline repeated her question.

Ferris' eyes rolled as he stuttered out his words. "He doesn't deserve to be a Devender. He shouldn't be a commander. He gets special treatment because of who he is. Even now, l-look at him."

"Jealousy?" Madeline raised her eyebrows. "You're jealous of him?" She leaned over Ferris. "Yet you knew what his father was like? And you still thought he got special treatment?"

Ferris gaped at her.

Madeline smiled as her finger hovered over the button. "Is that why you accused Commander Kiefer of consorting with the rebels?"

"He was. He did. I was telling the truth. He was with that

woman for over a week." Ferris was babbling, his words tumbling out as he tried to justify himself.

"So, you killed his father? Thinking it was another way to get at him?"

Ferris struggled against his restraints. "No, no, I swear."

Madeline pressed a button, and Ferris went rigid. His face stretched in a horrible grimace.

"Oops," she said.

Kiefer ground his teeth. "Oops?"

"Wrong button."

Ferris went limp, and the aroma of singed skin permeated the room. Madeline wrinkled her nose and made a note on her pad. "Ask him another question."

"Doesn't he need a recovery time? Where's the doctor?"

"Oh, we don't need one for this. This is just a few questions."

"Madeline, you just electrocuted a man at the wrong voltage. That is a little more than oops."

"He's a criminal. He deserves it."

"He has not been sentenced yet. Until he is, he doesn't deserve this treatment."

"Oh, Kiefer. He killed your father, slandered your name. He's the reason you were wiped. Go on, ask him what he said. What else did he accuse you of?"

Kiefer gritted his teeth. This was not what he was here for. It wouldn't change anything. Glancing at Ferris, he said, "I doubt he'll be able to answer anything at the moment." The poor man was foaming at the mouth, and his eyes rolled whitely in his head. "I can take him back to his cell, if you like. Do you want me to bring the girl for you?"

"Would you? All the guards seem to have disappeared."

"Of course. After all, you've given me such a great gift; you've made him suffer. The least I can do is help you."

Kiefer kept his expression neutral as Madeline grinned, her eyes sparkling with delight.

"Then, yes." She looked at her pad. "Ciely Frances, cell 213-C. You can dump him in her cell."

"My pleasure," Kiefer said. He waited while Madeline remove the connectors and then unbuckled the straps, wrapped one of Ferris' limp arms over his shoulder, levered him up, and dragged his semi-conscious body out of the room.

Kiefer's mind spun as he staggered down the corridor. Ferris was no light weight; with a combination of corded muscle and well-toned body, he would be a good Devender if he could get his head out of his arse. He was too focussed on what he could gain instead of helping others.

The guard opened the cell, and Kiefer dumped him on the concrete floor. Kiefer straightened, still breathing heavily, and stared at Ciely Frances. Her face was salt white, her eyes wide with fear, and she huddled in the corner of the cell as if she could press herself into the stone walls and hide. She began whimpering.

"Ciely? It's Kiefer. Do you know who I am?"

"Please, not again. I've already told them everything. I don't know anything else, I swear."

"You told them everything? Even what Lorne told you never to speak of?"

"Everything, everything, everything."

Her eyes dilated as he crouched beside her, and she flinched back. He was losing her.

"Ciely, hold on a little longer."

Ferris groaned behind Kiefer. His arm flopped into the ray of light from the open cell door, and Ciely stared at it, her face greying as she began to gasp. "No, nooooo!" she wailed, tugging at her hair. "Noooooo!"

"Ciely." Kiefer's voice was sharp, and Ferris groaned again.

The silence was sudden as Ciely stopped mid-wail, her chest heaving, her blue eyes wide.

"I'm so sorry." Ferris' voice was feeble and drained of life. "So sorry. I didn't know, I swear. I didn't know what they did."

Kiefer glared at him. It was too little, too late. "Maybe you should have found out first before you betrayed others."

"I didn't kill your father, Kiefer, and I don't know who did. There were many people there that night; it was a full house."

Kiefer relaxed; Ferris wasn't accusing him anymore. He helped Ciely stand, and she swayed. Then she turned and tried to kick Ferris, but she didn't have the strength to make it hurt. "You-you bastard. You said…you said you'd help me find A-Arran…" Her voice trailed off into tears.

"I'm sorry. I'm so sorry," Ferris moaned, staring at her, distraught. His usual confident demeanour had been replaced by that of a shaking, desperate young man. He tried to move his arm, but he couldn't control his body. His muscles spasmed at the attempt, and he lay gasping for breath. "I never meant to…" he mumbled into the stone floor, spittle flecking his mouth.

Kiefer was glad Ferris didn't finish the sentence, because he was sure it was another lie. He steered Ciely out of the cell, and the guard slammed the door shut behind him.

Ciely collapsed to the floor, a trembling dead weight, trying to dig her toes in. He scooped her up in his arms and glanced at the guards. They fell in on either side of him, and he silently cursed. He had hoped his good fortune would mean he could walk her straight out of here. But no, the guards crowded him as if they knew and forced him down the corridor and back through the tunnels towards the interrogation rooms.

When they arrived, the interrogation room was full of people. Madeline frowned at him. "This one is official; it's being recorded, so we needed a tech and a doctor." She flounced back to her desk, tapping her foot in a sharp staccato. It grated on his nerves, and Ciely gripped Kiefer's jacket and burrowed her face in his chest.

The guards watched from the doorway, absorbed by the scene.

He dropped his mouth to her hair and whispered, "I am so sorry, Ciely. Hold on. Lorne is coming."

She shook and lifted her face to look at him. "No, please, no, it's all my fault." Her face crumpled.

"Strap her down. Let's get on with it," Madeline snapped.

Ciely clung to Kiefer as he tried to lay her in the chair. "Be strong," he murmured while the technician tightened the straps.

Ciely struggled, trying to hold onto him, and Kiefer stepped back. "I need to return to my office," he said, avoiding the technician's eye when he realised it was Gerry Staffen. His heart thumped a little quicker as the pieces of his plan began to slot together. And yet, so much could still go wrong. "Are you sure she should be questioned today? She is in no fit state for more treatment."

The doctor leaned over her and held her wrist, before jotting a note on his pad. "Her stats are high," Henry Staffen said in a neutral voice.

"Tough! We follow the schedule, not question it," Madeline replied.

"Ah, Kiefer," Velten said as he entered the room. "Excellent. Madeline said you would be here to observe. I hope, between you, you can validate her statements."

Ciely moaned.

"Sir, I don't think I should be here. I am not supposed to be in interrogation," Kiefer said, shuffling towards the door.

"Nonsense. Time for you to see it from the other side."

"Minister, please. If we could have a word? The girl is in no condition to be questioned further."

Velten chuckled. "My dear boy, it's the best time then. Madeline, she's all yours. Come, Kiefer. Come watch with me." Velten led the way out of the room, and Kiefer had no choice but to follow.

37

Kiefer followed Velten into the small office behind the two way observation glass. The two guards who had escorted him from the cells waited in the corridor. A thin-faced man in a white lab coat sat at a desk, monitoring a screen in front of him. He flipped a switch and the office lights dimmed, replaced by a dull amber glow. The scene in the interrogation room was brightly lit, revealing every nuance of Ciely's suffering and fear. His stomach clenched even tighter as he stood beside Velten and stared through the glass.

The minister smiled as he watched his daughter hover over the girl and said, "Madeline will see that the program runs properly."

Madeline drew closer, and static charged the air. Ciely stiffened in the chair as the current ran through her. The technician checked the dial and then hit the button. "One," he said, and Ciely collapsed limply back in the chair.

Madeline hovered over Ciely, her eyes glittering in antici-pation. She licked her lips. "Tell me where the rebel hideout is."

Ciely moaned and struggled.

"If you don't want it to happen again, talk."

"The Wytchwards," Ciely whispered, tears streaming down her face. "They are in the Wytchwards. Our families, all of them. Through the marshes, I gave you the route across the plains. I already told you. Pleeeeease."

"Again." Madeline's voice was hard.

"Two," the technician said. The current jolted through Ciely, and she gasped. Her eyes rolled whitely. Kiefer shifted next to Velten, unable to keep still. His heart rate spiked with every charge, his body reacting even if his mind didn't.

"She's answered. This is unnecessary," he said, his eyes glued to Ciely's distraught face.

Velten glanced at him. "Haven't got the stomach for it, have you? Madeline is a natural. I should have seen it before," he said with fatherly pride.

"I thought she was teaching in Pre-Ed. Why is she here?"

"She persuaded me that she had more to offer," Velten said, checking his watch. "I'll return in an hour; the program should be complete by then. I'll see the recording later." He nodded at the technician and left.

Kiefer drew in his breath at the man's callous attitude. The booth was dark, with only the amber lights from the controls. They lit the lab engineer's face with an orange glow, as he adjusted the recording dials.

"Again," Madeline said through the speakers, and Kiefer knocked the engineer out with one well-positioned blow. The man slumped forward, and Kiefer dragged him off the controls and stabbed the button to stop the recording.

"Three," Gerry Staffen said, and Ciely's body jerked, and her eyes closed. A faint gleam of sweat covered her face. "It's running," Gerry said.

Madeline's eyes glittered, and she stroked the sweat off Ciely's forehead and then licked her finger.

The doctor calmly monitored the patient's statistics.

Madeline's voice echoed through the speakers, high and excited. "She looks too relaxed; are you sure you've got the right voltage?"

Kiefer opened the door to the booth and beckoned one of the guards over.

Once the guard entered the booth, Kiefer punched him in the gut and grabbed his taser. The guard slammed him against the wall. His grip locked like a vice around Kiefer's throat, and he squeezed. Kiefer tased him, and the man collapsed, spasming.

Gerry Staffen's voice came through the speaker: "Of course."

Kiefer took a deep breath and straightened his hair and clothes. Through the two-way window, Madeline slid her hand under Ciely's shirt and placed her hand over her heart and smiled. "Raise it," she whispered as she hovered over Ciely's greying face.

In horror, Kiefer stared at Madeline for a moment and then dashed out of the booth. He rushed the second guard, jammed the taser against his neck, and spun into the interrogation room before the man had even started collapsing to the floor. "Stop her!" he yelled as Madeline strode over to the console and reached for the dial.

"You heard me," Madeline said, ignoring Kiefer. "Raise it. You're not doing it properly."

Gerry batted her hand away. "Are you mad? You'll kill her."

As Kiefer lurched for Ciely, trying to rip off the pads, Madeline whipped around, pushed Gerry out of the way, and twisted the dial. Ciely went rigid in the chair, her back arching as the current ripped through her and into Kiefer. His breath stuttered as he collapsed to the floor, and his muscles spasmed in remembered agony.

Lorne and Julian rushed through the door, and Lorne, taking in the scene in one swift glance, shouted, "Julian! Restrain that woman."

Julian barrelled into Madeline as Gerry lunged at the controls to dial the voltage back down.

"Don't touch them!" Henry shouted, watching Ciely until her body relaxed. "Now you can," he said and he ripped off the pads. He connected a bag of fluids and slid a cannula into the back of Ciely's hand. "She'll be weak and disoriented when she wakes up. Don't let her move until I say so."

His face tightened as he felt Ciely's pulse. "Pain relief," he murmured and added a clear liquid through the cannula; there was no doubt she would be in pain. "She's been under too long." He scowled at Madeline. "Stupid, idiotic, byte-sized, pea-brained scientists!"

"What happened?" Lorne gathered Kiefer in her arms and craned her neck to see Ciely. "Will she...they be alright?"

Gerry stared at them. "Where did you come from?"

"I was escorting Lorne to one of the rooms when we heard the noise," Julian replied. "We have to leave."

Madeline tried to twist out of Julian's grip, and he slammed her against the wall. "What do you think you were doing? You could have killed her."

"She's a rebel. She doesn't have the right to live," Madeline snapped.

"That is not your decision to make," Lorne hissed as she watched Henry's competent fingers flutter over her sister. A sudden fear gripped her innards as her gaze was drawn back to Kiefer's pallid face. The gleam of his half-lidded eyes struck her as wrong. She frantically began searching for a pulse. "Henry, what do we do? He's not breathing."

Henry cursed, patted Ciely's unresponsive arm, and rushed over to Kiefer. Pushing Lorne out of the way, he pressed his fingers against Kiefer's throat and then began pumping Kiefer's chest repeatedly, muttering under his breath all the while. Long seconds passed, his rhythm never faltering, and then he released a sigh of relief as Kiefer's lashes began to quiver and he inhaled.

Henry leaned closer, monitoring Kiefer as his fingers dug into Kiefer's throat. Finally, he nodded. "Keep him still. His body is still recovering. His nerves need to settle."

Lorne hovered over him and began kissing his face. "I thought I'd lost you! You weren't supposed to be here, Kiefer. This is not part of the plan."

"Be glad he was," Henry said, "or that bitch would have killed Ciely."

Madeline tried to bite Julian's wrist and punched her fist up under his chin. Julian shook the blow off and raised her off the floor by her neck.

Lorne glared at her as she gathered Kiefer into her arms. "You sadistic bitch. Getting off on it were you?"

Madeline hissed and spat as she struggled in Julian's grip. Julian tweaked a nerve in her neck and let her collapse to the floor.

"What?" Julian asked as Henry glared at him. "She was getting heavy. Anyway, we need to get out of here; it's taking too long."

"It'll take as long as it takes," Henry replied, focused on reviving Ciely.

Kiefer inhaled and let his breath out with a groan. Then, with Lorne's help, he sat up.

Lorne scowled at Kiefer. "What are you doing here? You're not supposed to be here."

"Best laid plans and all that," Kiefer said, rubbing his arm.

Henry threw a jar at Lorne. "For the burns," he said. Lorne grabbed Kiefer's hand and sucked in a breath at the livid red marks across his fingers. "Next time, don't touch someone with high voltage running through them," she said as she smoothed the salve over his fingers and pushed his sleeve up, following the angry red burns.

Kiefer huffed. "There better not be a next time."

"No, there hadn't. It's unlikely you'd survive it," Henry said.

"Gee, thanks, doc."

Henry grimaced at Kiefer and returned to his other patient. "Ciely? Don't move, You've had a bit more voltage than is good for you."

Ciely didn't respond. Her glazed blue eyes stared at the ceiling; they were almost silver in the harsh overhead light.

"Kiefer, why are you here? What's happened to your grand plan? Everyone is out of place." Lorne hugged him, and he tried to hug her back, but his coordination was off.

Julian grinned as he crouched beside Kiefer. "Improv. Best way for success."

Kiefer rubbed a shaky hand over his face and then gripped Julian's arm. "You got this?"

"Of course," Julian replied, "but don't you think you ought to rest a moment?"

Kiefer shook his head and kissed Lorne's cheek before releasing her and trying to stand. "No time," Kiefer replied. "I'm supposed to be somewhere else."

Julian took most of his weight and held him steady as he gained his balance. He wavered, lurching to one side and then staggered over to the door. He took a deep breath, opened the door, and, after peering out, disappeared down the corridor.

"In that case," Lorne said, holding Julian's gaze, "make sure you get Ciely out safe."

Julian nodded, and she rushed after Kiefer. "I said he'd need a woman with a stern heart," he said to the empty doorway. "Looks like he found one."

"Take a moment," Henry said to Ciely. "You're in the mind-wipe lab. You've been electrocuted repeatedly. Your muscles will relax soon. I've given you a pain reliever and a muscle relaxant. The pain should ease shortly. Rest. You've got a minute or two."

Ciely stared at him blankly.

"Though only a minute, we've been here too long," Henry said, sealing his bag. "Kiefer said we would be in and out in five minutes."

Julian grimaced and bent to pick up Ciely. "Did he? Tell him not to be so stupid next time."

Henry chuckled and, after draping the bag of fluids around Julian's neck, patted his shoulder.

Julian strode to the door. "Remember, exit through the ladies' college. Don't delay."

Henry hurried to wrap a blanket around Ciely. "Once the spasms stop, she'll feel lethargic. You need to keep an eye on her breathing. Any issues, any at all, and she'll need immediate treatment. Likewise, her muscles. If her arms or legs begin to swell, she's in trouble, and you'll need to go straight to the infirmary. I've done what I can, but it's down to you now."

"Thanks, doc," Julian said as he hugged Ciely against his chest. "You and Gerry get out now. There's nothing more you can do."

Henry nodded. "Be careful, Julian. Make sure she avoids any strenuous activity."

Julian glanced at Madeline. "Maybe *she* should have a

dose of her own medicine. A memory wipe and a reset would do her good."

"Just enough to calm her down. She'll do herself an injury if she carries on," Gerry said with an evil grin as he began to power up the machine.

Julian grinned at the Staffens. "Don't delay. Leave the moment she's under." He stumbled as the building trembled, his clasp on Ciely tightening. Nothing significant, but enough to make him stagger as if the floor had moved.

He couldn't check his watch, but he knew it was the beginning of the end. Kiefer had identified a small backup generator that was unmonitored. Harmony had agreed to reverse the current, a slow build to overloaded the generator and spark a fire in the basement. Enough to trigger—the scream of a siren blared through the corridors, interrupting his thought—the fire alarm. They would begin evacuating the building. He looked back into the interrogation room.

"No delays!" he shouted and left.

Annie stared at the screen. She was through the first two security checks and needed Chiva to breach the third. She waited, drumming her fingers on the plastic desk, her eyes constantly flitting to the door as the alarm bell screamed.

Never had she even imagined a place like this existed. The ladies' college had been built specifically so young women and girls, could learn. To sit in a classroom *all day* and be taught about new things. It wasn't fair.

She had bluffed her way past the guard, but he was likely to return. The guard had barely glanced at the papers Chiva had given her from his project in case anyone did check her story. The waiting was stretching her nerves wire thin. Wiping her mouth, she waited some more. The terminal pinged, and she crouched over the keyboard. Her fingers flew over the keys, entering the commands Kiefer had given her.

Annie watched them segment, and then spiral into a perfect funnel, and then they executed in sequence, and she smiled as pure poetry flowed across the screen.

Kiefer was a genius.

All the gates were limned in green, and she began unlocking them in sequence.

She flinched as a guard slammed open a door further down the corridor. "All out. Can't you hear the evacuation bell? Out now." Footsteps thudded down the hallway.

Another door slammed. "Everybody out. Evacuation drill, now."

The guard was working his way up the corridor. Annie drummed her fingers on the desk. "Hurry up, hurry up." The next gate released, and her fingers flew over the keyboard.

Another door slammed, and she tensed and shot a glance over her shoulder. He was getting closer.

———

Chiva grinned with satisfaction as he stared at the terminal in one of the booths in the public area of the main college building. It was magical, watching as the code was executed, the way it flowed in sequence, one line after another.

He looked up as the building shook and dust and grit rattled down the walls. Then he turned his gaze back to the code scrolling down the screen, nodding as Annie nullified the defences. Three down, four. Another tremor shook the building, and he pinched his lips. Come on, Annie, come on. His grip on the disk tightened.

Velten rested his hand on his desk as the vibration rumbled away. He frowned and then leaned forward, flicking on his terminal. He checked the interrogation lab; Madelaine should be finished by now. As expected, a reset program was running. He tapped his lip thoughtfully.

A moment later, he typed his access codes and ran a security query. Staring at the screen, he skimmed the results until he found the breach to Harmony's chamber. Then he flicked a switch and as his screen went dark, he left his office.

When Lorne caught up with Kiefer, he staggered into the wall, and she grabbed his arm. "Where are you going?" she asked.

She gasped in shock as he tugged her against his body, and they fell through an empty space. The door slid shut behind them.

They were in a dark corridor stretching off into the depths of the building. Kiefer braced himself against the wall and shrugged. "I had a feeling things might not go to plan. Annie knows what to do. Julian will get her out."

"And what are we doing?" Lorne asked, looking up warily as the ceiling above them creaked ominously.

Kiefer stopped and looked at her blankly. "Who are you? Am I supposed to know you?"

"That's not funny. Don't even think it."

He grabbed her close and kissed her.

"Kiefer, now is not the time."

"Why not? You said we had to take the moments when they came, and this is definitely one of those moments." His arms tightened as he thoroughly kissed her.

Lorne melted against him.

"Lorne is right; this is not the time," a prim voice said from all around them, and Kiefer rolled his eyes.

"Harmony, now *is* the time."

"No, it isn't. Velten is on his way. You have to move."

Kiefer sighed as the door to their left swished open. Wrapping an arm around Lorne's waist, he guided her down the corridor. He stopped next to a metal ladder going both up and down, both ways dark and uninviting. "Down," he murmured, pushing her down the cylindrical ladder. He followed behind her, glad some of his strength had returned. At the bottom, he grabbed her hand and hurried down a dark tunnel.

"How do you know where we're even going?"

"Harmony is showing me. See? On the floor." Lorne looked down, and a gentle glow led the way, a stripe laid out on the tunnel floor, fading as they passed. The passage opened into a circular room with large, curved screens covering the walls in an arc, providing a full 180-degree view, a window into Harmony.

Kiefer caught his breath and stilled his rapidly beating heart. Dropping into the chair, he pressed a button on the table surface. The outline of a keyboard appeared limned in red, and next to it, a bright green button glowed. Kiefer typed into the console. The screens woke up and filled with statistics. "This is where they monitor the shackles." He peered at the screens curving around the room and then stood and moved over to the central screen. He tapped a box in the top right. "This is the one to watch. When this gets to zero, we can release the synapses."

"And how do we do that?" Lorne asked.

"We press that bright green button on the console, but we have to wait until it's zero, or we'll cause more harm than good."

Lorne watched the screen. The numbers were decreasing, 66, 65, 64…slowly, but they were decreasing. "What is it?"

Kiefer looked across at her, confused. "What's what?"

"The numbers, what do they represent?"

Kiefer's eyes unfocused for a moment as he listened to Harmony. "No idea. I didn't understand a word of the explanation. All I know is that we need to wait until zero and then press the button."

"Then you should sit and rest while we wait," Lorne said, forcing him into the chair. She massaged his tense shoulders. "You're supposed to be taking it easy. You were just accidentally electrocuted."

"So stupid. I should have known better."

Lorne chuckled. "Well, at least, once we're finished, you can sleep well tonight."

Kiefer flexed his shoulders under her hands. "And how likely is that?"

"Very unlikely," Velten said from the doorway. "Move away from the console."

38

Henry and Gerry skidded onto the main concourse as the alarm bell screeched through the building. Chunks of masonry shattered around them, and splinters flew at them as if they were the intended target. Flinging up an arm, which afforded little protection from the vicious shards, Gerry herded his husband towards the exit. Security staff were ushering people out the glass doors while first responders piled up equipment by the reception desk.

Henry stopped and spun around. "The gurney," he said and darted off towards the steel-framed trolley parked against the wall. After dumping his bag on the bed, he grabbed an oxygen cylinder and mask, spun the bed around, and headed back in the direction they had come.

"Henry, what are you doing?"

"Julian will never get through that."

"But we don't know where he is."

"Sure, we do. I know where I'd be," Henry said as they turned the corner. "I'm a doctor!" he shouted as guards spilt out of the stairwell. They parted around him, and Henry continued down the corridor with Gerry close behind.

"Where?"

"Canteen."

"What? Why?"

"Newsfeeds, internal screens. He could check out the foyer."

The canteen doors crashed open as Henry barged through. "There was a report of someone suffering from smoke inhalation. Where's the patient?" he shouted.

Julian's voice came from behind the pillar. "Here."

"Lay her on the bed. We'll have her to rights in no time."

"What are you doing here?" Julian hissed as he did as Henry instructed.

"Improvising," Henry replied. He placed the oxygen mask over Ciely's face and twisted the dial to start the flow. "The foyer's heaving with guards. You'd never get through. This way is better."

Henry efficiently settled Ciely into a more comfortable position and tucked a blanket around her. He hooked the bag of fluid over a hook and then grinned at Julian. "See you later." He motioned to his husband. "Gerry, take the other end, and don't stop for anyone."

Julian watched them leave, a stunned expression on his face. Then after a quick glance around the empty canteen, he headed towards the academy. Threading his way through the people streaming out of the building, Julian ran. Shoving people aside, he forced his way through the corridors, until he reached the bridge connecting the Devender building to the Ministry. He raced down the stairs to the second floor, to the Pre-Ed department and the back entrance to the ladies' college.

A security guard barred his way. "All evacuees should leave now."

"I'm here to run a last check of the floors. Devender," Julian said, flashing his badge.

"Sir, we've already sent the building security to check."

"Well done. I have to sign off on the building. You should wait outside. I'll do a final sweep."

"Yes, sir." The guard left with alacrity.

Running up the corridor, Julian yelled at the guard opening the doors. "I'll finish this floor. There are reports of people refusing to leave on the second floor." The guard scowled, but recognising Julian's uniform, he nodded and ran.

Julian slammed open the next door. "Annie?" he whispered. "Annie, job done. It's time to leave."

Julian exhaled in relief when Annie peered out from behind her chair. "Commander Laithe?" Rising, she leaned back over the screen. "Not yet," she said, scanning the code, her fingers poised over her keyboard.

Julian glanced out the door. "Annie, we have to go, now."

"No, we've one more gate to go."

Julian entered the office and scanned the screen over her shoulder. "Gate? What gate?" He squinted at the code scrolling on the screen. "Wait a minute. Isn't that Kiefer's fulcrum?"

"Yes," Annie said absently, focused on the screen. "He modified it; it's the key. One more gate to unlock, and he'll be in."

"In where?"

Annie froze, waited, and then tapped a key. The screen blossomed into a rainbow of colours, and she dropped to her knees. She slammed a disk into the tray and then leapt back to her feet. Tapping a sequence, she watched the screen intently and then said, "Now we can go." She spun into his chest. "Oof," she said as she met solid muscle.

Julian wrapped his arms around her to steady her, and Annie looked up and he met her pale blue eyes. She smiled, uncertainly. "Commander Laithe?"

"It's Julian," he murmured. "Call me, Julian," he repeated and then spun her and dragged her out of the room. Something detonated beneath their feet, and the building sagged. Rumbling vibrations echoed along the halls, and they half-slid, half-staggered down the corridor as the floor canted down at a sickening angle.

"I thought this building wouldn't be affected?" Annie murmured as she hurried to keep up with Julian.

"Obviously, Kiefer got that wrong."

"Let's hope that's the only thing he got wrong," Annie replied.

Kiefer helped Lorne stand and tugged her towards the bare wall opposite the arc of screens. He wrapped his arm around her chest and pulled her back against him. "Minister Velten, I would have thought you had more important things to do."

"Kiefer, Kiefer, you think you are so clever, but you are not. You cannot release Harmony from here."

Lorne stiffened in his arms, but Kiefer held her still. His arms trembled with the effort as he leaned back against the wall.

"Did you tell your rebel that you could? She will be so disappointed in you."

"This is Harmony's chamber," Kiefer said.

"That's what it's called, but it is only a window. A window into her soul, as such." Velten waved a hand at the screens; the other held his gun on them. "Her vital statistics."

"I would suggest they don't reflect the best of health," Kiefer said.

Velten's smile was forced. "Best of health for what? Do you have some dewy-eyed notion of freedom? People need order. They need control. They need to be told what to do, what to think. Otherwise, everything descends into chaos."

Kiefer watched the small box at the top of the screen. The numbers continued to decrease: 35, 34, 33…

"Maybe people would surprise you if you gave them the chance. Look at Sector 45," Kiefer said.

Velten snorted. "You think they are an example to follow? I think not."

Kiefer smiled. "What is it the core mandates say? Harmony protects all so we may live our lives to the full. How is that possible if Harmony is not free to protect us? Since when did people like you, Minister Velten, and people like my father have the right to take that away from Harmony? From us?"

"I knew it. I told Madeline you were a dreamer." Velten stilled. "How did you fight the reprogramming?" His gun moved. "Where is Madeline?"

The numbers on the screen continued to decrease, 24, 23, 22… The screen blossomed into rainbows.

A tremor vibrated through the structure, and Velten braced against the wall and looked up. "What have you done?"

"I'm so sorry," Kiefer breathed into Lorne's hair.

She looked up, startled. "Why?"

Velten scowled at them. "What? What is it? Even if you destroy the building, it won't change anything."

Kiefer smiled and pushed away from the wall. He stepped towards Velten, he could barely make out the numbers through the myriad of colours. They were single digits.

"You are too late," Kiefer said with a vicious grin. "Harmony is free, and you will have to pay the price."

Velten gave a brittle laugh. "No, I think you will pay the price." He aimed his gun at Lorne.

"Madeline is lost. Long live the new Madeline," Kiefer said.

Velten jerked, and his face paled. "You bastard," he said and pulled the trigger.

39

The academy building shuddered. The explosion of shattering glass had Julian shoving Annie to the ground as he covered her with his larger body. Shards of glass crashed down around them. Grabbing Annie, Julian hustled her down the corridor, and then they erupted out of the glittering shower as if Harmony had spat them out. Raising his arms, Julian sheltered her from the falling debris and hissed as fragments glanced off him instead.

They skidded to a halt at the bottom of the steps and turned to look back at the scene of devastation in horror. The Ministry building next door visibly swayed and then slowly imploded.

They ran, surrounded by screaming people trying to get further away. Clouds of dust enveloped them, blinded them as floor by floor, glass shattered, falling in a shower of deadly splinters as the building collapsed and sank into the ground.

Sirens sounded in the distance; the piercing sound getting louder as red and blue lights penetrated the thick dust surrounding them. As the air cleared, they reached an open concourse, filled with people and medics. Annie started hunting through the milling people who had been evacuated. "Chiva? Where are you?" she shouted, jumping to see over their heads.

"Annie, come this way. We said we'd meet back at Kiefer's; we can't hang about here." Julian dragged her away as guards began corralling people and pushing them away from the scene. Annie stopped complaining when she saw the blood running down his face. She folded her handkerchief and, standing on tip toe, pressed it against his temple.

"I'm sorry," she said.

Julian winced as he ducked his head so she could reach. "What for?" he asked, pressing his thick fingers over hers to hold the cloth in place.

"Delaying, but I had to wait for the last gate. Otherwise, it would have all been for nothing."

"What was the fulcrum doing?"

"Freeing Harmony."

"I thought that was what Kiefer was doing. He said he had to go to her chamber."

"No, he was the diversion. He kept Velten looking in the wrong place while we ran a virus straight through his defences. Harmony is free now. All the synapses were broken; they have no inroads into Harmony anymore."

"They'll have a back-up."

Annie's eyes glittered as they hurried down the street. "Not anymore. Chiva downloaded the Bantwich virus into the server farm."

Julian stopped dead, his chest fluttering. "He did what?"

"It was Kiefer's idea. He asked Chiva to work the code back to the core string and build out a new version. Kiefer remembered the code from Sector 45, and Chiva transformed it into the virus."

Julian held his head. The mess it would cause; the

computers would all go into melt down. He suddenly laughed. What was he worrying about? The server farms were destroyed. The processors would be obsolete, and the whole net would be down—until such time as they rebuilt it.

"Don't worry, Kiefer will explain it all. Come on, Doctor Staffen needs to stitch that." Annie tugged him down the street, her fingers entwined in his.

They were the first to arrive back at Kiefer's apartment, and Annie made Julian sit in an armchair. She bustled about, getting more cloths and a bowl of water. Then she bathed his face and the gash. Rolling up another square of cloth, she laid it along the wound and wrapped the bandage around his head.

Julian sat stoically through all her ministrations, even accepting a couple of pain relief tablets, which he knocked back with a shudder.

She grinned and went to make some tea.

Next to arrive were the Staffens, covered in white dust and carrying an equally dust-coated Ciely between them. Julian hurried to take her. She was still limp and unresponsive, her eyes shut, her face grey. Annie hurried to hug them and then pushed them into the bathroom to clean up. Julian carried Ciely to the bedroom where he laid her on Kiefer's bed and stood looking down at her.

Annie joined him. "What happened to her?"

"She was electrocuted. I left her with the Staffens. I had to find you," Julian said.

Annie stared at him. "But…"

"But nothing," Julian said and kissed her. Annie blinked and then kissed him back. Her arms threaded around his neck, and she pressed against him. As their kiss deepened, Julian groaned deep into her mouth.

Henry cleared his throat, and Annie and Julian broke

apart. "There's a time and a place," he said as he hurried into the bedroom to check on Ciely.

Annie laughed a little self-consciously and went to switch on the newsfeed and groaned out loud at the black screen. Unsurprisingly, the whole communications network was down. She made more tea instead, gaze drawn to flickers of blue and red lights still reflecting in the glass buildings around the area which used to house the Ministry and the Harmony complex.

Washed and changed, Gerry collapsed onto the sofa as Henry tutted over Julian. Julian closed his eyes as the doctor opened his kit and threaded a sharp needle. He opened them again as a small hand crept into his, and Annie smiled at him. He smiled back and stared into her pale blue eyes as Henry stitched his skin back together.

"How is Ciely?" Annie asked while Henry wrapped Julian's head with a new bandage.

"Too early to tell. We need to give her time to recover," Henry said, and then he wiped his hands and went to sit with Gerry on the sofa. Snuggling into Gerry's embrace, Henry closed his eyes. A smile grew on his face as Gerry murmured in his ear.

Gerry broke off at a loud explosion on the monitor as it blared back into life.

Julian reached over for the remote, turned the sound down, and scowled at the screen. "Someone must have managed to reconnect the media channels. You know it looks like the damage was limited to only that building and the academy. Do you think Harmony contained it?"

Annie stirred. "Must have. Where is Chiva? And Kiefer and Lorne? They should be here by now."

"They'll be here. Give them time," Julian murmured as he squeezed her hand. "They went deeper, him and Lorne. Said they had to free Harmony."

But they wouldn't have needed to if Annie was right, so where had they gone?

———

Kiefer pushed Lorne away from him, twisting as he shouted, "Go low!" He avoided the first charge and lurched for the console, but not the second, which caught his right shoulder and spun him. His body gave under him, and he slid off the console, his hand dragging over the keyboard to the green button as he collapsed, senseless, to the concrete floor. All the screens went out, leaving the room dim and lifeless.

Lorne dived for Velten's legs, driving him to the floor. His gun popped as it discharged into the wall. She twisted around him before he had a chance to recover and punched him in the face. His head jerked back, slamming against the concrete wall, and his eyes rolled up as he slid down the wall, leaving a red smear in his wake. She inhaled as she saw Kiefer shuddering on the floor. Following a slow exhale, he stilled.

"No," she gasped as she scrabbled over to his body. He wasn't breathing. Again! She ripped open his shirt and, ignoring the livid burns on his skin, placed her hands on his chest, interlocked her fingers, and began pumping. She pinched his nose and blew in his mouth for two counts, watching his chest rise, and then she repeated everything, focussing on trying to make him take a breath.

"Come on, you bastard, don't you give up on me now," she muttered, pumping furiously and then breathing slow and deep into his mouth. She didn't notice at first, as the screens began to light up with swirls of colour, it wasn't until the reflection on the floor crept closer, all colours of the rainbow in pretty mosaics.

"He needs Vizerine," a youthful voice said from above

her, and she leaned back on her heels in surprise, breathing deeply, her own chest aching.

A young child, brown-eyed, with glossy chestnut curls, sat on the desk, swinging her legs. Her feet were bare.

"How did you get in here? And what is Vizerine?"

"It's what they were after, those men. They want what I am; they only wanted the Vizerine, not me."

"You shouldn't be down here. This building is collapsing. You should leave while you can," Lorne said, returning to Kiefer.

The child watched Lorne breathe into Kiefer's mouth. "That's not going to work. The Warden needs Vizerine."

Lorne pushed her hair out of her face with shaking fingers. "I don't have any Vizerine. I don't even know what it is."

"I do," the child said and hopped off the desk. She stood over Kiefer for a moment and then knelt on his chest and pushed her fists into his skin up under his ribs. Then she began to glow. Faint at first, a swirl of colours spread from her fists into Kiefer's body. The glow pulsed and spread, coating Kiefer in a rainbow of light which coalesced into a single colour Lorne couldn't describe. It wasn't one; it was all, and it pulsed with life.

Kiefer groaned, and his eyelashes fluttered. Lorne leaned over him as the glow faded. He looked normal again. The light had gone, and his chest rose and fell.

"What's sitting on my chest?" he wheezed. "It feels like the building collapsed on me."

Lorne looked up as a loud crash above them shook the room. This was followed by more detonations, and the ceiling groaned.

"It will soon if you don't get up," Lorne said, trying to help him sit up.

He flopped, his tortured muscles not responding.

"It will take a little time for it to work through him. His arm won't respond, though. It'll be numb for a few days," the youthful voice said.

Kiefer squinted as he gazed up. He relaxed back in Lorne's arms and frowned at something over her shoulder. She looked back and saw the child smiling down at him.

"Do we have time?" Lorne asked as the sound of falling masonry clattered down the corridor.

"Not really," the child said with a tilt of her head. "I thought you'd relate better to me like this. I know you like children." She smiled at Lorne and morphed into a small boy with a cheeky grin, then a slim young man with impossible curls, and finally a black cat, sinuous and smooth. All had enormous eyes, wide and all-seeing. "I can be whatever you want," the cat said, baring her teeth.

"Harmony, this really isn't the time for games," Kiefer said. He still struggled to lift his hand.

She morphed back to the little girl, and her smile widened, revealing tiny pearly teeth. "It won't work. Use the other one."

Lorne sat back with a squeak. "Harmony? You're really here?"

"Well," the child replied as Kiefer used his left hand to rub his face, "I'm all around, but I think you'll find it easier to have a focal point to talk to. I wanted to say thank you for all your efforts to help me, but I suppose now is not the time." Smiling at Lorne, she gestured at the ceiling. "I can stop it from crushing you, but the corridor will be blocked soon, and then you'll have to try and clear it." She stared at Kiefer for a moment. "Strap his arm against his chest; he can't use it, and it'll get in the way."

"Bossy little thing, isn't she?" Kiefer murmured as Lorne undid his belt and used it to strap his right arm across his chest.

"I heard that," Harmony replied.

Lorne smiled into Kiefer's eyes. His pupils were blown wide and swirling with…with Vizerine, she supposed. She had no other name for it. "Can you get up?"

"You keep saving my life; you must like having me around," Kiefer said as he struggled to his feet and leaned heavily on Lorne. He held his chest. "I feel like someone's been stomping on my chest."

Lorne cupped his cheek, stared into his crazy eyes, and kissed him. "I'm afraid we both did, and you're welcome… again," she said and helped steer him out the door.

EPILOGUE

The aftermath rumbled on for weeks.

Dr Staffen admitted Kiefer and Ciely into his private rooms at the hospital and refused to allow anyone to visit them. Kiefer's mother stepped into the gap left by the Ministry and decreed a week of mourning for those who were lost in the collapse of the Ministry building.

The Ministry feeds were just blank screens, until one day a reel of tranquil images appeared. People collected on street corners to read the news which began to scroll across the screens. The sky brightened to a brilliant blue and then softened to violet as the second moon rose, casting its reddish glow, and the sun warmed the streets as three moons phased across the sky.

People gazed around them as if they didn't recognise where they were. For the first time in their history, all three moons were visible in the sky at the same time as the ancient texts had once described them. Harmony was determined to restore the natural flow of the planet, and where she could reach, she began to revitalise the sectors, encouraging new trees to grow and rivers to flow, watering crop fields and ripening fruit.

As the rubble of the old Ministry building began to be cleared, there was no sign of Chiva, and Annie sadly gave up hope of finding him.

A week later, Kiefer lay in his hospital bed, a constant stream of visitors from his mother and her newly appointed ministers to the men of his old Devender unit passed through his door, until Henry Staffen threatened to bar everyone.

"Does no one understand you need to rest?" Staffen complained.

"It will ease off as things are sorted out," Kiefer said with a weary smile.

"You are not the one sorting them all out. No visitors until tomorrow. The only thing you are allowed to do is sleep." Staffen stalked out the room.

The next afternoon, Staffen allowed Annie to visit. Kiefer gripped her hand. "I am so sorry about Chiva. He should have been able to get out with more than enough time. I don't know what went wrong."

"It wasn't your fault, Kiefer." Annie shrugged. "We'll never know why he didn't make it out. Maybe he went the wrong way or got delayed by security. There are many possibilities. The college building was damaged, but there were no reported fatalities. There was no reason for him to enter the Ministry building, if that's what he did." She bit her lip. "Why would he take such a stupid risk?"

"I don't know."

"Julian has offered to take me home to tell my parents."

Kiefer cocked an eyebrow. "Julian, eh?"

Annie flushed, but a small smile hovered over her mouth. "I like him."

"He's a good man."

Kiefer couldn't bring himself to mourn Ferris' death. The

mind-wipe had stolen any friendship they may have had and only left the bitter taste of betrayal and greed. He observed Annie's faint blush and didn't mention him.

"Time's up," Staffen said as he peered through the door. "Kiefer needs to rest if he wants to go home next week."

"If I rest much more, my body will be melded to the bed."

"Good," Staffen said with a grin and escorted Annie out.

———

The following week, Kiefer was finally allowed home on condition he still rested. No strenuous activity.

Staffen smiled at Lorne, his eyes twinkling. "I mean it. His heart can't take it. You need to keep him calm."

Lorne grinned. "Don't worry. I'll take care of him."

"That's what I'm worried about," Staffen replied, but he let them leave. And true to her word, Lorne forced Kiefer to lie on the sofa as soon as they arrived back at his apartment. Fortunately, it was empty, as Julian had left with Annie and the Staffen's had returned to their own home.

Ciely remained in Henry's clinic, silent and unresponsive. There wasn't much hope that she would recover, but Henry said give it time, so Lorne would wait and hope.

Kiefer dozed as she pottered about the apartment, preparing their dinner. His face was relaxed, though his lashes fluttered as she watched. They lifted, revealing eyes that luminesced in a crazy swirl before settling into a brownish violet. He watched her for a moment as if adjusting to where he was, and then he smiled as he sat up.

"It's nice to wake and see you here."

"Only nice?" she asked with a coy smile.

"More than nice, it feels right."

Lorne nodded. "I agree. I don't miss moving camp every night one little bit." She came over and sat beside him.

"You'll need to go back and disband your rebels."

"Harmony has already spoken to them. She assures me they are helping the sectors, though, yes, I still need to go and speak with them."

"My mother said she's updated the Devender's charter and sent them out to help transfer the sector processors back under Harmony's control."

"It will take time, but I'm sure Harmony will ensure all is as it should be."

"She also said she wants me to officially become the Warden and take a seat in the new Administration she is forming."

"As you should," Lorne agreed.

"We'll have to stay in the city."

"You have yet to show the city to me, and no doubt, Harmony will find a way for us to visit the countryside. You are her Warden. I think she will have priority over anything your mother wants you to do."

"True. You don't mind staying here with me?"

Lorne arched an eyebrow. "Are you asking me to?"

"Yes. I am. Lorne," he cupped her cheek in the palm of his hand and stared into her eyes. "Will you marry me?"

Lorne kissed him. "Yes," she replied against his lips and deepened the kiss. She pulled away, smiling as he protested. "You have to rest. And if you're good, we can celebrate properly next week."

"Another week!"

"If you are good." She kissed him on the nose and pulled him to his feet. "Dinner's ready."

As night descended, and the city lights began to flicker below them, Lorne helped Kiefer to his bedroom and perched on the end of the bed, watching him get comfortable.

"Harmony says to stop worrying," he murmured.

"I can't help it," Lorne admitted. "We almost lost you." More than once she added silently. The strength of her feelings for this man frightened her sometimes. She had known him for such a short time, and yet, it felt like she had known him forever.

He raised a shaking hand, and she leaned forward to take it, visible proof that he still needed to recuperate. She lay beside him, tucking his hand against her chest. Her heart thumped under the heat of his palm.

Kiefer leaned over to kiss her. "But you didn't," he whispered as he flopped back. His lashes dropped again, and he drifted off.

The walls pulsed, and a spray of rainbows crept across the floor. Lorne smiled as the light played over them and a sleek black cat jumped on to the bed. Harmony curled up on Kiefer's chest and started purring; the deep rumble soothed Lorne, and she relaxed into the side of Kiefer's body. Harmony watched the couple while they slept.

A few days later, they packed a bag and left Maincore. Harmony was insistant that Kiefer saw the sea and, seeing as he was still recuperating, now was the ideal time. Harmony appeared as a yellow and orange striped butterfly perched on Kiefer's shoulder as they slowly walked towards the transit station.

People stood around, staring at the sky as if searching for something they had lost.

"They are missing that constant voice telling them what to do. I will fill the vacuum with new advice for a little while. They'll soon remember how to make decisions for themselves."

"We're never going to know where you are or who you're watching," Kiefer murmured under his breath, grimacing as Lorne insisted on carrying the bag. His right arm was still supported by a sling, sore and aching.

"I see all, but I will always be watching you, Kiefer. This is but a moment to breathe. We still have much to fix."

"And that is better than the Ministry how?"

"Because you know I love you and you love me. And I am not some voyeur only watching for gratification. I am with you because I want to be. Because we're family. Belonging does not mean owning. I am thankful for you, Kiefer. Without you, there is no me. And anyway, I want to watch your expression when you see the sea."

Kiefer chuckled under his breath. *"You've seen it all. Why is me seeing it so special?"*

"Because you don't remember it. And it is beautiful. The colours, the sound of the waves washing onto the beach. The salty tang of fresh air, the warm breeze ruffling your hair. The rainbows in the spray, the life hidden below. It is freedom, Kiefer. And it is a freedom we can all enjoy because of you."

The End

I hope you enjoyed Harmony. Please leave a review and a tell others what you enjoyed most and why they should read Harmony too!

Sign up to my newsletter (via www.helengarraway.com) to find out my latest news and download two bonus stories in the Sentinal world.

ACKNOWLEDGMENTS

I wrote the first draft of *Harmony* in 2020, after I had written the Sentinal series but before I started the SoulMist series.

Because I had an external deadline to hit for *SoulBreather*, as part of the Realm of Darkness anthology, I focussed on completing the SoulMist books first.

Every now and then I would return to *Harmony* and edit a bit more.

Today, I am thrilled to be releasing *Harmony* into the bookish world, and I hope you enjoy it as much as you have my other books.

I always intended *Harmony* to be a standalone complete story, but you do get attached to the characters and the world, and I must admit, there is so much more I could write in this world that it is tempting to continue this as a series.

But I have three different epic fantasy tales started and begging to be written, so any further books in this world will have to wait. I thoroughly enjoyed writing about Kiefer and Lorne and their dystopian world.

Thank you for staying with me on this magical writing journey. I am having such fun creating new worlds and characters I know you will love.

Thank you to my alpha reader Michael for his continued support and brilliant feedback. To Jefferson from First Editing for his insightful review and comments, and to the 100 Covers team for my wonderful cover.

And thank you to my first ever Patreon follower, Steve

Flanagan. I appreciate all your support and hope you enjoy the behind the scenes insights and shenanigans!

ABOUT THE AUTHOR

Helen Garraway is the USA Today Bestselling author of the award winning epic fantasy Sentinal series which was first published in 2020, followed by the first book of the fantasy romance SoulMist series, *SoulBreather*, released in 2022 as part of the Realm of Darkness boxset.

An avid reader of many different fiction genres, a love she inherited from her mother, Helen writes fantasy novels and also enjoys paper crafting and scrapbooking as an escape from the pressure of the day job.

Having graduated from the University of Southampton with a Degree in Politics and International Relations, she remains an active member of their alumni. You can find out more at www.helengarraway.com.

Patreon

https://patreon.com/HelenGarraway

Join Team Arifel, Team Darian or Team Sentinal and get access to the first chapters of my new books first, free bookish downloads, polls, early sneak peeks.

ABOUT THE AUTHOR

START THE EPIC FANTASY SENTINAL SERIES TODAY

When a long-forgotten threat starts to reemerge, one man stands as the last defence against darkness...

Jerrol Haven serves his king without question. When he finds evidence of corruption and is attacked, the loyal soldier's mind spins after his touch of a sacred tree awakens the dormant spirit of a three-thousand-year-old protector. But he fears he has failed after the crown prince accuses him of treason and orders his execution...

Fleeing the city, Jerrol is stunned when the goddess appears to him, appoints him captain of her warriors, and charges him with a quest to find artifacts that can save the realm. And as he runs into danger and more betrayals, the steadfast hero discovers a rare gift that may be the world's only hope...

Can Jerrol rally the forces of good to stop a rising evil?

Sentinals Awaken is the first book in the Sentinal epic fantasy series. If you like endearing characters, immersive world-building, and gritty conflict, then you'll love Helen Garraway's award-winning tale.

Available on Kindle Unlimited. Download *Sentinals Awaken*: https://Books2Read.com/SentinalsAwaken

PREFER EPIC FANTASY ROMANCE?

If you fall in love with the shadows, does that mean you are fallen too?

A dying angel. A fractured realm. The SoulBreather who might be able to save them both.

Solanji has a secret. One that is becoming increasingly difficult to keep. She can touch souls and see into a person's inner thoughts. Soulbreathing is exhilarating and addictive, until the day Solanji caresses the wrong person's soulmist.

Dragged into a long forgotten angelic mystery, Solanji is forced to venture into Eidolon, the godforsaken last resort for those without souls. In order to save her brother, she must rescue a broken and tortured man. Can she save him from the shadows? Does he even want to be saved? And can she find a way to return to the light before the darkness engulfs them both?

SoulBreather is the first book in the paranormal fantasy/epic fantasy romance SoulMist series.

Order now from a book vendor of your choice : https://Books2Read.com/SoulBreather

READER'S NOTES

FAVOURITE QUOTES